WITCHES

EDNAH WALTERS

Firetrail Publishing
P.O. Box 3444
Logan, UT 84324

Copyright © Ednah Walters 2015
Published by Firetrail Publishing
ISBN: 0991251741
ISBN-13: 978-0-991251742

Edited by Allisyn Ma Edmonds
Cover Design by Cora Graphics.
First **Firetrail Publishing** publication: March 2015
www.firetrailpublishing.com

ALSO BY EDNAH WALTERS:

The Runes Series:

Runes (book one)
Immortals (book two)
Grimnirs: A Runes Book
Seeress (book three)
Souls: Grimnirs Book 2

The Guardian Legacy Series:

Awakened (prequel)
Betrayed (book one)
Hunted (book two)
Forgotten (coming June 2015)

WRITING CONTEMPORARY ROMANCE
as E. B. WALTERS

The Fitzgerald Family series

Slow Burn (book 1)
Mine Until Dawn (book 2)
Kiss Me Crazy (book 3)
Dangerous Love (book 4)
Forever Hers (book 5)
Surrender to Temptation (book 6)

Infinitus Billionaires

Impulse (book 1)
Indulge (book 2-Coming Fall 2015)

DEDICATION

This one is for you,
Toraine's fans

ACKNOWLEDGMENTS
§
To my editor, Allisyn Ma Edmonds,
I would not have asked for a more thorough, meticulous,
and professional editor. To my personal assistant Cheree
Crump, you rock!!! Nuns have nothing on you. So thank you.
To my beta-readers Irina Wo, Jeannette Oatman Whitus, and
Carolina Silva. Thank you for reading the raw version at such short
notice and your honest feedback. I could not have polished
this book without your keen eyes. My Street Team: This is for YOU!!
You keep me humbled, encourage me, make me laugh and cry
I love hanging out with you, sharing stories and pictures, and having
fun. Thank you for being so awesome. If I could thank all of you
I would. You know who you are. Love you, guys.
To husband and my wonderful children, thank you for
your unwavering love and support. You inspire me in
so many ways. Love you, guys.

TRADEMARK LIST:

Google
Harley
StubHub/LA Galaxy
FIFA
Nikon
Twizzlers
Supernatural
CWTV
Charmed
Beckham
The Scarlett Letter
Chevrolet
Petsmart
Honda Civic
World Cup
Dodge
Lays
Herbalife

GLOSSARY

Asgard: Home of the Aesir gods
Odin: The father and ruler of all gods and men.
He is an Aesir god. Half of the dead soldiers/warriors/athletes
go to live in his hall Valhalla.
Freya: The poetry-loving goddess of love and fertility.
The other half of the dead warriors/soldiers/athletes go to her hall in
Falkvang
Frigg: Odin's wife, the patron of marriage and motherhood
Norns: deities who control destinies of men and gods
Völva: A powerful seeress
Völur: A group of seeresses
Immortals: Humans who stop aging and self-heal
because of the magical runes etched on their skin
Valkyries: Immortals who collect fallen warriors/soldiers/
fighters/athletes
and take them to Valhalla and Falkvang
Ragnarok: The end of the world war between the gods and
the evil giants
Artavus: Magical knife or dagger used to etch runes
Artavo: Plural of artavus
Stillo: A type of artavus
Grimnirs: Reapers for Hel
Hel: The Goddess Hel in charge of the dead
Hel: Home of Goddess Hel, dead criminals, those dead from
illness and old age
Nastraad/Corpse Strand: The island in Hel for criminals and evil
Mortals
Yggdrasil: The tree of life or tree of knowledge that connects
the nine realms of Norse cosmology
Seidr: An old Norse term referring to a magical practice by the
Norse, it includes act of divination or prophecy performed
while in a trance.
Brísingamen: A beautiful necklace owned by Goddess Freya
Bygul: One of the cats that pulls Goddess Freya's chariot
skreyja vilfill: loosely translated from Norse as incompetent beetle
Baulufotr: cow foot in Norse
Beiskaldi: bitch in Norse

Jotunn: giants in Norse
Draugr/Draugar/Revenants/Wendigo: zombie-like creatures
Garm: Hel's hound
Daufi: Stupid in Norse
Idun: Norse Goddess of Spring
Nornsgard: Norns' Hall
Midgard: Earth in Norse
Valknut: the rune formed by three interlocked triangles

1. First Case

The stench of stale sweat woke me from a deep slumber, and I jerked upright, fighting the gag reflex. The source of the stench was Beau Hardshaw's sweatshirt on my pillow. Dang it! I'd fallen asleep on the job.

Naked jocks flashed in my head, images I was still trying to erase from my memory. Served me right for trying to steal something of Beau's. But what was a witch supposed to do when a Mortal was in danger of destroying his life? Brave the worst place in Kayville High School—the boy's locker room.

I picked up the sweatshirt with my thumb and forefinger like it was a rattlesnake, but that was all the contact I needed to get a vision. My room faded into darkness. Walls and cabinets appeared in its place, and then I was standing in the same room I'd visited earlier this evening—Beau Hardshaw's kitchen. The scene played out like my worst nightmare.

Beau raised the gun, green eyes fierce and crazed like a cornered animal, and pointed it at his stepfather.

The lumberjack stumbled back, an empty beer box dropping from his hand. He only wore underwear—tighty-whities, hairy chest and large stomach hanging over stick legs. Not exactly what I wanted to see in a vision.

"What do you think you're doing, boy?" Hardshaw senior snarled. "You'd better be prepared to pull that trigger, because I'm gonna teach you a lesson when I come over there."

Beau grimaced and shook his head. He either didn't like being called a boy, or he objected to being taught a lesson by anyone. Beau was tall and buff with serious tats and a killer smile. It didn't help that he was the co-captain of Kayville High's baseball team and a chick magnet with a reputation for girl hopping. Yep, Beau wore his douchebaggery on his sleeves and didn't care who knew it. Even I had noticed him, Kayville High's Number One Bad Boy, during my pre-Torin years.

"Get out or you're a dead man," Beau threatened.

"This is my home, boy, and she is my wife!" his stepfather bellowed.

"She's my mother and tonight is the last time you touch her." Beau angled the gun.

"Don't, Beau!" a woman cried out. I followed the voice to the corner of the cabinets, where a woman crouched, cowering. From the way she held her arm it was probably injured.

"He'll kill you if I don't stop him, Mama," Beau said in a shaky voice. He released the safety of the gun, the sound loud in the stillness of the moment.

"I'd never kill your mother, Beau," his hulking stepfather said, his voice now whiny. He moved backward toward Beau's mother. "I love her. Put the gun down, son." Then he grabbed his wife by her hair and hauled her in front of him, just as Beau pulled the trigger.

The sound of the gun wiped the vision, and I was back in my room. I jumped to my feet. At least that was my intention. I landed on the floor with enough noise to wake the dead. Lucky for me, Mom and my boyfriend, Torin, were out reaping souls. Dad was doing much better, but he was a deep sleeper these days, courtesy of some serious pain and sleep runes for his terminal cancer. Femi, his nurse, would understand once I explained.

As though my thoughts had conjured her, a portal appeared in my room and Femi peered at me. "You okay, doll?"

"Yes. Just a nightmare." *Go away now,* I projected into her head.

"Okay. Goodnight."

The portal closed behind her, and I wondered if I'd gotten inside her head or if she'd believed that I was actually okay. I didn't like getting inside people's heads and playing with their thoughts, but sometimes, it was necessary. Besides, I was new to these witchy powers. I improvised a lot.

I engaged my runes and started for the mirror. Before it responded to my runes and changed into a portal, I caught my reflection and grimaced. My hair was a mess, and I still wore my pajamas—shorts and a tank top. The silk robe only came to my thighs. And I couldn't remember where I'd put my slippers.

Oh well, I had more important things to worry about than my appearance. In the seconds it took for the mirror to turn into a portal, I mentally went over what I knew about Beau's life.

His stepfather was a bastard. If I hadn't seen him treating Beau like a punching bag in my earlier vision, I would not have fallen asleep holding his dirty sweatshirt. I needed to touch items belonging to people to get a vision. Being a Seeress had its perks, but when it involved a life-changing vision, it totally screwed up my day.

I'd received the first vision in the school cafeteria today, when Beau had brushed against me. The bloody scene and the gun in Beau's hand had been enough to make me lose my appetite.

The second one had happened after I'd deliberately followed him, bumped into him, and dropped my books. He'd probably thought I was coming on to him, especially when I'd grabbed his hand and hung on to it for dear life. My visions had never been so clear, but the look on Beau's face, a cross between shock and fascination, could lead to complications. My eyes glowed whenever I had premonitions. So he could either tell his friends that Torin St. James' girl was into him or was a witch. I'd been labeled a witch before I even knew I was one. Now I wore the label with pride. Too much had happened the past nine months for me to disregard my magical gifts.

Bottom line was Beau could kill his abusive stepfather and possibly his mother tonight.

The thought brought me back to the present, and I watched the portal form. The mirror changed texture until the surface looked like a rippling pool of water. Portals come in all sizes: some with hallways and others without, depending on the runes used. Tonight, the surface peeled back into a short hallway, the floor and the walls shimmering.

The lights weren't on in Beau's house. The fact that there were no flashing red and blue lights outside told me that the events in my vision hadn't occurred yet.

I stepped into his living room, and the portal closed. The runes glowing on my body gave me enough illumination, so it wasn't hard to get my bearings. I recognized the worn out sofas and pictures of Beau in baseball outfits on the walls and fireplace. There were a few pictures of a little girl, and I wondered if he had a sister. She appeared much younger than Beau, and in the pictures; he couldn't have been older than ten.

I left the mirror in the living room, skirted around chairs and tables, and went toward the hallway. During lunch, I'd followed Beau home in my car and searched his house for a gun, a very frustrating endeavor since I couldn't use my elemental magic.

Was it only a week ago I'd discovered I was linked to the world around me in ways that were both scary and beautiful? I could communicate with trees. Command the ground I walked on. And don't get me started on what I could do to the human mind. That wasn't elemental, but it was still pretty amazing. Even Torin, a powerful Valkyrie, was not immune to my magic.

I reached the basement door, and I found myself hesitating before creating the next portal. Doubts crept in. I hadn't found the gun during my earlier search. What were the chances I'd find it now? It was quiet. Maybe nothing was going to happen tonight.

I peered into the hallway. The house wasn't large, just a single story with a basement, where Beau's bedroom was located. He lived on the west side of Kayville, where most Chandler Lumber Corp's workers and their families resided. Chandler was the single largest employer in Kayville, Oregon. We might boast of being wine country with huge vineyards, but the wineries were actually in the neighboring towns. Half the kids I went to school with were from families like Beau's, with generations working or having worked in the lumber industry.

Beau, however, could break that circle. He had an amazing arm and a chance at a full ride to college on a baseball scholarship. Scouts were already coming to the games to watch him when he was only a junior. This mess with his stepfather might just prevent that from happening.

Why should I care about what happened to Beau? The guy I loved would definitely not understand. Torin was a Valkyrie, a soul reaper, and he strongly believed in letting one's destiny take its course. I was the opposite. I believed that everyone should have the right to change his or her destiny. You know, make mistakes, and pick themselves up, dust off their pants, re-evaluate, and try things a different way. And if they got a little help along the way, that was just great. As long as it was what they wanted, and not what some hag, deity, or supernatural being had decided before they were born.

So here I was, butting my nose into Beau's business. It might come back and bite me in the butt. Heck, I might even fail to help him. Beau with his tattoos and bad reputation was the worst candidate for a first case, but I didn't choose the visions I got. This one happened and I was dealing with it the only way I knew how. I was giving Beau a nudge off a destructive path. The rest would be up to him.

The Norns weren't going to like me interfering in their business, but then again, when have I ever done anything that made those hags happy? I just couldn't sit back and do nothing. Or I could have called the cops and told them... What? I saw a vision of a crime that hadn't been committed? They'd laugh at me or haul me off to a mental house.

Sneaking into the guys' locker room to find something of Beau's had been traumatizing. High school guys are gross. They fart, and scratch their asses and balls with no shame. I'd always thought my first naked guy would be Torin, the man I was crazy about. Unfortunately, I was wrong. I'd grabbed the first thing of Beau's and used an air portal to get out of there fast. Not fast enough though. The images of naked jocks were trapped in my head.

A door opened down the hallway, and lights flickered on. During my earlier search, I figured that this was his parents' bedroom. Sure enough, Beau's stepfather cursed as he staggered into the hallway. TV sounds said he'd been watching something. He wore his tighty-whities, the same ones in my vision. As though he realized he wasn't alone, Hardshaw senior looked up and scowled, staring straight at me.

I'd never made a portal through a wall so fast. It led straight to Beau's room, bypassing the creaky wooden steps with worn out carpet. Another thing I'd noticed during my first visit.

A shirtless Beau was on his back, an open laptop on his stomach. I'd never have guessed Beau was the type to stay at home on Friday night. The tattoos on his left arm extended to his shoulder and chest. In the vision, he'd worn a T-shirt with the same pajama bottoms. Yikes. I just realized his hand was inside his pants doing something I didn't want to watch. If he started moaning, I was so leaving.

I looked around. Where could the gun be? I'd checked everywhere, except... Ah, his school stuff. Where the heck was his backpack and gym bag? Like most ball players, he should own a Kayville High gym bag with the school name on it.

I searched around the room, the closet, and bathroom. If he noticed the draft caused by my hyper-speed movements, he didn't show it. He had headphones on and his eyes were glued to the screen. I tried not to listen to his side of the conversation, but couldn't help it once I found his gym bag and slowed down. At high speed, sounds tended to disappear.

I tried not to gag as I searched the bag. Dirty gym clothes, socks, and wet towels. Ew, and women's panties. Trophies probably. He had enough condoms to supply the entire baseball team. But there was no gun.

"Lower your hand," I heard him say. "Perfect. Closer. I don't want to miss a thing."

"Janice! Get your fat ass out here!" his stepfather bellowed from upstairs. Their walls were seriously paper-thin. "What happened to my beer? If that boy took them again, I'm going to teach him a lesson he'll never forget."

There were three empty cans of beer by Beau's bed. I spied his messenger bag hidden under a pile of dirty clothes by his desk. I left the bathroom and inched closer to the bed. He cocked his head. At first, I thought he'd finally sensed my presence. But then he said, "Yes, Ellie."

Ellie? I only knew one at our school. Ellie Chandler. She was the captain of the cheerleaders and Justin Sinclair's girlfriend. Justin played football with Torin. He was a total douche though. So what was his girl doing talking to Beau?

I couldn't help myself. I walked around the bed to see the screen. Her mouth opened and closed, but I couldn't hear what she was saying. Didn't want to. She was also in her panties and wore no bra. More images in my head I didn't need.

I went back to retrieving the backpack.

"My stepfather is being a shithead, again," I heard Beau say. "Don't stop." She must have protested because he added, "No, forget him. Let's finish this."

Lala lala lala… hmm-mmm… Lala lala lala…

I tried to drown out his words as I slowly pulled the backpack away from his line of vision. I wasn't sure what Ellie just did, but air left Beau's lungs in a rush and a quick glance over my shoulder made me wish I hadn't.

I went into hyper speed as I searched the pockets of his backpack. More dirty socks. Candy wrappers. Bikinis. More condoms. I got a few visions I didn't want to see and one that was very helpful. I now knew how he'd gotten a gun, but I still didn't see where he'd hidden it. Stupid visions. I slowed down, frustration setting in.

"Get your sorry ass down here, boy!" came from upstairs.

"Damn it." Beau growled. "Don't go anywhere," he said and closed his laptop. He grabbed a T-shirt from the floor. By the time he pulled it on, I'd disengaged my invisibility runes.

I blocked his path.

"What the... Fuck!" Eyes widening, he scrambled to get away from me. He bumped the edge of the bed and struggled to stay on his feet as he put some distance between us. "Raine Cooper? What are you doing in my house?"

I hadn't thought this far. My plan had been to find the gun, take it, and leave without revealing my presence. I improvised.

"What name did you call me?" I asked, faking ignorance.

"This is not funny, Raine. How did you get in here?"

"I don't know who this Raine is, but if that's the image you're seeing then that's what your mind conjured. Why you may ask? It's what Mortals do when they see me."

His jaw dropped. Then he shook his head as though to rattle his brain into place. "What?"

"I'm your, uh, Norn." I hated using that name, let alone admitting I was one, even though I was embracing my destiny. When he stared at me blankly, I added, "I'm what you Mortals call a guardian angel and I'm here to help you. The projection you see here,"—I waved a hand to indicate my body—"is what your mind chose."

He swallowed, ran his fingers through his hair, and grimaced. "You're screwing with my head, right? You're right here in front of me. I can see you."

"And now you don't." I engaged my invisibility runes and watched him look around in panic, cursing up a storm. I reappeared again and he grew paler. "Like I said, I'm your guardian angel and I'm here to make sure you don't do something stupid, Beau Hardshaw."

He gulped and blinked. "Stupid?"

"You have a gun that doesn't belong to you. I want it."

His eyes darted to his bed. "How do you know that?"

I sighed. "Because I know things, Beau. Remember the guardian angel part? Randy showed you his father's collection after school today and you took one." Randall Meyer's father was a survivalist with enough weapons to start World War Three. "Give it to me."

Beau frowned and stared at me, thinking things through. "I meant to return it."

"After using it."

He shook his head. "I'm not going to use it. I just want to threaten the ass-hat with it."

"Except it will go off." He was beginning to believe me. "You are an amazing baseball player with a bright future ahead of you, Beau. Don't blow it. He's not worth it."

Thuds came from upstairs followed by a scream. A tortured look entered Beau's eyes. "He's hurting her. I have to go."

I moved and blocked him. "No."

"He won't stop until I give him a different target."

Which explained the discolorations on his left cheek. Earlier, at school, he'd fibbed about sliding into a plate during a game and hurting himself. As a right-handed pitcher, he'd do everything to protect his right arm, which meant all his defensive bruises would be on his left. The tattoos could be covering scars from years of abuse.

Anger slammed through me. "I'll take care of him, Beau. Just give me the gun."

He glanced toward the door and I could see him trying hard to decide whether to trust me or not. More thuds, followed by, "You stupid bitch. You think you can hurt me?" More thuds and screams.

"The gun, Beau," I said firmly and with a confidence I didn't feel. Beau wasn't the type of guy a girl ordered about.

He reached under his pillow and pulled out a gun. I didn't know anything about guns, except you cocked it and pulled the trigger to shoot. I gripped the middle and made sure the muzzle was pointing away from me.

"Stay here," I said. Beau opened his mouth, but I shook my head. "No. Stay. I don't like to be interrupted when I work."

I engaged my invisibility runes, moved into hyper-speed, and created a portal. Beau stared around in confusion, probably wondering where I'd gone. His stepfather stood over his mother while she cowered in the corner of the room by the stove. She was holding her arm, just like in my vision. He had the empty box of canned beer in his left hand.

"You stupid woman. You can't do a simple thing unless I tell you over and over again how and when to do it." He raised his fist.

"I wouldn't do that if I were you," I said calmly.

He whipped around, ran his eyes over me, and leered. "Who are you? One of Beau's girls? Get out of here before I show you what a real man can do."

"Real men don't beat up helpless women and children, Joe Hardshaw," I said, sliding the gun behind the knife holder.

"This is my house, girlie. No one touches my things." He reached for his wife.

Moving fast, I closed the gap between us and gripped his wrist before he made contact. He stared at me as though I was crazy.

"You little slut," he growled, and stale breath fanned my face. My stomach rebelled. He tried to push me, but I had engaged strength runes. I twisted his wrist and a yowl escaped his mouth. He dropped the box and tried to jerk his hand from my grip, but he couldn't break my hold.

"Names? Really?" I twisted again and he adjusted his body into a weird shape to relieve the pain. "One more twist and I'll snap your wrist, Mr. Hardshaw. Stop struggling and listen carefully to what I have to say."

"How…" He took a swing at me with his other hand. I caught his beefy fist and squeezed hard. "Aw, my fingers," he moaned.

"I'm really trying hard not to hurt you, Mr. Hardshaw. If I squeezed hard enough, I would crush your bones." His face twisted in pain. "If you rammed me with your head, you'd only split your skull. If I pushed you, you'd fly through the window behind you, taking the counter and the sink with you. Now, are you ready to listen?"

He nodded.

"Good." I let him go. "Don't move." I turned and offered the wife a hand, but she cringed. "It's okay. I'm not going to hurt you. I'm here to help."

"Watch out!" Beau yelled.

I turned to see his stepfather lunge at me. I ducked, grabbed his arm and yanked. He tethered on his heel, then he went down, taking the counter with him. I lifted him by his tighty-whities, which gave me a nasty view of his butt crack. Didn't want to see or smell that.

I pushed him against the counter, careful not to break another section of it. He had bruises on his arms and back. "I'm trying to be nice and you're not helping," I said, annoyance lacing my words. Beau was attempting to help his mother to her feet. "Don't move her."

"She needs to see a doctor. The bastard broke her arm this time." He glared at his stepfather.

"No, call 911. Her arm *is* broken." Beau looked ready to argue. "Please." I needed to erase their memories and I couldn't if they left. He nodded and reached for the phone. I focused on his stepfather.

"I'm here to protect your wife and son, Joe," I said. "If you ever hit one of them again, I'll know and I'll come for you. You haven't seen what I can do. I'm strong and I'm fast. I'm relentless when I want something and mean when pissed. Everything about you pisses me off, Joe. Do you understand?"

He nodded, fear clouding his pale blue eyes.

"They won't remember what I did here tonight, but I want you to remember me. I know everything about you, Joe Hardshaw. You're a bully and you drink too much. Touch them again and I promise you, you won't live to see another day." I stepped back and removed my artavus. His eyes went to it. Beau was squatting by his mother consoling her, but his eyes were on us. Any second, I knew the police and EMTs would come barreling toward their house.

I turned my back to Hardshaw senior, knowing he wouldn't dare attack me again. "I have to go now, Beau. If he hurts her again, I'll know."

"How?" Beau asked, glancing at his stepfather before focusing on me.

Yeah, that was a good question. How, genius?

"I'll know," I said with a confidence I didn't feel. I glanced over my shoulder at his stepfather. "See you around, Joe. Be good. You've been warned."

I used invisibility runes to disappear, etched forgetful runes on Beau and his mother, and walked across the room to get the gun. Now to return it to Randy's before his father finds out it's missing.

"What are you doing?" a woman's voice cut through the air and my stomach dropped. That annoying, arrogant voice sounded way too familiar.

I turned, expecting to see the Norns assigned to me, the bane of my existence, and found myself facing a couple instead. Relief coursed through me. They were not the ones. Catie, Marj, and Jeannette, as I liked to call my Norns, always appeared to me together. It didn't matter whether they were men or women, they were always in threes.

The guy was handsome, tall, and slender with pitch-black hair that reminded me of Torin's hair, except Torin's was thicker and more luxurious. This guy was a walking ad for tattoos, which blended with his runes. The sleeves of his coat were rolled up and he wore biker gloves like Torin's. He was handsome with unforgettable violet eyes. The woman was exotic with high cheekbones and slanted eyes. She reminded me of someone, I just couldn't remember who.

"Follow us," she said and created a portal.

"What are you? Valkyries? Grimnirs?" The sound of an ambulance and flashing lights drew closer. "I gotta go."

The woman moved fast and blocked me. "No, you're not going anywhere. You just stole our soul."

Her tone of voice didn't surprise me. Most reapers were arrogant. But to stop me from leaving? "Excuse me?"

"You heard me. We were supposed to reap him," she pointed at Beau's stepfather, "tonight. You interfered."

Grimnirs. The trench coats should have warned me. I didn't want to antagonize them. "I saved his son from a fate worse than death tonight, guys. That's better than a soul bound for Hel. Maybe he just needs a little nudge to change his ways."

They looked at each other and shook their heads. "You can't interfere with our reaping by changing what is meant to happen."

"I'm a Norn-in-training, Grimnirs, so yeah. I can." I glanced over my shoulder at the kitchen. Beau stayed with his mother while his stepfather lumbered to the door and opened it for the EMTs.

"Thugs broke in here and attacked my wife and me. They ran that way," Mr. Hardshaw pointed down the street as he continued to lie. "If our son hadn't come upstairs, they would have killed us."

"Where's your wife, sir?" an EMT asked.

"This way. I think they broke her arm and ribs."

What an a-hole. From the look on Beau's face, I couldn't tell whether he bought his stepfather's story or not. Maybe I shouldn't have runed him.

While the EMTs went to get Beau's mother, his stepfather talked to two police officers, repeating the same lie about a break-in by thugs he couldn't identify because it had been too dark. Someone gave him a blanket. Through the door, I could see neighbors stepping out of their homes to gawk.

The Grimnirs were arguing softly, but the girl gave me a look that said she wasn't going to leave until she spoke with me further. Her partner hadn't said anything since they'd arrived. I had a feeling nothing bothered him much.

"I have to return this gun before the owner finds out its gone. I'm sorry you didn't reap the douchebag, but I couldn't let Beau kill him. He would have ended up in jail, which would have been a waste of his potential. He has an amazing arm." The Grimnirs scowled. "Baseball."

"We know what you meant," the woman said through clenched teeth. "That doesn't make it right. And you're not a Norn yet."

Her attitude didn't bother me. Soul reapers took their jobs way too seriously. Since I was all about helping living people, not the dead, we were bound to knock heads. "Then you understand that he might get a full ride to college. I had to do something to help him. If you have a problem with it, report me to the Valkyrie Council or whoever you answer to."

I brushed past them, but the girl reached for me. I jerked my hand away, but not fast enough. Her hand closed around my arm, and I wasn't surprised that a vision appeared. I had gotten used to them by now, but I really needed to learn how to close my mind to them. Beau's kitchen disappeared to be replaced by a familiar, brightly lit hallway.

The two Grimnirs stood at the end of the hallway as though waiting for someone. I couldn't hear what they were saying, but they didn't look happy. A blonde approached them. It was Cora Jemison, my best friend. No wonder the hallway had looked familiar. It was the nursing home where Cora volunteered.

Cora saw the two Grimnirs and broke into a run, but they stopped her, the woman grabbing her arm and the guy creating a portal. They disappeared through the portal with Cora.

The vision cleared, leaving me shaken. I jerked my arm from the Grimnir and stepped back. "What do you want with Cora Jemison?"

Surprise flickered across the woman's face. The guy had a poker face.

"Who?" the woman asked.

"Really? You want to pretend you don't know her?" Cora was dating a notorious Grimnir. There was no way they didn't know her. "Do not pay Cora a visit at the nursing home. Do not touch her, or do something stupid like kidnap her, because I'll know. She's under my protection, so if you mess with her, you mess with me. And where I go, the Valkyries follow. So leave her alone."

"You think we are afraid of the Valkyries?" the girl asked. The guy smirked.

"Oh, then you'd better be afraid of one of your own. You touch Cora and I'll tell Echo." That got their attention. The girl paled and the guy stopped smirking. "Happy reaping, Grimnirs."

2. Illusions

The lights were on in my bedroom when I returned. Torin was back! After going through Beau's gym bag, I wanted nothing more than to take a shower and curl up in my boyfriend's arms.

Surprise replaced the anticipation when I realized someone else was in my room. She was sitting in my computer chair. At first, all I saw was wavy blonde hair the color of sunbeams cascading to the floor like a waterfall. Only one blonde came and went into my room as she pleased, but it wasn't Cora. Her hair was lighter and shorter. As though she felt my presence, the owner of the glorious mane swiveled around and faced me.

My eyes widened with immediate recognition. She was gorgeous; her online pictures did not do her justice. Her white and golden dress flowed to her sandaled feet. Her roped belt matched the golden headpiece inlaid with red jewels that held back her hair from her face. A single jewel dangled between her startling blue eyes, and a gorgeous gold necklace with the same gems graced her neck. I recognized the necklace—*Brísingamen*. Internet pictures got that wrong too. It was more breathtaking. The gray and black tabby on her lap was also smaller than those often shown pulling her chariot.

What was Goddess Freya doing in my room?

"No need to be shy, Svana's daughter," she said, her voice musical and hypnotic. "Come closer."

I tried to resist, but it was as though she'd put a spell on me. Was this how she seduced the gods? She was known for taking many lovers, yet her heart belonged to one—her diseased husband.

"Do you know who I am?" she asked, standing, her bejeweled hand stroking her cat's head gently.

I nodded.

"Or would you prefer me to appear like this?" The words barely left her mouth when her golden gown shifted and changed texture until it was battle armor—golden breastplate, skirt, knee-high boots, and a headdress with wings. She looked totally badass. All she needed was her chariot drawn by her cats. I hid a smile.

"Or perhaps you're more comfortable with me like this." All the clothes disappeared, except for a shawl over her shoulder. Now I had a naked goddess in my room.

I closed my eyes. "The first one was fine."

She chuckled. "So you do have a voice. From what I'd heard about you, I didn't expect you to be shy or so modest. Nudity is something you should embrace, my dear. The same way you embrace your femininity or your destiny."

"What do you want?" I flushed when I realized how rude I sounded. "I mean, what are you doing here?"

"Sit, please." She took the chair she'd vacated a few minutes ago.

I sat on the edge of my bed, and angled my body so there was enough space between us. I still couldn't believe she was in my room, and that her cat wasn't attacking me. Cats hated me. As far back as I could remember, cats would hiss whenever Eirik and I walked past them. But then again, dogs would also either snarl or whine. I never understood it. This one watched me with eyes that seemed way too intelligent for a cat.

"I saw what you did to help that boy tonight."

"Oh. Is that why you're here? To tell me to stop?" I asked defensively and shifted uneasily.

"Maybe. Would you?"

"No."

She chuckled. "I like your attitude. I've been your champion even before you were born, dear, so I'm not here to stop you. I've watched you since you learned about our world. And I knew you would eventually figure things out."

If she wasn't here to stop me, what did she want? This particular goddess had been my mother's mentor. She'd fought for my parents to be together and even for Mom to rejoin the Valkyries. She could actually be nice.

"My champion before I was born? Why? Did you know I'd be a *Völva* and one of the announcers of Ragnarok? Was that why you supported my parents?"

She chuckled. "Ah, you are a suspicious one, aren't you? I cannot see the future like you or Frigga." A grimace crossed her face after she mentioned Odin's wife. "She never tells anyone what she's seen. So much pain and heartache would be avoided if she only shared. So, no, dear one, I didn't know what you'd become. I supported your parents because I'm the Goddess of Love. And I made sure you were born because I'm also the Goddess of Fertility. It was quite a fight challenging the Norns for you, but every child matters. I win some battles and I lose some, but I keep fighting. I fought for your birth without knowing why they didn't want you to be born. And once you were born, my job was done. If I'd known they'd try to manipulate you, I would have continued to keep an eye on you. Vile creatures, the Norns." She closed her eyes and when her eyelids lifted, her blue eyes were flashing with something I couldn't define—anger or determination. "You don't mess with the Norns unless you plan to win, my dear. And to win you must be willing to make sacrifices. Do you want to win?"

I'd gone to selective listening after she said one word: "Sacrifices?"

"Do you want to win, Raine?" she asked, her voice sharp.

"Of course," I shot back, not liking her bossiness.

"Then I'll help you. Tonight, I watched you appear to the young Mortal as yourself," she continued. "Why would you do that?"

"How was I supposed to appear to him?"

She leaned forward, her cat purring and angling its head as she scratched its ears. "He will remember you."

"No, he won't. I runed him."

She sighed impatiently. "Are you forgetting something? Runes' effects are not permanent. Just like the runes on your body, you must replenish them or their effect wanes. He will remember. It might take a week or a month, depending on his mental and physical prowess, but he will remember."

Deflated, I scowled. "Then what am I supposed to do? I mean how do the Norns do it?"

The goddess smiled. "That's the question you should have asked yourself before you went charging in. Norns get inside people's heads, selectively erase memories, and implant new ones. One day, you'll be able to do that."

Norns had messed with Torin's memories so he'd forget me. I'd hated them for that. "No, thanks. I would never do something so despicable to anyone."

"Circumstances can force you to do things you hate, my dear," she said, as a far-away look entered her eyes. "Sometimes, it's the only solution." She refocused on me. "Anyway, I have an answer to your problem, if you want to continue helping people."

Did I want to continue helping people? Yes. I might not be able to run from my destiny, but I planned to do things my way. Norns didn't marry. But I planned to marry Torin. Norns lived together in their own hall somewhere in Asgard and worked in groups of threes. Even though I didn't have two other Norns-in-training with me, I had Valkyries watching my back and I planned to someday share a home with Torin.

"Okay, what's the answer?" I said.

"You need to change your appearance whenever you appear to people."

"Shape-shift?"

She chuckled. "No, dear. You are not a shape-shifter any more than Norns are. Shape-shifting involves bones changing shapes and sizes. What Norns and Witches like you do is control what Mortals see. It's all an illusion. You connect to the source of your magic and work with it. You mimic."

I shuddered, remembering how an evil Norn-in-training had mimicked Cora and screwed with our heads. That was something I didn't want to learn. It left a nasty taste in my mouth, yet I had to hide my real identity if I wanted to continue helping people.

"How do I do that?" I asked a tad reluctantly.

She cocked a perfectly shaped eyebrow. "What do you mean?"

"I don't know what you mean by the source of my magic. When I want to use my magic, it just happens. I mean, I touch things and the visions appear."

She sighed. "I'm not talking about your ability to connect with the energies people leave behind. I'm talking about your core energy, the one that makes all of the magic possible. Have you ever projected your thoughts into someone's head?"

I nodded, remembering how I'd knocked out Torin just before the battle with his evil father. "Yes. I've spoken to people with my mind before."

"How do you connect with Mother Earth?"

"Same thing. I think it and it happens."

Confusion clouded her eyes. "But you had the entire forest following your wishes when you fought the Immortals. You must have felt it."

Last week, I'd connected with the earth for the first time and replanted the trees Torin had destroyed. A few days later, we'd battled his father, and I'd once again connected with nature and controlled it.

I shook my head. "No. I mean, I felt the adrenaline rush from anger and fear."

She chuckled. "That would definitely mask your connection. You've been so busy riding on emotions that you haven't paid attention to the source of your magic," she said. She pressed a hand to my chest. "It's in here. Find it, feel it, and channel it." She leaned forward. "Take a deep breath and dig deep."

I wasn't sure where I was supposed to dig, but I took a deep breath. Nothing happened. The goddess frowned.

"Let the need to connect with your magic fill you," she said.

I tried. I really did, but nothing happened.

"Hel's Mist! How can you be so powerful and be so inept?" Her eyes glowed then dimmed. "See how easy that was?"

"Yeah, for a goddess. I'm seventeen and have just barely acquired my powers."

Hands on her hips, she pinned me down with glowing eyes. "You didn't acquire anything. It's always been inside you. Find it."

Anger shot through me. "Listen, I can learn at my own pace and Lavania—"

"There's no time. The Norns will not leave you alone as you approach your eighteenth birthday. We need to speed up your education. Some Witches draw energy from others, so when they heal one person, another falls ill. Others draw from their surroundings, like evil souls, while others tap into the powers of their ancestors in burial grounds. You tap into a power that's inside you. You connect it to the energy others leave behind whenever you want a vision without even realizing it. You called it forth and linked it to nature's power to heal the trees and order the vines. I watched you battle and I was very impressed. Yet you're just sitting there looking very ordinary like a Mortal. You're not ordinary, Lorraine Cooper, so snap out of it!" She snapped her fingers right under my nose. "Find the passion, the burning desire to claim your birthright, the need to be more than ordinary."

"I'm trying," I whined. "It's just—" Then I felt it, a spark deep inside me. Like someone, or something, flipped a switch.

"Let it grow and flow."

Her voice was beginning to bug me. If anyone asked me how I did it, I wouldn't be able to explain it. The spark became a pulsing feeling that unfurled like petals of a blooming flower. It spread and grew until my entire body throbbed with it.

"Beautiful. Your eyes are glowing with it." She got up and extended her hand. "Come with me."

I took her hand and eyed her cat warily, seeing my face reflected in its dark eyes. If I made a sudden movement, would it pounce? I stifled a giggle.

"Get up, Raine," the goddess urged.

"Where are we going?"

"I want to show you something." I hesitated. "Trust me, child," she added softly.

After the Norns, I wasn't about to trust another deity. I didn't care how nice she was. She wasn't in my room helping me tap into my powers for nothing. She wanted something. I stood. Dizziness washed over me, and I would have fallen if she hadn't grabbed my arm and steadied me.

She chuckled. "The power can be too much and gives a buzz like you're drunk. You must learn to control it. Connect with it and when you're done, push it back."

I stared at her hand, marveling at the enhanced sensitivity of my skin. Even after she let go, I felt the imprint of her soft palm. I ran my fingers over my arm, expecting to see sparks. No sparks, but my skin felt like I had live wires running under it. I looked around and grinned. Everything seemed brighter and more colorful as though someone had turned up the lights and enhanced the hues.

A chuckle drew my attention back to the goddess. She was blindingly radiant, but now I noticed a few things I hadn't seen before. She had wrinkles at the corners of her eyes and mouth, and there was sadness in her eyes. She was also keeping secrets.

She sighed. "You're trying to read me?"

"What do you really want from me, Goddess Freya?"

"I promised your mother I'd stop by for a chat, so here I am. The Norns have taken too much from you, and they won't stop unless you stop them."

I frowned. Apart from friends I had lost during the swim meet, the Norns hadn't taken anything from me. As for stopping them, that was impossible. "I don't understand."

"Forget about that. Take a hard look at me. My hair. My eyes. What I'm wearing. Then close your eyes and let the image fill your mind. Once it does, will yourself to transform, so you look exactly like me. Whatever you want changed, focus on it. But do not let your power ebb. You need it for the shift."

I shot her a skeptical look. "I'm going to shape-shift—"

"Wrong choice of words," she said impatiently. "Mimic. You will see with your Mortal eyes and Mortal mind a new person, but it will still be you."

Mimic. The very word made my stomach roil. The only consolation was I had no intention of doing it unless it was absolutely necessary. I tried it, but it didn't work.

"You must want this, Raine," she urged softly. "Just like you did with your powers. Focus and let the need fill you."

Nothing happened. Annoyed, I walked to the mirror and stared hard at my reflection, then closed my eyes and tried again.

Nothing happened. Her cat meowed.

"No, no, *Bygul*. Pathetic is too harsh a word. She's still a novice."

Was she talking to her cat? I glared at the cat, and I could have sworn it smirked. No one calls me pathetic and gets away with it.

"Think of someone you love," the goddess said. "Someone whose gestures and facial expressions are so much a part of your daily life that all you have to do is hear their name and their image pops into your head."

We'll see who's pathetic now. I closed my eyes and let the image of my father fill my head. Not the way he looked now, but the robust man who'd loved life and adored his family. I wanted to see that man again.

Too scared to look and see my failure, I kept my eyes shut.

"See, that wasn't hard," the goddess said.

I opened my eyes and gasped. Instead of my reflection, Dad stared back at me. Same intelligent eyes I'd inherited, more brown than green. Same haircut, shorter on the side and longer on top. I had him in my favorite T-shirt, the one I'd bought him before he became ill. I turned and grinned at the goddess. The cat watched me from her arms.

Take that, feline. The cat yawned.

I faced the mirror, and didn't close my eyes as I went through another transformation. My long brown hair changed texture and shortened to wavy, raven-black. Brilliant blue replaced the hazel in my eyes. The gentle sloping of my jawbone shifted to a masculine

line, my cheekbones became chiseled. The rest of me changed too, breasts flattening to a broad chest and shoulders.

I lifted my tank top and grinned. I had a six-pack. When my eyes met my reflection, I was staring into the sapphire eyes of the man I adored. Torin St. James.

I giggled. I could have fun with this. Torin still managed to look masculine in my silky pajama bottoms and snug tank top. But it was weird being a guy. No wonder they adjusted themselves. I had to.

Goddess Freya laughed. "I think you're going to enjoy mastering this ability. For right now you can only transform into those you know and love, until you gain enough experience to look like anyone. When you do, choose carefully. You don't want to mimic people they'd recognize."

Yeah, like Maliina had done. The Norns had appeared to me in so many forms, some familiar and others not. Could I do that too? Pull any skin tone or hair color out of thin air, and keep the image intact without slipping back to me?

"Can anyone tell I'm fake?"

She nodded. "Only another powerful witch can *feel* that you're not real. That's how you see through the disguises the Norns wear. Keep practicing until it's as easy as breathing. Say your goodbye, dear," Goddess Freya added, lowering the cat to the floor.

I frowned. Was she talking to me? "Just one question. How do I hold on to the image?"

"Try not to think of yourself. Channel the person you choose. If you're using your handsome Valkyrie, think of nothing but him. And Raine?"

I was busy watching my reflection as I transformed back into me, except my eyes didn't go back to hazel. They glowed golden, something that happened whenever I used magic. My gaze met the goddess' in the mirror. "Yes?"

"Now that you've decided to use your magic, be very careful how you deal with the Norns. You can be like them without being one of them."

That was my plan. I had no interest in being a Norn, spinning destinies and messing with people's heads. I planned to give people choices, something the Norns never did. "What did you mean by sacrifices?" I asked cautiously, but my insides clenched with dread.

"Like I said, I cannot see into the future. But the Norns took something valuable from me the last time I pushed them too far." She smiled as though it was nothing, but I saw through the image she projected to the anger and hatred. She was the mistress of illusions too. "Be careful. I've left you a little present. She'll be an asset as your powers grow, and she can always find me whenever you need me."

A portal opened and she walked through it, two cats following her. I hadn't seen the second one until now. The black and grey tabby looked at me, fur rising as though in warning.

What was her problem?

I dismissed the cat, my mind on what the goddess had said. What had the Norns taken from her for defying them? Not that I planned to defy them. I only fought them for the right to be left alone, to decide my fate. I stepped back, my feet sinking onto something soft.

A shriek filled the room.

I screamed, jumped back, stumbled against the edge of my bed, and fell.

You two-legged klutz. You broke my beautiful tail.

3. Kiss My Paws

Torin burst into my room through the mirror portal like an avenging angel. I wasn't the kind of girl who expected a man to run to my rescue whenever I screamed like a banshee, but he did look really good. His expression said he'd annihilate anyone that hurt me.

"You okay?" he said, eyes darting around the room before coming to me. I grinned. He frowned, squatting. "You're smiling."

I nodded. "You're my hero."

He reached out and stroked my nose. He loved my freckles. Always had from the first moment we met. He slid down and sat beside me, bringing his warm and intoxicating scent. He always smelled nice. "Except you don't need me rescuing you, do you?"

"Not this time." I rested my head on his shoulder while he stroked my arm. I trembled. My reaction to his touch had never changed since we met. A touch and I melted. Heck, he didn't even have to touch me for my body to respond. A look across a room often did the trick and he knew it and loved it, the arrogant Valkyrie.

My mother and Femi joined us through the door, their eyes frantically searching my room. Usually, they'd react to my scream like it was the end of the world, but not today because they'd known I was with the goddess.

"You know, if I was being attacked and Torin wasn't here, I'd be dead by now."

At least they had the decency to look guilty. Mom recovered first. "What a terrible thing to say," she reprimanded.

"Don't even try it, Mom. You knew she was up here, didn't you?"

She gave a brief laugh. "Yes, but uh…"

But nothing. Her loyalty was to the goddess, I knew that and understood why. My focus shifted to the cat.

So this was my present? Coat sleek and black as midnight, emerald green eyes that reminded me of Mom's eyes, which was a plus, except they were slit like the cat couldn't wait to scratch the crap out of me.

"I'm sorry," I whispered.

Her fur rose as she arched her back. *You should be, skreyja vilfill. I'm being forced to live in this godforsaken realm because of you.*

"What's going on?" Torin asked.

"I stepped on the cat," I said, giving him a sheepish look.

His eyebrows shot up. "You have a cat?"

"Not really. She's a present, but she doesn't want to be here." I glanced at the cat. "Maybe you can take her back to Asgard."

The cat's arched back slowly lowered.

"No, you can't," my mother said in a horrified voice.

"Why not?" I asked. "Because your goddess brought it?"

One second Torin was beside me, the next he was on his feet. "We had a deal, Mrs. Cooper."

"I know, dear. We were surprised when she appeared and asked if she could see Raine. I had no time to prepare. And she came bearing gifts."

"So did the Greeks," Torin murmured, but I heard him. Did he mean that the cat was like the Trojan horse?

"She's very particular about who gets her kittens, Torin." Mom went down on her knees, studied the cat, and smiled. "No, this one is not a kitten. She's one of the goddess' own. The changeling from the last litter."

"What deal are you two discussing?" I asked, my eyes volleying between Torin and Mom.

"It's nothing, hun." Mom got up, and Torin gripped her arm, leaned in, and murmured something to her.

"Hey," I called after them when he started to lead her out of my room.

"Bond with your cat, Freckles," Torin said.

My jaw dropped. That sounded like 'mind my own business'. The arrogant...

I tapped into my magic. It wasn't easy getting the spark going, but I hoped it was enough. I let images fill my head and willed them into his. Torin stopped and squinted at me. I gave him an innocent smile.

"What did you just do?" Femi asked, surprise sharpening her blue eyes.

"Projected something to him. You felt it?"

She nodded. "Yes. Nice. You're getting stronger."

I grinned. "The goddess showed me how to find the source of my magic. It's not easy, but with time, I might do it without stressing about it," I said. My focus shifted to my unwanted feline present. "Cats have never liked me. This one will probably hate me forever because I stepped on her tail. It was an accident."

"Goddess Freya," Femi whispered, her expression dreamy. In fact, I doubted she'd heard anything I said. "I never thought I'd ever meet her."

Femi was an Immortal, which meant she'd never visited Asgard. The gods tended to ignore Immortals, since they were turned in order to serve Mortals.

"Was she nice to you?" I asked.

"Oh yes, very nice and gracious. None of my friends will believe me when I tell them I met her." She thumped her forehead. "For all that's holy, why didn't I think of taking a selfie with her?"

A selfie with a goddess. I laughed. Femi would have asked too. She might be pint-sized, but she was feisty. "Maybe next time."

"Maybe next time what?" Mom asked as she and Torin returned.

"Take a selfie with Goddess Freya," I said while studying their faces. Mom seemed the same. She even laughed at my response, but Torin... I was getting some weird vibes from him. He didn't meet my eyes. What had Mom told him? I knew he wasn't too crazy about me being a witch, but I thought he was adjusting. Maybe he didn't like the idea of Goddess Freya paying me a visit in the middle of the night.

I reached for his hand and tugged. He slid down beside me on the floor. I searched his face and got my answer when he flashed one of his sexy grins. He wasn't fooling me. Something was wrong. Mom tried to reach for the cat and she hissed.

"I can't keep her," I said. "She's feral."

Call me feral again, baulufotr, and you'll be sorry.

Baulufotr. Skreyja vilfill. They all sounded like curses. Part of me wanted to ask Mom if I was supposed to hear the cat or not, but another part shied from sharing that bit yet. Like I said, Torin wasn't too thrilled about my witchy gifts, especially after I'd put a whammy on him before he battled his father.

"Cats hate me," I griped.

Mom stood. "No, they don't."

"They do too. Don't you remember how often I begged for a dog or a cat when I was little? And how we'd go to the pet store or animal shelter, and they'd hiss at me and the dogs would snarl?" My eyes met Torin's. "Eirik used to call me animal repellant. I ended up getting fish and birds. Why couldn't the goddess give me a bird? Isn't she the patron of ravens?"

Mom dismissed my words with a wave of her hand. "Swallows and cuckoos, and Eirik didn't know any better. You and the cat will bond and work together. Returning her would only insult the goddess."

I knew about the bond between a witch and her familiar, but that didn't mean I had to have one. I was an elemental witch. I communicated with the elements of the earth. "Did you guys have cats?"

Mom nodded. "Saoria was a charming companion."

"Azhara saved my life more often than I care to admit," Femi said.

Mom had a Celtic background while Femi was an ancient Egyptian. Both were thousands of years old. I was dying to find out if Mom's cat ever talked to her, but I wanted to be alone with Torin and find out what was wrong. His hand let go of mine, leaned forward, and extended toward the cat.

There was no hissing. The cat left its hiding place and sniffed his hand, then rubbed her cheek against it. The little traitor!

"See? Just be as gentle as Torin," Mom said.

The cat continued to rub her neck against his fingers. Finally, Torin picked her up and lifted her up like a baby, hands under her front legs. The two had a stare-down. It was both cute and impressive. Both had hair the color of midnight and sapphire eyes— Torin's blue and the cat's green. Both were deadly. One swipe and the cat's claw could leave nasty gashes on Torin's handsome face. And with very little effort, Torin could crush the cat's skull. The effect of strength runes was scary to watch. I'd seen Torin bring down a tree with a blow. It was as though he and the cat were sizing each other up. When it seemed like they'd reached an understanding, Torin lowered the cat to his thigh.

And what do you know. The fur-ball curled up like they'd known each other forever. Seriously? Everyone adored Torin. He'd won Mom's heart a long time ago and earned Dad's respect. And now he had even bonded with my familiar before me.

He belongs to me, I forcefully projected to the little cat.

The cat purred and closed her eyes. *Jealous?*

I blinked, surprised she'd heard me. *Not of a four-legged fur-ball.*

Kiss my paws, baulufotr. You need me, not the other way around.

Great! I didn't just get any normal witch cat. She had to be smart-alecky. Torin glanced at me, saw my expression and smirked, but I saw through it. Something was wrong. I glanced at Mom. I wanted her and Femi to go. The cat situation could wait until tomorrow.

"Goodnight, Mom. Femi."

Mom glanced at Femi. "I guess that's our cue. Goodnight, hun. Torin. Don't keep her up late. It's a school night."

As soon as the door closed, Torin said, "Why were your eyes glowing when I arrived?"

"I'll explain after you put *her*," I pointed at the cat, "down. I don't even know what to call her or where she's going to sleep." The cat lifted her head and glared at me.

Torin scratched her neck. "You should name her. It might help with the bonding."

"No, thanks. She's going back to Asgard," I said even though I knew she wasn't. "Were you reaping?"

"No, scouting at StubHub Center. I'm subbing for a math teacher at a local high school and coaching a U-16 youth soccer team for LA Galaxy Academy in the evenings. Most of the team members go to the school."

Torin often befriended those whose souls he reaped. "And that bothers you?" I pried.

"Nope." He was such a liar. "It's just a job."

He didn't look too thrilled. StubHub Center was in Carson, California. It was the National Training Center for the U.S. Soccer Federation. There was no telling which team was about to have an accident because they held camps and competitions for all U.S. soccer programs in the area and for national teams. Even the International Federation of Football Association (FIFA) used the stadium. Torin and Andris could be waiting for souls of teenagers or grown men. Something about his present assignment was bugging him, but I couldn't figure out what.

"Can I come with you tomorrow and watch you coach?"

He chuckled. "Why? You hate sports."

I bumped him with my shoulder. "Hey, I cheered the loudest when you were the quarterback."

He smiled, but it didn't reach his eyes. "We have a game on Saturday at three, but I'm having them practice at five every day this week. They made it to the quarterfinals."

"Then I'll come tomorrow after I shop for her," I nodded at the cat.

"Don't you have after-school lessons with Lavania?"

Lavania Celestina Ravilla was my trainer and a Valkyrie. "Yeah, but I should be done by five." I stifled a yawn and the cat yawned too. Coincidence? "Seriously, where is she supposed to sleep?"

"The window blanket." Torin got up and placed the cat on the window seat. The cat moved around as though searching for the most comfortable spot, then laid down. Dang, my favorite throw blanket was going to be covered with cat hair. No more window seat for me.

"Cats are smart. They can sense when someone doesn't like them," Torin added and threw me a censuring look.

But do they project their thoughts into people's minds? "*She* doesn't like me."

"She doesn't know you yet." He pulled me up, wrapped an arm around my waist and lifted me off the floor. I wrapped my legs around his waist and my arms around his neck. "Once she does, you two will be inseparable."

"Since when are you okay with me being a witch?"

"Since you and your witch friends defeated the Earl." He grinned. "Now stop talking and kiss me. I haven't seen you since this morning."

He liked to order me around, but I didn't mind this time. I studied him. He was still the cocky and outrageous guy I fell in love with, but something was off with him tonight. His voice had changed when he'd mentioned his father. Four days had passed since we'd defeated the Earl of Worthington, but the Immortal was very much alive despite the fact that Torin had vowed to kill him. A fact that still bothered him. A trip to Florida over the weekend to unwind had appeared to help. I'd made sure of that. But now that we were back home in Kayville, everything must remind him of what his father had done to his mother, and the fact that he hadn't killed him.

"Don't look at me like that," Torin said.

I tilted my head. "Like what?"

"Like you're using your witchy powers to see stuff I'm hiding from you."

On a normal day I would have told him I could see through his bullshit and that hiding things from me only caused friction between us. "What stuff?"

"The hot California girls. The nude beach Andris found."

He was really trying to act normal and I loved him for it, but he didn't fool me. "He would. One day he'll catch something runes can't cure."

Torin frowned. "Sometimes I think that's his intention. He does the craziest things."

Nah, Andris loved life too much to have a death wish. On the other hand, Torin had known Andris for centuries and might know a lot more about him than what I'd seen in the past eight months.

I tilted back Torin's head and studied his eyes. Shadows drifted like a dark rain cloud across his sapphire blue irises. "What's going on?"

A spasm of something—anger or pain, I couldn't tell which—crossed his face. "You have five seconds to kiss me, or else," he threatened.

Or else what? He needed me as much as I needed him. I kissed him, pouring all my love into the kiss and hoping to erase whatever had caused his pain.

The next second, my back was on the bed and he was crushing into me. Not that I was complaining. The invasion of my senses sent a shudder through me and I pulled him closer, my fingers sinking into his hair, my other hand slipping under his shirt to caress his back.

He rained kisses down my neck, his mouth relentless, one hand holding my head in place as though making sure I didn't move. Shudders rocked him and he pulled back, but I wasn't ready to let him go yet. He, on the other hand, had his own idea. He trapped my arms above my head, easily circling my wrists with just one of his hands.

"Torin," I protested.

"Engage your runes," he ordered.

I didn't like being ordered around this time, but once again, I let him get away with it. He was in a strange mood. His runes were already blazing and as he lowered his head, I caught a glimpse of the grim determination in his eyes. He needed me to forget something. I just wished I knew what it was. I didn't push because he would eventually tell me everything. His mouth did its own exploration as he reduced me to a trembling mass of needs and cravings. I squirmed, getting frustrated fast.

"Let go of my hands," I begged.

"No."

"Yes."

He kissed me again, as though to shut me up. Then he stopped and rolled with me, so I was on top. I stroked his arms, loving the way his muscles jerked. He watched me from under half-closed eyelids. I loved that look on him. It was sexy, yet challenging. Like he was daring me to be bold. My hands skimmed over his broad shoulders, my lips following. When I nipped him, he jerked. I soothed the skin with my tongue.

He smelled nice. Woodsy. Exotic. Intoxicating. I burrowed my nose in his neck and breathed him in. Was it possible to want someone as badly as I wanted him now? I showed him and he groaned.

I glanced at him. "Do you want me to stop?"

"Don't. Don't ever stop loving me, Freckles," he growled. That was all I needed to hear.

I ran my tongue along his lower lip, then the upper one before slipping my tongue inside his mouth to play with his. His chest heaved with the strain of holding back. I trailed kisses down his neck as tremors shot through him.

I moved lower, my hands caressing his wide chest, his six-pack. He had the cutest belly button. My lips followed. Before I could move farther, he pulled me up and captured my lips again in a kiss that went on forever. Then he lifted my face and studied me.

"We need to stop now," he said.

"No," I protested. I could tell he didn't want to and I was tired of waiting for him to make up his mind. Tired of being a virgin.

"Shh," he added when I opened my mouth to complain. "If I claimed you and made you mine, Freckles, I wouldn't want to stop. I'd want to do it again and again, all night and into the next day. That's what honeymoons are for. I've waited for you for nearly nine centuries, I can wait a few more months."

Okay, put that way, I could live with it. Sort of. Why couldn't he be like most guys? You know, selfish with a raging libido? "What if we agree to stop after—"

He pressed a hand to my lips. "I will not negotiate with you when it comes to this, Freckles. There'll be no stopping and no going back once you are mine. And tonight…" He sighed. "In the mood I'm in, things could get out of control fast." He pulled me closer as though to absorb me into him and pressed a kiss on my forehead. I swallowed my disappointment and hugged him tight, the glow from our runes blending.

Once our hearts slowed to a regular beat, I lifted my head and studied him. "What happened?"

For a brief second, I was sure he'd blow me off. He tended to keep secrets in the name of protecting me, but after the fiasco with his father, I hoped he had learned his lesson.

"I saw my father tonight," he said.

His statement robbed me of words. One, Torin always referred to him as the Earl. Second, I hated that conniving bastard. Hated what he'd done to Torin's mother and what he was doing to Torin now. No wonder he was a mess tonight.

"Where?" I asked.

"StubHub. He watched me coach, then came over after we were done." Torin took my hand and pressed a kiss on my knuckles. Only then did I realize that I'd formed a fist. He uncurled my fingers and pressed a kiss in my palm as though to take away my anger.

I tried to relax and pretend we were discussing something mundane, but I couldn't. The Earl was pure poison. My anger grew. "What did he want?"

"Forgiveness."

"Screw him," I said before I could stop myself. Torin chuckled. It wasn't funny. "I know he's your father and all, but after what he did and the number of people who died because of him…"

"Andris reacted the same way," Torin said, speaking slowly, eyebrows flattening. "I'd never seen him move so fast. My father didn't fight back. I think Andris broke several ribs before snapping his neck. I did nothing," he added softly. "We were late coming home tonight because we had to wait for him to heal and regain consciousness."

Way to go, Andris. He could be a total douche, but he was loyal. "Maybe you did nothing because Andris was doing exactly what you wanted to do, but chose not to."

He interlaced our fingers and pressed our joined hands to his chest. "Very likely. I stopped Andris before he yanked his heart out." He glared at the ceiling. "I don't know why I did that. I should have just let him finish the Earl."

We were back to the Earl, thank goodness.

"He's not talking to me now."

"What are you going to do?"

He shrugged. "I don't know. He's trying to make amends."

In other words, he was willing to listen to his father. That man had some nerve. Selfish bastard. We had just barely finished fighting him and his renegade Immortal followers, and he was already back. He didn't even have the decency to give Torin time to heal. Give *us* all time to recover. We were all affected by what he'd started. I still had nightmares of what he'd done to the Seeresses. He and the Norns. All I had to do was close my eyes to see the smirks on the Norns' faces.

"Can I meet him?" I asked.

"No. I don't want him anywhere near you. I don't trust him."

Thank goodness he wasn't totally on a forgive-Daddy bend. I might not find the idea of snapping necks appealing, but I had a mean knee. A quick thrust and the Earl's nuts would get lodged in his esophagus for eternity. Or maybe I didn't need to meet the bastard to make him disappear. I could just change his destiny and find him a quicker exit to Hel where he belonged. I hated that the Norns were in charge of destinies. If I changed his, I'd be acting just like them.

"Can I come with you tomorrow?" I asked.

"No."

"Hey, you were okay with it earlier. I've never seen you coach."

He glanced at me and groaned. "You only want to come to confront the Earl, and I'm not letting him anywhere near you."

We'll see about that. My mind raced as I imagined what I'd say to his father if we ever met again. Torin stroked my temple. I could feel him relaxing. He'd definitely been worked up about this. Probably worried about how I'd react. He could be so sweet sometimes.

Sleep was beckoning me when he spoke next. "How was your day?"

I lifted my head. "I will summarize it into three sentences, so we can go to sleep."

He chuckled. "Okay."

"I snuck into the boy's locker room to steal a sweatshirt to confirm a vision."

Torin stiffened, but I ignored it.

"I went to his house and stopped him from killing his stepfather and ruining his life."

Torin's face had gone pale. He was taking this well, but the fact that he didn't say anything proved how much control he was exerting. Usually, he would be yelling.

"And I learned from the goddess that I shouldn't rune people to make them forget me, when I can do this instead." I focused on the source within, but the spark was barely there. I closed my eyes and let the need to connect with my powers fill me.

"Do what?" Torin asked. I opened my eyes and he blinked. "Your eyes are glowing."

He sounded wary. Grinning, I felt the connection grow and channeled the energy into changing his perception, my skin tingling with the surge of magic. Torin's eyes went from wary to shock. He moved so fast that one minute our limbs were intertwined and the next he was tripping on the chair in an attempt to put some distance between us.

"Hel's Mist. That's messed up."

I cocked my eyebrow and smirked, hoping I had nailed that habit of his I found so adorable.

"I don't do that," he protested. "And definitely not that," he added when I tossed my hair. He started to laugh. I sat up and watched him. I'd been sure he would be repulsed. "I told you before, Freckles. There can't be two of me."

I let go of the image. "You're not angry?"

"Because you can mess with people's heads and make them see you as someone else? No, I expected that to come with the witch territory. Do I want you to do it to me? No. When I'm with you, I want to see you, not someone else. When we are... Wait! You went to the boy's locker room? What were you thinking?" His voice rose.

"Shh," I hissed.

He came back to bed and scooped me up.

"Hey! Where are we going?"

"Somewhere where I can tell you exactly how I feel without waking up your mother," he said through gritted teeth, but I heard him. He went through the mirror portal to his bedroom, dropped me on his bed unceremoniously, and ran his fingers through his hair. His hair fell back into place, the locks in front almost reaching his eyebrows. He needed a trim.

"Did anyone see you?" he asked.

"Nope. I did the seeing. I saw and heard things I hope never to see again." For one brief moment, I was sure he'd laugh. Instead he scowled.

"Who did you see?" he made it sound like I'd committed some heinous crime. "The images you projected in my head earlier?"

I grinned. "Were real, but they weren't impressive. Pasty and not exactly drool-worthy. But you could take everything off and erase them from my mind. I'd rather have you up here," I tapped my head, "than them."

He stared at me intently as though actually deciding whether to do it or not. Then he gave me a slow, wicked smile and reached for his pants.

Alarm shot through me. "I'm kidding, Torin."

"I'm not. Don't you dare close your eyes." He continued down. That intriguing line of hair broadened. I closed my eyes. Then I wished I hadn't. Now I was too chicken to look.

"Open your eyes, Freckles."

I resisted, my heart pounding.

"Chicken," he added.

I opened one eye slowly so I could only see through my eyelashes. He stood in the middle of his bedroom, hands on his hips, expression saying he was no longer in a playful mood, but he wasn't naked.

Relief and disappointment vied for dominance.

"Now start from the beginning and don't leave anything out. How did you know where he lived? How did you stop him? You're not invincible. A bullet can get lodged in your heart you know. You and I are going to have a little understanding about your after-school activities." He stopped his rant and glowered. "Start talking."

I would if he would shut up. "It started in the cafeteria."

He interrupted every few seconds, cursing and running his fingers along his nape. When I finished, he gave me a long lecture until I lifted my hands in surrender.

"I get it," I said. "You are worried about me because you think I take chances with my life when I don't. I thought this through. You know, while following his truck home. I'm not going to stop helping people out of fear of what might happen to me, Torin."

He sighed. "Sadly, I know that."

"But I promise to be careful."

He shot me a skeptical look. "Right. Describe the Grimnirs."

I rolled my eyes. "Don't worry, I dealt with them."

"Describe them, Raine," he said in a hard voice.

I hated it when he went all intense and bossy on me. Just to shut him up, I did, not skipping on the guy's unusual eyes and his amazing tattoos. Torin's intelligent eyes slit as though he was compartmentalizing each image for retrieval later.

"FYI, no one should tell you what to do."

"Except you," I said.

"Damn right." He smirked. "I earned that right the moment I chose to love you."

My jaw dropped. "You chose to love me?"

"Oh yes. Falling in love with you was out of my control. But loving you is a choice and a responsibility I take seriously. It means worrying about you and saving you from shitheads like Grimnirs on power trips." He crawled into bed and pulled me into his arms. "I'm only gone one day. One freaking day and you go all guardian angel on me. I'm coming to school with you tomorrow. If Hardshaw looks at you wrong..." Then he went quiet and scowled. "What exactly were you wearing when you paid him a visit tonight? What was he doing?"

The answers were likely to cause another yelling session I didn't need, so I ignored the questions. "You can't come to school tomorrow. You're subbing at that school in California."

"Caesar Chavez High School, or CC High as the locals call it. They start later, so we're attending first period here for appearances, and to make sure you're not going out of your way to touch people just to see their futures and fix their miserable lives. Adversity creates character you know."

I didn't argue with him. What was the point? I made a face.

"I felt that," he said, then pressed a kiss on my forehead. "Go to sleep while I think up a way to save you from yourself."

I wanted to tell him he wasn't my keeper, but I knew where that would get me. Nowhere. Probably another lecture about worrying about me came with loving me. "How exactly did you go from having a full class load to just one class?" I asked instead.

"Andris altered the records and changed the rest of our classes to either completed or online classes."

Andris was the computer geek in the group. "Can he do the same for me? I mean, finishing high school won't change what I'll be doing in the future."

"So you can go around finding trouble? No-ooo. You're safer in school." I felt his lips move as he smiled. "No, you're safer with me. You should definitely come with me to California, where I can keep an eye on you. You could join the janitorial staff at my school."

Menial work? "Forget it. I'm staying right here." I was falling asleep when I realized he'd manipulated me into agreeing with him.

***

Torin must have used the portal and carried me back to my bed after I fell asleep because I woke up in my room. I slammed my hand on the alarm to turn it off. A quick look out my window showed him in his kitchen making breakfast. I loved that we were next-door neighbors. As though he knew I was watching, he looked up and smiled.

Do you do this every morning?

I turned my head to see Freya's present with her head resting on her paws, her ears twitching, and her head tilted sideways so she could look at me. Not wanting to bait her, I refused to ask what she meant.

What? Ignoring me now? Are we sulking? She stretched and rolled onto her back.

I turned away.

Cat got your tongue?

Snarky and funny. Still, I wasn't enabling her.

I guess you don't want to know why I'm here, what the goddess really wants.

I stopped. "What?"

She chuckled, the sound so human-like that a shiver shot up my spine. *I need a soft bed to sleep in, something with extra cushioning. I will not wear a tag like Mortal felines. I will not use a litter box unless it's self-cleaning, and I don't eat hard food. I like fish and liver. Once I'm comfortable, we'll talk.*

I slowly counted backwards from ten, and squatted so we were on the same eye-level. She hissed, but I didn't back down.

"Listen to me, you narcissistic *alley cat*." Her eyes narrowed at the insult and the hairs on her back rose. "Scratch me and you'll hit the pavement so hard you'll have eight lives left. I've had it up to here," I touched my forehead, "with you supernatural beings. Norns. Goddesses. Now you. You want a bed and nice things, you earn it."

The cat glared back.

"What does the goddess want?"

Her ears twitched.

"You think I'm kidding? I'll change your litter once a week and use the non-clumping, non-odor absorbent kind." I'd seen enough commercials for cat litter to know what cats preferred. "I'll buy you hard food and if you do anything to piss me off, you'll spend the night outside."

Her fur went down and her eyes closed. She meowed and rolled onto her back. *Want to scratch my tummy?*

I blinked. I was so pissed I wanted to pick her up by her tail. Yeah, I know. Totally cruel. But I didn't give a crap about animal rights at the moment. *Fur-ball.*

Beiskaldi, she retorted.

Another insult? I gave her the finger.

She stood and stretched again. *So what's for breakfast?*

I moved away from her and slammed my bathroom door. The shower didn't help my mood. I could feel the cat's eyes on me as I changed. I didn't look her way, just engaged my runes and headed for Torin's.

He met me with a latte and a plate of hash-browns, eggs, and bacon. He was still in his sweats, his hair wet from the shower.

"What's wrong?" he asked.

"Cat problems."

"Who's winning?"

I glared at him. "I will once I know how to shut her up."

"You two are communicating already?"

He didn't seem bothered by it, so I nodded. "Lucky me."

He chuckled. "You're probably hungry, aren't you?" He bent down and when he stood, he had the cat in his arms. Seriously? The fur-ball followed me here?

"Want something to eat?" Torin asked, his face close to the cat's.

Meow! She licked his nose.

The nerve. Torin gave her a whole slice of bacon and scratched her neck as she ate. "See? Give her something to eat and she'll be nice." He planted a kiss on my lips and swatted my butt on his way out of the kitchen.

I sat and started on my meal. Fur-ball finished her bacon and stared at me. I tried to ignore her. She inched closer. I took some of my eggs and offered them to her.

She shot me a condescending look. Sighing, I gave her my last piece of bacon. She ate it, then demolished the eggs, and went back to staring at my plate.

"You can't possibly still be hungry," I griped.

I'm miserable. Bacon is my comfort food.

Now I felt bad. I slid the entire plate across the counter to her just as a gentle breeze swept through the kitchen from the hallway. Someone had just used the hallway portal.

I put down my drink as Andris entered the room and walked straight to the coffeemaker. He was a grouch until he had coffee. Unfortunately, he lived with Lavania in the mansion, and she was a tea person. And so was Ingrid. Blaine wandered in here too for coffee.

Once Andris poured himself some coffee, black with no additives, he took a big gulp, gave a part sigh and part moan of appreciation, turned and smiled at me. "Morning, sunshine. Sleeping over here now?"

"Can I give you a hug without you acting weird?"

He took another gulp, put his drink down, and opened his arms. I hugged him tight, leaned toward his ear and said, "I love you. You know that, right?"

A weird expression crossed his face, and he gave an exaggerated sigh. "I always knew you had a thing for me from the first moment we met. Sorry, babe, but it wouldn't work between us." Then he smirked. "Unless you want a quickie when your man is teaching. Some of the closets at CC High are pretty roomy."

"You deserve better than quickies in the closet." I kissed his cheek and stepped back.

He reached for his mug and yelped.

"What's that?" He was staring at my cat, who hissed at him, her back arched as though marking her territory.

Why are you kissing him when you have the hot Valkyrie, she screamed in my head.

I rolled my eyes. *Back off, Fur-ball. He's like Torin's brother, and he was only joking.*

No, he wasn't. He has nefarious thoughts about you. He's a scoundrel. A knave. A Jotunn backside.

I laughed. She just called Andris a giant ass.

"Raine!"

I glanced at Andris.

"Why are you acting weird? Why am I asking an obvious question? You are weird and maddening. Where did *that* come from?"

"She's a gift from your goddess." Andris reaped souls for Goddess Freya's training field. I loved that she was so powerful that warriors were split equally between her and Odin. In fact, she got the first pick of souls. During Ragnarok, the final battle between the gods and the evil giants, she would lead her men into battle. "Let's talk about a certain earl. You should have yanked out the murdering bastard's heart instead of snapping his neck."

Andris' attention reluctantly moved from the cat, his brown eyes darkening. "I wanted to. He's going to screw with Torin's head. This forgiveness crap is just the bastard's new way of getting to him."

"We're not going to let him," I said.

"Damn right." He glanced toward the stairs. "Let's connect later and strategize."

"I'm coming to California after school to watch you guys coach."

"Good. We can talk while *he* coaches. I'm assisting him, but he's such a stick-in-the-mud I just let him run the whole damn thing. The Mortal assistant coaches are so in awe of him, they just pant after him when he enters the field. They think he's the next best thing since Beckham." He chuckled in derision. "I've watched Torin play and he can whoop Beckham's ass. And don't let me get started on the mothers. They're willing to carry and fetch things to catch the new coach's attention. Women. That's why I'd never settle for one." He pushed against the counter and stood straighter. "Later, sweetheart. Happy we're on the same page." His eyes went to the cat. "Witches and their cats." He shuddered.

You're not all that either, pretty boy, the cat shot back and hopped off the counter.

I fought a smile and followed Andris, waited until he was inside the mansion, then redirected the portal to my bedroom. Fur-ball walked ahead of me and went back to the window.

I gathered my school stuff and Beau's sweatshirt. With a quick glance at the cat I found her napping, or pretending to. She looked so peaceful. I didn't want to disturb her and hear another round of insults.

I headed downstairs, deliberately walking instead of creating a portal. I liked the exercise. Dad and I used to jog together before he became ill. I would swim with the swim team during regular season and with a local club in the off-season, but since I got immersed in the supernatural world, I'd dropped everything. I needed other forms of exercise to stay in shape. Moving at hyper-speed burned calories like crazy and my appetite had shot up exponentially to match it, but it wasn't something I did regularly. Maybe I should.

Mom was in the kitchen finishing her breakfast when I got downstairs. Someone had cooked eggs. Probably Femi. Mom's cooking sucked. Dad had done most of our cooking when I was growing up.

"Is Dad up?" I asked.

"No, honey. Do you want breakfast?" Mom asked.

"No. I already ate at Torin's." I placed my backpack on the counter and took a stool. "I guess I'm not exactly sure what to do about the cat now. Should I put newspaper down for her to use and a bowl of water? I'm not even sure what food she eats. I was thinking of shopping for her after school."

"Sounds like a good idea. Don't worry about her now," Mom reassured me. She got up to put her plate away and pressed a kiss on my forehead. "Femi will take care of her." She grabbed her bag. "Wish me luck. I don't want to be late for my first day at work."

"Work?" She was dressed in her Boho skirt and top, jewelry around her neck and wrists, and a Gypsy-inspired hairpiece holding her pitch-black, straight hair down. As usual, she looked like a hippie. A drop-dead gorgeous hippie. "Aren't you reaping today?"

"Yes, in the Seattle area. My partner got me a job at a jewelry shop, so we don't have to hang around doing nothing."

I frowned. "What partner?"

"Some young man. Just like Torin and Andris are paired, I'm paired with a Valhalla Valkyrie." She glanced at her watch, blew me a kiss, and added, "Love you, hun. Be careful. If you need me, portal to me."

I watched her hurry towards the den and scowled. Young man, huh? Of course young man meant he was a few centuries younger or he'd become Immortal at a much younger age. Mom might be over a millennium old, but she looked like someone in their late twenties or early thirties. Men were going to hit on her out there. Somehow I couldn't imagine her with anyone but Dad. In fact, I didn't know how I'd feel if she dated anyone after Dad died. My throat closed. I'd accepted that my father was dying. It was only a matter of when. Still, it wasn't easy.

Femi was checking Dad's vitals when I entered the room. For a moment, I studied him. His color had improved since Mom came back. It had taken months for the Valkyrie Council to reinstate her status as an active reaper, but it was worth it. She would reap Dad and find him a place in Goddess Freya's Hall. I hope. She wouldn't have to date some faceless man while Dad was in Freya's Hall because she'd see him whenever she escorted souls there.

I dropped a kiss on Dad's forehead and followed Femi out of the room. "How is he doing?"

"Better now that Svana is home." She glanced up the stairs, and I followed her gaze. The cat stood at the top of the steps watching us. "I'll take care of your cat while you're gone."

I nodded. "Thanks. I think she's hungry."

She extended a hand toward the cat. "Come here, princess."

The cat gave her a disdainful look, turned, and walked back toward my room.

"You need to give her a name, doll," Femi said. "Start bonding with her."

"We've already bonded. Hey, Fur-ball, there's bacon down here," I called out.

Beiskaldi.

That must be her favorite insult.

Femi laughed. "Fur-ball? That's a terrible name. Try Bastet or Isis."

The cat reappeared at the top of the stairs and sat, looking regal. *Ugly names,* she said.

"Isis sounds good," I said and got a mean glare from the cat.

Femi chuckled. "You might be right about bonding with her. Cats are ornery, but familiars tend to bond fast with their owners."

"This one bonds with whoever gives her bacon," I said.

"Is that so? Then she and I are going to be best buddies. I love bacon. Come on, pretty lady."

Femi knew a lot about magic. Without her help, I would not have sharpened my visions or discovered Torin's father's evil plot.

"How do you know if you've bonded with your familiar?" I asked.

Femi glanced at me and chuckled. "You'll be in sync. She'll know when you need her, know what you're thinking before you speak. If you're really lucky, she will communicate with you telepathically."

Yeah, lucky me. "Ok. Later, Femi. Bye, Isis." She ignored me.

Torin was already waiting in his garage. He watched me, an appreciative gleam in his eyes. I was wearing the leather jacket he'd bought for me in Florida and jeans. Nothing to go ga-ga over, but he had a way of telling me he liked what I was wearing without saying a word. I wanted him to look at me like that forever.

He snapped my helmet on and swept my hair away from my nape. My breath caught, reminding me of the first time he ever did that. The effect on me was the same, which might explain why he loved doing it.

"You look beautiful," he added, pressing a kiss on my lips. They tingled. "That's new. Tastes good."

"It's flavorless," I said.

He tilted his head sideways. "Did you do magic this morning?"

I'd practiced connecting with the source of my magic. "A little. Why?"

"Nothing. What's that?" He jerked his head to indicate the sweatshirt in my hand.

"Beau Hardshaw's sweatshirt." I dropped it in one of the bike's saddlebags while Torin stashed my backpack in the other.

"Are you getting anymore visions from it?"

"Nope. It's all good. He has a bright future now." I didn't bring up his 'nothing' response to my question about magic until he was parking his bike at school. "Nothing? Really? You never say anything unless you mean it."

"You feel and taste different after you do magic," he said.

I frowned. "Different good or different bad?" He waved to two of his jock friends, then lifted my backpack and gripped my hand. I dug my feet in. "I'm not moving until you tell me."

"Does it matter?"

He was procrastinating. Not a good thing. "Am I repulsive? Taste disgusting?"

"Freckles, you could never— Ouch!"

I'd elbowed him. It hadn't hurt, the faker. "This is important and you're screwing with me. Is it good or bad?"

"It's hard to explain." He ran a finger down my nose and frowned. "After you perform magic, it's like the energy inside you calls to me. You become my oxygen, something I must have. And when we touch, it only gets more intense. It's very unsettling and..."

I laughed and hugged him.

"Quit that. It's not funny. I hate being out of control."

That explained his weird intensity last night. "I think I'm going to enjoy this."

"No, you won't." He put his arm around my shoulders and pressed a kiss on my temple. "I could hurt you."

No, he couldn't. But a Torin I could control opened new doors. I was still grinning when we entered the main hall.

Students were everywhere. Prom courts seemed to be the topic. The junior prom was next week on Friday and the teachers would post the nominees the day before. The bigger event would be the senior prom several weeks away. I planned to attend both with Torin.

After yesterday, I tried not to brush against people as we made our way across the main hall. Torin bumped fists with his friends and a few slapped his back. They tended to treat me like one of them, which was totally cool with me most of the time. But since the visions started, I didn't want to be touched. And the way I clung to Torin's arm, like some insecure girlfriend, left little room for me to high-five anyone or do fist bumps.

My focus stayed on the people hurrying past us, hoping no one brushed against me. My premonitions were sporadic. I didn't know how to open or close my mind to them yet. Maybe tapping into the source when I needed it and pushing it back might do the trick. Lavania hadn't taught me that yet. She preferred to take things slow.

We turned the corner and almost bumped into Justin Sinclair and Darren Rassman leaning against the wall chatting. Both were seniors and had played football with Torin. Last night flashed in my head. Ellie, Justin's girlfriend, and Beau Hardshaw. Who would have thought?

"Seen Hardshaw this morning?" Torin asked them.

"Nah, but his fucked-up ride is outside," Justin said and leered at me before focusing on a group of girls walking by.

I never liked Justin. He was preppy, rich and entitled, and I found it repulsive the way his pale eyes ran over every girl that walked past, as though he was mentally undressing them. Ellie was better off with Beau, but loaded girls like her only dated loaded jerks like Justin.

Ellie and Amber Griffin left the restroom across the hallway and paused to giggle. I hated girls who giggled. Justin and Darren must have been waiting for them.

"Her hair looks hideous," Ellie said, glancing over her shoulder at the restroom door.

"Thank you. The bitch got what she deserved," Amber said. Then she saw us and flashed a smile. "Hey, Raine, Torin."

I gave them a stiff smile, remembering Ellie's camera make-out session with Beau. She walked into her boyfriend's arms and continued to kiss him. What did she see in him?

Amber took Darren's arm and pulled it over her shoulder. She and Ellie might consider me one of them now because we dated jocks, but six months ago, they'd made fun of me when I'd been labeled a witch. Who were they tormenting in the restroom this time?

"If you see Hardshaw, tell him to find me ASAP," Torin said and bumped fists with Justin.

As we walked away, a girl burst out of the restroom and brushed past us at a run. The vision that flashed in my head was brief, but it was enough to know the person behind her new hairstyle. Her hair was an ugly shade of pink.

Ellie and Amber giggled.

"She tries too hard," Amber said.

I frowned. "I thought McKenzie was your friend."

"Oh please," Ellie said and rolled her eyes.

"We tolerate her because her brother's hot," Amber said. McKenzie's brother, Luke, was the captain of the baseball team. "But not as hot as you, hun," she added, smiling at Darren. He lapped it up. Moron.

I waited until we were a fair distance from the group before saying, "I can't stand them."

Torin squeezed my shoulder. "I noticed."

"She did that to McKenzie."

Torin shot me a bewildered glance. "Who did what?"

"Cheer-bitch Amber colored McKenzie's hair. You should do something."

Torin's eyebrows shot up. "Why me? I don't even know who this McKenzie is or how her hair color is my problem."

I sighed. "Just find a girl with bright pink hair and say something nice to her."

He stopped. "Like what?"

"I don't know. You are the charming one. Make up something. Compliment her hair. Tell her she looks pretty this morning."

Torin laughed. "You're kidding."

I shook my head. "This incident will lead to another, then another, and finally she'll slit her wrists."

"Because a bunch of girls mocked her hair? Is she pretty?"

I punched his arm. "Does it matter? She's sweet and nice, but her hair is an ugly shade of pink." I grimaced. "But that's beside the point. She's been trying to fit in all her life and she thought Ellie and Amber were her friends. Now they did this. Please."

Torin groaned, but his expression said he'd do as I asked. He glanced at his watch. "If I used hyper-speed…"

I kissed his cheek. "You're the best."

"The things I do for you, Freckles," he murmured. "*You* can return Beau's stinky sweatshirt."

"Aw, come on."

He tossed it and it landed on some poor guy's face. At least the guy was graceful enough not to take offense and gave it to me. Torin, on the other hand, was aggravating. He laughed when I glared at him.

"I'll take it to lost and found." Just in case the guy he'd hit thought the smelly sweatshirt was mine.

I felt a little bad about using Torin, but I knew how it felt to be in McKenzie's shoes. To have your so-called 'friends' desert you while others looked at you like you were a freak was demoralizing. At least I'd had Eirik and Cora when the entire swim team had deserted me. McKenzie needed a confidence boost, and no one could deliver it like Torin.

4. A Helping Hand

I was running to catch up with Cora during lunch when I almost bumped into Beau and his entourage—Seth Renwick and Ryder Copeland. Seth was built like a viking: red hair, freckles everywhere, arms and legs like a tree. He was the serious one of the trio. Ryder was the opposite—skinny with curly dark hair, and a mouth that didn't stop yapping. Both played varsity baseball with Beau.

Beau didn't act like he'd seen me in my pajamas. He flashed the lopsided grin that had lured many naïve girls to his rundown truck.

"St. James said you found my shirt," he said.

"Yeah, but it's in my locker."

"Damn." He looked at his friends.

"We gotta go, dude," Ryder said and walked backwards. "They won't wait forever."

Beau looked undecided for a second, and then said, "I'll get it after school. Your last class is band, right?" He winked. "I've watched you walk past my class. I'll find you." He took off after his friends.

By the time I entered the bathroom, Cora had already used the portal and disappeared. She was probably meeting Echo for lunch.

Torin was waiting for me at his place with lunch by the time I got there. He only had five minutes because he was meeting a student. Once he left, I carried my food to our house and sat with Dad while I ate. I didn't see Fur-ball.

I headed back to school after lunch feeling a bit meh. I couldn't explain why. Maybe it was sitting with Dad or only seeing Torin briefly. I was used to spending most of my free time with him.

Hours later, I was on my way from the orchestra room when I heard, "You know the drill, Hardshaw. You don't improve your grade, you get benched."

I stopped by the door and shamelessly eavesdropped.

"Just one last chance, Mr. Gentry," Beau said. "I have a big game in two weeks and there'll be scouts from several colleges."

"This is the school policy, Hardshaw. If you're failing a class, you can't play sports. I'm sorry, but you should have enrolled in peer tutoring weeks ago."

No. I didn't sneak into the boy's locker room and kill my brain cells with the stench from Hardshaw senior's tighty-whities only to have some teacher mess with my case. I peered into the room. Beau was picking up his things while Mr. Gentry scribbled on a piece of paper.

I looked up and down the hallway. Students were hurrying home and half the hallway was already empty. I could disappear without anyone noticing. I lifted my oboe, waited until a group of girls walked past me and then engaged my invisibility and speed runes.

I entered the classroom just as Beau started for the door and went to where the teacher sat. *You will give him one more chance. Call him back and give him one more chance. Do it now.*

Mr. Gentry looked up just as Beau reached the door. "Hardshaw! Wait." He pulled out a packet and slid it across his desk. "Turn this in by next Friday or no more baseball. We'll have a test on Friday too. If you work through this packet, you should be able to pass. Otherwise I will have to contact your coach."

Yes! I took a peek at the packet. They were reading *The Scarlet Letter* by Nathaniel Hawthorne. Sweet. I'd read the book last year and could help him.

"Find someone to help you with it or enroll in the peer tutoring program. There's no shame in asking for help." While Mr. Gentry expanded on the value in seeking help, I left the room.

The hallway was almost empty. I got rid of the runes and pulled out my cell phone. Timing was crucial. I listened to Beau's footsteps and when he was closer to the door, I put my cell phone to my ear.

"That's okay, Mom," I said into the phone. "I know. I'll find a student to tutor for the rest of the semester. I don't know, Mom. Math or English lit." Beau entered the hallway, but instead of walking past me, he stopped. I gave him a brief smile. "Fine, Mom. I'll stop by Mr. Kent's office and sign up for peer tutoring." I closed my phone and smiled at Beau. "Mothers. They can be so pushy." I made a face. "I'm heading to my locker if you want to get your sweatshirt."

Beau nodded and for a few minutes, we walked without talking. Students heading to after-school programs turned and stared at us. I wondered what they were thinking. Kayville High bad boy and the QB's girlfriend together? Hmm, too cliché.

"So where did you find my sweatshirt?" Beau asked.

"I went to the boy's locker room and grabbed it, just so I can give it back to you." I gave him a toothy smile. "That's probably what everyone's thinking."

He smirked. "You can read minds?"

"Yep, and faces. You were thinking it too."

"Nah," he protested, but he couldn't look me in the eye, confirming my theory.

"Right. You think I haven't noticed how girls find a reason to have you, the great Beau Hardshaw, notice them? It's quite interesting to watch. It's like a special mating ritual."

He chuckled. "Okay, now you're shitting with me. They do that for your boyfriend."

"Only an idiot would think Torin could possibly be interested in them," I said.

This time he laughed. Several students looked at us before disappearing into a room.

"So you're saying you and Torin are tight?" Beau asked.

I crossed my forefinger and the middle one. "Like that."

"If I didn't know better, I'd take that as a challenge."

"And you'd lose. Besides, you have enough girls panting after you." We reached the lockers and I stopped in front of mine. "One more and your head would explode."

"You held my hand yesterday outside the cafeteria after deliberately bumping into me," he shot back.

My face warmed a bit at that. I'd done both and he was full of himself enough to have reached his own conclusion. "It wasn't deliberate. As for holding your hand, I saw bruises on your arm and knuckles. They looked painful."

He frowned and I wished I hadn't brought those up. The whole point was to make him feel at ease so he could ask me to tutor him. Sure I'd blown my chances, I unlocked my locker, retrieved his sweatshirt, and handed it to him. "I found it outside the boys' locker room and it happens to have your name. Ok bye, unless you want Torin to think you're hitting on me." I wiggled my fingers.

"Thanks." He turned to leave and my heart dropped. Maybe he had someone in mind. Ellie was smart and a senior. McKenzie and I just happened to be one of the few juniors in the AP class.

Beau stopped, pivoted on his heels, and faced me, a sheepish expression on his face. He shoved his hands in his jeans' front pockets and glanced around as though making sure we were alone. "So, you want to do peer tutoring?"

"Yeah. It will look good on my college application, but the few times I went to the resource room, they had more tutors than students." I hoisted my backpack onto my shoulder and started toward the school entrance. He followed. "I didn't want to hang around, so…"

"Do you *have* to do it here at the school?"

So that was why he hadn't attended peer tutoring. Embarrassment. No, an image or reputation thing. Guys like Beau liked to pretend that grades didn't matter. "When I did it last year, we worked anywhere. My place. Her place. The Hub."

He was quiet. The front hall was empty and so was the schoolyard. We crossed the road running in front of the school and reached my car first. The parking lot was nearly empty, but his battered Chevrolet truck stood out. It was old and rusty, but I could tell he was trying to take good care of it. Part of it was freshly painted.

"See you around, Beau," I called out.

He seemed undecided, and then he closed the space between us. "Would you consider tutoring me?"

"You?" I faked surprise. "In what?"

"English lit. Have you read *The Scarlet Letter?*"

I nodded. "First semester. It was a tough one, but I enjoyed it."

"You're kidding, right? I hate his style of writing. Anyway, if you can, cool. If you can't…" he shrugged, but his expression was hopeful.

I pretended to think about it then nodded. "Sure. When do you want to start?"

After we set a time and place, I headed straight to the nearest Petsmart and splurged on everything cat—self-cleaning litter box, odor-control litter, and some of the best food a cat could possibly have. I was tempted to get her a tag since they had a machine for making them right there in the store, but I needed a name first. Furball might get my eyes gouged out.

As though she knew I came bearing her things, she stood at the top of the stairs when I opened the door. "Missed me?" I asked her.

You wish.

"She did," Femi called from the kitchen. "We watched a little TV but she got bored and went to the window to look outside. Did you get her a flea collar? She could go outside to explore when she has one."

I placed my purchases at the foot of the stairs. "Yes, but I need a name before I can get her a personalized tag. Where do I put her food and water?"

"The laundry room is large enough. I moved the hampers and created room for her litter box."

"Good. I don't want my bedroom smelling like fish." I went back to the car to get the litter. Mrs. Rutledge pulled up into her driveway and nodded without smiling. I bet she didn't miss a thing.

No one in our cul-de-sac owned a pet. A few neighbors had dogs when I was young, but I couldn't remember what had happened to them. Then there was the Labrador on the other side of our backyard fence. The dog ran away so often Eirik and I were convinced dog snatchers, or dognappers as we had called them, got it. I didn't think my cat was in any danger of being snatched. I was more likely to be scared for anyone crazy enough to kidnap Fur-ball than for the cat herself.

I set up the litter box while she watched. Femi shook her head when she walked by and heard me explain how the box worked. I stashed the rest of the cat food in one of the cabinets, and headed upstairs.

I had an hour of homework, then studies with Lavania.

~*~

I peered into the mansion and listened for the housekeeper. All was quiet. It seemed like she'd already left for the day. I stepped into the room and the mirror portal from my bedroom started to change. My cat left her lofty place by the window and peered at me curiously before the portal disintegrated.

The silence was almost spooky, reminding me of the days when Eirik and his parents had lived here. The Sevilles had tried to act like Mortals, surrounding themselves with expensive paintings and knick-knacks. I'd always known there was something off about them. They'd been cold and standoffish towards everyone, including Eirik, their supposedly adopted child. Turned out I was right. Not only were the Sevilles Immortals from Asgard, they were bound to serve the gods. And their adopted child, my best friend since I was little, had turned out to be the grandson of Odin. How I missed Eirik. I didn't care that he was a god in his own right. We were raised together, like brother and sister.

I headed for the stairs, hurrying past the living room. The room was more inviting than when Eirik had lived here. The chairs were comfortable and the expensive paintings and works of art had been replaced by more cheerful contemporary pieces, thanks to Lavania. The two story foyer with its winding staircase was still imposing, but I was no longer scared of knocking down a vase or some museum worthy décor.

I headed upstairs and turned left past Andris' bedroom and into the library. Of course, Andris had chosen a room close to books. The guy was a closet nerd. I'd even spied a pair of glasses by his bedside. Not that he would ever admit to owning a pair or loving books. Ingrid and Lavania's bedrooms were on the other side of the second floor. Blaine's and Eirik's old bedrooms were downstairs by the pool. Torin could have taken Eirik's room but he chose to stay closer to me.

"I met your cat earlier when I stopped by your place," Lavania said as soon as I entered the library. The entire wall of the room overlooked the pool below, which wasn't being used today. The gang wasn't around. Blaine, being an Immortal, was probably out on an assignment. Ingrid was probably at cheer practice or out with friends. She'd gotten an intern position in New York with some editor, but I didn't know whether she still planned to take it. She was taking runic lessons from Lavania first.

Andris had turned Ingrid into an Immortal using his personal runic artavo, instead of ones specifically chosen for her. Runes were weird like that. Each person had to use his or her own artavo. If you use someone else's the effect only lasts a few centuries no matter how often you add runes. Ingrid was only a couple of centuries old, yet a few weeks ago, she'd found out that she was starting to age. Lavania was nice enough to get some artavo for her from Asgard. Lavania was also the one who'd given me my set, which covered artavo for body runes and special ones for surface runes that are used for creating portals or fixing things.

Lavania was what you called an Immortal Maker. She had the authority to rune people, or Mortals as they called them, and turn them into Immortals. It was a long process that took months and lots of runes. I was still etching runes on my skin though not as often as I did seven months ago when she started training me. She'd been doing this a long time. She was the one who'd turned Torin and Andris centuries ago.

I kicked off my shoes and sat on the mat across from hers. I'd gotten used to sitting on the floor on mats and using a low table when she taught. Usually the tables were lined up side by side and covered with runic text books, our books, and artavo holders for the three of us—Cora, Ingrid, and me. Since we weren't working on runes and she was doing a one-on-one session with me, she'd pushed the three tables aside to create more room. If anyone walked in on us, we'd appear to be meditating.

"Did you have a cat too?" I asked her.

"Yes, before I joined the Vestal Virgins. I even named her Vesta after the goddess. We had several cats in the Temple, where we lived. In my time, cats were seen as the Gods of Liberty and sacrifices were made to them."

She'd joined Valkyries during the period when ancient Rome was at the peak of its civilization. "There should be a manual for all this, you know," I said. "What to expect when a witch's abilities start to show? How to train your familiar? What to do about visions or Norns?"

She chuckled and took my hands. Torin poked his head inside the room and she shooed him away. Once the door closed, she focused on me.

"We'll figure things out," she said. "I'll show you how to channel your power, when to let it flow and when to shut it off. It will help you control your visions."

Yes! Exactly what I wanted to hear. "I know I have you, and some Witches like Rita and Gina have their mentors and parents to help them. But what about those who don't have anyone and don't belong to a coven? Do they freak out when their powers appear? I didn't even know what the Call was until the Witches appeared here and Gina mentioned it."

Lavania sighed. "That's because you're a lot more powerful than most Witches and your powers are appearing much faster. Most times, the gift of sight is passed from parent to child, and the child learns from the mother."

Yeah, except my mother was a Valkyrie but hadn't revealed that to me because she'd fallen in love with my father, a Mortal, and renounced her calling to be a soul reaper. The punishment was to never, ever mention anything to anyone about who she was. Not even me, her daughter. I was surprised the Norns hadn't wiped Dad's memories so he'd forget too.

"Andris' mother helped him understand his special connection with the spirit world way before he took lessons with the high priest," Lavania said. "Torin's case was different. His father wasn't willing to share his knowledge with anyone, not even his children."

Selfish butthead.

"Things were a lot easier for young Witches when we had schools," she added.

"Then why not open one again? After what the Earl and his Immortal followers did, there should be a safe place for Witches to go and learn. Norns could choose from among them instead of stealing Seeresses. Oh, and you could make sure the students not only learn magic in a controlled environment, but have expert teachers in all areas."

For a moment, she just stared at me. Warmth crept onto my cheeks. Like my mother, Lavania was centuries old. Though in her case, she could pass for a college student, which made it easy to sometimes forget she was my mentor. She was smart, patient, and wise. I liked that she was a good listener and often discussed my ideas without putting them down.

"It's scary when your powers blindside you," I said. "And things are easier when you're not alone. I mean, I have you, but—"

"I know, dear." She patted my hand. "I just don't think I can run a school. It's been so long. Centuries. I wouldn't know where to start."

"Right here. You are teaching the three of us, but we are surrounded by Immortals with a vast knowledge of the supernatural world. Femi. Hawk. Blaine. Mom. Torin and Andris. Then there's you. You're so good with students, so patient. And your students love you. Look at Andris and Torin. They look up to you and respect your wisdom. I'm able to face new challenges because of the confidence you've instilled in me."

Everything I'd said was true except the part about my confidence. Thatcame from my parents. They laid the foundation for me to thrive. Dad taught me to always plan for the unexpected while Mom taught me to embrace changes, no matter how hard. Lavania and my Seeress' adventures just benefited from that.

"I didn't even know I could shape-shift… I mean, mimic other so that people only see what I want them to see," I added.

She nodded, a far-away look in her eyes. "That's something you'll learn years from now. Right now, we need to focus on controlling your powers."

"But I did it last night. I'm not good at it, but the goddess helped."

Lavania glanced at me as though I'd yanked her from miles away. "What goddess?"

"Freya. She's the one who dropped off Fur… my cat."

Lavania's eyes widened. "Femi didn't say anything about Goddess Freya dropping off one of her cats. She just said the cat was yours. I assumed Svana got her while you and the others were in Florida. Tell me what happened. From the beginning."

When I finished, she was pacing. Finally, she pulled her black hair to one shoulder and sat. Her hair had grown so much she could sit on it.

"Show me," she ordered.

I closed my eyes and tapped into my power source. This time, I found the spark a little faster. As it bloomed, I let an image fill my thoughts. When I opened my eyes, Lavania was staring at me in awe.

"What do you think?" I asked.

She made a face. "Unsettling. You look exactly like him. How long can you maintain it?" Excitement laced her words.

"I don't know."

There was a knock on the library door and Andris entered. He frowned when he saw us. "When did you get here?" he asked. "I mean, I just left you in the field a few minutes ago."

I jumped to my feet, grinning and hoping I had nailed Torin's smoothness. I didn't. I stumbled a bit. Torin wouldn't. He was graceful. Adopting his easy loose-gaited stride, I sauntered to where Andris stood and dropped an arm around his shoulder.

"That's because I'm faster than you'll ever be, little brother." Then I kissed his temple with a loud smack, something Torin wouldn't do, and smirked when annoyance crossed Andris's face. "Shouldn't you be assisting me with the team?"

"You asked me to get Raine." Andris pushed me away and swiped his temple. "Put your lips on me again and I'll slug you."

I reached for him again, lips puckered up for a kiss. "Come on, Andris. Just one kiss. Plant it right here, hot stuff." I touched my lips.

He punched my arm hard. "You're an ass." Andris glanced at Lavania, who was watching us and trying hard not to laugh. "Stop enabling him. This shit is not funny." He turned to leave. "I'll be at the beach if you need me."

I blocked his path. He balled his hand and I knew he would slug me. He took a step back as I let the image of me fill my head. I knew I was transforming back to me when blood drained from his face.

"Hel's Mist! What… Since when…?" He stopped and glared when I started to laugh.

"You should see your face," I said between bouts of laughter.

He wasn't amused. "That was creepy. I should have guessed it wasn't Torin. How did you do that?"

"She's a Norn-in-training, Andris," Lavania said by way of explanation. "Give us thirty minutes, then you can take her."

"I prefer witch, or Seeress, or Völva-in-training," I said.

Lavania just chuckled. Half an hour later, I went in search of Andris and found him eating in the kitchen while searching for things online. He grinned when I sat next to him.

"Can you shift into anything?" he asked.

"Not yet. Right now, I can shift into those I love because I know them. You know, features, facial expressions, mannerisms." I showed him and from the way his eyes widened and color crept onto his face, I knew I had surprised him. "Hi, I'm Andris. Everyone wants a piece of me," I said, imitating him. "Men or women, it doesn't matter. Want to know why? Because I'm hot."

"That's so corny and so me." A weird expression crossed his face. "I wish…"

I shifted back to myself. "What?"

"Nothing."

I sighed. "You too? When are you Valkyries going to learn that 'nothing' is not an answer? It is a concept that has no meaning or value. You can't answer me with nothing."

He laughed. "You're so weird. And yes, smarty pants. The answer in this case is nothing. Let's go."

"I'm not leaving until you explain, dufus."

A glint appeared in his eyes. I was beginning to recognize that look on him. He was about to say something outrageous. Andris tended to be brutally honest.

"You should be mine instead of Torin's," he said.

He sounded serious. I didn't think he was into me or felt anything lasting, but watching Torin and I get closer the last few months while he flitted from lover to lover couldn't be satisfying. After all, he and Torin had been reaping together for centuries. He either felt left out or was simply jealous. And I knew there was only one way to deal with this.

"First of all, I'm not *his*. He's mine. Second, you and me? Really? First, you complain that I'm mouthy, stubborn, and I let emotions control my actions. Recently I've been promoted to weird. Torin might complain, but he loves those qualities in me. Second, you don't have a type. Third, faithful is not in your DNA, which means I'd bore you in no time and then you'd break my heart." I leaned and added, "And hell hath no greater fury than a witch scorned. I'd pay you back with a nastiest hex ever created and turn you into a eunuch. No, I'd make you see things." He was laughing by the time I finished.

"But you can shift into anyone. Think of all the famous people you could turn into. I wouldn't be bored or unfaithful because you can shift into, uh, actresses and actors. Models. Musicians. Tennis players. Lately, I seem to have a thing for tennis players."

"And where would I be in your twisted world?"

He smirked. "You could be you once a month."

"You're an idiot." I smacked the back of his head.

He chuckled. "Why? Because I'm honest instead of cheating?"

"No, because we all need a man who puts us first twenty-four-seven. When are you going to learn that?"

~*~

We appeared at the top stands inside the StubHub. Since it was only practice, there were few spectators. Probably parents and grandparents. In Kayville, the entire family usually came out to watch a kid play.

"Doesn't the US National Soccer Team practice here?" I asked Andris.

"They're on the road this week. I think they're playing Peru and Brazil."

"Did you rune lots of people in order to replace their coach?"

Andris chuckled. "Nope. The coaches are volunteers, so we just had their bosses promote them. With extra workloads, they had to step down from coaching. However, the LA Galaxy Academy soccer program is very organized, and I needed to bring my A-game to fix their roster of coaches." Now he was bragging. "I added our names in their system, threw in our qualifications making your man the next most qualified person, and sent a few e-mails. It helped that Torin had coached youth soccer in England and knows Beckham."

"Really?"

He shot me a disgusted look. "Of course not. But all he has to do is open his mouth and they believe anything he says. If I cared, I'd fake a British accent too."

Except Torin's accent was real. That he'd kept it for centuries was cool. I followed Andris down to where the parents were seated. Most were women.

Torin was walking up and down the side of the field, yelling instructions to the players. He removed his baseball cap, wiped his brow and slapped it back on his head. He took everything he did seriously. I sat behind some of the parents while Andris sauntered toward the field.

After a few minutes, I got bored. I should have brought a book. Sports weren't my thing, but this was different. Torin and Andris wouldn't be here unless some of these kids were going to die. Such a tragedy. The U-16 league was for sixteen and fifteen-year olds. I touched my seat to see if I could get a vision.

Nothing.

I touched the next seat and the stadium disappeared.

In its place was a park and to my right was a man at a picnic with his wife and two daughters. The scene changed to show him at their graduation, then a wedding. I grinned as the vision faded.

Nice to see a happy family for a change. I reached behind me and got another vision. Nasty divorce, but the wife seemed happy. The last one had me yanking my hand from the seat. Pervert.

Obviously, the seats could only give me visions of their last occupants, not the catastrophe that was going to happen at this center. I might have to touch the turf on the field to get a reading, or the boys when their mother's weren't looking.

I studied the women in front of me. Some had their heads close together as they talked, their eyes on their kids. A few were on their phones. One had her e-reader on. I eavesdropped on the whispered conversation from the ones near me.

"I'm still angry at the way Coach Taylor abandoned our kids," the brunette said. She wore white capris and a light blue top. She also had high-heeled sandals, not exactly what moms in Kayville wore to soccer.

"I'm not," her blonde buddy answered. Her white sundress went down to her sandaled feet and she had some serious boobs, though they looked too big to be real. "Taylor was a yeller. I mean, I knew his life was a mess, but still... Harry likes the new coach better. He's firm without being scary, and he seems to know a lot about what he's doing."

"I love his accent," White Capris said.

Blondie giggled. "Sexy, just like Beckham's."

"He's better looking," a third woman joined them. She was dressed more like a soccer-mom. Jeans and a T-shirt, just like I was, and a baseball cap. "Josh talked of nothing else but the new coach, so I had to come and see for myself. Who's the blonde?"

"He's friends with the coach," White Capris said. "He's just as good-looking. Probably European though he really doesn't have an accent."

"I love European men," Blondie said. "They're so cultured. Love the way they care about clothes. I mean, look at him."

Andris in white slacks and a trendy short trench coat with his collar turned up did look like he'd stepped off some runway of a European designer. He didn't join Torin at the other end of the field. He walked to a table with a pitcher of water and poured himself some first, then turned and lifted it toward the bleachers. He probably knew the attention he was getting and loved it. The parents waved or nodded.

I removed my phone and was checking my text messages when Soccer-Mom Number Three asked, "Is he the coach's boyfriend?"

I almost laughed.

The first two women looked at each other. "I don't think so," White Capris said. "Their body language doesn't indicate anything like that."

"My gay-dar didn't go off either," Blondie chimed in. "And the way he stared at these babies," she stuck out her chest, "confirmed he's batting for our team. I should have team dinner at my house on Friday before the Saturday game. We could all socialize and learn more about them."

A woman seated in front of them tilted her head and threw over her shoulder, "I'm having one tomorrow. Text Deidra. As the Galaxy rep, she schedules all pre-game and post-game dinners."

The first two women dove inside their purses for their cell phones and started texting furiously. Refusing to be left out, Soccer-Mom Number Three also reached for her phone.

I grinned. Torin had that effect on most women, young and old. Had he really stared at Blondie's boobs? Or were they talking about Andris?

I glanced at my chest. My breasts were modest and I had never worried about their size before. I mean, Cora had a serious rack and I never felt lacking because of her. Would Torin want a bustier girlfriend?

As though he felt me stressing, he glanced toward the bleachers and waved me over. At first, every woman near me assumed he was indicating her. They looked at each other with raised eyebrows.

Torin blew the whistle and the players headed toward the water table. He spoke briefly to Andris, then lowered his wraparound glasses and cocked his eyebrow.

I knew that look. If I didn't go, he'd come and get me. Necks craned when I stood, and eyes followed me down the stairs. Feeling self-conscious, I wished I had worn a jacket or coat over my T-shirt and jeans. It was easy to pretend you were invisible when wearing something bulky. Then I'd be sweating. The boots already made me feel overdressed. This was California. It might be spring, but it was already warm, the temperature perfect.

Torin was high-fiving the boys and cracking jokes when I reached them. He pushed his glasses into his hair and studied my face. "You okay?"

He could always tell when I felt out of place. I shrugged and gave him a sheepish smile. He could have kissed me or introduced me to the players as his girlfriend and made me feel even more self-conscious. Instead, he took my hand and went back to talking to his players.

They hung on his words and he seemed to have already memorized their names. The boys stared at me curiously and looked away when I caught their eyes. They might only be fifteen and sixteen, but they were taller than me. Most of them anyway.

It was hard to believe some of them would die in the coming month. Funny I used to wish I were a Valkyrie. Now the thought of knowing people were going to die and doing nothing to stop it made me a little sick.

Two more adults I hadn't noticed before joined us. They were part of the coaching team, Torin explained as he introduced me. I wondered if they'd make it.

"Okay, let's finish here and head home. Unless…" he paused for effect and got everyone's attention, "you want to grab pizza right here before going home?"

All the players looked at each other in confusion. "Coach, the food stands are opened during game days only," one of the boys said. He had a deep voice and was growing a moustache.

"And today, Bill," Torin corrected. "From now till we win the championship in June, we'll eat here at the Stadium Club whenever we practice here."

He got the players. Even the assistant coaches were surprised and thrilled by the news. I wondered how much he had to pay to make this happen. I did research StubHub after our talk and knew it was an exclusive restaurant only available by reservation on non-game days.

As the players ran back to the field for the last fifteen minutes of practice, one of the coaches went to talk to the parents. Torin focused all his awesomeness on me. "Can you hang out with us afterwards?"

"Sure. I've always wanted to see inside the Stadium Club."

He chuckled because he knew I was lying. I had very little interest in sports, unless he was playing. Hanging out with the players though meant I could touch them and see who was going to die. That sounded morbid, but I was curious, and maybe I could tweak a few things and save some lives. I glanced at the stands and found the parents' eyes on us. They seemed pleased by the news about pizza. Or was it a chance to talk to the coaches? I wondered if some of them would die too. Torin's target souls were hard to predict. They were told where to go and wait.

"Don't mind them," Torin said, misunderstanding my frown. He touched my cheek, flashed a cocky grin, and went to join the assistant coaches.

I was still staring at him when Andris planted himself in front of me, a Galaxy Academy hat in his hand. "As one of us, you get to wear this," he said.

"I don't see you wearing one."

"And mess up this?" He pointed at his perfectly tousled hair. He put the hat on my head and adjusted it. "There. Now those cougars know you're his. Let's sit down before we wilt in this heat."

The temperature was perfect. "Can we sit away from the parents?"

He chuckled. "You heard them talk about Torin, didn't you? I went invisible and eavesdropped. Shameless hussies."

"I don't care what they think." I slipped my arm through his. We started for the seats when I felt icy fingers crawling up my spine. I shivered and stopped. The feeling was so sudden I knew the effect didn't come from the Mortals.

"What is it?"

"We're not alone," I said, searching the stadium, but it was impossible to know where someone could be hiding.

"Lord Worthington?" Andris asked.

"I don't know." The feeling grew stronger and became more familiar. Norns. I remembered the smirks on their faces the night we defeated Torin's father and his minions. I'd like to pretend the Norns were just sore losers, but from our previous dealings, I knew they'd be back. Which group of soccer moms were they mimicking? The three that had gushed over Torin?

"I've changed my mind. Let's sit behind the parents."

Andris didn't argue. Maybe my face gave me away or maybe it was my body language, but he went all protective, arms on my shoulder, eyes vigilant, tension in his body. He was primed to act.

We sat a few seats behind the three women, so we could talk without being heard. Blondie turned and smiled at us. Andris winked at her, which earned him a chest thrust and a come hither smile.

She wasn't one of them. And neither were her two friends. I shivered again and the next second, Andris dropped his trench coat around my shoulders and added his arm. I leaned against him even though I knew he couldn't warm the chill. It had nothing to do with the temperature. It was the crazy mental link I had with the Norns.

Still, I mumbled, "Thanks."

He slipped on his sunglasses and casually glanced around the stadium. "If he's here, we should lure him away from the stadium and finish him off. Torin will never know."

I forced myself to focus on Andris. Even laughed. "Nice plans, except Torin and I made a pact never to keep secrets from each other. If we go after his father, we'll have to tell him what we did."

"I don't have to," Andris said. "Torin can be pissed at me, but once he calms down, he'll thank me. The Earl deserves to die."

"I was thinking of changing his destiny." After giving him a choice, of course.

"Too tame. Shift into Torin and finish him off. Would be a nice way too. He'd know his own son hated him so much that he gave him a one-way ticket to Corpse Strand."

Being tortured for eternity on the island of the damned in Hel was more than what the Earl deserved. "Sorry. It's the same thing, Andris. No matter who I mimicked, he or she is still me. I just can't do it and not tell Torin."

Andris growled in frustration. "Fine. Once you shift into Torin, tell him you don't want anything to do with him, but he should apologize and pay restitution to the family of every witch and Seeress who died last week. Then he must disappear and never contact you again."

I thought about that. "I like it. To make sure he's paid restitution, he should e-mail Torin some sort of evidence. A receipt of the transaction or... Wait. Weren't the Witches' memories wiped after the battle? They wouldn't remember how their parents or siblings died. An apology would be pointless."

Andris shrugged. "Anonymous donation with a condolence should suffice. And I like the idea of sending proof to Torin. This way, he knows his father's remorse is genuine without actually dealing with him. Once he's done with his penance, I'll finish him off."

He could be so bloodthirsty sometimes. "You kill an Immortal and you'll end up on Hel duty permanently this time," I warned him.

"Actually, the goddess might thank me. She gets another monster to fight on her side during Ragnarok." Runes covered his skin. "I'll be back in a few." He took off at hyper-speed.

I couldn't believe he just went invisible in broad daylight. But then again, that was Andris. He never cared who he pissed off. The problem was the Norns were around and might have seen him.

I closed my eyes and tried to find them, but all I heard was static.

I know you're here. What do you want?

No response, but the cold under my skin expanded. Goose bumps spread all over my body and my lungs hurt as though I was breathing in icy fumes. I looked around, expecting them to appear. Nothing happened. I tried to link with them, but it was as though a heavy veil was blocking me. My head hurt when I tried to push beyond it. This was different. I knew they were Norns, but they felt different. Did I piss them off that much they'd do this to me?

If you have something to tell me, show yourselves, I snapped.

Just when I was sure I couldn't take it anymore, the link broke and the feeling disappeared. I sucked in air and tried to regulate my breathing. My chest expanded as warmth replaced the iciness that had crawled under my skin.

I glanced at the field and saw Torin running toward the stands. I didn't have to see his face to know he'd sensed my distress. At least that was what he claimed. Valkyries couldn't feel the presence of Norns, but he and I shared a bond I still didn't understand. Eyes followed him to where I sat.

He squatted and frantically searched my face. "What happened?"

"I'm okay now," I said, aware of the parents watching us. "Go back and finish the game."

He touched my arms then cupped my face. His hand was so warm. "You're shaking. Was it my father?"

"No, Norns. They're gone now. I'm okay. Really."

"What did they want?"

"I don't know. I tried to communicate with them, but they locked me out. In fact, I think they blasted me with something and blocked my attempt to connect with them. It was like nothing I've experienced before."

His jaw clenched. "I'll let the assistant coaches finish while I take you home."

"No, Torin. We can't leave. The players need you, and I want to meet them. Go finish the game, then let's have pizza."

He studied me intently then glanced around. "Where's Andris?"

"He went for a run. He should be back any minute now. Please, go."

He nodded and stood, but I could see he was reluctant to leave. Andris appeared, saw the look on Torin's face, and yanked his sunglasses off. His eyes volleyed between me and Torin. "What happened?"

"Stay with her." He turned to leave, paused, and added. "Please." Then he hurried back to the field.

Andris looked thoroughly confused. "He just said please, right? He didn't just bark orders and expect me to follow them?"

I threw him a tiny smile. He wasn't even breathing hard after his run and his hair was still perfectly moussed. He had to tell me his secret. And why was I thinking about such mundane things when I had the Norns to worry about?

What were they up to now? They often appeared when they had a diabolical plan to lure me to their side. Maybe they knew what I was planning to do tonight and this was their way of telling me to back off. If that was the case, they got their wish. Whatever grandiose ideas I had about finding out what was going to happen to the players went out the window. Anything to keep those three bitches out of my life.

"Okay, you're ignoring me." Andris cut through my thoughts. "What's going on?"

I blocked my mouth like I was about to cough. "I can't talk to you while you're still cloaked, Andris. I'll look like an idiot. Wait for them to stop staring." Andris decloaked anyway. I should have known he wouldn't listen. "Seriously?"

He smirked. "When humans see something that doesn't make sense, they come up with a rational explanation and life continues. Was the Earl of Darkness here? Did he approach you while I was gone? I couldn't find him anywhere."

"No, he wasn't here."

He scowled. "Then why was Torin looking like he wanted to reduce the entire stadium into rubble?"

"We had a different kind of visitors." Before I could explain, he cursed.

"Why can't they just leave you alone?"

"You know why." I was one of the Völur who'd announce Ragnarok and they wanted me on their side. "There was something different about their presence tonight. It felt darker. Almost evil."

5. The Staff

Andris and I made it inside the American Express Stadium Club restaurant before the players and their parents. The view from the window was spectacular. It gave one the illusion of floating above the stadium. Two guys were staring at the field, boxes of pizza, drinks, paper plates and cups piled on a table behind them. Andris paid them and shooed them out.

I looked around, loving the blend of redwood tables with green chairs and booths. Even the sconces over the counter were green.

"Come on. Help me arrange these chairs."

I didn't contain my shock. "You?"

"Amazing, aren't I?" He carried the boxes to the gleaming counter. "Since I'm not running up and down the field with the pimply-faced players, this is my contribution." He engaged his runes and grabbed two chairs as one would plates and moved them to the other end of the counter, turning one upside down on top of the other.

I looked around to confirm we were alone, and then let the spark in my core grow and spread to my limbs. I pointed at the nearest chair, lifted it off the floor and directed it to the end of the counter. I focused on the second one, turned it upside down, and placed it on top of the first one. Getting bolder, I went for two at a time. Grinning, I lifted the rest. I was getting cocky, but by the time I was done, the chairs were grouped at the other end of the counter.

"Damn," Andris said.

"Thank you," I said, bowing. My skin still tingled with the effect of magic.

"Your eyes are glowing."

Dang it! I'd completely forgotten about that effect. I squeezed my eyes tight, pushed the magic away, which was something I was still learning, and opened them again. "Now?"

"Still glowing."

"I need to hide them before the players get here."

Andris shook his head. "Why do you care about what Mortals think? They'll just assume you're wearing color-changing contacts."

"If such things exist."

"Or is it Torin you're worried about? He hates what you're becoming."

"No, he doesn't." He did, but he was adjusting. A couple of weeks ago, he would have freaked out when I mimicked him. "I just don't like people thinking I'm a freak."

He laughed. "There you go again, worrying too much about Mortals. And FYI, you are a freak."

"What does that make you?"

"Master of all freaks. Here." He plucked his sunglasses from where he'd pushed them in his hair and slid them across the counter. "Chicken."

"Douche." I walked around the counter to join him and frowned. He was right. I was being ridiculous. These people didn't know me and wouldn't care about my eye color. "You're right. I don't need them." I tugged the brim of my baseball cap low. "I'm fine."

Andris chuckled. "Our little girl is growing."

"Oh, shut up." I swatted his arm.

We lined up the pizza boxes according to toppings, placed the plastic plates and napkins on one side of the counter and the plastic cups and drinks on the other. I was in charge of the drinks. Andris grabbed a plastic cup and pulled a bottle from the rack of spirits behind the counter. I didn't even bother to reprimand him. He lived by his own rules. He poured a generous amount and took a swig.

"Hmm, nice. Want some?"

"No, thanks." I got high enough on magic. Even now, I still felt the buzz.

By the time the coaches, the players, and their parents arrived, everything was ready. Torin's eyes found me when he entered the room with a boy who seemed younger than fifteen. The other kids elbowed each other and looked around with excitement. They'd probably never been inside the club either.

Somehow, they calmed down, lined up and picked up slices, then stopped by my end of the counter for their drink of choice. Andris removed empty boxes and flipped open new ones. Torin came around the counter.

"You used your powers," he whispered, his hand massaged my neck.

"My eyes are still glowing?"

"No. The other thing." He stole a kiss, but instead of leaning back, he angled his head and brought his lips closer to my ears. "Damn."

"It was just a little magic."

"Still packs quite a punch. Thanks for helping out," he whispered.

"It's nothing."

"It's something. I'll get us out of here as quickly as I can." He touched the corner of my mouth again as though he couldn't help himself, grabbed several slices of pizza, and bumped fists with Andris. "Thanks for taking care of this, bro."

Conscious of the stares from both players and parents, I poured myself a drink and gulped some down. Torin took the cup from me and winked. Sure my face was red, I shot him a glare. I was sure he was aware of the interest his every move generated.

"You two have a secret language now?" Andris asked.

"Hmm?" I asked, but my focus was on Torin. Several mothers tried to get his attention. Even the assistant coaches seated with some of the students waved him over, but he glanced around and headed to the table where a lone boy sat. It was the same boy who was with him when he'd entered the room. That boy was going to die. Torin never singled out someone unless death was coming for them.

I poured myself another drink and moved closer to Andris, who was demolishing a slice like a starved convict. I took a slice from his plate. "So are we going to join the others?"

"Nope. I have no interest in interacting with Mortals." I followed his eyes to Torin and the boy.

"Who's that?" I asked.

"Jace Taylor," he said.

"Coach Taylor's son?"

Andris nodded.

"Not very popular, is he?"

"Nope." He didn't elaborate.

I sighed. "Because you guys replaced his father?"

Andris shrugged. "We did what had to be done to put us here."

I think sometimes he said things to get a reaction. I tried to focus on eating, but I couldn't. "He looks too young to be playing with the others and now he's going to die."

"Is he?" Andris said mysteriously.

"Of course he is. Torin is palsy-walsy with him. There's only one reason for that." Watching the animated way the boy talked to Torin only made me feel worse. "How can he befriend those whose souls he plans to reap?"

"Why don't you ask him? He's taken a personal interest in the boy. And do you know who I blame for that?" He shot me a pointed glance.

"Me? Why?"

"You crushed the steel wall he'd erected around his heart and changed him. For centuries he got close to would-be souls, gained their trust, and reaped them without losing sleep. Our area of expertise is catastrophe, and he knew how to herd them without losing a soul,"—he grinned—"and I mean that literally. Why? Because they trusted him. Then he met you. For the first time, he's letting one get too close and not in a good way. They bonded over losing their mothers."

Now I was intrigued. "The boy's mother died recently too?"

"Last month after a long struggle with metastasized lung cancer. His father is up to his neck in debt." Andris sighed dramatically. "So first, we got his old man promoted so the man can take care of the little runt and we could replace him as the coach. Then an anonymous donor helped pay the huge hospital bill the mother left behind."

"Torin?"

Andris gave me a what-do-you-think glance. "I used one of his dummy corporations to make it happen. I've seen him give money to the people left behind, never to those about to die. He even promised Taylor he'd keep the boy on the team despite the fact that he's asthmatic and most of his pimply-faced teammates and their parents didn't want him playing. They only tolerated his presence because his father volunteered to coach."

The mothers were furtively watching Torin and Jace, probably envious their sons weren't getting the coach's attention. "Is the boy the reason you guys are here?"

Andris smirked. "No. I told you. We reap when a catastrophe hits. That's our specialty, not individual reaps. I don't know what's coming, but it will involve this team of kids. Jace is just a distraction." Andris frowned. "He's a talented player even though he becomes winded fast. The others are actually jealous of him."

My eyes went to Torin. He was smiling at something Jace was saying. "How do you know so much about him? You barely started reaping after the death freeze the Norns put in place, and you guys only started coaching yesterday."

"We started last week while waiting for the Earl to show up in Kayville. Scouting. Getting the feel of the place. If we'd hung out here a little longer, they would have tagged us as pervs, so we decided we needed to be more involved. It only takes minutes to alter records and set up a fake background."

Something else occurred to me. Since Jace's mother had cancer, she'd gone to Hel's Hall. And asthmatic Jace would also... Crap!

"Jace is not going to Asgard with you guys, is he?"

"Nope."

Now I was beginning to understand what Andris meant by Torin changing. He only befriended those he reaped. "Could you guys sneak him in?"

Andris laughed, drawing attention to us. "No, we can't. The boy is too frail and will stand out."

My father was too frail too. Did that mean Mom wouldn't reap him? "Remind me again how you know exactly who is about to die."

"We don't. They tell us where to go and what team to scout, and we do it. Your man does his thing while I wait on the sideline. We never, ever mess with Hel's souls. Like I said,"—he shot me a pointed look—"this is your fault. You've made him soft."

I ignored him. Was Torin really changing because of me? I knew he wasn't the uncaring Valkyrie I'd met months ago. That didn't mean I was responsible. The incident with his parents could have changed him. As for messing with Hel's souls, I did that last night.

I turned to say something to Andris and caught him winking at one of the mothers. He'd been playing eye tag with the short brunette since she arrived and it wouldn't surprise me if he did something about it. No woman was safe from him.

More boys came back for second helpings, then thirds. Andris cracked jokes with some of the boys. Across the room, Torin got up to do his rounds, moving from table to table, talking to the players, then the parents, who hung on his words. Jace reached the serving table and got more slices. He was such a timid boy. He even blushed when our eyes met.

"Did you ace the test?" Andris asked him.

Jace nodded. "Yes, sir."

"Good."

My jaw dropped. The fraud. "I see through you, you know," I whispered after Jace went back to his table. "Torin is not the only one changing."

"Please. I helped him with his homework while we waited for his father to pick him up. I had no choice. Torin was talking to his evil sire. It's not going to happen again."

Somehow I doubted him. Something about this boy had touched both of them. "The master of freaks is changing too."

He scoffed at the idea. "That's absurd. Have you any idea how many souls we reap and how pointless it is to care? I'm enabling Torin. I guess I owe him."

I kissed his cheek and caught Torin's eyes on us. He raised an eyebrow. I just grinned. Maybe they might not be too hard on me when I changed a few destinies, starting with Jace. I didn't care if the Norns were watching. This boy's future was worth altering.

"Where are we going?" Andris asked when I grabbed his arm.

"To talk to Jace."

~*~

I couldn't get a reading from Jace, which didn't make sense. If Andris noticed how often I patted the boy's hand, he didn't say it. He was busy playing eye-tag with the same brunette. Torin, however, hadn't missed a thing.

"Were you trying to get a reading from Jace?" Torin asked as soon as everyone left. The three of us were piling up pizza boxes in garbage cans.

"No," I fibbed.

Andris laughed, which earned him a kick. He dodged my foot and created a portal to the mansion. He turned once he was safe in the foyer and said, "He thought she was hitting on him. Now he's worried about what the coach will do."

I cringed. "Quit making things up. You didn't even talk to him."

He smirked. "You were too busy touching him you didn't see his face. I gotta go. Got a hot date with a smoking hot cougar."

"She's married," I called after him as the portal started to close.

"Divorced," he shot back before the portal disappeared. Torin was staring at me with a hard to read expression.

"Are you mad?" I asked.

"Would it make any difference?"

I started to nod, thought about it, and shook my head. "No. I want to—"

He covered his ears. "I don't want to hear it. You do what you have to do. Just leave me out of it."

Color me shocked. Was this the same man who'd yelled at me for going to the boy's locker room and putting my life in danger for helping people? He grinned at my expression.

"Come on, help me clean up."

Andris was right. Torin was changing, and for some reason, he wanted Jace's life spared. Did that extend to the other boys on the team too?

We finished cleaning up and opened a portal home. "I need to take care of something this evening, but I'll stop by later."

"Tell Jace I'm sorry for scaring him."

"Will do." Then he chuckled when he realized what he'd revealed. "Don't sneak into guys' bedrooms while I'm gone."

"Promise." His expression said he didn't believe me.

~*~

My cat was asleep on the window seat, despite the nice bed desk I'd bought for her and placed next to my computer.

I headed downstairs, following the sounds to the kitchen where Femi was cooking while watching TV. "I had pizza with Torin's soccer team," I told her.

"I know, doll. You texted me." She tasted whatever was in the pot and sighed blissfully. "You don't know what you're missing."

I made a face and hoped she didn't notice.

"Hmm, too bad." She laughed. We both knew I hated fish stew. I liked my fish fried or baked, and smothered with herbs. "Is Mom home?"

"She's with your father."

My parents were playing chess when I peeked in. It was nice to see Dad up and about. He seemed stronger, his color a lot less zombie-gray. Having Mom around seemed to be good for him, but then again, she had that effect on most people. Or maybe she was using unique runes to manage his pain. To use Mortal terms, he looked like a man whose cancer was in remission.

"Hi, sweetie," she patted my hand when I kissed her cheek.

"Who's winning?" I asked, looking over Dad's shoulder.

"Your mother." But his eyes sparkled. "Where did you disappear to?"

"California."

He shook his head. "Florida. California. Where next? Paris?"

"Maybe," I teased. We traded grins. I was still getting used to the ease with which I could move from one place to another without using transportation. I liked it, but at the same time, it made me uneasy. It reinforced the fact that I was no longer a normal person.

Last week, after the battle with the Immortals, we'd gone to Florida for a few days. Most parents would have worried about plane tickets or the drive. We'd rented a beach home for the weekend and used a portal to access it. We could have slept in our beds if we wanted to, but none of us had wanted to be in Kayville after dealing with evil Immortals.

"What's happening in California?" Dad asked, his focus on me.

That was something I'd missed the last few months while he'd been bedridden. The way he'd make what I did, however small, seem so important.

Grinning, I walked around and sat on the arm of his chair. "Torin is coaching the Galaxy Academy U-16 soccer team. He also subs as a math teacher at the boys' school. Caesar Chavez High."

"Poor kids," Mom mumbled.

"What am I missing?" Dad asked, his eyes volleying between Mom and me.

Mom glanced at me. "Do you want to tell him?"

Explain the logistics of reaping to my dying father? I didn't think so. I was still trying to get used to his imminent death. I shook my head.

"Torin and Andris are in California to reap the boys' souls," Mom explained.

Dad frowned. "Oh."

Mom and I exchanged a glance. Was he thinking of his situation?

"I guess I should have figured that out," he said, speaking slowly as though adjusting his perception. "He became close to the swim team here before the pool accident and joined the football team before the accident. Do you know who will die in Seattle, Svana?"

He sounded more curious than sad, but Mom's eyes welled with tears. Time to leave before I joined her. I was a sympathetic crier, but I refused to mourn my father while he was still alive.

"I have homework, so I'll see you two later." I kissed Dad's cheek and walked around the table to Mom, who was trying hard to control herself. Between us, I was usually the levelheaded one, like Dad. My flamboyant mother's emotions were more volatile.

I hugged her and whispered, "He looks great, Mom. Because of you. Because you're here, so please don't cry."

She hugged me tight and hung on. She was a hugger, but this time, I think she was giving herself time to calm down. She leaned back and smiled. Her tears were no longer threatening to fall. "Thank you. Now go. Your homework will not do itself."

"Why can't I quit school like Torin and Andris? It's not like I'm going to need a high school diploma in the future." I couldn't tell who was more shocked—Mom or Dad. "Just kidding. I plan to go to college and study something. You know, contribute to the world." They looked at each other and then at me. I threw up my hands. "Forget it."

I let myself out of the room. Femi looked up when I started upstairs. She and Mom used portals to go to and from upstairs, but I still insisted on doing a few things like a normal person.

Fur-ball stretched and eyed me as I pulled out textbooks from my backpack.

"Miss me?" I asked.

Why? You don't do anything remotely interesting or exciting. No potions or spells. Elemental magic is so boring. She rested her head on her front paws, closed her eyes, and sighed.

"How come you speak English so perfectly?"

Her eyelids parted and she studied me as though deciding whether to respond. *I've watched every movie ever made in the last hundred years. I speak most of the world languages fluently.*

"Hundred? How old are you?"

A lady never tells her age.

I rolled my eyes. "You're a cat, Fur-ball, not a person."

Don't call me that stupid name. I'm older and wiser than you. Didn't your Valkyrie mama ever teach you to respect your elders?

"Oh yeah, cat years."

Mortal years, Norn.

"Don't call me that." I settled down to do homework, but I could feel her eyes on me. After I read a line twice without understanding it, I sighed and glanced at her. She was sitting up. "What?"

When are we going to do something interesting around here?

"I do plenty of interesting things." She jumped up on the table and stared at my book. "Let me guess. You can read most languages too."

No. Never learned to read or write. What are you doing?

I sighed. "Math. I need to do this or my grade will slip."

She sat in the middle of my textbook and stared defiantly at me. *The goddess risked a lot to bring me here. You should be working on your magic and thinking up ways to stop the Norns from messing with you, not work on meaningless Mortal stuff.*

I'd stopped listening after her first sentence. "What did she risk? Why did she want to help me? You said she had a reason."

The cat shrugged, or at least it looked like a shrug. *What god or goddess does something without a reason? They only care about themselves. Most of them anyway. And just because I'm feline doesn't mean I don't see or hear things.*

"Like what?"

She stretched out on top of my book. *Why do you need to go to school? Don't you ever do anything fun? And when I say fun, I mean magical. And why do you live in such a small house? There's nowhere to go and explore.*

I leaned forward until we were nose-to-nose. "First, I'm fun. Second, my house is perfect the way it is. And third, I'll only share if you share."

She bumped me with her nose. *You can't blackmail me.*

"I just did. Start talking or get off my book."

Her eyes closed briefly. *She met with Goddess Frigga, and your name was mentioned. Several times. They talk a lot about you up there, but this was different. The two are not really friends. After their meeting, Goddess Freya decided to bring me down here.*

"What did they say?"

I don't know, but I could help you find out. Your turn.

Being blackmailed by a cat. How low I'd sunk. I sighed. "I went to watch a soccer practice and met a nice young man."

You ditched your Valkyrie for a Mortal? That's stupid.

"I didn't ditch anyone, Fur-ball. The boy is on Torin's soccer team, which means he and his friends will be dying soon."

The cat stood and tilted her head to the side, emerald green eyes not leaving mine. *Are we going to help them? Maybe stop them from dying?*

"I don't know. Maybe. I couldn't get a reading from the boy."

Then try again.

I remembered the way Torin watched out for Jace and knew I couldn't walk away. "I will."

Now.

"No, I'm not going to his house."

I want to meet him. Maybe I can keep an eye on him until you know for sure. That's what I'm here for. To be your eyes and ears when you're not around. I'll know if he's in danger and alert you.

I shook my head. "This boy lives in California, not here."

So? It doesn't matter whether he's in Moscow or Timbuktu. I know how to access a portal to anyplace. Probably better than you.

"Timbuktu, ha! You don't have a tag. You don't even have a name." I lifted her off my book and put her back on the window seat. "I'll think about it."

I don't need a tag. I'll always come back to you. But I need a name because I hate Fur-ball. She rolled on her back. *I want to meet this boy. Our first case.*

I sighed. "*Your* first case. I already helped two people, *Bastet.* That's a good name for a cat."

Not Bastet. How could you go on a mission without me? What kind of a partner are you?

"That was yesterday before you were dropped off here, Artemis."

No! You can't have helped anyone because I've been watching you since they said one of us would be your, uh...

"Familiar. Watching me? You mean you've been spying on me, Venus?"

Enough with forgotten goddesses already. And no, not familiar. Muse. I'm here to make sure you grow as a Völva. And I wouldn't call it spying. Keeping an eye on you. Making sure you are all right.

"Funny I don't recall getting help from you when I battled Immortals and Norns. Some guardian cat you are. I should call you, *El Diablo.*" I grinned when she hissed. "Celestia?"

She sighed and lay down again. *That's my middle sister's name and there's nothing angelic or celestial about her. She's self-centered and vain, and she's the goddess' favorite. You should have seen her face when she wasn't chosen to work with you.*

Okay, too much sibling rivalry. "Princess?"

My oldest sister's name. Be creative.

"Jade? Your eyes—"

No.

"Emerald? Moss? Mint? Pear? Chartreuse?"

She rolled onto her side and covered her eyes with her paw. *You totally lack imagination.*

"Amber might suit you. I know a girl at school called Amber and she's a PITA." The cat peered at me. I expected her to hiss. Instead, I could swear she smiled. "Yeah, I should call you PITA?"

You'd name me after bread? Really?

I grinned. "Pain in the ass."

She laughed and rolled onto her back. Slowly, she wiggled as though scratching her back. *Keep them coming.*

"Ebony. Jet. Slate. Obsidian. Onyx."

Pathetic. She rolled back on all fours, hopped down, created a portal small enough for her to walk through. *I'm going to find something to eat.*

"Onyx is perfect," I called after her. I couldn't believe I'd once begged for a cat.

I got busy finishing my homework. An occasional glance out of the window told me Torin wasn't back. Was he still at Jace's? When I finished, I debated whether to go to Cora's and see what she was doing. She volunteered at a nursing home and her hours were odd. I texted her anyway, then booted my laptop.

Checking for new releases at book sites was something I hadn't done in a while. Between school, lessons with Lavania, and doing things with Torin, I never seemed to have time for leisure reading anymore. Reading to Dad didn't count.

I ordered a couple of books, all sequels to series I'd started last year, then started my rounds on social websites. Five minutes in and I lost interest. Selfies, movies and music seemed to dominate the lives of people I knew from school. My life was so complicated that their issues seemed petty by comparison.

Onyx sauntered back inside my room and hopped onto my desk like she owned it. *Let's go see the boy now. I know you can get a reading if you focus hard enough.*

Would Torin still be there? "It's not a question of focusing. My visions are unpredictable."

They shouldn't be. Not for you, the most powerful Völva of this generation. Onyx walked behind my laptop and pushed it shut. Her eyes glowed briefly. *Try it again.*

Glaring ensued. "Ass-kissing will get you nowhere with me."

Her whiskers twitched as though she was fighting a smile. I wanted to try it again. I changed into black pants and pulled on my leather jacket.

Where's your staff?

"I don't own a staff."

No one can be this ignorant. Of course you own one. She padded to my bedside chest of drawers and pawed on the lowest knob. She managed to open it. *What's that?*

I peered inside. "Oh, that. That's a dagger the Norns gave me months ago."

That's it. Pick it up. Whoa, watch where you point that thing, she added and leaped out of the way when I picked it up. She crouched behind my desk and peered at me.

"What are you doing?"

Hiding in case you use it. That's a Norn's staff.

"Norn's what? Whoa…" Something was happening. The magic deep in my core stirred and blinked into existence without my help. I didn't even have to focus on channeling it. It swelled and shot to my arm, gunning for the dagger.

The dagger responded, the runes on its blade and handle glowing. I tried to drop it, but it was as though my hand was fused to the handle. Panic surged through me and my stomach hollowed out. But the freak show wasn't over. The wooden part elongated while the iron blade coiled into a weird-looking knot the size of a baseball. Its core looked like a blue crystal. Or maybe the runes gave that illusion. The shaft hit the floor with a thud and stopped stretching, but the blue core continued to glow.

Onyx said something I didn't catch, but my mind was slow processing everything. The Norns had given me the dagger months ago to use it on my best friend Eirik. Eirik was Hel's son, raised with me on earth so he wouldn't turn evil. They'd thought he was turning evil, but I'd refused to use it on him. Eirik was many things—confused, growing, dark, trying to find himself. But evil? No.

However, the hags had known about my powers. They'd always known. What the hell was I to do with a staff anyway? I was a modern *Völva*. I couldn't walk around with a staff.

I remembered something Cora had told me. Echo's scythe was the size of my dagger, until he held it and engaged certain runes. Then it shifted and grew into a full length, scary-looking reaper's weapon. He didn't just use it to create portals. The light from the blade could disperse a soul. I'd never seen it happen, but Cora swore by it.

I lifted the staff and pointed it at my dresser.

Not inside the house, Onyx screamed inside my head. I studied her. She still crouched behind my desk. *Turn it off.*

How? I wanted to ask her, but she already thought I was a complete idiot. No point giving her more ammunition. I focused on reversing what had happened. I pulled back the energy linking to the blade, and pushed it away as though rejecting it.

And what do you know? It receded back to my core.

The crystal core at the tip of the staff dimmed and disappeared as though sucked into the staff. The wooden part shrunk and the tip uncoiled, until once more, I was holding the dagger. It now looked like any ordinary weapon without my magic.

So the Norns had known about the dagger. Was their intention to make me use my magic to hurt Eirik when I didn't even know I had it in me? Why? That was obvious. So they could control me.

I opened the drawer, threw the dagger inside, and closed it. I was never touching that thing again. Shaken, I sat on my bed, then lay on top of the covers and stared into space.

Onyx joined me, curling up a few inches from my head. For once she kept her thoughts to herself. Just stared at me without saying a word as though she knew just how shaken I was.

Their presence at the StubHub might be another attempt to control me. Maybe to stop me from helping those kids. I sat up.

"Come on, Onyx. We are visiting Jace."

6. Draugar

I could see part of Jace's bedroom while we were still in my bedroom. Pinpointing people's whereabouts by thinking about them as the portal formed was becoming easier now. Previously, I'd only focused on familiar places—the mansion, Torin's place, our shop, or the school. Now I created air or wall portals anywhere. I bet I could find Torin if I wanted to stalk him while he was out reaping.

Air portals were tricky because it meant literally etching runes on invisible air particles. Runes had to hang in the air before they dissipated, and since they were made of light, you had to be fast. Torin and Andris made it seem so effortless. Me? It was a hit or miss. I preferred mirrors and walls.

A shirtless Jace was at the other end of the room, head bowed low as he did something on his desktop computer.

The room was filled with soccer paraphernalia—flags, posters of soccer players, teams, and trophies. He was a serious LA Galaxy fan. Among the posters was a corkboard with pinned school events and pictures. He must have been playing since he was young. He looked about five in some of the team pictures. There were also scattered pictures of a red head. She was smiling in almost all of them. Must be his mother. None showed her when she was sick. In a few, there was also a man with her. Former coach? I didn't see any of her with Jace.

I touched the pictures, the board, even the soccer stuff and got nothing. Strange.

What is he doing? Onyx asked, her voice startling me.

"Shhh," I said.

Jace glanced over his shoulder and I froze, my grip tightening on Onyx. Had he heard us? I noticed something else. Bruises on his back like someone had hit him. There was no way they came from soccer. Could his father be abusive? Like Beau's?

Carefully, I skirted around the dirty pile of clothes, socks, and cleats on the floor. I was done touching dirty gym clothes to get visions. I stood behind his chair. No reading on the chair. He was on a popular social website.

"Faced my bullies tonight. Got a black eye, but made sure they'll never come after me again," I read what he'd just posted on his timeline and my eyes flew to his face. He was pressing a bag of frozen peas on his left eye, but I could still see the split lip and the cut above his right eye. He also had bruises on his knuckles, which explained the online comment.

He chuckled at a response to his post and clutched his side. He dropped the peas to respond, and I slapped my hand on my mouth to stop from gasping. His eye was almost swollen shut.

Oh, poor kid, Onyx murmured. *His eye is swollen.*

Thanks for stating the obvious, Onyx.

Beiskaldi! Don't call me Onyx.

Runes could take care of his wounds. I could add just enough to lower the swelling without arousing suspicion. *You use that word a lot, Onyx. It had better mean sweetheart or gorgeous.*

Onyx gave a gleeful chuckle that said it was none of the above.

If I put you down, can you stay invisible? I'd forgotten to ask her before I scooped her up in my bedroom.

Oh, I'm perfectly happy being carried around.

I put her down. *Self-serving Beiskaldi!*

Who are you calling a bitch? I'll have you know—

Stop yapping for one second. I need to think. Surprisingly, she clammed up. From the way she sat on her hind side and lifted her chin, she was pissed. Too bad. She had called me a bitch first. I pulled out my artavus.

What are you going to do? Onyx asked.

I should have known she wouldn't stay quiet for long. Ignoring her, I engaged speed runes and etched on Jace's back just enough to take care of severe damages. By tomorrow, his face wouldn't look like his attackers had used him as a soccer ball.

He turned suddenly and looked around, almost brushing against me. I stepped back, careful not to make any sounds. His eyes zeroed in on my position as though he felt my presence. Someone rattled the door and Onyx practically leapt into my arms. We backed away from Jace.

He dove for his T-shirt and yanked it on before yelling, "Come in."

I was by the mirror, ready to create a portal when a man stuck his head inside the room. Taylor senior. His pictures had captured him perfectly, brown hair with a receding hairline, gray eyes, and a nicely trimmed moustache. The dark shadows under his eyes and the gauntness weren't in the pictures though.

"Mr. Worthington is leaving now," Coach Taylor said. "Would you like to personally thank him?"

What? Torin's father was here? Unless there were two Worthingtons in L.A., the evil bastard was up to something. Could I sneak into their living room and confirm it?

"I already did," Jace mumbled.

"He wants to know if you're ok, son."

"He shouldn't have interfered. It was none of his business. And he creeped me out by following me home."

His father sighed and stepped into the room. "He witnessed those boys attack you, Jace, and did what any decent man would do."

Decent my ass. I bet he knew of Torin's interest in Jace and had been following Jace around. What did he want?

"I intend to file charges against LA Galaxy, and Mr. Worthington said he's willing to testify. All you have to do is tell us their names."

"No, Dad," Jace said, standing up. "Please. You'll only make things worse for me. Let it go."

His father moved closer. "Why are you protecting them? If they get away with it, they'll do the same thing to someone else. That's what bullies do until they're forced to stop." His father peered at him and frowned. "Hmm. The swelling on your face is down and the redness in your left eye is gone. Even your lip seems less swollen." He stopped and straightened. "Jace, I need the names of the boys who did this to you."

Jace sighed. "I didn't see them. It was too dark."

"Son..."

"Dad, please. Just let it go."

His father sighed. "Fine. Here." His father held out a locket on a gold chain. "He found this on the ground by the bus stop."

Jace took the necklace and stared at it, a weird expression crossing his face. "I didn't know I'd lost it." He opened the locket and his face crumpled. "If I'd lost this..."

"I know." His father patted his back. "Come on. Your mother raised you better than this."

Jace pocketed the locket and followed his father out of the room. Once again, Jace's eyes swept the room as though he knew they weren't alone. Then he followed his father. I wondered what was in the locket.

Follow them, Onyx said.

Do you know who could be in the other room?

I know who the Earl of Worthington is. He's your boyfriend's father and an evil Immortal. We watched the battle last week, and I overheard your conversation with the pretty Valkyrie.

Relieved I didn't have to explain, I followed Jace and his father. Voices came from straight ahead—Jace's high-pitched one and a deeper voice. British accent. I'd only heard the Earl yell during battle, but I'd seen and heard him in my vision and knew what he looked and sounded like. I slowed down as we got closer. Jace's father was talking about filing a report with the police. How to look at them without alerting Worthington? As an Immortal, he'd see me cloaked.

An idea popped in my head and I went with it. I lowered Onyx to the floor. *Go and see if he's facing us or not.*

Glowing runes were visible through Onyx's fur. She padded to the entrance, then crouched low and peered inside. Immediately, she scooted back and came back to my side. *He's a big man.*

I know.

He looks like your Valkyrie, only older.

I know that too.

He's facing this side and might see you.

Damn it.

"Isn't that right, Mr. Worthington?" Jace's father asked. I'd missed part of his question.

"Yes, the boys responsible should be held accountable," the all too familiar British accented voice said and a shiver crawled up my spine. "If this was an attempt to force him to leave the team, the league should be notified. I played football in England growing up and know that every league has a code of conduct. You break it, you get a suspension. Physical altercation means immediate expulsion from the team. It is within your father's rights to report this to the police and file charges, young man. He's only looking after you."

Which century did he play football? This was clearly an attempt to make himself look good, and crawl back into Torin's good graces. I picked up Onyx and backed up. *Let's go home.*

And leave him with them? I can keep an eye on him and come home once he leaves. Even better, I can follow him.

No. He'll know you're there. Chances are he can feel our presence right now too.

Then I'll keep an eye on the boy only and report to you.

Are you that bored?

YES!

Fine. Stay here until he leaves. Listen to anything he says and does. If you're not back in thirty minutes I'm coming to find you. And do not follow Lord Worthington.

She nodded again.

Jace's father was explaining the mentality of bullies when I lowered Onyx to the floor. This could be disastrous. If Worthington saw Onyx, he'd know we were onto him. I bit my lower lip, wanting to call her back. Then she did something that didn't make sense. The runes disappeared then she meowed.

"What is a cat doing in our house?" Jace asked.

The last image I had of her before the portal closed was Jace bending to check for a tag. I was so happy I hadn't put one on her.

~*~

In twenty-four hours, Onyx had become a fixture around my bedroom. It seemed empty without her. I actually missed the ornery cat. Lights were on at Torin's, but there was no one there when I stopped by. I had to talk to him about his father. Talking to Mom was out of the question because this was a private matter for Torin, which left Andris.

I went to the mansion and followed the sounds to the pool. Blaine and two girls were in the hot tub. From the looks of it, he was making out with both. Finally, he was letting go of his dead girlfriend. He'd been pissed since Casey died during a football game.

One of the girls saw me first and said something to Blaine. I didn't recognize her, which meant she was either a local girl who'd graduated high school before my time, or a college student. Kayville had one private university.

Blaine was out of the tub before I reached them. He shrugged on a robe. "You didn't have to get out," I said.

"The look in your eyes says I do." He waved to the two girls. "And they're not going anywhere tonight," he added in a whisper.

"Two of them?" I asked.

He grinned. "Why not? I've accepted that Casey is gone, so this is me moving on. So what's wrong?" he asked after we left the deck and the pool door closed behind us.

"I'm looking for Torin and Andris. Have you seen them?"

"Torin stopped by hours ago then left for L.A. Andris said he had a date. Lavania is visiting her husband and Ingrid is in her room. You know, just in case you want to see them next before you decide to ask me for help."

I winced. He was newer to the group and tended to be overlooked. "I wasn't."

He shrugged. "I know I have to earn my stripes. So, what is it?"

I couldn't tell him about Torin's father any more than I could Mom. That was Torin's story to share. "Someone I know might be in danger."

He sighed and chuckled. "Oh, phew. I thought you were about to tell me you saw the Earl."

I blinked. "You know?"

"That he's back? Yes. Torin told me. I'm to keep an eye out for him in case he decides to pay you a visit at school."

I shook my head. "He wouldn't dare return to Kayville, the scene of his crime. He couldn't be that bold. And I don't need to be protected."

"This is not about protecting you."

"Yeah. Sure. I think he's after someone Torin plans to reap."

"The asthmatic boy?"

Okay, so he was in the loop on everything. "Yes."

He swore softly under his breath. "That bastard. I need to find Torin ASAP. Jace cannot be touched."

"I left my cat to keep an eye on him." Saying the words sounded ridiculous, but Blaine didn't miss a beat.

"Good move. Meanwhile I'll track Torin down." He started to walk away then glanced at me. "Stay away from the boy. You don't want to spook him."

"I'm always careful," I called after him.

He chuckled. "He's different."

Different how? Because Torin had taken a special liking to him? Back in my room, I watched the clock and paced. Lights were still on downstairs and I could hear a band playing. Femi was probably watching TV while Mom was probably with Dad. She slept with him downstairs sometimes, even though they didn't share a bed. I hoped Torin and I would be like them. Loving. Supportive. There for each other, in sickness and in health.

Minutes crawled by. Getting restless, I texted Andris. Nothing from him. He was probably lost in some woman's arms, the man-whore.

The portal opened and I stopped pacing. Andris glared at me from a bathroom which looked too fancy and sterile to be someone's home. He wore a robe and from the logo on the robe, it was hotel issued. The bare legs and visible chest said he was naked. He smirked when my cheeks grew warm.

"Never mind," I said. "Sorry, I bothered you."

"I was just getting ready for round," he counted his fingers, "three. What's going on? Lost Torin?" he asked, peering behind me.

A woman's voice called his name. Andris ignored her and stepped into my room, concern flickering in his eyes as he studied me. "What's wrong?"

I felt silly pulling him away from his latest conquest. But by the time I finished talking, the lover was gone and a warrior had taken his place.

"Where's Torin?"

"I don't know, but Blaine went to find him."

"How did Jace seem?"

"Okay. I gave him enough runes to bring down the swelling and left Onyx to keep an eye on him. Onyx is my cat," I added when he shot me a questioning look.

Andris didn't even crack a smile. "Good. I'll be there in a few." He turned and re-entered the hotel bathroom. "Something has come up, sweetheart," I heard him add. "A family matter. Let's do this again." The portal closed. A few minutes later, it reopened and he entered my room fully dressed. "Engage your invisibility runes. Once you get your cat, you come straight home."

Yeah, right. I went to my drawer and pulled out the dagger. Was it only an hour ago I'd sworn never to touch it? I had no idea what was going on, but this boy was important enough to pull both guys from their ladies. I was going prepared. Besides, Onyx wasn't back. The Earl might have her.

"What's that for?" Andris asked suspiciously.

"For kicking ass," I said.

"Which part of 'come straight home' didn't you get?"

I pushed the dagger in the pocket of my jacket. "I'm getting Onyx back by whatever means necessary."

He frowned, opened his mouth as though to say something, then closed it and sighed. "This is going to screw up Torin's surprise," he mumbled, but I heard him.

"What surprise?"

"Let's go." The portal to Jace's room opened so easily for him I knew Andris had been there before. Jace had picked up his room, and he was back at his desk either doing homework or online. "We find your little fur-ball then you head straight back home and to bed. End of discussion. You have school tomorrow," Andris added.

"Don't call her Fur-ball," I shot back. "Her name is Onyx."

"Okay, sheath your claws. Come on."

Jace looked over his shoulder and like before, stared straight at where we stood. My feet faltered and Andris' hand rested on my shoulder reassuringly. We waited until Jace went back to his work, then cut across his room.

"Did he hear us?"

"Of course not. We are cloaked. That includes sounds. Don't touch or move things in his room though."

I looked around and refused to panic. "Onyx is not here."

"Call her," Andris said and opened another portal. This one showed Jace's father in the kitchen, cleaning up. Cheering and sports announcers discussing a game came from the TV. It couldn't be easy being a single dad, but Jace's father seemed to be pulling it off. But then again, if his wife had been sick all those years, he'd probably gotten used to taking care of the house, himself, and Jace.

Onyx? Where are you?

Once again, just before we left his room, Jace glanced over to where we were and frowned. Andris didn't seem bothered. As soon as the portal closed, he removed his artavus and started toward the man.

"What are you doing?"

"I need to question him," he said.

"About what? The cat is not here."

Andris sniffed the air. "Yes, but something was. Don't you smell it?"

There was a rotten stench in the air. "So he's not the cleanest father in the world, but he's trying. It's not easy being a single parent. You've seen my mother. She's great at everything except house chores." I looked around. Jace's father was turning off lights. "The house looks clean and Jace is a well-adjusted guy."

Andris shook his head. "Sometimes I forget how green you are. I'd know that scent anywhere and it's not garbage." His eyes locked on me. "You know what? I'll find your little fur-ball on my own. Go home."

Something in his eyes set off warning bells. "What is it?"

"It's getting late, Raine."

He was hiding something. He opened a portal to my room and pulled me out of the path of Coach Taylor, who turned off the kitchen light, plunging the room into darkness. The runes on Andris' and my body gave us enough light to see our way. Andris nudged me toward the portal. "Go."

"Fine. Find Onyx, okay? She might be a pain, but she was just starting to grow on me."

I turned to enter the portal, but a flash of light appeared in the corner of my eye and I whipped around. Squinting, I peered out the window and into the darkness. I could recognize runic lights anywhere. It had come a fair distance from the house. I had no idea where Jace's family lived, but I knew StubHub was in Carson, California. The area appeared to have medium-sized houses with trees in the distance. The lights zig-zagged again to the right, then a howl filled the air, rattling the windows.

"What was that?" I asked.

"*Garm*. Go home, Raine." He shifted to hyper-speed, created a portal, and disappeared through it.

Garm was the hound guarding the gates of Hel, the realm of the dead, definitely not Valkyries' territory. Something was wrong. I engaged my runes and followed Andris before the portal closed.

He zipped around homes and headed for the trees, then stopped so suddenly I almost bumped into him. We were inside a fenced basketball court at a neighborhood park or a local school. I couldn't tell which from the surroundings. There was a building to our right, bushes and trees adjacent to it. No one was playing basketball. Instead, headless bodies and ripped limbs littered the ground. The carnage was straight out of a horror movie, the stench suffocating.

Some of the limbs were too big for regular humans, the skin gray like mummies, but they were definitely human cadavers with long, stringy hair. Most were male in tattered gray pants and no shirts.

Even more puzzling was the lack of blood. Just red flesh inked with black gooey stuff.

A flash of light zipped across the basketball court. Even at hyperspeed, I recognized Torin chasing one of the gray men. Things. Or whatever they were. It was huge.

Torin leaped and tackled it. A loud roar escaped its mouth as it lost its balance and started to fall. Moving faster than I thought possible for something its size, it turned and tried to grab Torin, but he was no match for Torin. He turned and rammed his fist into its back. Bones cracked. A bellow left the thing's mouth as the impact of the blow propelled it forward. Instead of hitting the ground, it disappeared through it and was swallowed by the earth.

Okay, that move was definitely not human.

"What are these things, Andris?"

"You've got to be shitting me," was his answer.

"What?" I glanced at him, but he was looking to his right, where Blaine was fighting one of the creatures. But Andris wasn't staring at Blaine. His focus was on the second man fighting further ahead. The Earl. Despite the beard, I recognized the Earl of Worthington.

"Raine!" Torin yelled. "What the hell, Andris?"

"I told her to go home, but you know how she is," Andris said, his eyes still on the Earl. "Do you guys need my help or shall I just take her home? Because I think you need our—" He didn't finish his question and I saw why.

One of the things was moving toward us. Andris pulled out two artavo and went to meet him. He leaped up, landed on its chest and severed its neck with a blow. Inky goop dripped from its neck and I could have sworn I saw a dark head-shaped shadow inside the body before it disappeared.

Badass Andris. Guess the next one will be gunning for me. I shouldn't have followed Andris. Death and mayhem wasn't my thing. I was a witch. A Seeress. A healer, not a killer. Worse, my presence was distracting Torin. He kept trying to keep an eye on me while kicking heads off of the humanoids as they slithered from the ground.

"Behind you!" I yelled when one reached for his legs.

He whipped around, grabbed the head, and ripped it clear off the thing's neck. Most of the body was still partially buried. No wonder the place was littered with heads. This time, I was sure I saw a second head. It was the soul of the thing. It looked like a regular person. There was even something familiar about him. Like we'd met before. Torin pointed a glowing artavus at it and snarled something. Light shot from the artavus, but the soul sank into the ground with the rest of the body. Torin cursed.

"Miss, can you take me home, please?" a voice asked and I turned. A boy around ten stared at me with round eyes, a skateboard under his arm. What the heck was he doing here?

"You shouldn't be out here this late," I said.

"I was going home from a friend's when I saw you. There are weird noises coming from the trees."

Weird, he could see me when I was cloaked? Lavania often said children were sensitive to the supernatural. Still... I put some distance between us. "Where's your home?"

"Over there," he pointed past the trees.

"Okay. Come on." We barely reached the line of trees when his body started twitching, bulging, and stretching. In seconds, the boy was a man. Not just any man, a Native American with markings on his face and long straight hair. I stumbled backwards and reached inside my pocket for my dagger.

"Hungry," he growled, saliva dripping from his mouth. "Food."

He dove for me, but I already had my speed runes. I leaped to the side and brought my dagger down, aiming for his neck, but he seemed to be growing larger. I caught him in the chest instead, leaving behind a gaping wound oozing black blood. He kept moving, like the wound was nothing. He loomed down to grab me, his breath hot and stinky, a gurgling sound escaped his mouth.

I turned to run, but he was faster. He grabbed my leg and pulled. I lost my balance and landed on the ground, rocks digging into my hands. His head lowered, rotten teeth bared. He didn't have fangs, but I was sure he didn't need them to eat me.

Someone yelled my name, but my mind was focused on the blood-thirsty brute. Desperation kicked in and with it, an instinct to survive. I kicked at the thing's chest with my free foot. He staggered backwards, letting go of my leg.

Torin appeared in a streak of light, eyes blazing under the glowing runes. He went for the guy with a snarl, but the thing sank into the ground and disappeared, leaving Torin holding a tuft of hair. He cursed and threw it away.

"You okay?" Torin asked, helping me to my feet.

I nodded. I didn't think I could speak.

"Good. See if you can connect to the earth and stop the souls from robbing more graves." He turned, walked to the middle of the basketball court and yelled, "Listen up, scum of the earth! You want revenge? Fine. Here I am. Come and get me." He spread his arms.

Was he nuts? These creatures didn't seem like the kind you reasoned with. I glanced around and realized I was wrong. The weird creatures appeared to be listening to him. Even the ones crawling from the ground turned to look at him. I noticed something else. They all had long hair and tribal markings on their faces like Native Americans.

"You touch her," Torin continued, pointing at me, "and I will personally make it my mission to find your worthless souls and escort them to Corpse Strand."

He'd gotten a kick from me for pulling this crap before. This time, I had no problem letting him be my hero. These bastards were scary.

"And once I'm done with you,"—he pointed at the creatures— "I'll go after each and every one of your *living* relatives and send them to join you." He glanced at me and grinned. I rolled my eyes. Such arrogance. "Work your magic, Freckles. Strip them of their stolen bodies. Keep an eye on her," he added and was gone.

I turned to see the person he'd spoken to, but there was no one there but bushes and trees. He was back fighting and none of the creatures were coming after me. That would have been great if more weren't slithering from the ground like worms. In fact, they seemed to be an extension of the ground.

Stolen bodies, Torin had said. Were they zombies? They didn't move like any zombies I'd seen in movies. Maybe Hollywood got that wrong too. And then there was the one that had changed its shape right before my eyes. The problem was they were just as fast as the Valkyries.

Torin was busy fending off three of them. He yanked off a head and the light from his artavus caught the soul in the face. It disintegrated and the headless body crumbled to the ground.

Hmm, so the light from an artavus was just as deadly as that from a scythe.

Blaine and Andris had their hands full too, and several more were crawling around the Earl. Not that I cared what happened to his sorry ass. Let them bury him alive for all I cared. But Torin was right. If I connected with the earth, I could stop the zombie-like creatures and end this nightmare.

I put my dagger away, went on my knees, and pressed my hands on the ground. Something snarled behind me in the bushes and I jumped. My eyes darted around, searching for the source. Nothing. Not even a rustle of trees.

Come on. Connect with me, please.

The spark flickered, but before it could bloom, beefy arms closed around me from behind, trapping my hands. So much for Torin's warning. My attacker obviously hadn't gotten the memo.

Humid hot breath drenched my neck. My strength runes weren't enough to break his grip. Grinding my teeth, I pushed down the fear threatening to drown me and dug deeper. I needed my magic now. The spark dimmed and flickered out.

Damn it! Time to scream and be rescued again. I hated that.

I opened my mouth, but I caught a movement from the corner of my eyes. Something black and huge crept from the bushes and leaped toward us. It moved so fast all I saw were streaks of light and eyes. So many eyes.

Fear trapped the scream in my throat as the thing with glowing eyes moved closer. Heart pounding, I struggled to reach for my dagger. I didn't stand a chance against the two of them, but I'd go down fighting.

The next second, I was free. I turned and caught the sight of fangs before the animal sunk its teeth into the neck of my attacker and whisked him away.

I had no time to wonder what that animal was, but the enemy of my enemies was my friend. I went back to trying to connect with my magic, before I became chow to another one of the things. The desire was there, but I was too rattled to focus.

Torin yelled something and shot past me, taking one more down. The thing disappeared, leaving poor Torin rolling across the basketball court with an arm he'd hacked off. He hit the fence, taking it with him and smashing into a nearby building with a sickening thud. I cringed, knowing he must have broken something.

Maybe it was the concern for him that did it, but I connected with the source in my core again. This time, it exploded and spread. I pushed my fingers into the earth and closed my eyes. Lavania had said sometimes a rhyme worked faster than just a command.

Reclaim what has been taken
By souls foul and wrong
Let the dead never awaken
From your cradle where they belong

I opened my eyes to see the earth suck the creatures like a giant vacuum cleaner, leaving behind the souls defenseless. I counted about a dozen. Fifteen. Nineteen. Some of them so black all I saw were their outlines. The one nearest to me looked ready to bolt. I pulled out my dagger and pointed at him. The energy still pulsing through me connected with the dagger and transformed it into a staff. The blue crystal inside the round knot at the tip glowed.

"Don't even think about it, pal," I snarled.

Torin laughed. "That's my girl." He was still on the ground, half-buried by the metal fence and bricks from the wall, exposing what appeared to be a classroom. The building looked new.

"You okay?" I called out, a little giddy from the magical buzz.

"Yeah."

He was still taking his sweet time getting off the ground and was starting to worry me. He was usually Mr. Invincible. Keeping my staff leveled at the soul, I waved my hand and the fence and bricks lifted off him.

"Thanks, luv." He stood and walked toward me with a slight limp, a glowing artavus in his hand. He looked a mess, blood and dirt all over his face and clothes. Just how long had he been fighting these things?

"You're sure you are okay?" I asked.

"Yep. Just tired of dealing with *Draugar*. Where did you get that?" he asked, his eyes on my staff.

"The Norn's dagger. It transforms into a staff." The words barely left my mouth when the dark soul I was guarding decided to run. "Hey!" I yelled and pointed the staff at it. Light shot from the tip. I expected the dark soul to disintegrate into pieces. Instead, the light wrapped around him and pulled it toward the staff like a tracking beam.

This was not good. I didn't want that dark soul anywhere near me. "Torin?"

"Got you." His hand gripped mine. "Relax. Hold it in place. You are in control."

The beam continued to pull the soul toward my staff. My instinct was to let it go.

"Focus on your magic and control it," Torin whispered, but Andris drowned his words from the other side of the basketball court.

"Give me a reason to disperse you, you worthless, bottom feeders." Andris had had both his artavo leveled at the souls. "I'm not in the mood to chase you all over the goddamn world. Get your sorry excuses for souls in there." He pointed at a portal he'd opened.

"Get over there, you worthless soul," I yelled, copying Andris. Sure enough the soul moved toward the ones Andris was ordering. Blaine also had his artavo leveled at some. When the one tethered to my staff reached the others, the beam of light dimmed and retracted, until only the tip of the staff glowed. I glanced at Torin and grinned. "I did it. I reaped a soul."

"Yeah, you and Blaine."

Blaine peered at the portal, a broad grin on his face. As an Immortal, reaping souls was not his job. The Earl stood on the side. I wondered whether he was thinking of jumping in with the souls. This could be his chance, except he'd be heading to Hel, not Asgard.

Please go! I dare you.

Andris wasn't smiling and appeared to be keeping an eye on the souls and the Earl. He'd definitely get the Earl if he dared to cross the line. "Andris looks pissed."

"That's his favorite jacket drenched with *Draugar* juice," Torin said.

That was the second time he had used that word. And yeah, Andris *would* get pissed over that. "*Draugar?*"

"Grave robbing souls," Torin explained. "They possess dead bodies." He winced as he sheathed his artavus.

"Like zombies, except zombies don't shape-shift and disappear into the ground."

"*Draugar* are not zombies. They're fast, strong, and ravenous for human flesh, which makes them a menace and hard to kill. Powerful ones like the ones we faced tonight use bones and clay, can change sizes, and disappear into the ground. The trick is to go after the souls inside them instead of cutting off their supply of dead bodies or bones." He looked at me and grinned. "But now we have you. *Draugar* killer."

"Zombie killer sounds better," I murmured.

He grinned and reached out as though to touch my face, but I stepped back. The pull he felt was from the magic coiling under my skin, but I didn't want *Draugar* juice on me either. "You stink."

He stepped closer, smirking. "So do you, luv."

Before I could evade his hand again, he palmed the back of my head and kissed me. I forgot about the *Draugar* and how filthy he was. It was always like that whenever we kissed. When he lifted his head, his eyes blazed. Not because of runes.

"Go home, Freckles," he whispered. "You've helped us enough tonight."

"We need to finish here first."

"We," he pointed at Andris and the others, "not you."

Andris was still directing the souls into the portal. The Earl was now collecting bones and piling them up like a stack of wood. He glanced up and our eyes met.

No matter how much he helped, I didn't trust him. The *Draugar* that had been caught halfway out of the ground were gone, the clay disintegrated, leaving behind the skeletons. The limbs and the heads were also all skeletons. Others had skin on them like mummies. Guess it depended on how old the graves were.

Blaine walked over to join us. He still held a skeleton arm like it was nothing. I tried not to cringe. "Thanks for the fight, Torin. It's been a while since I hunted *Revenants*."

"Dealing with them is a joint effort. Do you think you can get our resident Grimnir? This lot," he indicated the souls, "belongs in Hel."

"Sure." Blaine dropped the arm and created a portal.

"*Revenants?*" I asked as soon as Blaine disappeared.

"That's what his people called them in Ireland and England. I've been hanging around Asgard for so long I think of them as *Draugar* now."

Torin squatted and started to etch runes on the ground. The basketball court was totaled, fissures criss-crossing the ground, but the right runes would take care of that. Torin's father was back at his favorite pastime—watching us. Why couldn't he just leave? I couldn't look at him without wanting to punch him in the nose, or put a whammy on him and make him disappear. The souls were all gone, but something kept teasing my memories.

"I think I recognized one of the souls," I said.

"That's because a couple of the ones we fought in Kayville last week were here," Torin said, sounding preoccupied as he etched the right bind runes. "They masterminded this attack. Someone told them we were in Carson."

Someone like his father? My eyes met the Earl's again. Funny how the *Draugar* appeared after he did, and they were his friends to boot. Or former friends. Maybe it was him they'd come after because they were dead and he was alive. Or maybe it was because he'd failed to lead them to Asgard as he'd promised and they were out for revenge. The bottom line was he was the only one outside our group who knew Torin and Andris were in California. Throw in his presence at Jace's place and he was my number one suspect.

"Someone is controlling them," Torin added. "*Draugar* might be intelligent and ruthless, but they rarely attack in packs." He stopped etching and glanced at me. "Go home, Freckles. Not to your parents. Mine. Shower. *Draugar* stench doesn't go away without thorough scrubbing and you do not want it in your house."

"I still haven't found Onyx. My cat," I explained when he frowned.

"She's at home. If she hadn't recognized the three *Draugar* watching Jace's house tonight, we would not have stopped them. I assumed the two of you paid Jace a visit and you left her behind to...?"

"Keep an eye on him," I said.

"Then thanks." He stood and studied his handiwork. The cracks on the ground sealed like a zipper closing. He threw me a smug smile. "I'm good, aren't I?"

What a show off. Even though he had a right to be. He was good with runes. He etched them on my car so often I could now recognize his handwriting. "Yes, you are."

He shot me a side-glance. "Humoring me now, Freckles?"

There was no winning with him. "Okay, you suck."

He ran a finger down my nose then opened an air portal. "Go home. I'm happy you helped tonight, but you shouldn't have been out here. You shouldn't deal with death." His eyes went to my staff. "You are a healer."

I was happy he understood that. I had no problem with Valkyries and Grimnirs reaping or retrieving souls. I could even tolerate Norns, but ravenous zombie-like creatures that shape-shifted and disappeared in the blink of an eye were so not what I'd signed up for.

A howl filled the air and I shivered. That was the same sound I'd heard when Andris and I were in Jace's kitchen. There was also a drop in temperature I hadn't noticed before. When the sound came again, I realized it was coming from the portal Andris had created. The souls were gone, but Andris and Torin's father were throwing bones and skulls through the portal, probably feeding the howler.

"Is that *Garm*?" I asked.

"Yeah," Torin explained. "We fed him the ones we killed earlier."

Was *Garm* the black animal that helped me earlier? "How long did you battle the *Draugar* tonight?"

"Hours. Go home, luv."

My eyes went to his father. In his hand was a skull. I remembered the markings on the cheeks and forehead. They were all members of a tribe, which meant this was an old burial ground. Native Americans held such grounds sacred.

"Tell them to stop feeding the hound and close the portal." Torin stared at me as though I'd lost my mind. "It's not right. They need to stop."

"We can't leave the bones here, and *Garm* eats anything."

"You don't understand." I looked around. "This must have been a burial ground for a Native American tribe. Those bones belong here."

Torin frowned. "Are you sure?"

"Yes. You guys were so busy fighting you didn't take a proper look at the re-animated bodies. Burials grounds are sacred to Native Americans. Hawk will want to know about this."

Torin cupped his mouth. "Hey! Stop feeding *Garm*, guys. Close the portal."

"Why?" Andris asked. "What's going on?" He still sounded pissed.

Torin looked at me. "Tell them."

"The basketball court must have been built on top of a Native American burial ground," I said. "I saw the faces of some of the *Draugar*. They had tribal markings. They don't deserve to be fed to

Garm." I went on my knees and pressed my hands on the ground. "I need to put them back where they belong."

This time, it was easier to connect with my powers. As it flowed to my hands, I mumbled, "I give you back what was taken, by souls dark, angry, and strong. Let them rest and never awaken. From your core where they belong."

The pile of bones slowly sunk into the ground until nothing was left. Torin helped me to my feet. I heard him say something to the others. Then he led me through the portal.

"You are supposed to help the others," I protested.

"I will once I have you under the shower." He led me straight to the bathroom, turned on the shower, and rummaged through a cupboard for a new bottle of shampoo. "I'll find you a change of clothes. Throw everything away because the stench will cling to them."

"You bought me this jacket," I protested.

"I'll buy you more."

I studied his face. He looked even more tired under the light. "Don't trust the Earl, Torin. No matter what he says or does. Do not trust him."

"I know." He reached out and touched my cheek. "I'll deal with him tonight."

7. The Staff

I didn't care what the Earl wanted. He was back in Torin's life for only twenty-hours and his former buddies attacked? I bet he'd known they were coming. They'd probably followed him to Jace's house.

I used all of Torin's shampoo and body wash, but I still didn't feel clean. After dumping all my clothes in the garbage, wrapping them up in several plastic bags, I pulled on Torin's T-shirt. Then I headed home.

Onyx was asleep on the windowsill. I wanted to hug her, and at the same time scold her for disappearing on me. She lifted her head, gave me a bored look, and lowered her head back on her paws. I pulled on tights.

I was sure she'd gone back to sleep, until she said, *You stink.*

"I do not."

It's not your job to fight Draugar. What if something had happened to you? What if a soul had body-hopped from a Draugar to you?

"Torin would never let that happen, and tonight, I helped."

I know. I saw it.

I stopped just before entering the bathroom. "You did?"

Best free show I've watched in a long time, except when you were almost mauled by one of them.

"You don't have to sound so pleased about it. I still shudder when I think about it." I disappeared inside the bathroom and brushed my teeth. Onyx entered the bathroom and jumped on the counter. She sat by the sink and watched me without saying anything. Her fur looked different as though freshly washed or brushed. She'd probably licked herself and laughed with glee while watching us fight.

"Want to brush your teeth too?" I asked her, rinsing.

Her whiskers twitched. *No. Tell me how you escaped the attack.*

"I thought you said you'd seen everything."

I couldn't stand watching you get eaten, so I closed my eyes.

I laughed. "Some familiar you are. *Garm* came to my rescue."

Now why would Hel's hound come to your rescue?

I shrugged. "Cause I'm important in the grand scheme of things. So, yeah, *Garm* did it. What other explanation is there? One second I was *Draugar*-food the next, this huge black animal leaped from the bushes. He moved faster than earthly animals and looked twice as ferocious. And he had many eyes. *Garm* has what? Six eyes?"

Daufi, she said and faced the window.

"You know what, Onyx? If you're going to curse me out, do it in a language I understand. Otherwise the insult loses its impact."

It means stupid.

I crawled under the blanket. "Why are you cursing me anyway? What did I do this time?"

You are a dodo brain.

I chuckled, switched off the lights and tried to fall asleep, but I kept seeing *Draugar* crawl from the ground like worms every time I closed my eyes. Then there was the Earl. Why couldn't he just leave? I had enough to worry about with the Norns to add him on to my People I'd Like to Destroy list. The smug grins on the Norns' faces were haunting me more and more. Why had they seemed so happy after the battle?

It was almost one a.m. when the portal opened and Torin walked in. As usual, he only wore sweatpants. He didn't bother to turn on the lights. He knew his way around my room. The mattress dipped as he joined me under the blanket, slid an arm under my head, and pulled me closer. I turned to face him.

"Not asleep?"

"I can't." He smelled nice. He was one of those guys that made you want to burrow into his neck and just breathe him in. Unfortunately, his hair was still wet and in the way. "Sorry I used all of your body wash."

I felt his lips move as he smiled. "That's okay."

"Everything fixed?"

"Yes. The building, basketball court, and fence."

"The souls?"

"Echo added them to his list. As if he needs more to stay ahead of the other Grimnirs."

"They count how many souls they reap?"

"Goddess Hel keeps tally. They get a break from reaping depending on the souls they've collected. The more evil and darker the better. Echo just scored almost two dozen, which means he owes us."

"No wonder the two Grimnirs were ticked off about Beau's father."

Torin pressed a kiss on my forehead. "Forget them. You call the shots and they'd better get used to it."

His blasé attitude toward my Nornish activity was beginning to worry me. It was so unlike him. He'd hated it when I became Immortal. Hated it when my witch powers started to show. And now he was okay with everything? I didn't buy it.

"Maybe we should ask Echo to share the souls. You know, give the two Grimnirs some."

We both chuckled. Echo and sharing in the same sentence was unheard of. Even though Cora and I had been best friends since elementary school, he didn't like it when she spent too much time with me.

"How's Andris?"

Torin rolled onto his back and draped my leg across his hip, so I was partly on top of him. It was his favorite sleeping position. "I promised to replace his jacket, so he's happy," he said.

I snorted at the idea. "Why? He can afford a hundred of those jackets."

"It was one-of-a-kind, and since he blames my father for what happened tonight, I figured I owe him one."

That was the dumbest thing I'd ever heard. "You're going to track down some designer just to get him a new jacket?"

" Mmm-hmm. One of a kind, he kept saying."

Andris can be such a baby sometimes. "Why can't the Earl do it?"

Torin sighed. "Because he's gone."

My first reaction was to say, "YES!" But I reigned in the elation. "Oh. Why?"

"His presence here was bothering you guys. I can't have you looking at me the way you did yesterday, or Andris threatening to beat some sense into me. He might get hurt."

I grinned, and then I remembered what he'd said about me. I lifted my head and engaged my runes so I could see his face. "How did I look at you?"

"With disappointment." He stroked my cheek, his runes flashing and dimming. "I didn't like how it felt. I never want to disappoint you that way again."

My insides melted. Now I felt bad. "I was worried, not disappointed."

He stole a kiss, and tucked my head under his chin. "No, it's okay to admit it, luv. I can't be perfect all the time."

I rolled my eyes.

"I felt that," he said, then sighed. "It's too soon for my father to ask for forgiveness anyway. Even though the information he'd given me proved to be useful."

I frowned. "What information?"

"About the souls. He said they were angry and plotting revenge for what happened in the forest. He was right about someone organizing them."

Yeah, I knew who that someone was. The conniving Earl. He set himself up to be the hero too.

"The attack tonight was too well planned. Souls don't move or attack in groups," Torin mused.

Unless they were being organized by their mentor. I kept my thoughts to myself, but not about what had happened earlier. Torin had a right to know. "The Earl was at Jace's tonight."

Torin stiffened. This time, he was the one who lifted his head to study me. "Did he see you?"

"No." I explained what happened.

"Thank you for taking care of him. I'll talk to Jace during lunch at school tomorrow and find out what happened. I'm happy you left your cat to keep an eye on him. If she hadn't, Jace and his father would be dead right now. Most *Draugar* don't care who they terrorize as long as they feed."

Now more than ever, I was convinced his father was behind the attack. I burrowed under Torin's chin and let his warmth chase away the cold. Now that I was in his arms, I felt safe and sleep came easy. And when *Draugar,* who looked like Norns, chased me in my dreams, he cradled me close and promised he'd never let them get me.

It wasn't until morning that I realized I hadn't asked him why Jace was under his care. He was a reaper. They don't protect those about to die.

~*~

Torin had left the Harley at his fake apartment in Carson, so we took my car to school the next day. Cora and Echo were prolonging their goodbyes and steaming up the windows of her car. Typical. We were crossing the street when I noticed a girl with pink hair hurrying across the parking lot. Then a girl with blue hair stepped out of a green Honda Civic. Another with blue and pink joined her. I grinned.

"I think you started something," I whispered to Torin.

He arched his eyebrows, totally clueless. We caught up with the girl with blue hair in the hall. "Nice hair style, Chelsea," I said and nudged Torin. "Isn't her hair gorgeous?"

"Yes."

I nudged him again.

"Stunning, uh, Chelsea." After, we met two more girls with neon streaks. He pulled me into a doorway, his eyes searching my face. "Are we on one of your rescue-some-poor-girl missions again?"

"Nope. This is me campaigning for the coveted junior prom queen and you,"—I gave him a toothy grin—"my super-hot and popular QB boyfriend are my ticket to getting it."

He smirked. "That's so lame, even for you."

My jaw dropped. "You didn't just say lame. Lame? You hate that kind of lingo."

He shot me a disgusted look. "You don't care about prom."

I didn't. "Do too. Mom already ordered my dress, and you need to find an outfit to match mine. The theme is All That Jazz. Lame, right? Say it again. I dare you."

"If I ever say that word again, put a whammy on me and put me out of commission for a few hours. And I refuse to compliment girls dumb enough to dye their hair with a paint gun."

"Shhh. They might hear. Think of it this way. You are making their high school experience a memorable one."

"I don't get it."

Most popular people never realized how invisible the rest of the students felt, but I expected better from him, an Immortal who'd attended hundreds, maybe even thousands of high schools.

"Let me put it this way. For two years, I was a dot in this school, but I didn't mind because I had Eirik and Cora. Others are not so lucky. A compliment from you," I patted his chest, "goes a long way."

He crossed his arms. "No. Not happening."

"Come on. Yesterday, I helped you with the dead. Today, you help me with the living. If you don't, I'll join Onyx and watch the next time *Draugar* attack."

"Are you threatening me?" He leaned in, invading more of my space. Instead of feeling crowded, my senses leapt. If we were alone, I would have jumped him.

I reached up and gave him a chaste kiss on his cheek. "No. I'm promising you."

"Would you two get a room?" Cora teased. I peered around Torin and waved at her. She fanned herself.

I shook my head and focused on Torin. He wore an expression that said he was going to be difficult. "Please?"

"No. I'm done. I adore you, but enough is enough." He planted a kiss on my forehead, turned and grinned at Cora. "Looking nice, Cora."

Cora blinked. "Oh, thank you." She looked at me and made a face. "Someone is chatty this morning."

"He's being difficult." We hugged and turned to watch Torin walk away.

"That man can wear the crap out of jeans," Cora said.

"He can wear the crap out of anything, or nothing."

Cora's mouth dropped. Then she slapped my arm. "You've been holding out on me! So you two...?" As if he knew we were watching him, Torin turned and spread his arms as though to say, "What?"

He was so cocky. "Not yet." And since I didn't want to discuss my virginity, I switched to her favorite topic. "How's Echo? You guys were steaming up the windows of your car a few minutes ago."

Cora laughed and looped an arm around mine. "He's such an amazing kisser. I could make out with him for hours." We put our backpacks away, and grabbed our books for morning classes. I had English, which was in the western wing while Cora's first class was upstairs. "Are you having lunch with Torin?"

I shook my head. "He's scouting in California. StubHub."

"Ooh, soccer. My father is really getting into soccer this year." She made a face. "I don't understand it. Oh, you should join us for lunch. A restaurant delivers soup and sandwiches everyday whether Echo is there or not."

"I don't know. I was thinking of eating with Dad. You know, make the most of things while I can."

Cora stopped walking. "How is he doing?"

"Better. He and Mom were playing chess last night."

"Like old times?"

I grinned and nodded. Cora and I had had enough sleepovers at my house to know how my parents played chess. Dad put his game face on and did his best to let Mom win.

Despite being alive when chess, or *chaturanga* as it was called, found its way from India to Europe, my mother hadn't mastered the game. But that was how she was. Never caring about new inventions and technology. If people were to go back to the days when humans walked around naked and ate only what nature provided, Mom would be perfectly happy. Watching her use computers was pretty hilarious. She cursed and yelled. Dad used to say she'd do great once the interactive computers hit the market.

Cora touched my arm. "If you change your mind, I'll be in Florida."

Ellie and Amber overheard her as they walked past. "You're going to Florida again?"

"Again?" Cora asked and glanced at me.

"We were planning on throwing a party last weekend, but Torin told Justin that you guys were headed to Florida for the weekend," Ellie said. "So we switched it to this Saturday. Please say you'll be there."

"We'll start around four then go clubbing afterwards," Amber added.

Cora made a face. "I volunteer at the Moonbeam Nursing Home until evening, so I don't know."

Crap, the two Grimnirs I'd met two nights ago were going to grab Cora at the nursing home. I couldn't even warn her, because she'd already made it clear she didn't want me reading her future. She worked at the nursing home on Thursdays and Saturdays, which meant I had to keep an eye on her from afar without her knowing.

"Oh, come on, Cora. You have to come," Amber said.

"Bring your boyfriend, uh, Echo," Ellie added, then she exchanged a glance with Amber. Seriously these two lusting after Echo? The reaper was so crazy about Cora no one else mattered.

"Not promising anything," Cora said and started upstairs, but I'd seen the expression on her face. She had no interest in partying with those two. Neither did I. Torin's team had a game on Saturday afternoon. I started to walk down the hallway leading to the English wing. Ellie and Amber hurried to catch up with me.

"You and Torin are coming, right?" Ellie asked.

I shrugged. "I don't know. I have prom on Friday."

"Junior prom blows," Ellie added.

"Is Beau Hardshaw going to be at the party?" I shot back, knowing that would make her quit bothering me. Sure enough, Ellie clammed up, her cheeks growing pink.

"Why would we invite that stoner?" Amber asked.

When Beau became famous, I hope she regretted not being nicer to him. "He's a student here," I said, looking at Ellie.

"You don't know him like we do," Amber continued. "His family is messed up. His father is a drunk. Do you remember last month at my party? Beau was so wasted he punched Justin in the face over nothing. Like father like son."

Ellie didn't defend Beau. He was good enough to hook up with, but not defend? Bitch. She kept her eyes down. Disgusted by both of them, I fell back and let them walk ahead.

Things got worse in class. One of McKenzie's friends was in our English class. As soon as she entered the room, Ellie and Amber looked at her blue hair, whispered, and laughed. Even after she sat, they kept turning and looking at her. Worse, they got two other girls in class involved. The girl slid lower in her seat, her face turning red.

I bet I could come up with a nice curse to make their gorgeous hair turn into knots. Who should I target first?

Eeny, meeny, miny, mo
Who do I dislike more
Turn her hair a shade of blue
And don't change till she gets a clue

I landed on Amber and grinned. The class ended, but her hair didn't turn blue. So much for my witchy powers.

I didn't see Cora again until lunchtime. When she linked our arms, the same vision flashed in my head—the two Grimnirs snatching her and disappearing through a portal.

Once again, I was tempted to warn her about them as we headed to the third floor bathroom. It was the top floor in the building and it emptied fast during lunch, so the bathrooms were perfect for creating portals.

"When do you volunteer at Moonbeam again?" I asked.

"It keeps changing, but Saturday afternoon for sure after group lesson with Lavania."

"This Saturday it's just you and Ingrid." Maybe I should drive to the nursing home with her, make sure she was okay before heading to StubHub. "I'm working on tapping into the source of my magic now." We looked up and down the hallway. Then we slipped inside the bathroom. "You go first." I watched her pull out an artavus and etch runes on the mirror. "Not bad."

She rolled her eyes. "You're faster. You even do air portals. I still can't. You know, I've seen portals like this in your store. All nicely runed." She entered the Florida house and turned. "We should just replace this ugly mirror with one of yours and no one would ever know."

Echo wasn't in the kitchen, but a paper bag with a restaurant logo sat on the kitchen counter. "We would know," I replied. "And then we wouldn't get better at creating portals."

"You stink," Cora grumbled.

"Lazy bum," I retorted.

She laughed. "You sure you don't want to join us?" Cora asked, peeking inside the bag.

"I'm good. Later." I shifted the entrance so it led to my house. Femi had lunch ready and Dad was waiting. He was watching a game when I arrived.

"You think the U.S. team will make it again?" I asked. Despite being wraith-like, there was more life in his eyes. They sparkled as he discussed teams and players. I never even knew he liked soccer. But then again, soccer was never that popular in the U.S. until recently. We were almost done with lunch before he switched topics.

"Your cat came to visit me. She spent the entire morning with me and only left when Femi brought food. Have you named her yet?"

"I call her Onyx, but she…" I almost forgot he was Mortal and hearing that I could communicate with my cat might seem weird. "I don't think she likes it."

"She'll get used to it."

No, I won't. Onyx entered the room, jumped on the couch, and curled up beside me. Mom had bought the couch right after she came back from Valhalla and placed it by Dad's bed. It pulled out into a full size bed, so she could sleep near him. Onyx's eyes closed, but I was sure she was listening. She even allowed me to stroke her before ordering me to stop messing up her fur. When it was time to go, she followed me to the portal.

I'm bored. Can I come with you?

"No. Cats are not allowed at school."

They were at Harry's school.

I knew she meant a certain fictitious young wizard, but I faked ignorance, "Who?"

She squinted. *I can stay invisible and walk all around your school. Mortals are entertaining, especially teenagers.*

"Uh, no. You'll bump against one and start a riot, or worse if one stepped on you and you screeched—"

I don't screech. Just say you don't want me there.

Actually, it might be entertaining to have her around in some of my boring classes. "You'll distract me, or get me in trouble for bringing a pet to school if you decloaked. Why don't you do what most cats do?"

And what is that?

"Sleep and clean yourself."

She hissed. *Baulufotr.*

"Sticks and stones, Onyx."

Femi laughed. She could see us from the kitchen. Our downstairs portal mirror was in the living room, but visible from the kitchen. "She's impossible, Femi! Give her something to do or watch. Animal channel. That should be entertaining." I turned my head towards Onyx. "You might even see your cousins."

If she could scratch me and get away with it, she would have. Instead, I received a toss of her tail and an indignant walk to the couch.

"Don't worry. I'll keep her busy," Femi said.

"Thanks. Bye, Onyx."

I hate that name.

"You are stuck with it, Fur-ball."

Bite me.

I was still laughing when I entered the bathroom at my school and the portal closed behind me. Onyx was growing on me.

~*~

When I left the band room, Beau and his friends were outside his classroom. He winked at me, but I just shook my head.

"Dude, that's St. James' girl," one of his friends said.

"So what?" was his cocky response. "I don't see his name tattooed on her ass."

My jaw dropped.

"You'd tap that?" another asked.

I didn't hear his answer, but the laughter that followed said it was outrageous. He and I were going to have a talk about that. If we were going to sneak around for these tutoring sessions, he should come up with a better reason than hitting on me.

I stepped outside the school and shivered. The weather had nothing to do with it. The sun was up and spring flowers were blooming in the flowerbeds lining the entrance.

I felt the telltale prickly feeling on the back of my neck. Someone was watching me. Not the Norns. I could always sense them. This was different.

I glanced around furtively, but nothing seemed out of place. Students hurried to the school buses parked at the curb, while others headed to their cars or bikes. For Oregonians it was already warm enough for biking.

McKenzie and two of her friends were talking and laughing as they hurried to her car. They were rocking their crazy hair colors with renewed confidence. I hadn't seen Ellie and Amber since English. Not that I needed to see them to confirm what I already knew. I was a good witch, which meant my hex probably had no effect.

Still, none of my observations gave me a clue as to who was watching me. The feeling grew stronger the closer I got to my car. Then I noticed the fresh runes.

My car had permanent protective runes, courtesy of my ever-vigilant boyfriend. Torin added more every other month, same with the ones on the doors and walls of my school, and the trees to and from my house. I now recognized his slanted runic writings. The new ones on my car weren't written by him. Even worse, I didn't know what they meant. Refusing to panic, I removed my phone from my backpack and took a picture.

"New runes?" Cora asked from behind me and I turned.

"Yep."

"What do they do?"

"I have no idea. They weren't here this morning." And Torin had hitched a ride with me and used a portal to go to California. I searched the parking lot for Blaine. He should be able to know what they meant. He was an Immortal, possibly as old as Andris.

"I can give you a ride home if you don't want to drive it," Cora offered.

"Nah, I'm good. I'm going to the store first." I had to tell Hawk about the burial grounds the *Draugar* had disturbed in Carson. I touched the runes, but I couldn't get a reading. "I can't run scared every time someone runes my things. It's probably Torin. You know how overprotective he gets," I lied.

"Yeah. I know," Cora said, but she sounded worried.

I should have kept my mouth shut. I couldn't lie worth a damn, and we both knew it. Determined to prove that the runes didn't bother me, I got behind the wheel and took off. I noticed Cora kept watching. She followed me in her car to the first traffic light. I appreciated her vigilance. We'd been through way too much to take chances.

She stayed behind me all the way to my store. As usual, the only available parking was behind the building. I removed my phone and texted Cora after I parked.

"U didn't have to, but thx," I said.

"Idk what u r talking about," she responded.

I sent her an emoji with hearts. Cora might act like she only cared about Echo, but she was a loving, loyal, and dependable friend.

The feeling of being watched returned again. I glanced up and down the back parking lot and shivered. Maybe I was imagining it.

The bell dinged when I pushed the back door open. Hawk looked up, surprise flickering in the depth of his dark eyes. He was still in charge of the store even though Mom was back. Full time reapers didn't run businesses.

"Have you come back to work, Ms. Lorraine?" Hawk asked.

He was just teasing. As an Immortal, he was very much a part of my life and knew everything that had happened in Kayville the last several months. He'd even rescued me from the Witches right here in the store.

"I wish," I said. "Between lessons with Lavania and school, I'm way too busy." I glanced around, but didn't see Jared, our other employee. Not that I considered Hawk an employee. Immortals might offer support to Valkyries, but they were based on earth and had opportunities that went with it. Like investing money and buying properties. Chances were Hawk was secretly a gazillionaire. He was the kind of guy that didn't welcome personal questions. I didn't even know whether he lived in Kayville or some mansion in the middle of nowhere.

He stepped from behind the counter and locked his hands behind him as he approached me. He always treated me with respect even though he was probably born a couple of millennia ago. He never cracked a smile or wore anything but black. His hair was tied in the back with a leather thong and at first glance, he could pass for a forty-something year old. But in the right setting and clothes, war paint and feathered hat, I could easily see him as a spiritual leader to his tribesmen.

"What can I do for you, Ms. Lorraine?" he asked.

I glanced around again. "Can we talk alone?"

"Of course." He disappeared into the room where he worked on frames. The Mirage did custom framing, but our most popular commodity was portals, mirrors with runes etched on their frames.

Hawk came back with Jared, who'd been our employee for years.

"Miss Raine, are you coming back to work? I told Celine the crazy customers probably scared you away."

His wife was a sweet woman who'd decided I needed mothering after Mom had disappeared for months. Being Mortals, they didn't know she'd been facing the Valkyrie Council in Asgard to get her position back.

"No one scares me away, Jared. I've just been busy with school and helping Mom take care of Dad." Taking care of Dad was a good enough explanation for Mom's absence these days. "Tell Celine that I'm fine."

"I will. She'll be happy to hear that."

I disappeared into Hawk's office. He closed the door and indicated a chair, then waited until I was seated before sitting. Now that I was here, I didn't know where to begin.

"It's okay," Hawk said reassuringly, reading me. "Is this about money?"

The last time I came to see him, I'd wanted money to buy a prom dress. Then Mom returned and took complete control over my prom preparations. The way she talked on and on she must think I have zero fashion sense.

"No. Last night, I fought *Draugar* in Carson, California, with the Valkyries."

He leaned forward. "*Wendigos?*"

I'd watched enough of the TV series *Supernatural* to know what a *Wendigo* was—a creature controlled by an evil spirit. "So *Draugar* and *Wendigo* is the same thing?"

"*Draugr* is one, *Draugar* means more than one. And yes, they're the same thing." He leaned closer, a strange light in his eyes. "Every culture has its own version of an evil spirit that devours humans, but it's the same thing, an evil soul possessing a dead body. They even possess living people and make them go insane or corrupt their souls, so when the people die, they run from reapers and possess others too. It's a vicious cycle To Mortals, these creatures have superhuman strength, speed, and are impossible to kill. It's our job to hunt them down, and then hand over the souls to the reapers. I've worked with a few Grimnirs and Valkyries over the years and taken down quite a few. When and where did this happen? How many escaped?"

By the time I finished telling him, he was on my side of the desk. He looked visibly disappointed when I told him how I'd helped get rid of them.

"These *Draugar* sound like they were part *Golem.*"

"What's that?"

"Creatures made of pure clay. I would have loved to see them. It takes powerful magic wielded by a powerful soul to use bones and clay to create a body. Most just find the nearest grave and crawl back into the fleshiest body they can find. I saw a pure *Golem* once, centuries ago. A rabbi created it using a different kind of power. It was completely under his control, doing his every wish." He walked back to his side of the desk and sat, then leaned forward and steepled his fingers. "I'm happy you shared this with me, Ms. Lorraine. It seems like your team took care of them."

"According to Torin, a couple of the souls were from the Immortals we defeated last week."

Hawk straightened, his brow furrowing. "I see. So more will be coming?"

"No. I mean, I don't know." I couldn't repeat what Torin's father had told him about angry souls without revealing the source. "But it doesn't hurt to be prepared."

"No, it doesn't. But between the Immortals and the Valkyries around here, we should be okay."

"But that's not the only reason I came to see you. The souls didn't use bones from a nearby cemetery. They found some under the basketball court at the school. I think it is an ancient burial ground."

"My people?" he asked, his features taut.

I explained what I'd seen.

He stood. "Show me."

A bunch of guys were shooting hoops when we opened a portal. Staying inside the office while using the portal as a window, Hawk studied the surrounding area. After a few minutes, he closed the portal and faced me. Gratitude and something else was apparent in his eyes.

"Thank you, Ms. Lorraine. My people are no longer as powerful as they used to be, but a group of us, Native American Immortals, have worked tirelessly with them over the years to preserve part of our culture in any way we can. We'll take care of this."

My throat closed a bit listening to him. This was the most vulnerable I'd ever seen him, and the first time he'd mentioned anything personal. "What are you going to do?"

"We can declare the site to be sacred. The school or the basketball court *will* be rebuilt elsewhere." He bowed briefly. "Thank you, Ms. Lorraine."

"It's Raine. All my friends call me that."

He smiled briefly. By the time I closed the door, he was on the phone. Jared was talking to a customer and didn't see me leave. As soon as I stepped out of the building, the same telltale chill I'd felt earlier skidded down my spine and I knew I wasn't alone. Then I saw him, the Earl of Worthington standing by my car. My stomach dropped.

8. Tea with a Warlock

My first instinct was to engage my speed runes, turn around, and run into the building for Hawk. I didn't have my dagger, just the artavus I carried to school to create portals. I was sure it was completely useless against a powerful Immortal. Still my hand closed around it. There were lots of trees and bushes nearby, and the earth at my disposal should he try something.

Tapping into my power, it burst and flooded me, bringing with it renewed confidence. I walked toward my car, my glowing eyes locked on him.

"There's no need to reach for your dagger, Miss Cooper," he said in a voice that sounded too much like Torin for my liking. Although his was colder, more menacing. The smile on his lips was condescending.

"I don't carry my dagger," I said, proud that I sounded calm. I wasn't sure what to call him. He didn't deserve the title of a Lord or the Earl of Worthington. "The world is my weapon." A localized rumble rippled through the ground and shook nearby trees and shrubs.

He glanced around, his smile not changing. "Impressive."

"What do you want?" I asked, wishing I could knock out his teeth and wipe that smirk off his face.

"Just to talk. Can we go to a nearby café for coffee or tea?"

Talk to him? I didn't think so. I opened my mouth to tell him no, but the look in his eyes said he expected me to refuse him. I needed to prove to him that I wasn't scared, even though I was.

"Sure. Why not? My favorite Greek restaurant is just a few doors from our store. We should be able to talk there." I was sure he could see the runes on the building and wouldn't miss the ones inside Café Nikos. Torin tended to get carried away.

This time, I threw him a challenging look before turning and going back to The Mirage. The door dinged when he followed. Jared was still with a customer, and Hawk was probably still talking to his contacts in the office. I might refuse to be intimidated by Torin's father, but I wasn't an idiot either. If he wanted to kidnap me, he could do it and disappear through a portal before my runes could alert the protective ones etched on the building.

I went straight to the office, knocked, and pushed the door open. Hawk scowled, but his expression cleared when he saw me. "Could you come outside please?"

Something in my voice, or maybe it was my expression, had him standing up quickly and without asking why. I opened the door wider. He followed me into the store.

"I'd like you to meet the Earl of Worthington, Torin's father," I said, waving toward the evil Immortal.

Hawk studied the Earl without offering his hand, but his eyes grew darker. Ignoring the guy, he glanced at me. "What's going on, Ms. Lorraine?"

"He was waiting for me when I left the store. He and I are going to Café Nikos for a drink, alone."

Hawk nodded, indicating he understood he wasn't supposed to interfere. "Of course, Ms. Lorraine." Then his focus shifted to the Earl. "Warlock. Do not do anything you'll regret. The young Norn is under our protection."

The Earl chuckled. "I'm sure she is. Shall we?"

There he goes again, sounding like Torin. I really, really wanted to wipe that smug smile off his face. My hand fisted, and I wasn't surprised when the mirrors in the room rattled. Interesting. When angry, I used my powers without channeling it by words or thoughts. I would so like to do that when I practiced good magic too.

I led the way out of the store and even slowed down so we walked side by side. "So what's next, Warlock Worthington?"

His lips tightened. I hoped he didn't like being called a Warlock because that was his name from now on. Warlock Worthington or just the Warlock.

"Let's sit down before you start interrogating me, young lady."

The authoritative way he spoke had me clamming up and hating myself for doing it. Café Nikos was packed as usual. The owner, Nikolaus, saw us when we entered.

"Raine! *Koreetsi mou!*" He came around the counter and clasped my hands. "How are you doing? How's your father?"

"I'm fine, and Dad is hanging in there." He and Dad went way back to high school. His exuberance could sometimes be embarrassing. Like now. We had the attention of everyone in the room. "I'm here with a family friend who wants to try some of your famous pies."

Nikolaus glanced at Warlock Worthington. "Lord Worthington. I didn't know the family you were visiting was the Coopers. Any friend of Tristan's is a friend of Nikolaus."

Completely blindsided, I stared at the Warlock's annoying smirk, but I recovered fast and exclaimed, "Uncle Warlock! You came here without me? You know how much I love Nikos' *baklava*. Was it last month when you excused yourself after dinner?" I glanced at Nikolaus, praying he gave me answers.

"No, no, it was last week in the afternoon with the twin boys from South…" His voice trailed off and I saw why. Warlock Worthington was glaring at him.

Twins? There was only one set of twins in Kayville last week— Alejandro and Matias Torres. Except the Norns had resorted to trickery once again and mimicked the Torres Witches and their cousin Bash to trick me.

"This way, Lord Worthington. Miss Raine." His voice carried, and once again the customers looked up and stared at us. I didn't care this time. Had Warlock Worthington met with the real twins or the Norns?

Once we were seated, he ordered a large slice of *baklava* and coffee. Black. Just like Torin. I mentally pinched myself. Just because the man looked like an older version of the guy I was crazy about and talked like him didn't mean they were alike. He was evil personified. Torin wasn't. I didn't want to eat anything, but I ordered custard pie anyway.

"Is this together?" the waitress asked, deftly pouring water into two glasses.

"Yes," Warlock Worthington said.

"No," I said at the same time. "I'll pay for mine."

The bastard chuckled as though my show of independence amused him. We had barely sat down and he was already pushing my buttons. Hopefully, my anger wouldn't get the better of me. I was likely to create a vortex under his seat and suck him into oblivion.

"You are a prickly little thing," he said.

I objected to being called a thing, but I let it go. He looked disappointed when I just shrugged.

"You are also very powerful for one so young."

I objected to being praised by him too, but this time, I couldn't help myself. "And you are such an evil Warlock for someone so old. I always thought wisdom came with age."

His lips pressed into a line. Score.

"The last time someone called me a Warlock, they died a painful death," he said so calmly a chill crawled up my spine.

I tried to cover it with a chuckle and sipped some of my water. "The last person to call you a Warlock was Hawk and he's very much alive."

"Ah! That's the name. I knew our paths had crossed before. As for his fate, that can be changed."

I stopped smiling, anger coursing through me. With it came the power. The table started to lift. Dang it. I needed to calm down. Taking deep breaths, I pushed the magic back. "You touch him and I swear, I'll forget you are Torin's father."

The smirk was back on his face. "Be careful, young *Völva*. Once you cross that line, there's no going back." He smiled at the waitress. "Thank you, luv."

I nodded briefly at the waitress, and waited until she was gone before saying, "No, Warlock. I don't kill. I change destinies. You touch Hawk or anyone I know, and I'll change yours like that." I snapped my fingers for emphasis and something flickered in the depth of his sapphire blue eyes. Anger? Surprise? Maybe fear? Wishful thinking. Somehow I doubted the man was afraid of anything or anyone.

"No matter how powerful you are, you're not a Norn and therefore cannot change anything," Worthington said. "The training doesn't begin until you're eighteen."

I shrugged, ate a slice of my pie, and almost gagged. I was more nervous than I'd thought. Putting my fork down, I studied the Warlock. He'd already demolished his *baklava*. He must have really been hungry or he had a sweet tooth.

A prickly feeling told me we were being watched. My sixth sense, which seemed to have sharpened since my witch powers emerged, picked up signals faster than normal. I didn't dare look around, so I wrapped my hands around my glass and let my gaze lock with the Warlock.

"So here we are," I said.

"I'd like to reconcile with my son," he said.

Wow, right to the point. "Then talk to him."

"I can't. He asked me to leave. I'm supposed to try in a century or two."

Way to go, Torin. "That seems reasonable."

"No, it's not," he snapped. "He was willing to listen until that idiotic Roman boy intervened."

"That *idiotic* Roman boy has a name, Andris. He's also a powerful Valkyrie, unlike you. He's been with Torin for centuries and is like a brother. Family. So I'd be very careful how you talk about him, especially to Torin."

He leaned forward. "I am his father. My blood flows through his veins."

He made it sound like he was the wronged one. Like Torin owed him something. "Oh gee, you think you'd win Father of the Year award with that? Blood means nothing if you hurt the people who share it. You hurt Torin by what you did. If he wants time before he can forgive you, give it to him."

He leaned back against his chair. "You're an opinionated young woman, aren't you?"

"You make it sound like it's a bad thing," I shot back. "Aren't you here for my opinion? Isn't that why you runed my car, stalked me to my shop, and invited me to this little meeting?"

"I thought the Roman was holding Torin back. That maybe they had a special relationship, but—"

"They do," I shot back. "But no one holds Torin back."

"It's you," he said like I hadn't spoken. "I saw it last night. He'd do anything for you, and you string him along."

"String him along? I would do anything for him too, including sit here,"—I looked around, noticed that we were drawing attention, and lowered my voice—"and share a drink with you. You want forgiveness? Show some humility. Some contrition. Prove that you've changed."

His expression didn't change, so I couldn't tell whether I had hit a nerve or not. "Why should I change? I didn't do anything wrong."

Was he serious? "For starters, you,"—I glanced around again and lowered my voice even more—"sacrificed Seeresses, Immortals, and Witches for your crazy cause."

"I didn't twist their arms to join me or force anyone to go against me," he said in that annoyingly calm voice.

"Wow. You are completely incapable of feeling any remorse."

He sipped his drink and watched me like I was some lab rat he was about to dissect. I didn't want my pie anymore. In fact, I didn't want to be in the same room with him. I needed to get up and leave without destroying Nikos.

"I see why he loves you," he said.

"I highly doubt it."

"You don't take crap from anyone, which is very surprising in one so young. You'll make a fine Norn." He leaned forward again. "You accuse me of being unfeeling, my dear. What about you? You'll never give him what he seeks. You're living on borrowed time because Norns don't mate. When you turn eighteen, they will come for you to start your formal training. When you're gone, what will become of Torin? The pain he's feeling now will be nothing compared to what he'll feel once you're gone. So why not let him go now? I may not win the Father of the Year award as you so eloquently put it, but I'm not toying with his soul. You are. You will destroy him."

I wanted to tell him to shut up. To just shut the eff up. If I could give up my magic to be with Torin, I would. Since I couldn't, I planned to have it all—the ability to help people and Torin. I just didn't know how yet.

I hoped my feelings weren't transparent as I stared at his father. "That's where you are wrong, Warlock. Torin and I will have our forever. I'll make sure of it. And if you don't change, you'll never have a relationship with him. I'll make sure of that too." I stood, pulled out my cell phone, and removed a twenty-dollar bill from its case. I dropped it on the table, aware that he watched my every movement. "My treat."

As I walked away from the Warlock I felt the table near the door watching me. I glanced over and my eyes met Femi's. She was seated with three men that had wise eyes. Immortals. My feet didn't falter. I didn't know how I made it to The Mirage, but I did. Hawk called out my name, or maybe it was Jared, but I kept walking. It wasn't until I reached my car that I started to shake.

As I tried to calm myself down before driving home, Femi opened my door. "Scoot over, doll."

~*~

We had barely left the parking lot when a warm draft filled the car and Torin appeared in the back seat. Who had contacted him? I didn't want him to see me like this. I was still processing and needed to get my emotions under control.

"Are you okay? What happened?"

The concern in his voice triggered all kinds of emotions, and I didn't care what he could or could not see. I could always hold it together when he wasn't around. As soon as he appeared, eyes blazing as though he was ready to annihilate anyone who touched me, all my defenses crumbled. I wanted his arms around me so badly my shaking got worse. I unbuckled my seatbelt, scrambled over to the back seat, and straight into his arms. He pulled me onto his lap and held me tight, rubbing my back while pressing my face on his neck.

"It's okay, luv. I'm here now. Shhh."

I burrowed deeper and held on to him until his warmth chased away the numbness that had crawled under my skin.

"What happened, Femi? Hawk opened a portal in the middle of the soccer field and said I should come home."

"I'll let Raine explain."

"If someone hurt her, I need to know. If they said anything to cause her pain, I need to know. That's why we have the code. The explanations can come later. Was it the Norns?"

Femi mumbled something in her native language. "She's okay, Torin. Just a little shaken. Raine, if you haven't noticed, is a tough one."

"But there's just so much any person can take. What was she doing before—?"

I lifted my head and he stopped. He searched my face frantically, fury sharpening his eyes. I imagined losing him and the sickening feeling in my stomach returned. I pushed it down. "I'm okay now. I just needed you to hold me."

He stroked my cheek with his knuckles. "Was it the Norns?"

I shook my head and decided to stop the conversation in the only way I knew how. I kissed him and time stopped, fear and frustration morphing into comfort, then passion. Or maybe it was his need to reassure himself that I was okay that made him ruthless in his possession of my senses. I didn't complain, I just clung onto him and allowed him to erase his father's smug face from my head.

When we resurfaced, we were alone in the car. Femi had already parked outside our house and left. Torin pressed a thumb under my chin and lifted my head, so he could study my face. The storm in his eyes still raged on, but it was less ominous.

"I want to know what happened," he whispered.

I nodded. We'd vowed never to keep secrets from each other. He got out of the car first and then pulled me out and scooped me up.

"I can walk," I protested.

"I know." He studied my face and grinned. "I hate that I can't protect you all the time, so allow me these little pleasures." He started for his place. "Besides, you weigh nothing. Hello, Mrs. Rutledge."

"Is Raine okay?"

Was that actual concern in my neighbor's voice?

"She twisted her ankle, but I plan to take good care of her," Torin lied smoothly.

"Is there anything I can do to help?" she asked.

I groaned. Torin chuckled. "No, but thanks for asking, Mrs. Rutledge. I got her."

He did. No matter what his father said, Torin and I had each other. As for Mrs. Rutledge, her attitude towards me had thawed a bit in the last few months because of Dad's illness, but she was still nosey and liked to watch my every movement from behind her curtains. I was amazed she hadn't noticed how often we had company without anyone arriving in cars.

The door opened before we reached it to reveal Andris. "Is she okay?"

"No," Torin said.

"Yes," I said at the same time, trying to mask my dismay. "What are you doing here?" I peered over Torin's shoulder at Andris as he closed the door.

Concern clouded his brown eyes until he caught me watching him. He winked. "Couldn't miss a chance to watch Torin act romantic."

I wiggled to get down, but Torin's arms tightened as he continued on to the kitchen. I opened my mouth to tell Andris to leave, but then I realized I might need him.

Once Torin learned about the Earl, he was going to go ballistic. Probably go after him, which might have been the Warlock's intention all along. That thought had flitted through my head during the drive, and the more I thought about it, the more it made sense.

The Earl was sneaky and mean. It didn't mean he was wrong about all of the things he'd said. Some were true. If I ever left Torin and joined the Norns, he'd lose his mind and soul.

"What he's trying to say is after last night, if anyone hears the code, they alert the others," Blaine said from the kitchen and I almost got whiplash trying to see him.

He was leaning against the counter and munching on an apple like he hadn't a care in the world, but his topaz eyes stayed alert. Even more surprising were his clothes. Blaine was usually a meticulous dresser. Today, he wore cargo pants with grease stains and a T-shirt that looked like a reject from a second hand store. He hadn't shaved and more grease strains competed with the stubble on his chin, and his bronze hair was covered with a woolen cap. He could pass for a mechanic at Joe's Corner, a local car repair shop.

"Put me down, please," I begged Torin, but I might as well have been talking to a brick wall. He set me on the kitchen counter and pushed my hair away from my face to study my expression. He was babying me again, and I hated it. I swatted his hand out of the way, but that didn't stop him. Worse, I couldn't get off the counter because he stood between my legs. Fighting him was useless. "What code?" I asked.

No one spoke.

"'Come home' is an SOS code for you," Ingrid said, entering the kitchen. She must have just come from the mansion.

She and I hadn't spoken since we battled the Earl, even though she'd joined us in Florida during the weekend. As an Immortal, she was part of our group, but she'd always been in the shadow of her sister Maliina—Andris's evil ex-girlfriend. Now that Maliina was rotting in Hel, Ingrid was slowly coming out of her shell. She and I had never been close, but she'd helped me understand a lot about Seeresses.

"What does that mean?" I asked.

"It means *you* are in danger," Ingrid said.

I gawked at her, and then glanced at the others, my eyes stopping on Torin. "When exactly did you guys come up with this code, and how come I wasn't told? No, how come I wasn't in the meeting?"

Torin's usual smirk was missing, which told me how seriously he took this. "Cause I knew how you'd react. Just like you're doing right now."

I smacked his chest. "Damn right. I'm not helpless and you know it. I have runes and elemental magic. I don't need you guys running to my rescue." I glared at them, but Blaine continued to eat his stupid apple. He had grease under his fingernails. This was a Blaine I'd never seen before. Andris just smirked. Neither one of them showed any contrition. Ingrid was the only one who seemed uncomfortable. Torin wore a long-suffering expression as though I was making a big deal out of nothing.

"You can't fight, Freckles," he said, pulling up a stool with his foot as though he knew I'd create a portal and disappear if he gave me breathing space. He sat and wrapped his arms loosely around my hips. "Waving a staff around doesn't count."

I gripped his hair and yanked his head back so he could see I wasn't amused. He didn't even wince. "I don't need to fight, pal. I point and BAM, things happen. I just didn't get a chance to use my staff last night."

I had no idea what that staff did, but they had to understand I hated being treated like I was helpless. I let go of Torin's hair and stroked it. He needed a haircut. And why that mattered now was beyond me.

"I can move things." I pointed at the wooden bowl of fruit and it lifted. "Smash heads without lifting a finger."

Blaine moved away from the hovering bowl. Ingrid picked an apple from it and came and sat on a stool. Andris rolled his eyes and muttered, "Show off."

"It's the only way to stop you knuckleheads from acting like I'm an idiot. Do you want a demonstration of my elemental magic?"

"No," they all said in unison.

"We get it," Torin said. "You're bad-ass. Still, I want to know what happened." He indicated the others with his head. "Do you want them here? Because I left the assistant coaches in charge and they could use Andris' help. And Blaine was...?"

"Undercover," he said.

"Studying my runes," Ingrid said.

The humiliation of being treated like a baby aside, I needed them here to stop Torin from going postal on the Earl's ass.

"This won't take long. Your father etched some runes on my car." Torin stiffened and sat up. This time, I was the one who stopped him from leaving. I slid off the counter and onto his lap. "I didn't know what they meant, so I ignored them."

Andris created a portal to my car, and then closed it. "Locator runes," he said.

"Go on," Torin said in a voice I'd only heard him use once, the night he'd vowed to kill his father for trapping his mother's soul on earth.

"He appeared outside The Mirage just as I was leaving and asked if we could talk."

"The bastard!" Andris ground out. "I hope you said no. I hope you created a sink hole and ordered the roots to trap him there for the next millennium."

"Andris!" Torin snapped.

"Actually, I said yes." Andris groaned, but Torin's eyes didn't leave mine. They were quickly acquiring an iciness that would have scared me if he were someone else. "He said he wanted to talk and I wanted to hear what he had to say."

Torin nodded, though I doubted he agreed with my decision. His body had gone rigid, his hands forming fists around my waist. I quickly summarized my conversation with his father and finished with, "He wants me to let you go now, rather than later when I join the Norns."

Torin didn't speak. He was probably plotting his father's demise.

Andris, on the other hand, had plenty to say. Most of it was things we already knew, but no one stopped him. "He obviously didn't get the memo," he said, pacing. "You are the one Seeress the Norns can't control. You don't have to deal with them or fear them. You're—"

"Shut up, Andris!" Torin snarled.

"Screw the rules. She has a right to know."

I sat up. Torin looked ready to slug Andris, who stared defiantly back at him. Blaine and Ingrid stopped acting indifferent. They either had no idea what was going on here, or they knew and were bracing themselves for my reaction.

I cupped Torin's face and forced him to focus on me. "What do I have a right to know?"

"I can't tell you. We,"—he tried to glare at Andris, but my grip tightened on his face—"are not supposed to influence you."

"You have to choose a side, Raine. You can't stand on the sidelines. You are either with the gods, Hel and the evil giants, or neutral like the Norns. Whichever side you choose, that's where you will reside. If you choose the gods, you'll head to Asgard when you turn eighteen. If you choose Hel, you'll join Eirik in Hel's realm. If you decide to stay neutral, you move in with the Norns. Those ugly hags lied again. They are not with the gods. They're only after their own survival, and having you with them ensures that. Eirik was given a choice and he chose his mother. At least that is how the gods see it since he turned eighteen and never went back to Asgard. No one knows whose side you're on or where you're going to live."

My heart was pounding so hard I swear everyone could hear it. Where I was going to live? Earth was my home.

My eyes met with Andris', then the others. From their expressions, this wasn't the first time they'd discussed this. Could this be why Torin hadn't said anything when I'd helped people at school? He hadn't wanted to influence me?

"But I'm with you guys," I said.

"Then you are on the side of the gods," Andris said.

I started to nod, then shook my head. "No, I don't want to live in Asgard. I mean, I want to live here. Why can't I live with you guys?"

"Because they will continue to try and influence you," Andris said, frowning. "The Norns tried and failed, but they won't stop. The gods might try next. If I didn't know what the Earl is after, I'd say those *Draugar* were really after you. They were watching Jace's house after you visited him. You have to decide—"

"Hey!" Torin said firmly, his eyes locked on Andris. "Leave her alone. She'll decide when she's ready."

"We don't have the luxury of waiting for her while they screw with us. She needs to go before the gods and declare her position, Torin, before things get worse. You know it and I know it, and you,"—Andris raised his arms and turned around—"bitter hags know it too. There. I told her the truth. Send a bolt of lightning and finish me off." Then he lowered his arms and smirked defiantly at Torin, as though daring him to say something.

Torin shook his head. "You're an idiot."

Andris bowed. "I aim to please, and they," he pointed at the ceiling, "can kiss my perfect Roman ass. I'm heading back to StubHub. Oh, and you may want to tell her the truth about the Earl, or I will."

"You're begging for it, bro," Torin warned.

"Bring it." Then he glanced at me. "I don't baby you. He does." Then he opened a portal and disappeared.

Silence followed. I had no idea what had just happened. But I had questions. How did they know about all this? And what was the truth about the Earl?

Torin glanced at Blaine. "Sorry Andris pulled you from your work, but I want you with us later this evening. You think you can make it?"

Blaine grinned. "After last night? You don't need to ask." He engaged his runes and disappeared through an air portal. I only caught a glimpse of his destination before the portal closed. It looked like some biker bar.

"What happened last night?" Ingrid asked. "No one tells me anything. I'm part of this team until I leave for New York you know."

She'd gotten a position with a fashion editor, but had to put it on hold while she learned more runes. "You were gone when we came back last night, but I'll explain later this evening."

A rebellious light flashed in her light blue eyes. Then she nodded and left for the portal. Torin lifted me off his lap and sat me on the counter. He planted his hands on either side of me and asked, "What do you want to know?"

"Everything. When did you find out about everything Andris said? And do you really think the *Draugar* were after me?"

"We don't know that. As for the rest, we only found out last night from the Earl."

That self-serving bastard. "Why would you believe him?" I asked.

"Because he was showing off when he said it. He wanted to prove he could be useful. It backfired. Bottom line is I cannot influence your decision in any way, or there will be consequences. Even telling you has consequences. Even though the Norns tried and failed, chances are they will try again. The gods also."

"Could Onyx be spying for the goddess?" I whispered. I explained the tidbits the cat had shared with me. "She said she could find out what the goddesses wants, but I don't know if she's lying or not."

"I don't know. Time will tell. But she saved you last night when she took out the *Draugr* that was attacking you, and her presence stopped the others from coming near you."

I shook my head. "Really? When?"

"Do you remember a large black cat jumping from the bushes and dragging a *Draugr* away?"

The animal that had saved me. The sneaky little cat. "That was Onyx?"

Torin grinned. "She's a shape-shifter, just like her parents. That's how they pull Goddess Freya's carriage. Not as puny cats, but as large ones. She kept an eye on you throughout the battle."

That lying, beautiful cat. What had she said? That she'd been cleaning herself while watching us fight. I was going to give her everything she wanted from now on. "What about humans? Is helping them being on the Norns' side?"

"Nah, that's sticking it to them." He smirked, clearly loving the idea. It also explained why he hadn't tried to stop me when I'd helped Beau. "You're changing destinies they've already set. They won't be happy, but there's nothing they can do to you."

"What if they come after you to punish me?"

Torin grinned.

"It's not funny." His grin broadened and I knew he was keeping something from me. "What is it?"

"I got a promotion. That's why the Earl was here."

"What promotion?"

"You know how I became an Immortal?"

I nodded, getting impatient. "Lavania found you half dead during the crusade and runed you." He shot me an annoyed look and pushed away from the counter. "Is that not right?"

He turned and shot me a derisive smirk.

I hopped off the counter and approached him. "She watched you fight valiantly, and when you were fatally injured, she gave you the choice of death or Immortality."

He smiled with approval.

"And because you,"—I pushed his chest with my finger—"in all your glorious arrogance, wanted to follow King Richard all the way to the Holy Land, to defeat Saladin, and go back to England a hero, you chose Immortality, which you've regretted since."

"No, I regretted *until* I met you." A cocky grin curled his sculptured lips. "You gave me a new purpose."

I grinned. Loving me grounded him, he always said. Gave him a reason to live. The things he said could go to a girl's head.

"Although at times you try my patience with the crazy things you do."

He had just spoiled a perfect moment. I slapped his arm. "Just tell me about the promotion," I said.

"Your impatience is another trait I'd like us to work on. Okay, okay," he added, rising his hands in mock surrender. "Whenever those eyes change color, I know you're about to zap me. I'm now an Idun-valkyrie."

That was a new term. "What's that?"

"It's another name for Immortal Makers, chosen to pacify Goddess Idun."

Never heard of her either. "Who's she?"

"The Goddess of Spring."

I shook my head. "I don't see the connection. Why did they need to pacify her?"

"The gods made her angry. Do you know why Odin and the other gods and goddesses are old, yet they're also immortal?"

"They've been around since the beginning of time?"

He chuckled and pinched my nose. "Yes and no. Odin has been around since the beginning of time, not the others. A long time ago, all the gods were young and strong because they eat the golden apples from Goddess Idun's orchard. But one day, Loki helped the giants kidnap Idun and her apples left with her. The gods grew old and their powers weakened. But with their last strength, they forced Loki to bring her back. They went back to eating the apples and once again, stopped aging, but the process could not be reversed. Because of the incident, the gods decided not to share the apples with Mortals and Valkyries, angering Idun. Like Freya, she's a big supporter of Mortals. So Odin came up with the right bind runes for immortality, and to appease Idun, named Immortal Makers after her. Idun-valkyries."

Norse stories never failed to awe me, and from the grin on Torin's face, he liked the idea of being an Idun-valkyrie. "Like Lavania?"

He nodded, his sapphire blues sparkling. "Yep, like her. I not only get to decide who becomes Immortal, but also which Immortals become a Valkyrie."

It all made sense. "No wonder your Warlock father came back so fast."

Torin scowled.

"The Warlock," I corrected. "He's hoping you'd choose him. Do you think he created the situation with the other souls just so he could prove he's changed? Or is he working with Norns to lure me to their side?"

"Andris thinks he's working with them. Personally, I think he hopes I can promote him to a Valkyrie. He knows I already have a candidate in mind."

"Who?"

"Jace."

My jaw dropped. I laughed. Now everything made sense. "No wonder you've been pals with him."

"He's a bit young, but he's the perfect candidate. Despite being asthmatic, he's an amazing athlete. I need to be there when the accident happens so I can reach him before he dies. That's where you come in. You get the visions of when and how they'll die, and I'll make sure I'm there to offer them the choice of either immortality or a position at a table in Valhalla."

A table in Valhalla. Ha! Nice way of saying death. No wonder he hadn't minded my attempts to get a reading from Jace. What if I wanted to stop their deaths? We'd probably knock heads. "So we would work together."

"We *are* working together. Aren't you trying to figure out how and when Jace will be injured?"

And save the others. I nodded.

"Since my work will be here, I'll spend even more time here and not in Asgard. Maybe I'll get a place to train new Immortals. Andris will get a new partner."

I chuckled. "Immortals are trying to go to Asgard while you're thrilled to be here."

"That's because you are here." He cupped my face, until I focused on him. "So you see, the Earl was wrong. You and I are going to be together for a very long time. Nothing can come between us. Not the Norns or the gods, and definitely not my self-serving father." He pressed a kiss on my forehead. "Now, I have to go."

"Don't go after him. I think he's hoping you will."

"No one screws with you while I'm around, so yeah, he and I will have a talk. Just not tonight. He's expecting us and will be prepared."

"Us?" I asked.

"Yes, us. When I meet with him, I want you there. Not just because you can have Mother Earth immobilize him, but also because he's afraid of you."

I blinked. "Excuse me?"

"Love is a powerful force, and you have it in its pure, unadulterated form. When you do something, you do it from your heart and without an ulterior motive. You face your opponents with one truth, that what you're doing is the right thing to do. Not for you, but for those you love. It makes you a formidable foe. The Earl cannot fight that. He's an amazing strategist. He plans every move and calculates every outcome. He's methodical and relentless. He's fought in wars Mortals won't admit were ever fought. Wars against monsters like *Draugar* and other forms of dark souls used to torment the living. Fighting him on his own terms is useless. We would have lost last week if it weren't for you. Our united front, our love is the one thing he can't defeat, and that's why he came to see you today and tried to guilt you into letting me go. Thank you," he said.

He had a way with words that was so humbling. I wish I could explain our love the way he did. It was almost like he saw me in ways I didn't see myself.

I had to clear my throat before asking, "Why are you thanking me?"

"For believing in us." He stroked my cheek. "Because things are going to get a bit bumpy before they get better." He stepped back and stretched. The T-shirt hiked up and bared his ridged stomach. When I looked up, he was grinning. "Now I need to have a long chat with Andris. Are you coming to watch the boys practice?"

I shook my head. "Not today. I have a group lesson today. An hour and a half."

He frowned. "I still need you to try and get a reading on what's going to happen."

"I know. I will. I'll be there tomorrow. No, Friday."

Torin didn't look too happy, but he didn't push for an explanation. I'd promised Beau I'd work with him the next two days. Maybe I could change the times. He had a game on Friday, so no lessons, and I'd told him I could squeeze him in on Sunday. No promises. Saturday was out because of the soccer game.

I knew why I hadn't told Torin about Beau. It had nothing to do with Beau being the Kayville High bad boy. Torin knows I love only him and doesn't need to worry about Beau. Helping Beau was a choice. My choice, not one I was forced to make by the Norns or the gods, or even my feelings for Torin.

Maybe it all boiled down to choosing a side. It bugged me that I had to do that and if I didn't they—the Norns, gods, and whoever Hel's people might send—would keep making my life a living hell. What if I didn't want to live with the gods? What if I wanted to be on the side of humans and stay here? Torin was here. He might not want to influence me, but by being promoted to Idun-valkyrie and making earth his home, he just made it easy for me to choose earth. Or maybe their intention was to separate us.

As for the belief that Eirik had chosen his mother's side, it was another load of crap. Eirik was not evil. Had it occurred to them that he might be with his mother now because he cares about her? I wish I knew where he was.

9. Whose Side Are You on?

Cora and Ingrid were already waiting at the mansion when I arrived for lessons. They were seated on the floor by the low-lying tables. Each had a knife belt with all of their artavo neatly arranged. Some of the artavo were for etching runes on skin, others were for surfaces and air, and of course we each had a book for runic writings. Every rune we etched onto our skin also appeared in the book. It made it easy to keep tally of which runes we added and how often.

"You're late," Lavania said.

"Sorry. I'm tutoring a new student and had to make sure everyone understood they can't use portals while he's around. Won't happen again."

Actually, I'd been online researching Norse mythological creatures, monsters and insults, thanks to Onyx, and lost track of time. That shape-shifting ball of fur had called me everything from fat cow to a dung beetle.

"Why are you tutoring a student?" Lavania asked.

I hadn't told her about Beau's problem when we'd discussed my new ability to mimic. "He's struggling in English lit and might be kicked off the team."

Her expression said she didn't understand. "Do you think using your place is a wise idea? We have plenty of rooms here or at Torin's. I'm sure he won't mind."

"Yeah, uh, I haven't exactly told Torin about it yet. I meant to, but it slipped my mind." My eyes connected with Cora's. I could tell she was curious. Ingrid grinned. "What?"

"He's not going to like it," Cora murmured.

I knew that, but yeah, well, too bad.

"Okay, let's get started," Lavania said firmly.

We worked on creating air portals, and covered when and how often to add more runes onto our bodies. Lavania might be laidback in her flowy gowns, love herbal teas, and have weird habits like sitting on the floor while studying, but when it came to lessons, she was serious. I could easily see her as a teacher.

"Who is it?" Cora asked as soon as the lessons were over and Lavania had left.

"It's definitely a jock," Ingrid added.

I headed downstairs, but they fell in step right beside me. "I can't tell you guys. I promised."

Cora's jaw dropped, and I knew what she was thinking. We didn't keep secrets from each other. "When are the lessons?" she asked.

"I can't tell you that either, and no stopping by to see who it is, nosey. He's very sensitive about private tutoring. You know, he has an image to uphold and that includes acting like grades are not important."

Cora harrumphed. "You started this. Don't get mad when I keep secrets from you."

"Seriously?"

She nodded. "Uh-huh. Just because you're a Seeress doesn't mean you can see everything. Remember, no reading my future," she reminded me and exchanged a knowing look with Ingrid, who watched us from the doorway as we left the mansion.

Cora kept bitching about it all the way to her car. I wondered if she'd understand if I explained. Helping Beau made me stay in touch with my humanity, the positive side. The inner drive or ambition that made a Mortal want something and go after it, instead of relying on a path someone had mapped out for him. Just like watching Dad battle cancer, in a way, affirmed his mortality.

As soon as Cora drove out of the compound, I went back inside the mansion. Ingrid was waiting. "Don't start on me too," I warned.

"If you want to have a fling behind Torin's back, who am I to tell you no?"

My cheeks warmed. "There's no fling."

"A boy around your age. Mortal. Needs your help. Bet he's gorgeous too."

Beau was, but he had nothing on Torin. "Torin needs me too."

"Oh, sweetie. He's invincible. But as his woman, I'm sure he does." She gave a look that implied all sorts of intimate things. My face flamed. "But that blush says this boy you're tutoring means something to you."

Beau did, but I had no intention of explaining anything to her. Time to change the subject. "Found any wrinkles lately?" I shot back.

She blinked and for a few seconds, I thought she was insulted. She and I were barely getting to know each other. A grin curled her lips. She pointed to the corner of her eye. "One, but I'm working on it."

"You know there's nothing there, right?"

"I know, but this way, I won't be too devastated when I finally get them. Tell me about last night. What happened?"

"*Draugar* happened. Ever met one?"

"Oh yes, but Andris, Torin, and Maliina took care of them."

I heard the annoyance in her voice. "Would you have liked to hunt with them?"

"Yes." She shuddered. "No. I'm much better with people than monsters. It happened in a village not far from my hometown and I kept the people calm. I just wish people wouldn't assume things about me."

"Maybe they will stop if you stopped looking like a model."

She laughed, then sobered up. "You think I look like a model?"

I grabbed her arm and pulled her in front of the hallway mirror. Her pageboy hair cut suited her delicate face, the combination of pale blonde hair and light blue eyes striking. "What do you see when you look in the mirror? A troll?"

She shuddered again. "Don't joke about trolls."

"Have you met any?"

"Oh yes," she said. "They're fast and mean."

"Okay, it's official. Next time we're going to face *Draugar* or some monster, you're coming with us."

She grimaced then shook her head, her pale blonde hair brushing her cheeks. "No."

"Yes." I engaged my runes and the ones on the mirror frame responded. "I was scared but I made it. We can keep each other company. Besides, it's nice to watch the guys kick ass."

She laughed. Then her expression grew serious. "Andris has been acting weird."

I had a theory about that and it might be the perfect topic to cement our newfound camaraderie. "That's because of Torin. Have you heard his latest news?"

Ingrid shook her head. "No."

"Do you want to hang out at my place for a few minutes? We could brainstorm about ways to help them. Unless you have a date."

"With who? Guys around here are so young and boring. I need someone my age. Just a minute while I tell Lavania where I'm going." She engaged her runes and took off upstairs.

My eyes swept the foyer while I waited for her to return. Despite having fought Maliina and Grimnirs twice in this room, the foyer remained my favorite place in the mansion. The marble floor, the winding iron and wood staircase with a dark carpet runner, the soaring two-story ceiling, and the enormous crystal chandelier. Looking at the walls, you couldn't tell they'd come tumbling down. Not even a ding was visible now. Mrs. Willow, the housekeeper Torin had hired, did an amazing job of keeping the place clean though. The floor was spotless, every surface polished.

I opened a portal and could see inside my room. When Ingrid returned, I led the way. Onyx was still sleeping when I entered my room, but as soon as Ingrid appeared, she opened her eyes and watched her, then got up and stretched.

"Ooh, what a beautiful cat," Ingrid said, walking to the window. She stroked her fur. "What's her name?"

"Onyx."

Stupid name, Onyx said.

"But she thinks it's stupid. Can I get you a drink? Something to eat?"

"Oh, I'll come downstairs with you. I want to say hi to Femi." Then she picked up Onyx and lifted her until they were face to face. "I've heard about you, but no one told me what gorgeous eyes you have. I would have named you Emerald because of your eyes."

I like Emerald, Onyx said.

I suggested it and you hated it.

No, you didn't.

Yes, I did, but you were being a real PITA at the time.

"Raine?"

I glanced at Ingrid. "What?"

"I said I think Onyx is actually perfect for her. I bet she looks amazing with glowing runes, like a real black onyx."

I like her and she's gorgeous.

The green monster reared its ugly head. Onyx and I had started off on the wrong foot. Literally. I'd Googled all the insults she kept hurling at me and most had something to do with a foot. Clumsy foot. Cow foot. A few bugs and rodents, things she could squash. I couldn't help but feel jealous. It was petty and childish, but damn it, she was *my* familiar. We were supposed to be pals, not knocking heads at every turn. I had yet to thank her for saving me from that overzealous *Draugr.* Maybe that would change things between us.

"Yeah, she's amazing," I said, then led the way downstairs. Femi had already started dinner. Sometimes I wondered how long she planned to stay with us. Until Dad died? Even though she lived with us and helped take care of him, I doubted she got paid for it. Like Hawk, she was probably loaded and this was just a dot in her vast experience.

"How come you didn't tell me about battling mummies?" Femi asked.

I grinned. I guess it didn't matter what culture the Immortals were from, they'd all met the same monster and given it a name. Femi and Ingrid had more stories to add when I finished telling them what had happened.

"I was teaching her how to get visions, and now she's using her elemental magic to destroy monsters. How fast she's grown."

"Better watch it," Ingrid warned. "She hates being treated like a child."

"Or being discussed like she's not here," I added.

"But you are a child, doll," Femi said. "In Immortal years. I will remind you of this conversation five hundred years from now. When you've saved the world a few times and had torrid affairs with some infamous men and... Oh, never mind. You're taken. But you'll know what I mean some day. I remember meeting this young Romani when I was working as a..."

Femi and Ingrid traded stories about their past jobs. With her pale blue eyes and blonde hair, Ingrid could easily be a model, yet she'd been everything but. Most of her jobs centered around people—a teacher, nurse, social worker, marketing, lawyer, and a therapist. Femi was also great with people, but she hated institutions, which explained why she was taking care of Dad instead of working at a hospital. She had an unusual beauty that most men found intriguing: blue eyes, golden-brown complexion, black pixie hair, and a petite figure with a larger than life personality. I could see her wrapping some poor guy around her fingers.

"Every fifty years or so, I open a shop and sell magical trinkets," Femi said. "It doesn't matter where I live. And I've also worked with entertainers who need spiritual guidance before and after performing. Married a few too."

Finally, we left Onyx downstairs with Femi and disappeared upstairs. Ingrid pushed her fur-covered blanket aside and took the window seat while I plopped on the chair. Beau wouldn't be stopping by until seven.

"You've led a colorful life," I said.

She smiled. "So will you. You're just starting out." She waited patiently for me to begin talking. That was something I liked about her. She wasn't pushy. As I talked about Torin's new assignment, she went pale. When I finished, she was pacing.

"This explains Andris' weird mood since we came back from Florida. I thought it was because..."

"What?"

"I met this nice guy in Florida, but Andris thought he was a creep and made a big scene." She shook her head, her bob cut brushing her cheeks. "He's so overprotective it drives me crazy."

"Do you think anything could ever happen between the two of you?"

She chuckled. "You've asked me that question before."

"Maybe. I guess I'm hoping you two would one day wake up and realize you are meant for each other."

"I don't think so. Once, a long time ago, maybe, but I stopped hoping when I realized he'd never settle down. That's why I wanted to go to New York." She went back to the window, stared at Torin's place, which was still in darkness, then turned and faced me. "Can you find out if Torin plans to get Andris another partner?"

"He mentioned it. Do you have someone in mind?" She raised a perfectly shaped eyebrow. "Like you. I mean, have you ever thought of being a Valkyrie?"

She made a face. "Not really. I don't like souls. But I wouldn't mind helping Torin train new Immortals. I like to teach."

And that could keep her in Andris' circle. I didn't care what she said about Andris. She liked him. He was the one hopping from woman to man to woman.

By the time Ingrid left, I was sure of one thing—our little group was slowly disintegrating. I finished my homework then went downstairs for dinner. Onyx sat on the counter and watched us. I fed her a few pieces of my steak.

Mom arrived while we were eating.

"Get off the counter, Onyx," she said and shooed the cat down. Onyx wasn't too happy. She disappeared upstairs. Mom went to eat with Dad, but left the den when I was taking care of the dishes. It was ten to seven.

"So who is this boy you're tutoring?"

"A Mortal that needs help." I was aware of Femi seated a few feet away.

"Why? Don't you have enough on your plate?"

"He needs help, Mom. I don't want him to fail."

She studied my face and sighed. "How many times a week?"

"Today and tomorrow. Sunday. Next week too. If he passes on Friday, that's it. If he needs my help until the end of the semester, that's fine too."

She sighed again. "Okay. Fine. Help him, but talk to Torin about it so you can use his place. We have too many things going on here without worrying about Mortals underfoot."

I went upstairs to get my copy of *The Scarlet Letter*. Torin's place was in darkness, but I wasn't worried. Now that I knew the Earl was out of the picture, I could breathe easier. I'd bet he'd already been imagining Torin turning him into a Valkyrie or helping him form an army of Immortals. He looked like the type that would have delusions of grandeur and plot to take over the world.

Then there was Andris. I felt bad for him. I bet there was something Torin could do to keep him here. We'd gone through so much together and he was part of our group. A group I might no longer be a part of if the Norns or the gods had their way.

Seven o'clock came and passed, and no truck pulled up outside our house. I alternated between checking my watch and outside.

Seven-ten. I started getting pissed. I had cleared my schedule for him. Blew off my boyfriend.

Seven-fifteen. Onyx hopped onto the window seat and sat on her hind legs. After a few minutes of feeling her eyes on me, I glanced down. "What?"

What's wrong?

I really didn't want to deal with her right now. "Thanks for saving me from that *Draugr*," I said.

Your boyfriend told you?

"His name is Torin. Just like mine is Raine. Not cow foot. Or fish belly. Or mouse." Hel's Mist, I was taking out my frustration on a cat. "Sorry. I'm disappointed by someone and I'm taking it out on you." I sat next to Onyx. "Yes, Torin told me. He said you shifted into a larger cat."

Onyx nodded. *I have to when I deal with larger prey.*

"Can you show me sometime?"

If you promise to practice with me. You haven't mimicked since the night the goddess left me here.

"Actually I have. I practice in the shower or bathroom, but it's a deal." I extended my hand, palm up and she placed her paw on it. How human-like she was. She curled up next to me. It wasn't my lap, but we'd made progress. I glanced outside again.

Nothing.

I couldn't believe Beau had blown me off. I'd even given him my cell phone number.

I can hear your teeth grinding. What's wrong?

"I was supposed to tutor some guy from school, and he stood me up. I hate flaky guys. And then there's the problem with Andris."

Pretty boy?

"Andris," I corrected.

What's wrong with Andris?

Should I trust her? What had she told me before? The gods didn't do anything without a reason. She'd been honest with me from the beginning. Even hinted that Goddess Freya and Odin's wife might be plotting something. "Yes. He might be in trouble."

She lifted her head, ears alert. *What kind of trouble?*

"He said something he shouldn't have and everything is changing too fast for him to catch up."

Are you going to help him?

"Yes." Andris would do the same for me.

Can I help?

Only if she could convince Goddess Freya to make Andris an Idun-valkyrie too. "Do you know who promotes Valkyries to Idun-valkyries?"

The Council. It has Odin and Freya, and other gods. Why? What are you planning? She sat up.

I stroked her head. "I'll let you know when I have a plan, Fur-ball."

She didn't push me away, and her voice wasn't scathing when she said, *you do know I hate that name as much as I hate Onyx.*

"Would you prefer Emerald?"

No. I only know one Emerald and she's a boyfriend-stealing, attention-hogging meinfretr!

I laughed. "Do tell. I thought you only reserved insults for me. When and where did she steal your boyfriend? And where is she so I can pull her tail?"

Your boyfriend is here.

The words barely registered when the portal opened and a barefoot Torin entered. His hair was wet and his sweatpants rode so low on his hips I could see the skin between his waistband and the white T-shirt.

"Where did you shower?"

He grinned. "I went for a swim at the mansion. Why? Did you want to join me?"

"I didn't even know you were back. Onyx knew you were coming before the portal opened. How smart is that?" I stood and realized I was still holding *The Scarlet Letter*. I put it on the headboard bookshelf, careful not to knock over the blown glass gifts he'd bought me then walked into his arms.

He leaned back and studied my face. "What's wrong?"

"Nothing."

"Definitely something." He scooped me up, and we settled on the bed. He wrapped his arms around my mid-section and rested his head on my chest. "Hmm, you smell nice. I'm here when you're ready to talk. And FYI, there's no way Onyx can feel me coming. She's linked to your energy, not mine."

I tried to remember something the cat had told me about Torin's energy. "Onyx, what was that you said about our energies?"

Don't remember. I say a lot of things. Now can you zip it? I'm trying to sleep here.

"She's in one of her moods." Torin's eyes were closed, his ridiculous lashes forming canopies over his cheeks. I stroked his hair away from his face. His birthday was next week on Friday. On prom night. "We forgot to talk about your birthday."

"Not important. Can you turn off the lights? I'm exhausted."

I ignored his request. "It's only seven…" I looked at the clock. "Seven-thirty." I glanced outside. "How old are you going to be?"

"Eight hundred and something," he mumbled. "I stopped counting after five centuries."

I lifted his head, but his eyes stayed closed. "I'm not going to let you go to sleep until we talk. We need to do something fun, and I want to know what you plan to do about Andris. He's one of us."

Torin opened one eye, then another. "I just spent the past several hours trying to talk to him. Several times. Each time, one of us ended with a broken neck. I'm exhausted. He's impossible. Can you let go of my head now?"

I did. "What did you two fight about?"

"No idea. I tried to find out what's wrong with him, and he kept acting like a douche."

Men! "Do you know why?"

"Nope." He was getting pissed. "I can't read his mind."

I sighed. "You two have been together for... what?"

"Almost seven centuries."

"And you're about to leave. Since he reaps for Goddess Freya's Hall, they'll have to find your replacement to reap for Valhalla. He's having a hard time with that. Your relationship is going to change and he's dealing with it."

"By being a jackass?"

"No, by putting some distance between you. This way it won't hurt so much when you finally go your separate ways."

Torin sat up. "The idiot. Why didn't he just say so?"

"Didn't you realize your promotion would change things between you two?"

"Not really. I mean we'd still stay together and... Oh." He cursed. "Okay. I'll take care of it."

"How?"

"I don't know." He planted a quick one on my lips and scooted off the bed. "Thanks, luv. I'm going to talk to him now. Idiot," he murmured again before the door closed.

Shaking my head, I changed into my pajamas and went to brush my teeth. As I stared at my reflection, it finally hit me. I was the idiot. Beau might have blown me off. Or maybe he couldn't come. Or maybe his car broke down or...

Crap! What if his stepfather had decided to forget about me and what I'd threatened to do three nights ago?

"Onyx." I walked to where the cat slept and yelled, "Onyx!"

She jumped, hair sticking out, eyes wide. *What? What's going on?*

"You're coming with me. We're going to check on our first case."

Jace?

"No. Beau. Engage your runes, so he can't see us." I let Beau's bedroom fill my head, then engaged my runes. In seconds, I was staring at his empty bedroom.

Sounds were coming from upstairs. Muffled voices. An awful sputtering sound and thuds.

10. First Session

If his stepfather was hurting them again...

Using Beau as my focal point, I created a portal. It led to their driveway. A one-eared dog rested on the steps, and several people sat on their porch. His mother stood to my right. She had a cast on her arm and was wearing a sling. His stepfather chugged beer with some guy a few feet away and sat on a rocking chair.

I was so relieved there was no fighting, I laughed. I looked around for Beau. His truck was in the driveway, and a man had his head in the hood. He must have been the one making all the ruckus. Despite the darkness, I recognized Beau behind the wheel of his Chevrolet.

The mechanic straightened and yelled, "Try it now!"

Beau cranked up the engine and it sputtered and coughed to life. It sounded like it was on its last breath. The mechanic laughed and slammed the hood shut, then walked to the window and bumped fists with Beau.

"Thanks, Uncle Heaney," Beau said, then looked over his shoulder straight at me. The instinct to step back was natural. I always forgot Mortals couldn't see portals. When he said, "Ma, my phone," I realized he was looking at his mother, not me.

"I'll try and find it. I hope you make it to your class."

His uncle stepped from the truck and opened the door, and said, "In, boy."

The dog trotted off the porch and hopped in the passenger seat. Beau took off with squealing wheels.

His mother entered the house. Before the door closed, the stepfather yelled after her, "Bring us more beer, Janice!" Then he reached into the pocket of his plaid shirt and removed something. I recognized the skull and crossbones on the cell cover. That was Beau's phone. "That boy thinks he can lie and get away with it? Study group. At night? He's probably late for a humping date with one of his girlfriends."

The mother, who was still in the doorway and overhead him, went back and tried to snatch the phone from his hand. "How could you do that, Joe? Beau is not lying. He cares about school."

"He cares about baseball and how many girls he can screw. But he'll end up like all of us here. Yep, breaking his back at Chandler for a woman who doesn't know how to listen. Where's my beer?"

"Give me the phone first," she said and reached for it.

He pushed her arm away, then for whatever reason changed his mind and shoved the phone into her hand. She left the porch and headed toward the kitchen, which still had dirty dinner plates on the counter. How the hell was she going to clean those with one arm? I checked my watch. It was going to take Beau ten minutes to get to my house, which was enough time to teach step-daddy a lesson.

I turned and almost stepped on Onyx. She'd been quiet since we arrived. I reached down and picked her up. *You okay?*

She glared. *No. I'm assuming the one who left with squealing wheels and a dog is coming to our house.* She shuddered. *I hate dogs.*

Really? You can shift into something bigger than a dog and you have claws.

Her eyes narrowed. *And your point is?*

His stepfather is a bully who likes to beat his mother or Beau, if he gets in the way of his punches. He and I had a brief chat and I thought that he learned his lesson. It's time for lesson number two. Go home and keep an eye out for Beau. If his truck makes it to my place, come get me.

As long as he's not bringing that mangy canine inside our house.

I didn't respond, just put her down and followed Mrs. Hardshaw to the kitchen. She had already removed one can of beer and was pressing it against her chest with her injured hand as she reached for a second one. The first one slipped and fell. I almost stretched out my hand to catch it, but stopped myself. For seconds, she stared at it, fighting tears, shoulders drooping with fatigue.

You're tired and sleepy. So sleepy you cannot keep your eyes open. Go to the bedroom and lie down. If you hear noises, ignore them.

She put the can of beer back on the counter, ignored the one she'd dropped and staggered out of the kitchen. I followed her, stopped in the doorway and watched her go down the hallway to their bedroom. When the door closed behind her, I checked my watch. I had time.

Grinning, I pointed at the front door and opened it. Slammed it shut. Opened. Shut. Opened again. Slammed.

"Damn it, woman!" Hardshaw senior bellowed and got his fat ass off the rocking chair. "Where's my beer? And why is the door..." He realized his wife was not in the kitchen. He gripped the door and looked behind it. "Huh?"

I grinned. I had so many ways I could screw with his head. I dragged him inside the room and then slammed the door shut, forcing him to jump out of the way. His friend was still outside. I got rid of my invisibility runes and his eyes widened.

"You," he said in a strangled voice.

"Mr. Hardshaw, I told you I'd be back." I crossed my arms. "Taking Beau's phone? That was just mean. Did you mess with his engine too?"

He looked at the door as though deciding whether to bolt or not, and shook his head. I walked toward him and he inched away from the door. "What do you want?"

"Checking on how things are going. He wasn't lying about studying. You should have given him your truck."

"He's lied before."

"He didn't this time." I locked the door and turned. He was already halfway to the kitchen. "You should have a little faith, Mr. Hardshaw. One day he'll thank you for taking care of him and his mother, but only if you do the right thing. I don't understand why you are so mean to him and his mother. She has a broken arm and can barely lift a thing and you have her running up and down, fetching drinks for you. Why are you so determined to be a terrible father and husband?"

"You don't know anything about me," he said.

"Actually I do." I engaged my speed runes and appeared beside him. Before he could react, I grabbed his arm and prayed I got a vision. At first, I got nothing and he tried to break free from my hold. "Stand still."

His life flashed by. I checked my watch and was surprised to see that only a minute had passed. I let him go and he staggered backwards and grabbed a phone.

"Who are you trying to call now?"

"The police," he said.

"And tell them what? That someone they can't see is harassing you?" I engaged my invisibility runes for a few seconds and watched him look around frantically. I got rid of them and reappeared. The look on his face was hilarious. "Put the phone down and listen to me, because if I have to come back here again, I'm coming back with soul reapers."

That got his attention. He put the phone down and swallowed.

"You were a star athlete too. Kayville High's finest until you were injured." He blinked. "I told you I knew about you. With your knee shot, you lost your chance of making it to college on a scholarship. The woman you loved, Lucy Carmichael, left you. You lost everything, and all because of a stupid prank. Without the scholarship, you followed in your father's footsteps and started working at Chandler Factory. You don't like it, but you do it anyway. Why? For your family, because you are that kind of man. The one who gets up every morning and goes to do a job he hates, because he wants to put food on the table and a roof over the head of his family."

He was finally listening to me. But I didn't have much time to continue stroking his ego without throwing in how he could help Beau. Any second, I expected a portal to open and Onyx to appear.

"You make sacrifices every day for your family, Mr. Hardshaw. You take more night shifts to make more money. You stopped driving the trucks because you were spending too much time away from home. You almost drove off the road the other night because you were so tired." I'd seen that in my vision and had no idea when it happened, but he nodded. "You could have been killed." He nodded again. "And that back ache problem you complain about will only get worse."

"You know about my back?"

"Of course." I leaned against the counter and crossed my arms. I was beginning to get cold. The pajama bottoms didn't cover much and the robe was flimsy. "But a time will arrive when you can't provide for your family, and guess who will help you?"

A sheepish expression crossed his face.

"Yes, your wife and your son. You might have been in love with Lucy in high school, but Janice, the girl you didn't notice when you were a star football player, was the one who came to see you at the hospital. You weren't nice to her, but she came anyway. And years later when you met her again, you saw the goodness in her and fell in love with her. You didn't care that she had a son with another guy. You raised him as your own. Beau is smart, and he works hard at school. Encourage him and he will be there for you when you need him. All the sacrifices you're making now will be worth it."

He was frowning now. I had him. His friend was knocking at the door, but he ignored him.

"Your wife and your son need you, Mr. Hardshaw. Stop pushing them away. She's sleeping now because she's exhausted and her arm hurts. I told her to go rest, please don't take it out on her. Show her you are the man she fell in love with. Help around the house a bit. Give Beau some attention. Go watch him play. Ask him about school."

A small portal opened and Onyx stared at me.

"I don't want to come back here, Mr. Hardshaw. I have other people who need my help. You don't. You can change whenever you want to. You can stop drinking and be a loving father and husband, or you can choose not to stop. The choice is yours."

He didn't nod this time. He was lost in thought.

"I have to go now. See you around." I engaged my runes and cloaked. He didn't even look around. I opened a portal. The last image I had of him was reaching down to pick up the can of beer his wife had dropped.

~*~

Voices reached me as soon as I entered my room. I pulled on sweatpants and a sweatshirt, and then headed downstairs. Mom had opened the door for Beau and was laughing at something he'd said. He stood on the step, one hand in his pocket and the other on his dog's neck.

"I'm here," I said and started down the stairs.

"Were you...?" Mom caught herself before she finished the sentence, but I knew what she was going to ask: was I out of the house?

"Yes. Thanks, Mom." I waited until she left before inching closer. Any second, I expected Beau's dog to start growling. "Hey." I glanced at my watch. "Seven-forty-five."

He shot me a lop-sided grin. "Sorry about that. You won't believe this, but my engine conked out and, uh, this might sound even lamer. I lost my phone, so I couldn't call you to cancel. So here I am, apologizing in person."

He got kudos for that. "Does that mean I rearranged my schedule for nothing?"

"It depends. How much can you show me in fifteen minutes?"

That was a cheap come on. I shook my head. "You didn't bring your books and you have a dog."

"Bono. Sit." The dog sat.

This was the first time a dog wasn't growling at me. "What breed is he?"

"A mongrel."

"It has only one ear."

Beau shrugged. "Made him stand out from all the ugly ones at the pound."

So he deliberately chose a deformed dog. I knew there was more to him. "Right. Do you have a copy of *The Scarlet Letter*?"

He pulled it from behind him along with the packet Mr. Gentry had given him. "I always come prepared."

He and I needed to discuss his flirtatious behavior. I nodded at the dog. "Will he be okay out there? I mean he could come inside, but I have a cat and she doesn't like dogs."

"He'll be fine. Bono. Stay."

Onyx was on the stairs and watched the dog until Beau closed the door. She followed us to the kitchen. Mom and Femi were having tea and catching up on the news on the kitchen TV.

"Femi, this is Beau. Beau, Femi, a family friend. You've already met my mom. Could we use the kitchen?" I asked, my eyes volleying between Mom and Femi.

Mom patted the table where they were seated. "Sure, hun. Don't mind us."

Was she serious? "Mom," I said. More like whined. "We talked about this and you promised you guys wouldn't be here."

"I'm just kidding." She stood, planted a kiss on my temple, and patted my cheek. "Come on, Femi. Nice to meet you Beau."

"The pleasure is all mine, Mrs. Cooper." Then he had the nerve to turn and watch them walk away. He even turned his head sideways.

"Hey!"

He gave me an innocent look. "What?"

"That's my mother you are ogling, you perv," I whispered.

He shrugged. "She's hot." He glanced toward the living room. "And so is her friend."

This time, I grabbed his head and forced him to face the window. Mom and Femi disappeared toward the wet bar in the living room.

"Sit." I waited until he sat and placed his book on the table. "Okay, before we start. Some ground rules. No flirting. No winking at me in school and come up with a better reason for this." I pointed at the book. "You can't tell lies to your friends about us or no more tutoring."

"Damn, you're tough."

"No, I have a boyfriend who will make you wish you were never born if you mess with me. Now, how far have you read?"

"Halfway, and it's the hardest book I've ever read. His writing is so weird."

"Mr. Gentry didn't ask you guys to read other books by Hawthorne to understand his style?"

"Nope."

I sighed. "Okay. I'll explain as we read the chapter you were supposed to cover."

Fifteen minutes became thirty. Then forty-five. He was sharp, but not afraid to say he was lost when he didn't understand something. When we finally stopped, an hour had passed. He tried to apologize, but I brushed it off.

"As long as I didn't confuse you," I said, getting up.

"No, you were perfect." He took my hand and covered it with his, then studied me with half-lidded eyes. "I hope you don't mind if I borrow your copy of Hawthorne's Short Stories. I promise to take good care of it."

I could see why he had so many girls chasing him. Those long lashes shading moss-green eyes, the lop-sided grin, and his tendency to be touchy-feely could make any girl think she was the center of his universe. Too bad all his moves were wasted on me.

I eased my hand from his. "Sure. I'll get it." I headed upstairs. When I came back he was talking to Femi and Mom by the bar. I walked him to his truck, his dog trotting quietly beside him. Once again, I was surprised by how friendly the dog was towards me.

I waited until he was inside the truck before repeating what I'd said at the beginning of our session. "Explain to your friends what's going on without making our tutoring session into something it's not. And quit flirting with me."

"What did I do?" he protested, then spoiled it by smirking. "I can't help it. There's something about you. I just can't put my finger on it."

As long as his memories weren't coming back, I was fine. And if they did, I hoped he assumed it had all been a dream. Mom and Femi gave me strange looks when I came back inside.

"Watch out for that one," Femi said. "He'll break your heart."

"Not mine." I kissed Mom's cheek. "Goodnight, Mom. Night, Femi."

"I hope you know what you're doing," Mom said.

"Tutoring," I said.

"Why didn't you tell Torin?" Mom asked.

I turned and faced them. How did she know that? "I will. Right now he's busy with other things."

"Whatever this is, I hope you get it out of your system fast," Mom added.

"Sheesh. I'm tutoring someone who might fail a class. Nothing more." I turned to go upstairs and almost stepped on my cat. "Onyx! Quit lurking around."

She hissed as I headed upstairs. I knew she was behind me, but I just ignored her. I changed into my pajamas and headed to the bathroom.

As I brushed my teeth I tried mimicking different people, experimenting with changing facial features and hair color and length when Onyx hopped onto the counter and perched herself near the sink. She watched me with those annoyingly intelligent eyes. I could feel wheels turning in her head. When she didn't make snarky remarks at the people I mimicked, I knew she wanted to talk.

"Out with it," I said.

He's a handsome young man.

"Don't start."

He flirts too much.

I ignored her.

I know why you're doing it.

I couldn't ignore her anymore. "No, you don't."

The pretty, uh, Andris one said you have to choose a side.

"You weren't at Torin's. How do you know that?"

I heard your thoughts. Sometimes I hear you even when you're not talking to me.

My jaw dropped. "You eavesdropped on my thoughts? That's invasion of privacy."

We're linked, Raine. Deal with it.

I flicked my toothbrush and splashed her. She just shook herself.

You shouldn't worry about choosing sides. I've watched you and Torin deal with worse situations and win. You'll make the right choice. She hopped off the counter and went back to the bedroom. *Splash me again, little girl, and I'll scratch your eyes out.*

I grinned. She was right. I was stressing over nothing. Torin and I would fix this. The lights were still off at his place. I hoped his talk with Andris was going okay. We had enough to deal with without them being pissed at each other. I went back to my bedroom, turned off my lights, and crawled into bed.

Sometime later, he entered my room and Onyx growled. Silly cat. I shushed her again and went back to sleep. I heard her growl again, then a man's voice. He didn't sound like Torin.

~*~

When I woke up in the morning, Onyx was a dead weight on my chest. Torin's side of the bed didn't look like he'd slept in it, yet I was sure he'd come into my room the night before. There was something about last night I tried to remember, but it eluded me.

"No sleeping on me, Onyx." I lifted her off my chest. "Or on my bed."

Not even if it's for your own protection?

"From what?" I looked out the window. Torin wasn't in the kitchen. Weird. "No one can walk in here without runes lighting up like a Christmas tree and warning Torin."

You're so naïve. One day you'll kiss my paws and thank me. For now, I forgive your arrogance because look what Torin gave me. She angled her head, so I could see the collar and the tag. *I'll be the envy of all the cats in Asgard.*

The collar was bedazzled and the platinum star had what looked like real diamonds. I turned it and read the inscription, Onyx and my phone number. "Your name is officially Onyx."

Depends on whether I respond.

I grinned and rubbed her head. "It'll grow on you."

You may want to check on Torin. He looked bad when he stopped by this morning.

My stomach dropped. "Bad how?"

Like he'd been up all night.

Had he spent the night fighting *Draugar* again? My eyes went to his bed when I entered his bedroom. He was asleep on his stomach, a pillow covering his head as though he was trying to block out the light. He was shirtless as usual, but there were no marks on him or weird smells. Still, he never slept late.

"Torin." The mattress dipped when I knelt on it. I lifted the pillow, but he mumbled something and turned his head the other way. "What happened?"

"Go away, Freckles."

"You're going to be late for school."

"Don't care."

Not the response I was expecting. I went and yanked open the curtains. Morning rays streamed into the room. He groaned and muttered, "Close it."

"What about California and teaching? What happened last night?" I grabbed the pillow covering his head, but he caught my wrist before I could fling it aside. A slight tug and I landed on top of him. I sniffed. He smelled different.

I lifted the pillow and frowned. Was that lipstick on his cheek? The corner of his lips had more color. He'd been kissing some girl. Change that to girls because his other cheek had a darker shade.

Anger slammed into me. He was so dead.

He opened an eye and squinted at me. "What time is it, luv?"

I pushed him. "Where were you last night?"

He smirked. "Andris and I went to some of our old haunts. Good memories."

I marched to the bathroom. I didn't think I was the jealous kind, but enough was enough. I was ready to take our relationship to the next level and he'd said no. No to me, and obviously yes to some other women. Jerk.

Hoping my voice didn't betray my soaring rage, I called out, "Really? Like what?"

"There's this club in Paris we used to hang out at a few years ago. Nothing's changed. Do you like your leather jacket? I bought it in Milan before we hit a string of clubs."

I dumped the contents from the small garbage can on his bathroom floor, put it in the tub, and turned on cold water. "What leather jacket?"

Silence.

I walked back to the door and peered at him. He'd dragged a pillow over to cover his face again. Let's see if he sleeps through this.

I marched back to the bathroom and got the water. Without stopping to weigh the consequences, I closed the gap between the bathroom and the bed, lifted the bucket, and dumped the water on him.

Onyx screeched and jumped off his bed. In my rage, I hadn't seen the cat. Torin came up swearing, arms and legs flailing.

"Hel's Mist, Raine! What was that for?"

I threw the bucket at his head, but he deflected it and sent it flying across the room. "I hope that cooled your raging libido, you jerk. Next time you feel an urge to sleep with someone, jump off a cliff because I will kill you in so many ways you'll wish you'd never met me."

I started for the mirror portal.

"Sleep with another woman? What are you talking about?"

I turned and pointed at him. "You do not want to go there with me, Torin. You do not want to act innocent and outraged." I shook my head when he opened his mouth. "One more word from you and I swear, I will snap your neck."

He raised his hands. "I don't want to fight with you, Freckles. You know how I feel about—"

Too late. I raced toward him, engaging my other runes seconds before I flew at him. I landed on the bed and heard the frame crack. The drenched bedding soaked my pajama top and bottoms. I whipped around to see him at the end of the room by the bike posters. How the heck did he move that fast?

He smirked and a fresh dose of anger flooded me.

"Some girls kissed me at the club. Not exactly my fault."

I got off the bed, pissed and humiliated that I'd lost it. "Stay away from me."

"Freckles…"

I lifted my hand toward him and curved my fingers, focusing on his neck. "I don't have to touch you to break your neck, jerk face. All I have to do is twist it from here."

Blue flames leapt in his eyes. He was getting pissed. Good. "Do it."

He was pushing his luck. Even his arrogant stance, arms crossed and legs apart challenged me to do my worst.

"I will not sink to your level, Torin."

"And what level is that? You drenched me already. And last night, you were so busy flirting with that shits-for-brains Beau you didn't even see me come into your house."

For one second, I was too shocked to react and just stared at him. "Oh. Do not make this about me. I was helping him study, while you... You allowed some girl to place her lips all over you and worse, you didn't even have the decency to wipe away the evidence. I had to see it on your stupid face." I whipped my hand toward him, but he disappeared, leaving behind an air portal.

His laughter reached me from downstairs. "Crazy witch," he called from downstairs. "You'll have to catch me first."

I created an air portal and he turned and cocked an eyebrow at me. That arrogant gesture made my blood boil. He was removing eggs and bacon from the fridge. I closed my eyes and projected images and thoughts into his head.

"Explain to me what's going on with Beau while I make us break..."

His body relaxed and his eyes rolled into the back of his head as he fell into a deep slumber. He landed on the kitchen floor. I barely stopped the eggs from falling on him. I should have let them.

Grinning and feeling a little better, I placed the eggs on the table and bent down to check on him. He was out cold. "You don't mess with a witch, Valkyrie."

11. Oh My, Didn't Expect That

Andris was waiting for me when I pulled up at school. "You're the last person I want to talk to," I said, walking right past him.

"Then you shouldn't have texted me and asked me to wake him up," he said, following me. "He's pretty pissed with you right now."

My stomach hollowed out, but I ignored it. "Well, tough."

"I'd be worried if I were you."

"Then it's a good thing I'm not you." I stopped suddenly. He almost bumped into me. When I faced him, he took a step back.

"No, Raine. Do not use your crazy witch powers on me," he warned.

"He deserved it, you don't. You were being your usual man-whore self. However…" My eyes locked on the girl walking toward us. With the baseball cap low over her forehead, it was hard to see her face, but I recognized her outfit and backpack. Amber. Did my mojo work on her hair? Because if I wasn't mistaken, she was wearing a wig under that hat. I lifted my chin and the hat lifted from her head. She grabbed it and hurried past us. Okay, so I can throw down with bad Witches.

"What are you plotting?" Andris pulled my attention back to him.

I glanced at Andris. "What?"

"Amber. You got a gleam in your eyes when she walked past us. Just because you're pissed at Torin doesn't mean you can take it out on everyone."

"Amber already got what she deserved. The curse will lift when she learns her lesson."

"Raine, you're headed down a dark—"

"Where was I?" I asked, cutting him off. "If you ever take Torin to one of your brothels, I will do things to you that you'll never forget."

He grinned. "On a normal day I'd be thrilled by that threat cause whenever a lover says that, they usually mean much more enjoyable things. You, on the other hand, are scaring me."

"Good, because he's mine Andris. No woman touches my man."

He realized how serious I was and stopped smirking. "Okay. I get it, but you need to calm down because your eyes have started to glow."

I shrugged. "So?" Then the sound of Torin's Harley drew closer.

"Now they're glowing brighter."

That was because the person responsible for pissing me off was finally here. "See you."

"You're not going to talk to him?"

"Nope." I glanced over my shoulder, but Torin had already started toward us. He wore a look that said he would mow down anyone who stood in his way.

I ignored him and continued into the building. Andris stayed behind to intercept him. Hopefully he would calm Torin down.

As if the Norns were plotting against me, Beau and his friends were in the hall. As soon as he saw me, he called me over. Not just by waving. He called out my name and drew the attention of everyone in the hall.

Men! I was so not in the mood to put up with their bullshit. Still, he was my first case, so I needed to play nice. Image was everything to him. I glanced over my shoulder just as Torin entered the hall. His eyes volleyed between Beau and me, and I could read the warning in them from across the hall.

Bite me, Valkyrie. I walked to Beau and his friends.

Beau caught my arm and pulled me closer. "Tell them."

If he had noticed that I stiffened, he didn't show it. "Tell them what?"

"How you helped me appreciate Hawthorne's writing style. Without her, I would not have known that the letter A becomes more than a symbol for adultery." He grinned at his friends, who watched him with slack jaws. A few girls inched closer.

I'd asked him to explain to his friends our association, not announce it to the entire school. "Huh?" one of his friends asked.

"You see, Hester changes the meaning of the letter by her behavior. The townspeople end up forgetting what it means and even grow to respect her. I'm telling you, it's like the letter has a life of its own."

The discussion became heated as more people chimed in. I didn't have to look over my shoulder to know that Torin was close by. A delicious shiver scuttled through me, a reaction I was unable to control whenever he was around.

"What do you think about the ending, Beau?" a girl asked.

"Babe, if I knew that answer, the lovely Raine and I wouldn't be hanging out after school." He glanced at me, and the smile disappeared from his face. His hand dropped to his side. "St. James."

"Hardshaw." Then Torin slipped his arm around my waist and pulled me back against him. My backpack slipped from my shoulder, but he caught it and took it from my hand.

I wanted to create some space between us. I really did, but the heat from his body had a way of wrapping around me and screwing with my senses. The conversation continued around me, but I didn't hear a thing. I was too aware of Torin's silent presence. Most guys would cause a scene when they thought another man was poaching their girl or if they had a fight. Not Torin. He let his presence do the talking.

He lowered his head and whispered, "We need to talk, Freckles."

I shivered as his warm breath teased my neck. I swallowed, turned my head, and whispered, "Not now. We're discussing Hawthorne."

"You knocked me out," he added.

"You deserved it."

He groaned. "You have five seconds to leave with me or I'm carrying you out of here."

I blinked. "You wouldn't dare!" Of course he would. "Don't embarrass me, Torin. Please."

"Time's up, luv. Excuse me, guys," he said and scooped me up.

Before I could protest, he turned around and cut across the hall, past snickering students and sighing girls fanning themselves. Idiots. Couldn't they see he was being a total ass-hat? I had no choice but to put my arms around his shoulders and try not to throttle him. I even pasted on a smile for our audience.

I leaned closer to his ear and vowed, "I'm going to kill you for this."

"You were ignoring me and I hate being ignored," he said, nodding at his friends.

"He's so romantic," a girl said as we walked past them.

"I know. I want a guy just like him," another added.

Seriously? They didn't even try to keep their voices down. He lowered me down by my locker, looked at the other students nearby, and they actually took off as though he'd ordered them to leave.

"Put your bag away and take the books you need. We'll talk while I walk you to class." I glared. "Or I'll carry you. Take your pick."

I hated that I actually had to put my books away just like he'd said. It made it seem like I was obeying him. I slammed the door shut and started for the hallway.

"So no apology?" he asked.

"I don't feel like talking."

"So that's a no. Fine. I'll do the talking while you listen. The way it's supposed to be. Why? Because I'm older and wiser."

I clenched my teeth. He was pushing his luck.

"First, let's make something clear. You are never to use your powers on me again."

I made a face. How I wish I could stop him from talking. Listening to him made me feel worse. I guess I shouldn't have knocked him out.

"If you do it again, I'll spank you."

I stopped and looked at him, my eyes wide. "You wouldn't dare."

He smirked.

I waited until a few girls walked past us and threw him adoring glances before whispering, "I hate you."

"You adore me," he shot back.

He was so lucky we weren't alone. I walked ahead. Cora entered the hallway, saw us and shook her head. "Hey, you two. Why is everyone whispering about you?"

"He decided he didn't like me talking to Beau and carried me out of the hall like I was his personal *property*," I said.

Cora laughed and high-fived him. "Way to go, Torin."

Disgusted by both of them, I hurried toward my class. He caught up with me before I entered the class. "Freckles…"

"Not now." I disappeared inside the classroom.

Ellie and Amber were talking in whispers, probably discussing Amber's hair. I knew I should feel some guilt, but I didn't. Let her enjoy her new hair for the rest of the day. Maybe I'd fix it. But with the mood I was in, I doubted it.

Kelly, the girl whose hair she'd laughed at didn't seem to be having any problems holding her head up. In fact, she was looking at Amber and Ellie as though she knew something was wrong.

"Morning, guys," Torin said and my eyes flew to the front of the class. What was he doing? "Mr. Quibble is running a little late, but he said you need to read the next chapter in your book. Raine, may I see you outside?"

A buzz filled the class. Of course, no one was going to read the chapter. A late or an absent teacher often meant 'pull out your electronics and get online' or catch up on the latest gossip. As for my boyfriend...

Torin was behind Mr. Quibble's absence. He was bratty when he didn't get his way. He still stood at the front of the class, waiting like some king who'd summoned his minion. Worse, other students noticed I was still seated and glanced my way.

Grinding my teeth, I got up and walked past him into the hallway. He closed the door behind him. For once he wasn't smirking. If he had been, I would have sucker punched him. And no one would have noticed because the hallway was empty.

"What did you do with Mr. Q?" I asked.

"I slipped him sleep runes." He smirked. "He's having a short nap in the boys' restroom. Don't worry; I'll wake him when we're done."

In other words, my English class depended on me. From his expression, he was dead serious. "Torin, you just can't go around runing teachers to get your way."

He shrugged. "I just did. Now, are we talking or just standing here for the entire next period? I warn you though. I could do this the whole day. From class to class, until we talk."

I yanked my arm from his hand and marched to the nearest door, which happened to be the girls' restroom. Thankfully, it was empty. He locked the door and just stood there.

"Well?" I asked.

"That's my line. You owe me an apology."

I laughed, scoffing at the idea. "Then we'll be here the whole day because I will not apologize for putting a whammy on you. You don't go out and make-out with some girl behind my back." My voice rose. "You don't kiss or touch them. You—"

"Belong to you, body and soul," he finished, closing the gap between us, eyes flashing. "From the moment you opened your door and stared at me with those gorgeous hazel eyes, I've thought of no woman but you. I've wanted to touch and kiss no one but you. I've *waited* for you. I'm *still* waiting for you." He angled his head, the smile on his lips turning predator-ish. "Maybe that's the problem. I haven't given you a reason to believe I'm crazy about you, or need you, or crave you." He cupped my face and I swallowed.

"Torin," I started to say, not liking the direction of the conversation.

"Shh. I'm not done. I'm going to show you." His mouth captured mine in a searing kiss that drove all my protest and anger from my head. His tongue slipped between my lips to caress mine as his arm circled my waist and pulled me to him. Every inch of his body and every muscle pressed against mine. Soft and hard complementing each other. He reached down and pulled my leg around his waist as he inched me backwards until my back was to the cold, smooth surface of the mirror.

"Engage your runes," he ordered.

I did, all of them. Not caring which ones. My arms circled his neck, never wanting to let go. He'd taken over all my senses. I breathed him. Tasted him. Felt him. Thought of nothing but him. He trailed kisses along my neck.

"I want you, Freckles. Only you. No other woman will do." He punctuated each sentence with a kiss. "Do you want to know why?"

I couldn't speak.

"Yes or no?"

"Yes," I gasped.

"Because no woman makes me feel and want and need the way you do. Your response when I do this,"—his hand slipped under my shirt. I gasped and trembled as he showed me how easily he could control my body and reduce me to a blubbering idiot—"is pure and honest and breathtaking."

He went into hyper-speed and undid the buttons of my shirt, his mouth replacing his fingers, my silk bra offering no barrier to his tongue and teeth. I was panting, adrenaline pumping through my veins. This was what I'd wanted. To have him kiss me like he couldn't get enough.

"I've never wanted to break rules for anyone, but you," he whispered. He lifted his head as his hand inched lower, past the waistband of my jeggings. I gasped. He'd never done this at school. "Engage your invisibility runes."

I did, my heart pounding so hard I was sure it would stop. I whimpered when his touch became bold. He licked my lower lip with his tongue, then took it between his teeth and bore down so hard I was sure he broke the skin.

"Look at you." He tilted my chin until I could see our reflection in the mirror. "You're beautiful. Breathtaking. And you are mine. Body and soul." Then his words became naughty and descriptive, and I realized that I loved it. Loved every second of his wickedness and every seductive whispered word that left his lips. He pushed me to my limit and beyond, until my existence ceased to matter, except as an extension of him.

The moment went on forever. It was beautiful and naughty, and so Torin. I clung to him until reality returned. He kissed me gently, soothing my bruised lips. "I'd never do that with anyone but you. Do you understand that?"

I nodded.

"Good. That was lesson one. I have several dozen more." Then he was gone.

It seemed like forever before I turned and faced the mirror. My lips were swollen, but I didn't care. My eyes glowed. Didn't care either. Nothing had prepared me for what had just happened and I'd loved every second of it.

I splashed water on my face, patted it with a paper towel, and raced to class just before Mr. Q entered.

~*~

The rest of the morning was a blur. My life was as perfect as it could possibly be. Andris was back to being Andris. The Torin I'd fallen in love with was back. His evil father was out of our lives. Everyone kept telling me I was a shoo-in for the junior prom queen, not that I coveted the title, but who wouldn't want it? I was only human. Or rather an Immortal determined to cling to her humanity.

Despite my near-perfect life, I kept expecting something to happen. The smirks on the Norns' faces the night we defeated the Earl kept taunting me. Andris' words that I must choose a side. I couldn't imagine living anywhere else but here in Kayville, Oregon.

Dad was asleep when I called Femi before lunch, so I decided to eat at school. I didn't see Cora around, which meant she was eating with Echo. Or making out. Those two couldn't get enough of each other.

Ingrid and her friends waved me over, but I was already headed to the swimmer table where Kicker and Sonya, and other members of the swim team sat. It didn't matter that I no longer swam with the team, and I was dating Torin. Or that the jocks embraced me and even Ingrid's friends—the "cheerbitches"—actually acted nice towards me. At heart, I'd always be a geeky swimmer, who'd rather discuss books during lunch. When I indicated my destination, I was surprised when Ingrid left her friends to join me.

"All they ever talk about are which couples are hooking up and breaking up," she whispered as we got closer to the table. "This morning is all about you and Beau, and how Torin swooped in and carried you out of the hall. So he's the one you're tutoring," she added slowly with a knowing gleam in her eyes.

"Don't say it like that. Why is it everyone assumes he's rotten to the core?"

"Cause he is." She grabbed my arm. "Do you know how many cheerleaders he's slept with? From their expressions back there, probably all of them. One even said it's not fair because you have Torin, the number one hottie at school. Now you have number two."

Girls could be such idiots. "They're welcome to him."

Kicker and Sonya weren't used to Ingrid and stared for a few minutes, but their unease didn't last for long. They usually discussed books and character crushes. Not today.

"Is it true you're tutoring Beau Hardshaw?" Kicker blurted out.

Ingrid rolled her eyes. Luckily, the girls didn't notice. I shrugged. "Yeah. It's just for a week."

"Can I be you for the week?" Sonya asked.

"Is he coming to your house today?" Kicker asked, twirling a lock of her hair. "Cause we could swing by to visit and accidentally bump into him." She and Sonya elbowed each other and giggled.

"Don't you have a boyfriend?" I asked, staring at Kicker.

"Yeah, but Cliff is not as exciting as Beau," she retorted.

"Or Torin," Sonya added. "Was he really jealous and carried you from the hall to get you away from Beau?"

"Torin would never be jealous of Beau." I took a bite of my burrito and chewed without tasting it. I was the insecure one. He still hadn't explained the lipstick to my satisfaction. Instead, he'd reminded me of how easy it was for him to make me forget our fight. "He has no reason to."

"So I hear they'll be announcing Junior Prom Court soon," Ingrid cut in, probably hoping to change the subject.

"Raine will definitely be nominated," Kicker said.

"Cora too. She's popular because of her blog. If only Torin was a junior. He'd be the king," Sonya added.

"Or I could be king if you went with me," Beau said, taking the seat beside me. His friends, Seth and Ryder took up the seats beside Sonya and Kicker. "I'm starting a petition that seniors shouldn't attend junior proms."

I rolled my eyes. I wasn't going to the prom if Torin wasn't taking me. Beau had everyone at the swim table hanging on his words. When he turned those green eyes on Ingrid, she flashed him such a naughty grin I wondered if she'd decided to mess around with him.

"I don't think we've ever been properly introduced," he said.

I didn't hear Ingrid's response because Torin entered the cafeteria, his eyes zeroing in on me. The look in his eyes had me remembering this morning and my face warmed. It was probably stupid that my breath caught as he sauntered toward our table.

"Hey," I said. That sounded so lame, but I couldn't think of anything else to say.

"Hey," he whispered and stroked my cheeks with his knuckles, completely ignoring the entire table. He wore his fingerless biker gloves, yet his fingers weren't cold, which meant he hadn't ridden his bike. Lowering his head, he claimed my lips possessively.

Boy, did that kiss go on forever.

When he lifted his head, he handed me a caramel frappe, my favorite. I hadn't even noticed he was carrying it. "Can you take my ride home? I want to borrow your car."

I nodded. "Sure."

"Thanks, luv." He knew where I kept the spare key just like I knew where he kept his, both places protected by runes. He smiled at the table, lingering on Ingrid, and pressed a kiss on my temple and left. I didn't turn to look but the girls at the table did. When I glanced at Beau, he wore a calculating look.

"Nice chatting with you, Beau," Ingrid said and stood. "Raine, see you later."

"You ride his Harley?" Beau asked.

"Yes." I stood.

"Want to give me a ride home after school?" he asked.

"No." I grabbed my drink and tray, nodded at Beau. "Seven, not a minute late."

"She's so bossy, I like it," I heard him as I followed Ingrid. I caught up with her by the cafeteria dumpster.

"I now see why Torin should worry about your evening diversion," Ingrid said. "That boy is something else and I should know, I've met and dated a few bad boys."

"Torin trusts me."

Ingrid laughed. "Of course, he does. You're crazy about him. Doesn't stop guys like Beau. The more unavailable you are the greater the challenge. They're in for the chase."

We threw our uneaten food away and returned the trays. "Spoken from experience?" She just grinned. She could be so mysterious sometimes. "You're not going to mess with him, are you?"

She shook her head. "Nah. I told you. I'm off Mortals."

"What are you doing after school?"

She looked toward her table and shrugged. "Practicing my runes after we're done with Lavania. Why?"

"You want to watch the guys coach in L.A.?"

Surprise flickered across her face. "Sure. Thanks for the invite." She touched my arm and went toward the cheerleaders' and the jocks' table. I headed for the exit.

As soon as I cleared it, I felt them. Norns.

I headed for the library. I needed a reading book while I waited for the books I'd ordered to arrive. Usually, I borrowed books from the local library, but with all the mess going on in my life, I didn't seem to have time anymore. Maybe I should buy an e-reader. No matter how crazy my life got, I loved to read. It relaxed me.

The first person I saw when I entered the library was Matt Langer. Boy genius. From the lunch box by his books, he'd brought lunch from home and eaten alone somewhere before slipping inside the library.

I waved when he saw me. His cheeks grew pink. Instead of heading to the aisles, I changed directions and grabbed the seat by his. I put my drink on the floor in case Mrs. Larsen saw it. Drinks were not allowed in the library.

"How did you know that question was wrong today?"

His face grew redder. "I just did."

The teacher had given us a pre-test in class earlier and not only had Matt aced it, he'd also corrected the last question. "I missed it along with everyone in class. You should just skip twelfth grade and head to college."

"Uh, my parents don't think I'm ready."

"Have they met you? Do they know how fast you compute a math problem?"

He grinned. "Kind of. My father is a neurosurgeon and my mother is a nuclear physicist."

"Double genius genes." The librarian caught my eyes and shot me a warning look. Our voices weren't even carrying. But I recognized the three girls that entered the library. They stared at me, and disappeared toward the fiction section. Catie, Marj, and Jeannette. "Okay, later."

I pushed back the chair and stood, but I'd forgotten about my drink and knocked it over. Matt and I reached for it at the same time and our hands touched. His future flashed before my eyes. I grinned when the vision ended. "Thanks."

He shrugged. "No problem. Hide it. She's looking over here."

Sure enough, Mrs. Larsen was glaring at us. I used my body to hide my drink. "Thanks again. Uh, Matt, about college. You should ask Mr. Finch to talk to your parents."

Matt frowned and whispered, "That's weird. I was just thinking about asking him this morning, but then I changed my mind when I realized the deadline for registration at the schools I want has passed."

If what I'd seen was right, he didn't need to worry about that. "Don't give up without trying. I dare you to register for the SAT. If you get accepted, you owe me one of these." I tapped my drink.

The librarian shushed me this time. I shot her an apologetic smile, waved to Matt, and took off. I headed toward the aisle where the three Norns had disappeared. I didn't see them.

I found the book I'd come to get, a dystopian novel everyone was raving about. I was thinking of leaving when they appeared. They were in their true form, all wrinkly and ancient when seconds ago they'd looked like teenagers. Long gray gowns and matching cloaks with hoodies hid their frail bodies, and it was impossible to tell what color their gray hair used to be. Everything about them was gray. Even their eyes were grayish. They reminded me of a character in the TV series Charmed.

Still, I recognized them based on their sizes. The shorter one was Catie. The tallest with hands crossed under her nun-like sleeves had to be Marj. That left the third one, Jeannette. I wondered if those were really their names. I should just name them Norn-one, Norn-two, and Norn-three. Since I knew they were invisible, I looked around first before engaging my invisibility runes. Then I waited.

"You haven't fixed the forest," the one I called Catie said. A week ago, I'd thought she was the nicest of the trio. Guess she didn't need to hide her true colors anymore.

"Excuse me?" I asked.

"We told you to take care of the forest after you battled the Immortals. It needs you," she said.

I shook my head. "Are you saying the trees are still down? It's been a week. They're probably dead."

"Then you better move fast and save them," Catie continued.

"No, I'm not cleaning up your mess. You let this happen."

"As long as you're involved, it's your job to clean up after yourself and your friends," Catie continued.

"Involved? The Earl came after me because you sent him. You did the sending, you do the cleaning."

They looked at each other and disappeared, leaving me fuming. Just when I thought I was finally happy, they had to come along and screw with my head. I wasn't fixing the forest and that was it.

12. The Vision

Ingrid and I appeared by the top of the stadium and walked down toward the field. As usual, the parents were occupying the bottom seats. Torin, Andris, and the two assistant coaches were in the field with the kids.

"I can't believe I've never been in here," Ingrid said, pulling my attention from Torin. He wasn't expecting us. "It's huge."

"They're playing a game tomorrow afternoon right here. Quarterfinals. You should come with me."

"What time?"

"Two."

The parents noticed us before we sat, their eyes lingering on Ingrid. As usual, she looked amazing in an off-white miniskirt, a print shirt, and boots. Her pageboy hairstyle and impeccable makeup gave her a sophisticated look. I stopped feeling underdressed and not put together around her months ago.

There were more parents this time, quite a number of them fathers. I caught myself before waving to Jace's dad. I might know him, but he didn't know me from Adam.

We took the empty seats to the right of the parents. Andris saw us first and waved. If he was surprised to see Ingrid, he didn't show it. I touched the seats next to ours, the backs, even the armrests and fought frustration. Why couldn't I see anything except soccer players and fans?

"Still trying to get a reading?"

I nodded. "It's so frustrating. The one time Torin needs me, and I can't come through for him."

Ingrid chuckled. "Stop being so hard on yourself. You can't control the visions. Most Seidr Witches need a lot of preparation before going into a trance. You don't even have to do that. How had Lavania put it?"

"Open your mind and reach deep inside you," I said, imitating our trainer's voice and gestures.

Ingrid laughed, the sound carrying. More glances were thrown our way, some of the woman scowling. Andris glanced at us again. Torin was so focused on the game we might as well be invisible.

When he blew the whistle, signaling a break, he stayed by the table with drinks and snacks to give pointers to the boys before walking over to where we sat.

"What are you two doing here?" he asked.

"Lavania let us off early because she," Ingrid pointed at me, "wasn't paying attention. She kept spacing out."

"I did not. Tattle."

Torin just grinned as though he was taking credit for my absentmindedness, but it wasn't what he did at school that had me on edge. It was the damn Norns. I'd need a repeat performance by him to erase them from my head. But what if the Norns continued to ignore the forest?

"See? I told you," Ingrid said and I realized they were talking about me. Warmth spread to my face when Torin chuckled, touched my cheek, and went back to the field.

"What's going on with you?"

I glared at her. "Quit tattling on me."

She rolled her eyes. "If I wanted to do that, I would have told him you almost crashed his Harley today," she whispered to me as Torin left.

I'd been busy studying and listening to the trees while riding and almost hit a car in front of me. If Ingrid hadn't honked, I would have gone flying over the hood. "Come on. We're going to the Grass Berm."

"What's that?"

I pointed at the grassy patch to our left. It overlooked the stadium. "I need to connect with Mother Earth without an audience."

She groaned. "It's so far. Can't I just open a portal and get us there faster?" she asked, looking at how far we had to go before we could open a portal without being seen by the parents.

"Sure, lazy bum. Then we'll have to come back here and rune everyone. As it is, if anyone sees us there, they'll wonder how we got there so fast. So we're doing this my way. I need to test something." I took her hand and pulled her up.

"Don't you just hate the way people stare?" she mumbled, taking my arm.

I grinned.

"What?" she asked.

"They're staring at you. You're gorgeous."

"War paint," she mumbled. "You're a natural beauty."

"Oh gee, I'd like to see you without makeup, Ingrid. Oops, I already did and you were even more gorgeous."

She made a face and bumped me with her shoulder. "When? I always make a point of never leaving my room without makeup."

We walked past the parents and I caught snippets of their conversations. U-17 Roster. Bradenton, Florida. Men's National Team. U-17 World Cup. After lunch with Dad, I knew enough about soccer to understand these parents' lofty goals.

L.A. Galaxy Academy was like college football, a place to shine and be noticed by the pro scouts. If you were good, a player could get selected to join a team of talented seventeen and younger players in Bradenton, Florida to practice for the U-17 Men's National Team. Apparently, once selected, the boys stayed in Florida for an entire year, training in the morning and attending classes at a private high school in the afternoon. If they won enough tournaments, they could even participate in the U-17 FIFA World Cup.

We walked along the perimeter of the field. I let Ingrid's arm go while I touched the ground, the grass, and the seats. Each time, Ingrid sat and sighed like she'd walked a mile and fanned herself. Then she listed various inventions that had made walking obsolete, from unicycles to airplanes.

"Okay, you stay here and wait for me," I said.

"Oh no." She jumped up, hands gripping her patent leather boots. "If you can do it so can I."

"Then stop complaining or I'll… grrr." I clenched my fist.

"Bitch slap me into next week?" she asked with a deadpan expression. "Put a whammy on me. Did you put one on Amber's hair?"

Where the heck did that come from? Andris. "Yes."

Ingrid laughed, which only proved what I'd started to suspect. She had a sick sense of humor. "I can't stand her. The way she and Ellie treat the other girl, uh, what's her name?"

"McKenzie," I said.

"Yes. You should have heard them during lunch on Tuesday. So when Amber said her hair just turned that ugly shade of blue on its own, I knew a witch was involved." She tilted her head and studied me. "I knew there was a mean streak behind all that sweetness. I like it. Have you really seen me without makeup?"

"No, but you ugly cry."

Her jaw dropped, then she lunged at me.

I raced up the steps all the way to the top with Ingrid threatening to punch a hole in my head with the heels of her boots. I stopped at the top and she almost bumped into me. StubHub's Grass Berm was on the other side of the fence.

I created a portal and we stepped onto the grass. It sloped toward the stands. I turned around. The view of the field was spectacular. Ingrid sat on the grass and sighed. I wondered whether she was worried about grass stains on her skirt.

"Now what?"

"Now I open my mind." I removed my ballet flats and lay on my back. I didn't have to worry about my clothes. My tights were black and my shirt had more black than yellow. "It's such a beautiful day."

Ingrid looked up. "Clear sky. No smog…"

I closed my eyes and fisted clumps of grass. Funny how touching the ground felt so amazing. Taking a deep breath, I opened my mind. I let the need to connect with the stadium fill me.

At first, all I heard was the crowd cheering and singing, the sounds rising and falling. Slowly, sunlight streamed in like a shaft of light into a dark room. It spread, until I was in the sun, standing on the Grass Berm on a sunny afternoon.

Fans on blankets sipped drinks and snacked on nachos, popcorn, and corndogs. Couples, parents with their kids, a few even had babies. A girl, about five in braids and a floral dress, played with her baby sister, completely indifferent to the game going on below. Two boys in LA Galaxy T-shirts alternated watching the players in the field and the trading cards of the players in front of them. Others watched the big screen at the other end of the stadium showing the close-ups of the players. The stadium was crowded, every seat filled.

Then a different sound mixed with cheers and the songs. It grew louder and closer. I shielded my eyes and searched for it. At first I saw nothing, but I recognized the droning engine of an airplane. Then I noticed people pointing at something. I followed the tip of the nearest finger to a low-flying airplane with smoke streaming from its rear end like a comet's tail. I didn't know if there was an airport nearby, but it looked ready to land. It already had its wheels out.

While the people on the grass no longer watched the game, the crowd in the stadium was still clueless. Then the plane appeared to crumple as though giant hands were breaking it into two. It changed direction and headed straight for the stadium.

Around me, the crowd gasped and panic swept over their faces. In seconds, chaos erupted. Parents grabbed their children. Husbands reached for their wives. They ran every which way, but there was nowhere safe. They were out in the open and the plane was faster.

Below, the ones in the stands were now aware of what was happening. Another pandemonium. Panic translated into screams and people started shoving and jumping over each other.

The plane hit the Grass Berm, the tail breaking off and the wings collapsing, taking people down. Blood-curdling screams filled the air. The impact slowed down the body, but not enough for it to stop. The sloping landscape did the rest. It tipped and rolled toward the stands and the running people. Some of the passengers were still trapped in their seats, unconscious. Others lay around the carpet of grass like broken dolls.

Bodies were everywhere, the injured screaming for help, the ones incapable of speech moaning. The rest were silent, their deaths swift. Their souls separated from their bodies to stare at the carnage.

The little girl with braids and floral dress was trapped under her father a few feet from me, crying and calling for her daddy. Her mother and the baby were gone.

I closed my mind and darkness replaced the gruesome scene. Then I heard Ingrid beg, "Come on, Raine. Come back."

I didn't open my eyes right away, but I felt the wetness of tears run like rivulets down the side of my face and into my ears. So many dead. And that poor little girl… All alone. I sat up and wiped the tears, but more kept appearing and I couldn't stop shaking. I tried to tell myself it was just a vision, that I could stop it from happening.

Ingrid put her arms around me and rested her chin on the crown of my head. "Shh, it's okay. It was only a vision."

"The screams. So many dead. Going to… to…die."

"What happened?" Torin asked sounding like he'd sprinted to reach us.

"She got a vision. A bad one."

Torin's arms replaced hers and for a few minutes I clung to him. So many were going to die. We had to do something. I wiggled out of Torin's arms. "They have to cancel the game. You could convince them. Or we could call the airlines. I saw the logo on the plane. It's wasn't an American airline. We have to save them, Torin. That little girl…"

"Shh." He wiped the wetness from my cheeks. I could read the frustration in his eyes. He hated seeing me in pain. "We will."

No, he couldn't be involved. "No, I'll do it. You stay out of it. The Norns might use it against us."

"Okay, luv. Whatever you say."

I frowned. He was patronizing me, but I lacked the fire to get angry at him. "I just need to know who to call. LA Galaxy people? Maybe the airline? I could tell them something was wrong with their airplane." I tried to remember the colors of the teams playing so I could pinpoint the exact day of the accident. I opened my eyes and looked into Torin's. "I have to do it again. I didn't get the team uniforms."

"Are you sure?" he asked.

"No, but I must know which team is playing that day. It's the only way to know the day of the accident."

Torin looked over his shoulder. His team wasn't done. He must have taken off in the middle of practice.

"I'm okay now. Go. Finish the game. I can do this."

He glanced at Ingrid. "Take care of her."

She nodded. I wanted to protest that I could take care of myself, but the vision was more important. I lay down again and opened my mind. This time, I willed myself away from the grass and into the field, and studied the uniforms, the names, and even the players' faces. When the plane crashed, I watched the catastrophe from the field.

The people seated in the northern section, right below the Grass Berm were not going to make it. Their mistake was running toward the field. If Jace was going to be injured that evening, he would be seated in that section of the stadium.

Crap! I couldn't stop the crash. If I did, Torin wouldn't save Jace and get his first Immortal. If he failed, would the Valkyrie Council take away his promotion? My eyes flew open and I stared at Ingrid in horror. She reached for my hand.

"What is it?" she asked.

"I can't stop it. I can't stop the accident from happening."

~*~

As soon as I got home, I went straight to Lavania when all I wanted to do was strip, get in a tub and have a long bath. The bloody scene was etched in my brain, and my skin crawled with it. Worse, I felt like all the deaths would be on me. Like I was going to fail all those people.

Lavania wasn't in the kitchen, but Ingrid heard sounds coming from her quarters. The spacious bedroom had a sitting area with a large-screen TV, and a private study attached to it. It used to be Eirik's parents'. He and I would hide there when we played hide-and-seek as children.

I knocked and was surprised when a man opened the door. The guy had red hair, a nicely trimmed beard, and piercing blue eyes. He had Norse god written all over him. Could he be Lavania's mate from Asgard? I heard she'd married a minor god. He only wore a towel and from the looks of it, he must have just stepped out of the shower. I tried to keep my eyes on his face.

"I'm, uh, looking for Lavania," I said.

He studied me with unnerving intensity. "You are Lavania's young protégée. It's a pleasure to finally meet you, Miss Raine." He bowed.

I blinked. "Oh. Thanks."

"I'm Belmar, Lavania's mate. Do come in." He stepped back and indicated the room. "She went to get us something to eat and should be back shortly."

I didn't move. "Uh, I didn't see her in the kitchen."

"Oh no, she went to our home in Asgard."

I bit my lip. "Could you just tell her I stopped by? I'll talk to her later." I turned to leave then glanced at him and offered a tiny smile. "It was nice to meet you, sir."

"No, my dear. The pleasure is all mine." Then a twinkle entered his eyes. "Maybe I could be of service to you?"

And what would he want in return? Gah, I was becoming suspicious of every god now. "No, but thanks for the offer." When he smiled and bowed again, I changed my mind. He had kind eyes. "Unless you know something about Idun-valkyries like Lavania."

He nodded. "She and I have been together for centuries, so I know of her work."

"Is she given a list of people to turn into Immortals or does she get to choose?"

A thoughtful expression settled on his face. "At first, she was given a list to prove herself. From my understanding, if she didn't succeed in getting the people on the list, they'd assume she wasn't ready."

My interference could screw Torin's chances. Lavania entered the room with a tray brimming with covered plates and bowls, and frowned when she saw me. She smoothly shooed her husband away and joined me, closing the door behind her.

"What is it?" she asked.

I quickly explained about the premonition and my concerns.

"Oh dear," she murmured and my heart sank. "A Norn's and an Idun-valkyrie's works don't complement each other very well. He can only offer them Immortality just before they die."

"Have you ever lost people?"

"Oh yes. Not everyone wants to become Immortal. Although at the beginning of my training, the Council gave me a list of people they hoped would accept Immortality." She peered at me, her brow furrowing. "This is a test, Raine. Torin can either pass or fail it. If he fails, it goes on his record and it will be centuries before he gets nominated again."

Great! "Who provides the list?"

"The Valkyrie Council. You may have to let this one go, honey." Lavania touched my arm. I nodded, turned, and left.

There had to be another way. Every time I closed my eyes, I saw the plane crash and that little girl trapped under her father. Tears rushed to my eyes again.

How could I let this happen? All those people would die if I did nothing. Yet, I couldn't take this opportunity from Torin.

I stripped and entered the shower. For what seemed like forever, I stood under the hot sprays and cried. What was the point of being a Seeress and not helping people? My bathroom door opened and I looked over my shoulder, my eyes widening. Torin? I covered my breasts, my back still to him. He'd never seen me naked.

"What are you doing?" I asked in a strangled voice I didn't recognize.

"Joining you," Torin said.

183

My heart trembled and my stomach dropped. I was naked while he wore shorts and a T-shirt, yet a feeling of deja vu washed over me and images that made no sense flashed in my head. We'd never showered together or made out in his shower. Yet the images said we had. Wishful thinking on my part perhaps, or a premonition? I shook my head.

"Is that a no?" Torin asked, reaching behind his neck with one hand and pulling off his shirt. He flashed a smile that said he'd try to make me change my mind if I denied him.

I swallowed and shook my head.

"So it's okay to join you?"

I nodded.

"Use words, Freckles."

He was being his usual impossible self. When he slipped his fingers under his waistband, my eyes widened. He chuckled. When I realized he wasn't stopping, I faced the wall, my heart pounding with anticipation and panic.

What was he doing now? I wanted to check, but I didn't dare. I heard the door close. He slipped his arms around me and pulled me closer until I felt every inch of his naked body. All of him. Pressed against my back. Holy smokes.

"I hate to see you cry," he said.

Was I supposed to respond to that? I was too busy trying to control my erratic breathing, and my mind had stopped working except to monitor his every movement. I listened to his breathing, stared at his arms around my waist, and my flushed skin was aware of his every muscle pressed against mine. I didn't think I could speak or move. In fact, I was sure the only thing holding me upright was his arm.

"Was the vision that bad?"

He seriously wanted to talk about that now? How about the fact that we were in the shower together? I nodded.

He dropped a kiss on my shoulder and swept my hair away from my neck. "Want to tell me about it?"

Hel's Mist! I opened my mouth, but I couldn't remember what I was about to say. My body was still reacting to the kiss he'd casually dropped on my shoulder. Worse, he was gently stroking my stomach and rubbing his cheek against mine. But the most distracting of all was all that skin and body parts pressed against me. I couldn't think, let alone speak.

He chuckled and whispered in a husky voice, "It's okay. We can talk later. Do you want me to wash your hair?"

I must have nodded because he reached for the shampoo, squirted some on my hair and gently lathered it. I pressed my hands against the wall since he'd let me go and my knees were like Jell-O.

"Close your eyes," he said, fingers massaging my hair and scalp. "I've always wanted to wash your hair. It's so thick and silky."

I wasn't sure how I was supposed to respond to that, so I kept my mouth shut. He rinsed my hair and squirted conditioner on it.

"Funny how I've had all these fantasies about you that I swore I wouldn't act on until you were my wife, but now I realize I was a fool. We could have been living them." He chuckled, rinsing out the conditioner. "Some of them at least. The others might shock you."

Wife. We'd never really discussed marriage although I'd hoped we'd be together for eternity. For now, I was more intrigued by, "Fantasies?"

Yay! I finally found my voice.

"Oh yes. So many and," he lowered his head and whispered, "so naughty you'd kick me out of here if you knew."

Kick him out? Never. "Like what?"

"Memorizing the perfection of your body." He poured bathing soap on his hand and slowly rubbed it down my arms, until our hands met. He slid his fingers between mine. Again, his movements were slow and hypnotic. I never knew the skin between my fingers was so sensitive. "You have soft skin."

He ran his knuckles back to my shoulders, his touch light and reverent as though he was worshiping my skin. He stepped back, soaped my shoulder blades, upper back, then slowly down the small of my back, even lower to my feet. Slowly, he came back up. He squirted more soap all over my front.

If we did this often, I'd be out of shampoo, conditioner, and soap within a week. Not that I was complaining.

"Close your eyes."

He hadn't been kidding about the memorizing part. My breath hitched at times and other times I just stopped breathing as he explored every curve and dip, his touch gentle, reverent, teasing. He had me completely under his spell. I forgot about the plane crash and the dilemma I was facing, and focused completely on him and the moment.

Sensations cascaded through me. I shivered and shuddered. I even begged him at one time though I wasn't sure whether I wanted him to stop, or never stop.

He turned me around and said, "Open your eyes, luv."

I stared at him in bemusement. He stroked my cheek and I leaned against his hand. "That was…" I couldn't describe it. Better than this morning? He set a new bar every time.

He smirked. "Amazing, I know. Now put your arms around my neck."

His arrogance was rearing its ugly head. I grew bolder, my voice returning. "Is ordering me around part of your fantasy?"

"Oh yes. Do you have a problem with it?"

Part of me didn't like being ordered around, but another part got a kick from it. "Yes."

"Get used to it. Now, kiss me."

I cupped his face and kissed him, pouring all my love into it. When I lifted my head, I looked him in the eye and ordered, "Turn around."

"This is not part of my fantasy," he complained.

"No, but it's mine." He let me wash his hair, but before I could do my exploring, he was out the door. All I could see was his back. "What… Where are you going?"

"Home. This was about you, not me." He grabbed a towel and wrapped it around his waist, picked up a second one and held it out for me.

How come he got to see me naked, but I couldn't see all of him? I hated double-standards. I turned off the water and allowed him to wrap the towel and his arms around me. The towel was nice, but unnecessary. All I needed was his warmth to chase away the sudden chill. I sunk against him, never wanting this moment to end. He pressed a kiss on my temple. "Did I mention what an amazing body you have? Every curve and dip."

My face warmed. I had no response to that. "What do you mean this was about me?"

"You don't trust me."

I rolled my eyes. "You had lipstick all over your face and lips."

"Slight exaggeration, but I forgive you." He lifted my chin so I could see our reflections in the mirror. "Look in the mirror," he said, eyelids dropping and lips curling in that slow, sexy smile I loved. Then he opened my towel. I tried to cross my arms. "Don't do that."

Again, images flashed in my head. Me in his bathroom trying to cover myself while he ordered me not to. How was this possible? It couldn't be a premonition. I couldn't see my own future.

"Look at you. You are breathtakingly beautiful."

I didn't see it. My hips were too wide and my chest too small. With my hair plastered to my head and no makeup, I looked like a drowned rat. He tucked the towel around me.

"Why would I want any woman when I have you? You're it for me, Freckles. My alpha and omega." He nuzzled my neck. "I'll prove it to you every day if that's what it takes for you to believe me, and I'm going to enjoy every minute of it."

My throat closed. He'd proven in more ways than I cared to count that he loved me. But I wasn't saying no to what we just did. No, what *he* just did. I wanted more of that. A lot more.

"The fantasies?" I asked, reaching up to caress his cheek.

He turned his head and pressed a kiss in my palm. "I'm going to live them with you, one at a time. You can have your turn when you're about a century or two." He stepped back, his towel threatening to unwrap. I didn't mind.

I lifted my chin and used my abilities to loosen it just a few more inches.

"Now get dressed," he ordered, spoiling my moment. I should have just yanked the damn towel off. "I'm cooking us dinner. We can discuss your vision and what to do about it, then you can tutor that airhead."

"Beau is not an airhead. Besides, people at school think you're jealous of him."

Torin scoffed at the idea and spread his arms. "Me? Jealousy stems from puny minds with trust issues." He blew me a kiss when I glowered. "I trust you. Completely. I just don't like that bonehead, so tonight you're tutoring him in my house." He turned to leave.

Puny minds? Just for that. I waved my hand and the towel flew off him. I covered my mouth to stop the laughter from escaping. Without an ounce of shame, he turned and put his hands on his hips, giving me full frontal.

Oh, my. Did I get my fill? He was magnificent.

Once again, images flashed in my head. Images of him. Naked. In his bedroom. Another premonition?

"My face is up here, Freckles," he said.

That line had me flustered the first day we met. Not this time. If I couldn't touch, I was going to look and memorize. I had ugly images of jocks to get rid of and a few fantasies to create. "Turn around."

Torin sighed, turned, and posed like a body builder while looking over his shoulder and wiggling his eyebrows. He looked completely ridiculous, but I adored this goofy side of him.

13. No More Visions

I was still grinning when I finished getting dressed. Torin was visible through the window. As though he knew I was watching, he looked up and straight at me, and raised his glass. I waved.

Feeling better, I see.

I smiled down at Onyx. She hopped on to the window seat. "Yes. Where have you been?"

Downstairs. Femi was cooking steak. Why were you crying earlier? Did someone hurt you? The Norns again?

She and I had discussed the Norns after school. "No. I had a premonition of an accident I can't stop. Many people are going to die."

There shouldn't be an accident you can't stop.

"Unfortunately, this is one of them."

Then get help.

I frowned. "What do you mean?"

If a job is too much for you, you need other Witches. I can find some for you.

The little girl at the crash site in my vision flashed into my head. Maybe I could save her family. I'd rather go for saving a few than none. "Can you find anyone for me?"

She sighed. *Magical people. All you have to do is think about them and project their images into my head.*

Too bad. She hopped onto my desk and watched the screen as I booted up my laptop.

Who are you looking for?

"A non-magical person." After ten minutes of searching for the airplane in my vision and getting nowhere, I grabbed a piece of paper and pen and sketched the logo, and headed downstairs. Mom was setting up a dinner tray for Dad.

"Where's Femi?"

"On a date. She'll be back tomorrow morning. There's food in the oven." She scooped more casserole onto a plate. "We're going to watch Hitchcock, if you want to join us."

I was not into black and white oldies. "No, thanks. I'm having dinner with Torin. Mom, have you ever seen a plane with a logo like this? It had Middle Eastern script on the side."

She studied my drawing. "Hmm. You know me with modern technology, hun. I've never flown anywhere and don't particularly care for things I don't understand. Ask your father."

Despite the tumor eating his brain, Dad was still the most brilliant man I knew. He studied the picture and gave me a solution in seconds. "Most airlines will have the name of their country on one side in English. Look at the other side of the plane."

Not the answer I was looking for. It meant revisiting StubHub and accessing the same vision. My stomach hollowed out at the thought. My visions weren't two-dimensional like images on a screen. I was part of it, which made them real and traumatizing. Dad identified the team faster, thanks to the names on the shirts and the team colors.

"Uruguay," Dad explained. "They're in the roster to play Team USA in two weeks. If we lose to them we'll be out of the World Cup. We have an amazing goalie, but Uruguay has experienced players. Since when do you like soccer? You could barely focus on the game a few days ago."

"Since Torin started coaching at LA Galaxy Academy." I couldn't tell him about the plane crash. Mom, on the other hand, wasn't easy to evade. She followed me out of the room.

"What's going on?"

"I had a premonition about a plane crash."

A thoughtful expression settled on her face. "Are you thinking of stopping the crash? Alone?"

I shook my head. "No. That would be too much."

"There's a reason Norns work in threes, my dear. It takes a lot of their power to change things. And don't forget who is in charge of accidents."

Evil Norns. I'd been so focused on what I could do; I had completely forgotten evil Norns were behind most disasters.

"If you take on something like this, you'll be going against them." She touched my cheek and went back to join Dad.

Sighing in defeat, I texted Beau and headed to Torin's. He had already set up a picnic for two on the floor in front of the fireplace. He had gone all out. Stir-fried chicken on a bed of rice topped with shrimp scampi and fresh garlic bread sticks. Chocolate dipped strawberries completed the meal. I had soda while he had a glass of wine. Since he was barefoot, I kicked off my flats and joined him on the rug.

As usual, he cooked everything to perfection and there was plenty of it. I couldn't believe I was ready to kill him this morning, and now we were playing footsie while he fed me strawberries. He even offered me a sip of his drink.

"Argh. How can you stand that? It's so bitter."

"I like spice in my life, which explains why I'm crazy about you." He swept my hair over my shoulder. "You, Freckles, are ice and fire. Sweet one second then my worst nightmare the next."

I bumped him with my shoulder. "Hey, that's mean. I'm sweet."

He smirked. "Sweet is boring, and that,"—he stroked my nose— "is something you'll never be." He tilted his head as though listening and yelled, "Get lost, Andris!"

I hadn't even felt the draft that usually accompanied a portal opening. Andris appeared in the doorway between the living room and the family room. He studied us.

"Hey, you," I said.

"Don't mind me. Just checking to see if everything is ok."

"Everything is fine. Now go away," Torin said rudely. Good thing Andris wasn't easily offended. He leaned against the doorway. For once, he wasn't smirking.

"How are you doing, Raine?"

"Two seconds bro, then your neck. I have a date," Torin warned.

I put an arm and a leg over Torin in case he decided to make good on his words. He shot me a questioning look. "I'm holding you down."

"I could run with you on my back."

I glanced up at Andris. "Everything is perfect."

"Did Torin explain?"

"No, but he's apologized in his own way."

Andris groaned. "You bullied her? Listen, I owe you an apology. Torin would not have gone to that club if I hadn't suggested it. But he behaved like a gentlemen the entire time. He told the girls he was taken."

That didn't explain the kisses. Andris looked so apologetic I decided not to go there. "It's okay. Really."

"The kisses were really goodbye kisses. He sat there and took it."

He should have pushed them away. "It's alright."

"Until Sylvie decided to get creative."

Moving fast, Torin threw his empty wine glass at Andris. Andris caught it and bragged, "Told you I was faster."

"Who is Sylvie?" I was more than curious. I was jealous.

"The girl who's probably wishing she'd never tried to seduce him. What did you tell her?"

"Please, let me shut him up," Torin whispered.

I grinned. "No, I want to hear this."

Torin groaned and buried his face on the rug.

"She'd have to be five-foot-seven with hair like silk, mouth meant to be kissed, and a smile that lights up a room to interest him."

I lifted Torin's head from the floor and kissed him.

"And, uh…"

"Say one more word, Andris," Torin warned.

"Lavania would like to talk you, Raine. I think she's taking off and won't be back until next week."

Nice. No lessons tomorrow morning. I could sleep in. "I'll stop by after Beau leaves."

Andris laughed. "He's still coming? You're losing your touch… Okay, I'm leaving," he added when Torin sat up, taking me with him. "I'll just take a few of those." He picked up two breadsticks from our plate, put the wine glass on the floor, and smirked as he left.

Torin lay on his back and pulled me down on top of him. I propped my elbows on his chest and studied him. Whatever insecurities I'd had were gone. "So everything is cool between you and Andris?"

"It will be."

"And with the Idun-valkyrie business?"

"All I have to do is turn everyone on my list and impress the Council. I'm keeping an eye on all of them. Jace will be my first."

"Isn't he too young to become an Immortal?"

Torin chuckled and traced my nose with the tip of his finger. "They're recruiting them younger. He can decide later if he wants to age a little and adjust how often he uses the right bind runes." He looked at his watch. "Tell me about your vision."

He didn't speak when I described what I'd seen. I didn't realize tears were running down my face until he wiped them. Then he pulled me down for a hug and pressed a kiss on my temple. "I hate what these visions do to you."

"Sorry."

"Hey." He lifted my face. "Don't be. You care, which is more than I can say for most Norns. Not that you are one of them," he added quickly. "It's one of the things that make you special. If you want to stop the crash, go ahead."

And mess with his promotion? No way. I was going to be a supportive girlfriend. "I can't."

"Why not?"

"I don't want to go against evil Norns."

"You did before at the pool, that first time, and stopped them," he said.

"I rescued a few students, Torin. I didn't stop the lightning. For me to stop the crash, I'd have to stop them before they mess with the plane. Oh, and it's three of them against one."

Torin sat up, dislodging me off his lap. "Giving up without trying doesn't sound like you. Who told you that you shouldn't stop the crash?"

Mom and Lavania, but he didn't need to know that. "No one did. I can make my own decisions, you know." He squinted, but headlights swept over the window and I looked at my watch. "Beau is here."

"Beau can wait," Torin said firmly and gripped my hands. He peered at me. "Why don't you want to stop the crash? You've cried three times since you saw the premonition."

"Stop interrogating me. I have enough to deal with without taking on evil Norns. My usual trio paid me a visit today at school."

That got his attention. "What did they want? Why didn't you tell me?"

"They said I'm supposed to heal the forest. Can you imagine they didn't?"

He frowned. "It's been a week. We haven't heard anything in the news."

"I know."

He stood, clearly bothered by this more than the fact that I wasn't going to stop the crash. He walked to the door and stopped before opening it. "Are you going to do it?"

"Yes. No." I shook my head. "They're trying to manipulate me."

He grinned, his expression saying he agreed with me. The doorbell rang and he growled. "If we ignore him, do you think he'll go away?"

"No. He's my first case. Kind of like Jace is yours, so be nice."

He yanked opened the door. "Hardshaw, right on time."

"Raine is worth it," I heard Beau say. "She texted me to meet her here. Where's she?"

Torin slammed the door in Beau's face. "Every time he opens his mouth, I want to punch him."

"You're better than that. Let him in." The doorbell rang again. "You're messing with my case, Torin."

"He's an asshole. Mine is a nice young man." He yanked open the door.

"You live here?" I heard Beau ask.

"What do you think?" Torin stepped back, then he saw what I was doing, picking up our plates. "I'll take care of that. Take him to the, uh, kitchen. You guys can work on the counter."

Where he could keep an eye on us. He was so transparent. Beau was busy looking around with interest, but his eyes kept going to our picnic. I saw the hunger in his eyes. With his mother's broken arm, chances were he'd left home without eating.

"Come in, Beau," I said and his attention shifted to me. "Have a seat. I'll be with you as soon as I take these to the kitchen. Torin, you cooked, I clean." Torin looked ready to argue, but I ignored him and focused on Beau. "Do you cook, Beau?"

He shook his head. "I'd love to learn. Someday." His eyes lingered on the breadsticks. Poor guy.

"Then you must try Torin's food. I insist. It's amazing. I'll get you a plate." I hurried out of the living room before either of them could protest. Torin followed me.

"What's going on?" Torin asked.

"He's hungry," I whispered. He rolled his eyes. I smacked his arm. "Be nice. Remember? His stepfather broke his mother's arm." He disappeared back into the living room while I warmed a plate for Beau.

~*~

I'd never seen someone wolf down food so fast. I even got him a drink, but he was done before Torin and I finished taking care of the kitchen. Torin might be an amazing cook, but he used way too many utensils.

"Hey," he said from behind us and we turned. He had his plate and fork, but was still chugging the soda. "Thanks for the food." He handed me the plate.

I inclined my head to indicate Torin. "He cooked it. I just come here to eat."

He shot Torin a weird expression. "I still can't believe it."

"Believe what, Hardshaw?" Torin asked in such a hard voice I was sure one wrong word from Beau and he'd boot him out of his house.

"That you two are next door neighbors," Beau said. "So you live here with your parents?"

"No." Torin didn't bother to explain. He focused on me instead. "Are you using the kitchen or the dining room?"

"Dining room. Come on, Beau."

I was sure Torin would hover, or worse, pull out a chair and join us just to be difficult, but he disappeared into the garage. Tinkering with his bike was his favorite pastime.

"So he lives here with his parents?" Beau asked.

"No. They're in England. In fact his father, the Earl, was here a few days ago to visit." Wow, nice. I could never lie to save my butt. My eyes met Torin's. He'd come back inside the house and was shamelessly listening to our conversation. He shook his head.

Beau was facing me and didn't see him. "So he's some kind of royalty?"

"Nobility," I said.

"What's the difference?"

"Royalties are blood relatives of the king and queen. Nobility has to do with titles. So what do the tattoos on your arm mean?" I asked to distract him. He wasn't stupid and might want to know more about Torin's family. The present Earl of Worthington didn't even know of Torin's existence or his father's.

Beau rolled up the sleeve of his sweatshirt and flexed his arm. In the kitchen, Torin leaned against the counter and rolled his eyes.

"What do you think they mean?" Beau asked.

"The butterfly is a symbol of the soul in many cultures. It emerges from a cocoon after being a lowly worm. A soul is believed to change with time too. So the tattoo must mean something happened to make you change for the better. I'm not sure what a snarling dog with red eyes means. Anger?"

He smirked. "Not bad."

"But the way the butterfly overshadows the dog says there's a connection between the two. And the last one is a dream catcher. In Native American mythology, they catch the bad dreams and let in the good."

Silence followed, then I realized I had slipped. The dream catcher was on his shoulders and covered his left chest. Only one of the dangling feathers was visible on his arm and no one would be able to tell what it was from that. I'd seen all his tattoos while I was at his place.

"That was amazing," he said, his eyes studying me with a speculative gleam.

"Was I right?"

"How did you know about the dream catcher?"

I should have known he wouldn't let me get away with that. "During baseball," I said, stammering.

He smirked. "What about it?"

"Well, you guys sometimes run around shirtless. I must have seen it then."

"So you've been checking me out?"

I rolled my eyes. "No."

The smile he gave me said he didn't believe me, but I'd rather he thought I'd checked him out than the truth. He pulled down his sleeve, and then he lifted up his bag and removed the books.

For the next hour, we went over the chapters he'd read since yesterday. He was serious about finishing the book by next Friday and ahead of his class. Torin got tired of keeping an eye on us and left. Soon after, sounds came from the garage. The hour crept by. I got us sodas and water. An hour turned into one and half.

"That was amazing. Now I can go clubbing without feeling guilty," Beau said, packing up his things.

"Where are you going?"

"We haven't decided yet. Do you want to come with us?" he asked and wiggled his eyebrows. "You can bring Torin." Or not was implied.

"No, thanks. I have..." I almost said I had lessons. "To help my mom and Femi take care of my dad."

His expression grew serious. "How is he doing?"

I shrugged. "Pretty well, actually, but it's terminal and he doesn't have long."

Beau shook his head. "I don't know how you can stay so positive and nice. I'd be fu... a total mess."

"No, you wouldn't. You're a survivor, Beau. Besides, death can sometimes be merciful. My father won't have any more pain, and his soul can finally rest in a better place."

He studied me as though seeing me for the first time, then rubbed his nape, pink coloring his chiseled cheeks. He looked down and murmured, "You're a lot different than what I thought."

I made a face. "What do you mean?"

A lopsided grin curled his lips. "A girl like you is supposed to be the Queen B. I mean you're hot, the most popular girl at school, and you happen to date him,"—he jerked his thumb toward the garage—"Mr. Royal Blood."

"Noble," I corrected, laughing.

"Same difference. I thought you agreed to help me just to get something to write about in college essays or to tell your friends that you were helping the school's fuck up, but you're nice and sweet. I mean, you're just like a normal girl."

I laughed and punched the air. "Yes!"

"What?" he asked looking thoroughly confused.

"That's the nicest thing anyone has said to me in a long time. Normal. Yeah, I like being normal." I wagged my finger at him. "But just so we're clear. You're not a fuck up, and if anyone asks why I'm doing this, it's because I can have something to write in my college essay. I have a rep to protect too."

Beau laughed. I walked him to the door. A thoughtful expression settled on his face when we stopped. Then he appeared to come to some decision because he smiled.

"You were right about my tats." He yanked off his sweatshirt and tucked the sleeve of his T-shirt. "This," he pointed at the snarling dog near his wrist, "represents my father. He left when I was five, a year after my sister Becca was born with a rare genetic disease. He couldn't handle the fact that she wasn't perfect. She died when I was twelve." He pointed at the butterfly hovering above the dog, overshadowing it in beauty and size. "That's Becca. Death freed her from pain and the vicious people who pointed and stared. She was beautiful. People didn't see how her smile lit up a room. How sweet and kind she was, how pure her heart was." He smiled, his eyes full of nostalgia. "She loved dream catchers. Hers is keeping my demons away."

My throat closed and I tried hard not to show it. "Do you see your father?"

He shook his head and rubbed his eyes. "Nah. He plays for the Muckdogs, but I plan to become a better player than he'll ever be."

I had no idea who the Muckdogs were, but I now knew what motivated Beau and it was heartbreaking. If he failed, then what? Torin entered the house, saw us, and paused when he saw us standing by the door. I gave him a weak smile.

"Thanks for the food, man," Beau called out to Torin and patted his stomach. "Good stuff. I'll see you Monday after school, Raine," he added, his attention shifting to me.

I nodded and opened the door. Then I saw his truck. "Oh, you're driving…" I caught myself before saying your father's truck. "A new truck?" I finished.

"Hardly new. It's my stepfather's Dodge. Mine conked out, so he let me borrow his." He chuckled. "Which is like saying turtles flew today."

Somehow I knew what he meant. His stepfather had surprised him. Maybe our conversation had finally penetrated the old man's thick skull. I waved to Beau as he took off then went back inside the house.

"An hour and a half?" Torin asked.

I ignored his griping, walked to where he stood wiping his hands on a paper towel, and hugged him. "The world is a cruel, cruel place. That guy has been through so much."

"You're getting too close, Freckles. The trick is to help them without becoming emotionally involved."

Easy for him to say. *I trust you. Completely.* He'd lied. The display at school today was all about putting Beau in his place. I might have been insecure about us, but he was possessive. His behavior this evening just confirmed it.

I grabbed his hand and pulled him to the family room couch and sat on his lap. "Just hold me and never let go."

He chuckled. "I don't intend to." It was a while before he asked, "Tell me what's wrong with him."

"There's nothing *wrong* with Beau. He's on the right track, and I am going to make sure he stays on it if it's the last thing I do."

Torin groaned. "I was afraid of that." He planted a kiss on my temple. "How about I make us popcorn while you pick a movie?"

"Really?" He always bitched about my selection. I got up and went for the remote. "Anything?"

"As long as it's not reruns of *Supernatural.*"

"Aw, come on. I didn't complain when I sat through five Furious This and Furious That movies."

He laughed. "That's because you fell asleep. No Supernatural."

"Oh crap! Lavania." I raced to the mirror portal and engaged my runes at the same time. It opened into the mansion's foyer.

The lights were on, but the mansion was too quiet. "Anybody home?" I called out, angled my head, and listened. "Andris? Ingrid?"

A door opened upstairs and Lavania appeared in the balcony. I met her at the foot of the stairs.

"About your premonition..."

"It's okay. I'm not going to stop it and interfere with Torin's case."

She smiled. "Good girl. It's not going to be easy doing what you do, honey. You'll have to choose your battles. And even then, you'll win some and lose some."

Beau's face flashed in my head. "No. I plan to win the battles I choose."

She chuckled. "Spoken like a true teenager. Sometimes I forget you're one. Okay. No lessons tomorrow. I have to talk to the Council about something. I might have some good news to share when I come back."

I hoped it was about Andris becoming Torin's partner. "Well. Knock 'em dead." I waved and headed for the portal.

"How's your tutoring?"

I stopped just before using the portal. "It's going great."

"Make sure you don't get too attached to him."

Lavania too? "I won't."

~*~

Coffee woke me up. There was a cup by my bed and it was still hot, which meant Torin had just left. Onyx was curled up at the foot of my bed, cleaning herself.

"Good morning, Onyx."

Is it?

Okay, she was in one of her moods. I got up and walked to the window. When I didn't see Torin, I headed downstairs. The smell of something burning reached me, and I knew Mom must be cooking.

Sure enough, I entered the kitchen to find her cracking eggs, and something was bubbling on the stovetop. She was still in her pajamas, flowing lingerie, and a matching robe.

"Something smells good," I fibbed, turning off the stove. Whatever she was cooking had spilled over. Worse, it looked like puke.

"Morning, sweetheart." She cracked an egg. "Did you bring your laundry downstairs?"

"No." I looked around. "Is Femi with Dad?"

"She'll be here. I'm taking care of you and your dad this morning before I head to Seattle to check on things. I'm only going to be gone for a few hours, then I need to talk to Hawk." She picked up a whisk and started beating the eggs. The bowl was slowly creeping toward the edge of the counter. I watched it with morbid fascination. "Oh, and I promised your father we'd go for a drive today. It's a beautiful day. Did you know Torin took him out yesterday while Femi was out shopping? You have a winner there, hun. Can you check on that?" She pointed towards the stove.

My head was starting to spin from the way she hopped from topic to topic. I had no idea Torin took Dad for drives, but it explained why he'd borrowed my car.

I studied the mess. "What is this supposed to be, Mom?"

She chuckled. "Cream of Wheat?"

More like lumps of wheat. I used the spoon she'd set by the stove and tried to stir the mixture. It was stuck to the pan. I dumped the whole thing in the sink and got a different pot, and started another batch. Dad's appetite had improved, but he was still on a low-fiber diet.

"Oh no, it got overcooked?" Mom wailed when she saw the pot in the sink.

"Yep. Why don't you let me finish here while you, uh, get ready for reaping?"

She looked relieved. "You sure?"

"Dad likes my omelets better than Femi's," I fibbed.

"Thanks, sweetheart. The bacon is in the microwave." She blew me a kiss and took off. Just before she headed upstairs, she stopped. "Did Torin tell you where he and Andris were headed so early in the morning?"

"No." I got out my cell phone and called Torin. It went unanswered. I tried Andris. Again, no response. Strange. He and his cell phone were joined at the hip.

I finished making the Cream of Wheat and omelet. The bacon might be in the microwave, but she hadn't started it. I hated microwaved bacon. I threw some in a pan. Breakfast was almost ready when Dad walked out of the bedroom. I hadn't seen him on his feet in weeks.

"Are you sure you should be doing that?" I asked, hurrying to his side. I put an arm around his waist.

"What do you think Femi and I do when you're at school?" He put an arm around my shoulder. "We run and jog, and throw parties."

"Ha-ha, very funny." I waited until he sat, handed him the paper, then finished with the bacon. He put aside the newspaper when I joined him.

"Mom! Breakfast."

Dad shook his head and shot me a censuring look. "You can do better than that. Find her, or create an air portal to where she is."

I grinned. "I need an artavus to create a portal, Dad. Otherwise, I have to use a mirror portal with runes. Besides, she's changing. Well, what do you think?" I indicated the table.

"This looks nice, pumpkin," he said. "And now for the taste." He served himself, his movements slow and unsteady. Then he picked up a spoon and sampled the Cream of Wheat. "Nice. I can taste cinnamon, nutmeg, and fresh apples." He took another scoop. "Granny Smith. Cooked to perfection. Have you been taking lessons from Torin?"

I grinned. Even if it tasted like goop, he'd say it was perfect. I never did wrong in his eyes. I was Daddy's girl. "Nope. I watched you. Next time, I'll make blueberry pancakes."

He pointed his spoon at me. "No. I plan to make those one more time before I check out."

My throat closed and tears rushed to my eyes. He always made blueberry pancakes with extra berries on my birthdays. I hoped he'd be around for my next one. In less than four months, I was going to be eighteen.

"Here I am," Mom announced as she floated into the room. As usual, she nailed the Boho chic style. Long skirt, lacy duster, charm bracelets galore and a necklace. She looked like my idea of a witch, not me and my jeans and layered tees.

"You look beautiful," I said.

"Thank you, sweetie." She dropped a kiss on Dad's forehead and took the chair beside his and scooted closer. "We need to talk accessories for your prom dress. Then I want you to try it on for us. I'm thinking..."

We let her dominate the conversation. I didn't care. I couldn't remember the last time the three of us had sat down for a meal together. Watching them reminded me how lucky I was to have them as parents. They raised me with love and laughter. Open displays of affection and passion, sometimes embarrassingly so. But I wouldn't trade them for Beau's. Thinking about Beau reminded me of his sister and death. The crash...

Dad headed back to the study after breakfast, and Mom left. After cleaning the kitchen, I threw my laundry in the washer and headed back to my room. Femi wasn't back yet.

I booted up my computer and went online. Half an hour of researching the airplane in my vision was enough to convince me to go back to StubHub and revisit the scene. I couldn't explain why I was doing it. It wasn't like I was going to do something about the crash. And watching the scene play out was gut wrenching. I couldn't explain my need to know every detail of that day, including where the heck the plane was coming from.

I changed and created a portal. Someone was cutting the grass. I groaned in disappointment, but then I felt magic stir and surge through me at the smell of freshly cut grass. I needed to connect with Mother Earth. It was calling to me as though I was tethered to it.

Could I get away with lying on the grass in my backyard? Or would a neighbor see me and call PMI, our local crazy house? They would. That left going to the forest. I could use the opportunity to check on whether or not the Norns had fixed it.

I pulled on my boots and reached for my new leather jacket.

I stood in front of the mirror and opened a portal. Lush vegetation stretched before me and animal sounds teased my ears.

The pull to connect with the land grew stronger. I wanted to reach out and touch every leaf and flower. Kick my boots off and feel the earth underneath my feet.

I took a step forward and froze as two hikers walked by. This couldn't be the place. The battle had taken place far from regular trails. I spent the next hour opening the portal to different parts of the forest. The tug on my magic was there, but a sickening feeling accompanied it, like something bad was lurking in the woods. It grew stronger.

Did I want to go out there alone? I didn't need someone holding my hand, but at the same time, I wasn't an idiot. Something was out there, but with lost souls after me and the Norns playing their stupid mind games, there was no knowing what could be hiding. I needed to go with someone.

Ingrid.

I checked the mansion, but it was quiet. Their housekeeper was humming under her breath while cleaning. She didn't see me, of course. Humans couldn't see portals. Ingrid was still in bed, so I didn't dare wake her. I grinned and fought the temptation to take a picture of her and tease her with it later. She'd never forgive me if I took a picture of her without makeup.

With Ingrid out of the picture, that left Cora. She was volunteering at Moonbeam Terrace this afternoon, which meant she was free this morning. Crap! I'd forgotten to tell her Lavania was gone.

I grabbed my phone and texted her. "Lessons canceled. Lavania left this morning. Going to the site. Want to come?"

When she didn't respond right away, I knew she was probably still asleep. Oh, well. I could either spend the rest of my morning frustrated or just go ahead and do it. Onyx could come with me. I needed a weapon. My shape-shifting dagger should do. I pulled open the drawer and reached inside.

It was empty.

Refusing to panic, I emptied the drawer. The dagger was gone. I hadn't moved it, which meant someone else had. The only person usually in my room was my shape-shifting cat.

"Onyx?" She wasn't in my room. I checked the closet and the bathroom, "Fur-ball, come out, come out wherever you are." She didn't hop onto my bed and lob sarcastic words at me. Frowning, I checked downstairs. She wasn't there either. Dad was watching news.

"Have you seen Onyx, Dad?"

"Not today. Is everything okay?"

"I can't find her."

"Check with Femi. She follows her around while you're gone."

Whoever took my dagger had known exactly where I kept it. My phone dinged. Cora. After a few back and forth messages, she agreed to come with me. But I didn't care about the forest anymore. Someone had stolen my dagger, the only weapon that could kill anyone, including gods and Valkyries.

14. The Forest

Maybe Torin had borrowed it. He'd seen what it did to a soul. Plus, he and I were connected in such a way that he might just have the right energy to connect with it.

I headed to his place and continued the search. Within seconds the portal opened and he walked in. My heart dropped. He looked filthy, and his clothes were ripped as though something with claws had mauled him. And what looked like blood spotted his clothes. Worries about my dagger flew out the window.

"What happened?" I asked, running to him.

"Are you okay?" he asked at the same time.

"Fine, what happened to you?" I searched his face and arms for wounds even though the runes had probably healed them already.

"The damned souls just graduated from dead bodies to animals. Soon it will be humans. What's wrong?" He stroked my cheek and my tears threatened to fall. I was such a girl.

"My dagger..." My voice hitched. "It's gone."

"How?"

"I don't know." My voice rose. "I was going to go to the forest to check on things and I wanted to make sure I had a weapon, but when I checked the drawer, it was gone. I thought you might have borrowed it."

He shook his head. "I wouldn't touch your weapon without asking you. I don't have the magic or the right." His eyebrows slammed down. "Listen, we'll get to the bottom of this. I promise. As for the forest, leave it alone."

"But the Norns—"

"Are manipulating you, again. It is their job to take care of the messes they make, not yours. We'll figure out what happened to your dagger when I come back. Right now, the others need my help." He engaged bind runes for cleansing, and the dirt and blood on his skin and clothes disappeared. "I'll be home as soon as we round the souls up and hand them over to Echo." He pressed a kiss on my temple, created an air portal, and was gone.

For a moment, I just stood there.

Why would anyone take my dagger? It didn't make sense. I headed home.

Sounds from downstairs told me Femi was back, so I headed her way and found her in the laundry room putting clothes in bags at hyper-speed. She slowed down when I appeared.

"You didn't have to do your laundry, doll," she said. "I take all of it downtown to Carly's and pick them up when they're cleaned, pressed, and folded."

Carly's was a laundromat on 4th Street. They offered self-service, but also did laundry at a fee. I had begun to wonder how Femi did laundry so fast, because I have never seen her fold anything. Made sense though since she wasn't really our employee.

"Have you seen Onyx? I've been searching for the last hour and it's like she just vanished."

"She's probably visiting her family. She disappears sometimes when you're at school too. What's going on? You look worried."

"I wanted to go for a walk and take her with me. Could she be reporting what's happening here to the goddess?"

Femi shook her head. "Why would you think that? Most familiars are loyal to their owners. Especially after you link. You two are linked, right?"

I felt a little bad for suspecting Onyx. "We are. I hate doubting her, but after my dealings with the Norns, I don't trust my judgment when it comes to supernatural beings. Although, she did save my life when we fought the *Draugar*."

"It is her job to be your eyes and ears, and warn you of any imminent danger." She went back to sorting clothes. "It was nice of you to tell Hawk about the burial site where the *Draugar* attacked your team. He's taking care of it. In fact, it was all he could talk about last night."

Femi was gone last night. Could she have taken my dagger? Once again, I felt bad suspecting someone I cared about, but I had to know.

"So Hawk was your date last night?"

She dismissed my words with a wave of her hand. "You don't call someone as distinguished as Hawk a date. Dates are fruit. Hawk is a man."

"So where did you and *your man* go yesterday?"

"He escorted me to a Broadway show and then we spent an enjoyable evening together at his secluded, beautiful mountain home." She sighed, and threw me a conspirator's glance. "I thought

I'd have to dance naked in front of the store for him to notice I was interested."

That didn't give me the answer I needed. "Have you seen my dagger?"

Femi frowned. "Your artavo?"

"No. My special dagger."

She shook her head. "I didn't know you had a special dagger."

I sighed. "I'll ask Mom." I turned and almost stepped on Onyx. "Onyx! Thank the gods. Where have you been?"

Valhalla. What's wrong?

"Come on." I took the steps two at a time. She raced up and was already waiting when I got to my bedroom. I closed the door. "My staff is missing."

She went to the other side of my bed and pawed on the handle of my trundle bed. *I hid it in here.*

I couldn't remember the last time I used the trundle bed. Eirik used to spend nights on it until he left for Asgard. The dagger was wedged between the mattress and the wall of the bed. "Why?"

Onyx hopped on my bed. *He told me to move the dagger around every day. Several times a day actually.*

I frowned. "Who?"

The young god who came to Asgard and left to join his mother.

I blinked. "Eirik? When did you talk to him?"

A few nights ago. I wasn't letting him come close to you, but I recognized him. He said to hide the dagger because they will come for it.

"Who?"

The Norns.

Air rushed from my lungs. Eirik. Always playing the hero, then disappearing. How did he know about the Norns? And why hadn't he come to see me during the day? "Why didn't you tell me?"

Onyx lay down. *He said to only tell you when you need the dagger, because the Norns can link with you any time and know where the dagger is hidden.*

I stood. "I want you to find him."

Onyx sat up. *What?*

"Eirik. You said you could find anyone. Find him and tell him I want to talk to him."

I don't like him. He joined the other side.

"Really? If he's evil, would he be warning me about the Norns? I want answers, Onyx, and he has them."

Why can't you just open a portal to wherever he is?

"I tried when we were in Florida and got nowhere. He's powerful." The doorbell rang. "Please, Onyx. Find him. I gotta go."

I left the dagger inside the trundle bed and ran downstairs. My eyes met Echo's when I opened the door. He was carrying boxes of pies. I hadn't expected Cora to bring her boyfriend. He winked.

As soon as Cora and I hugged, everything faded to black before a bright hallway appeared. Moonbeam Terrace. Again. I hadn't opened my mind, yet I was having a vision. It was the same premonition I'd had the night I met the two Grimnirs.

Cora entered the hallway, saw them and broke into a run. As she got closer, she slowed down and talked to them. I didn't hear their conversation, didn't need to. They didn't grab her or open a portal. After a few minutes, she disappeared inside a room. The Grimnirs opened a portal and left.

They'd listened to my warning. I wondered what did the trick. Probably threatening to unleash Echo on them.

I blinked and the vision disappeared, my eyes connecting with his. He stared at me with a weird expression, and I knew why. He must be seeing my glowing eyes and knew I'd gotten a vision. I held on longer to Cora, not wanting her to see my eyes and start asking questions. I hoped my magic didn't have the same effect on them as it did on Torin. I pushed the magic back. Echo nodded when my eyelids lifted and I shot him a questioning look.

"Hey," I said in greeting, hoping he didn't blurt out what he'd seen.

He grinned. "Do I get a hug?"

Of course, he wasn't going to let it go. "You're carrying pies." Cora, completely oblivious to the vibes, plucked the pies from his hands and nudged him toward me. I had no choice but to hug him.

"What was it?" he asked.

"It's nothing. She'll be okay." I stepped back. "Come inside."

Cora glanced around. "Where's Femi?"

There were no sounds coming from the laundry room, "With Dad," I said. Cora glanced toward the study, but Echo continued to stare at me. He was beginning to annoy me. "Are you coming with us?"

He nodded. "Cora insisted."

Cora elbowed him and a look I couldn't explain passed between them. She started for the kitchen and called over her shoulder. "I'll put these in the kitchen. Two are for your family and one is for Mrs. J at the nursing home."

"Quit worrying," I whispered to Echo as I walked past him. "You are the first person I'd tell if I saw something bad happening to her." Echo tended to react first and ask questions later when it came to Cora. I didn't want to give him a reason to turn on his fellow reapers over something that might be nothing.

"Promise?" he asked in a hard voice.

"Promise."

Cora was arranging the pies on the counter and didn't even notice our exchange. Her devotion to Mrs. J, the old woman she'd adopted at the nursing home, was cute. The Cora I knew a year ago wouldn't have lasted a week at a nursing home. But a stint in a mental institute because of her ability to see souls changed all that. She went two to three times a week to read to Mrs. J and keep her company. According to Cora, the poor woman's family dumped her at the nursing home and ignored her. They never visited or called.

"Someone should track down her daughter and force her to visit. It's been what? Three months since you started there and she's never visited?" I asked.

"The nurse said it's been six months. Maybe there's something you can do." The glance she gave Echo said she was only teasing. Echo's response was classic.

"Sure, hun. I can scare Mrs. J's daughter to death, then take her soul to Corpse Strand for being ungrateful."

"Good one," I said laughing.

Cora sighed and shook her head. "Don't encourage him."

I led the way to the mirror and opened a portal, going for the last area I'd seen during my search. The foreboding feeling was there, only stronger. I stepped into the forest and it hit me from all sides like thousands of ants crawling all over my skin. Goose bumps spread across my skin despite the blazing spring sun and my jacket.

~*~

Cora and Echo stayed behind me. "You're sure this is the place?" he asked.

It was. There was nothing evil lurking in the trees. It was the forest itself. It was suffering. Where was the source? I closed my eyes and let the power surge to the surface. It was coming from our left.

"I've spent the last couple of hours searching different sections of the forest, but I couldn't see—"

I gasped, the pain so sudden it paralyzed me. I stopped and pressed a hand against my stomach, but it only grew stronger. Cora ran to my side and said something. I could barely hear her above the pain. The trees were dying.

I followed the scent of death, and the closer I got the more excruciating the pain became. I should have come here right after we came back from Florida to make sure the Norns did their job.

I reached the clearing and fought tears. The devastation was too much. The trees were either snapped off at their trunks or completely uprooted. The leaves drooped, starving for water and nutrients. The roots of the uprooted ones were caked with dry soil. It wasn't just the trees. They were crushing the vegetation underneath them.

Cora appeared beside me. She didn't speak, which I really appreciated because any sign of sympathy and the tears I'd been fighting would escape.

"I hate them, Cora," I whispered. "They could have fixed this, but they chose not to." No, I should have listened to them when they'd said I must fix the forest. They said it the night of the battle and yesterday at school. This was also my fault. I was the nearest witch with the ability to communicate with nature. Why hadn't I felt their cry for help?

Cora put her arms around me and whispered, "Can you contact them to fix this?"

Yes, I could contact them, the manipulative hags, but what good would it do? I shook my head. "I'm fixing it. It's my fault."

"How do you figure that?"

"It just is." My chest hurt and my stomach felt gutted. In the back of my mind, I wondered if they were deliberately making me feel their pain because I'd failed them.

I'm so sorry, forgive me.

I wiggled out of Cora's grip and reached down to connect with one of the fallen plants. Then another. The pain in my core grew, making me feel worse. A sob rose from my chest and escaped my lips. I felt, rather than saw, Cora squat beside me. I knew she spoke, but I didn't hear a thing.

I engaged my strength and pain runes, closed my eyes, and pushed my fingers into the soil. The connection was instant. Magic flowed through my fingers and into the earth. I struggled to find the words of apology and ended up repeating the same words.

I'm sorry I have been gone so long.

There was utter silence. Even the birds stopped chirping. Yet I felt the forest come alive. I didn't need to see them to know that roots sank back into the earth and trees lifted. Branches reattached themselves to the bigger stems, and water flowed upwards again to the leaves and flowers.

The birds and the insects went back to their singing. Leaves swayed in the breeze and hugged the sun rays. I felt weak and drained, yet my magic still burned hot. I still didn't understand my powers.

I opened my eyes, stood, and looked around.

Beautiful.

Every tree, bush, and vine was thriving again. They whispered their appreciation. I laughed, moving from tree to tree. Branches swayed as though to show off leaves that no longer looked starved for food and water. Flowers showered me with their scent, their colors so vibrant it hurt to look at them.

I felt rather than saw Torin arrive. My connection to him was equally magical. I had stopped trying to understand it.

Images of him walking toward me while I danced with the trees flashed in my head. Same indulgent smile. Same intense look in his eyes. Like he couldn't take another breath unless I was in his arms. I wanted him to look at me like that every day.

I floated to him and he lifted me up, arms tight around my waist, sapphire blues reflecting the skies.

"You just couldn't resist coming here, could you?" he scolded.

"It was hurting, Torin. I created a portal to this place and all I felt was decay and pain. Now look at it. I fixed it. It's beautiful, isn't it?"

"Yes," he said, frowning.

"Stop frowning and dance with me," I whispered.

He chuckled. "There's no music."

"There is. You're just not listening."

He angled his head and pretended to listen. "Now that you mention it, I think I hear it." He turned around, laughing. He was so graceful. I closed my eyes and welcomed the energy pulsing through me. When I opened my eyes, Torin had stopped moving. Funny, I hadn't realized it.

His eyes were brilliant in their intensity. "I'm crazy about you, Freckles."

I grinned. "I know."

"Even when you disobey my orders, get drunk on magical energy, and dance in the woods like a wood nymph, you complete me."

Tears rushed to my eyes.

"No, no, don't cry." He lowered me to the ground, hands tightening around my waist. "Don't spoil this perfect moment."

"Nothing could ever spoil this moment." I put my arms around his neck and kissed him. For a brief moment, everything else disappeared except us. The moment. The kiss. With both of our runes blazing, my magic flowing through my veins, every nip, lick, and touch became enhanced until I couldn't tell where he began and I ended. And I could swear that the forest became a part of us.

When he lifted his head, I rested my cheek on his chest and we continued to sway while he stroked my hair. I liked to believe that he could hear the music in the forest, but I knew he was only indulging me.

"I keep having visions of us," I said.

He chuckled. "You're not supposed to see your own future."

I hated leaving his arms, but this was important. I had to see his reaction. "I know, yet I keep seeing us. When I saw you walk towards me, I saw visions of us in these woods. I was dancing and you were watching me. Then you lifted me into your arms, but it was different from today. It was dark and we were alone. Then there was the shower yesterday." My cheeks warmed, remembering the moment.

His eyes darkened. "What is it?"

"I think another witch is projecting images into your head again."

I nodded. Before the battle against the Immortals, a witch had created illusions and totally screwed with my head.

"I haven't sensed any Witches at school or in town since last weekend." I frowned, trying to remember some of the things the Norns had said that night. The euphoria from winning had made me forget their annoying presence, except for their smug smiles.

Someone was playing mind games with me. Eirik might help me figure things out. He was chummy with Witches and had issued the Call that had brought them to help us. If a witch were in town, he'd know about it.

"Let's ditch them," Torin whispered.

I blinked, focusing on him. "Who?"

He chuckled and turned my head, so I could see Cora and Echo. They were by the trees to our right. I'd completely forgotten about them. But then again, whenever I was in Torin's arms, nothing and no one else mattered.

"Say yes," he whispered, his breath warm and stimulating on my ear. "I can open an air portal right now that leads straight to my place. We could spend the afternoon just the two of us. I have these things I've been dying to try." He bit my earlobe, sending sensations through me. "You'll love them."

More fantasies. I would love nothing more than to make-out with him the entire afternoon, but I knew he was under the influence of my magic. He probably forgot his soccer team was playing this afternoon. "Okay, but what about the game?"

Torin looked at his watch and swore softly under his breath. "Hel's Mist. I'd completely forgotten about it. I'm meeting the students in less than two hours. Are they coming too?"

"No, Cora is volunteering at a nursing home this afternoon, but I'm bringing Ingrid. I may have to drag her out of bed. When I checked on her earlier, she was still asleep."

"They didn't come home until this morning. I had to drag Andris out of bed too. It's like every pissed off Immortal's soul had minions of dark souls. This time, they're using dogs."

"Bastards."

"Nice souls use electronics to communicate, but evil ones don't care what bodies they use. When they get tired of animals, they might target humans."

My eyes flew to Cora and Echo. Souls were attracted to Cora like moths to a flame because of the runes Maliina, Ingrid's evil sister and Andris' ex, had etched on her. It didn't matter whether the souls were good or evil. I'd seen her become unconscious for hours after a soul entered her body. The effect of being possessed by an evil one could be permanent. "We have to protect Cora, Torin."

"Echo said he'd deal with any soul that dares to come near her."

"That's ridiculous. He can't be around her twenty-four-seven. I'm telling Cora everything. Then we'll sit down and come up with a way to keep her safe."

"Okay, Freckles. We'll do this your way, but be warned. Echo won't like it."

"I don't care. This is about her, not him. Cora would not be going through this if it weren't for me," I reminded him.

"No, luv. Maliina targeted her because she thought Andris liked you. Her insane jealousy did this, not you."

I sighed. That was true too, but still...

Torin chuckled and pressed his forehead against mine. "Will you take a rain check for this afternoon? I'll make it up to you on Friday after my birthday surprise."

His birthday. Crap! I'd completely forgotten about it. I needed to buy him something special. "What surprise?"

He pinched my nose. "If I tell you, it won't be a surprise, will it? Come on."

We walked toward Cora and Echo. I blew out air; my head was ready to explode. So much was happening when all I wanted was a moment to breathe and be a normal teenager in love with an awesome guy. I should be planning his birthday party, shopping for his birthday present, not worrying about Witches projecting images into my head, dark souls possessing my best friend, and Norns.

Cora might have some birthday ideas. She'd dated before and knew what guys liked while Torin was my first real boyfriend. Eirik didn't count because our attempt to date had been doomed before it had even started. Having grown up together, we were like brother and sister.

Dang it, I had to tell Torin about Eirik and the dagger. Another thing we had to deal with. Maybe this evening after the game. If I told him now, he'd want to track Eirik down himself. Unfortunately, Eirik was an expert at disappearing until he was good and ready to be found. For once I wish he would make one of his dramatic entrances.

Just before Torin created a portal, I felt the Norns' presence and looked around. Were they happy now? I'd done exactly what I swore I wouldn't do—follow their order.

15. Stupid Posters

My life should be simple. Filled with love and new discoveries, not worrying about Norns and their shenanigans, and evil souls coming after my best friend. I deserved to have Torin to myself just once without dealing with them. I deserved to be happy, even if it was just for one day.

"You two need the forest to yourselves?" I teased Echo and Cora, trying to act like I didn't care that the Norns were around.

Cora pulled from Echo, her face turning red. Echo wore a smug smile. I walked past them and through the portal Torin had created. Torin followed then Cora and Echo.

"Let's hang out, guys," I added. Cora had to know about the dark souls.

"What she means is we need to talk, so grab a seat while *I* make lunch. You forgot to say please, Freckles."

Hearing the teasing in his voice only hiked my frustration. I closed the gap between us, savoring the moment, the love in his eyes.

"Like this?" I asked, then reached up and claimed him with a kiss that dared anyone to deny me the moment, until I was drunk with the taste of him. When I stepped back, he stared at me with amazement and staggered.

"Hel's Mist, Freckles," he muttered then turned and stumbled toward the kitchen.

I grinned, saw the shocked look on Cora's face, and shrugged. "I needed that."

"What was that all about?"

"Using my powers unleashes this thing inside of me, and I just want to—" Why was I lying to her? This had nothing to do with my magic. This was me, claiming my man. There shouldn't be an explanation. It was one of those things that happened because it was right. My face warmed, I shrugged. "Kissing him makes my world right again. Come on, let's go eat."

Femi grinned when she heard me. I'd been so lost in my funk that I hadn't noticed her. She winked at me and made a beeline for Cora and Echo. While she talked to them, I followed Torin to the kitchen.

"Need help preparing lunch?"

"No, sit." Torin pointed at the stool. "You distract me."

"And that's bad how?"

"Because I have a game and my head needs to be with my team, not my girlfriend. Quit pouting."

"I don't pout." But I was, and hated myself for it. Self-pity was such a wasted emotion.

Sighing, I sat and watched him get bread and cold cuts from the fridge. I loved that he was so comfortable in my house and knew where everything was. Eirik used to be just like him. He came and went as he pleased. Cleared my fridge without worrying that my parents would be pissed. I wanted that Eirik back, not the one that appeared in the middle of the night with a dire warning.

I reached for one of the pies Cora had brought and grabbed a knife to cut a slice, but Torin snatched the pie out of the way. "No pie *before* my sandwiches."

I glared at him. He touched the top of my nose and left a dollop of mayo. I swatted at his hand and tried to lick it, but failed. He just laughed.

"Stinker. I'll get you for that." I went to get a paper towel. When I turned around, Echo and Cora were in the kitchen, and something was up. What had I missed? Cora's eyes volleyed between the two men. She looked ready to read them the riot act. Echo's arms were folded, his expression unyielding.

Torin shot him an exasperated look, then focused on Cora. "The Earl lost about six Immortals, and their souls disappeared before the fight ended. They might be gunning for us."

With a whole army of dark souls. Why was he making it sound like it was no big deal? "*We* just want to make sure we're on the same page on what to do if they bother *you*," I chimed in, my eyes meeting Cora's.

She frowned, but she didn't seem scared or worried. She just nodded and turned to whisper something to Echo. Cora never ceased to amaze me. Ever since Maliina etched dark runes on her, she was like a different person. Confident. Serious. Nothing seemed to bother her. But then again, it takes a lot of guts to willingly allow souls to possess you just so you can listen to their last wishes. I was kind of proud of her. Instead of whining about what Maliina had done to her, Cora had embraced her runes and found a new purpose—helping souls find closure.

Torin and I exchanged glances.

"Did you already talk to her about the *Draugar* attacks?" he asked.

"No, but he,"—I indicated Echo with a nod—"might have."

We all sat down at the table, and I tried to appear happy during lunch. I even fooled Cora because she didn't once look at me questioningly. Torin wasn't fooled though. He pulled me down onto his lap, and stroked the palm of my hands until I relaxed against him.

"I think you should go on helping souls freeze until we round up all the souls of the Earl's Immortals," Torin suggested. Echo seemed to like the idea, but not Cora.

"What if I knew the people before they died?" she asked. "I've helped quite a few from the local hospitals and nursing homes, and I'm not going to stop just because of a few angry souls."

The guys protested, but I knew Cora. You didn't tell her what to do once she made up her mind about something. She and I were alike in that aspect.

"Don't gang up on her," I jumped in, which earned me a censuring look from Torin. It didn't bother me. There was nowhere written I had to take his side on every issue. "I agree with her. She can't stop helping others out of fear." Both men groaned. "We have to come up with another way to protect her."

"Thanks for the support," Cora said, and we high-fived.

Torin glared at Echo. "You need to reason with your woman."

Echo laughed. "How about you focus on yours? I don't see her agreeing with you. One kiss and you turn into a doormat."

Torin glanced at me. "Really?"

"We don't kiss," I said, leaning into him. "We affirm. With a touch, a look, or a smile." I kissed him again. But he took over and ran with it, making me forget we had an audience. Or maybe it was payback for the kiss I'd given him earlier, because when he lifted his head I didn't want him to stop.

"Where were we?" Torin asked, having recovered. I was still trying to come back to earth. "Oh yeah. You said you had everything covered when Cora's not at school," he said, looking at Echo.

"Yep. They won't bother her, or if they do, I'll know."

"What if you're at the bottom floor in Hel?" Torin shot back.

"I'll know, Valkyrie," Echo vowed.

I was sure an argument between the two was inevitable, and then I'd have to kick them out of my house. My dad might have accepted my new life, but I didn't want him subjected to a supernatural testosterone showdown. Since I was already on Torin's lap, I did what I could to calm down the situation. I linked our hands and stroked the back of his neck, until he calmed down.

"Alright, the others will cover the school," Torin said. "If you see any soul you don't recognize, find Raine, Blaine, or Ingrid. Yeah, I'm bringing them into the loop," he added when Echo scowled. "Andris and I are gone most of the day. We only have one class this semester, and even that's for show. Do you carry your artavus to school, Cora?"

"Yes. I've used it to threaten a few difficult souls."

"Make good on your threat next time," Torin said. "Immortals' souls are not like Mortals'. They're sneaky and will not leave your body until they're good and ready. By then it'll be too late."

"Not if I have anything to do with it." Echo's voice was chilling.

"Your scythe won't work on them the way it does on regular souls, Echo," Torin shot back. "Once they're inside her, there's not much you can do unless you slice her open."

"Is that supposed to be funny?" Echo shot back.

Things were getting heated again. This time, I took his hand and slipped it under my shirt. And just like that, he was distracted. "No, it's not," he said, speaking calmly. "She's one of us and we'll do whatever it takes to protect her, but I want you to be realistic."

While Echo cursed, I elbowed Torin. "You didn't have to be so graphic."

"We're dealing with dark souls, Raine. Graphic is all I have."

"If a possession happens, I can take care of it," I said. "My staff is a lot more powerful than a scythe or an artavus. You've seen what it can do." Torin didn't look too happy with my suggestion, but I got Echo and Cora's attention. Echo smirked for reasons I couldn't explain and shot Torin a mocking look. He had a twisted sense of humor so I rarely tried to understand him.

"Staff?" Cora asked.

"The dagger the Norns gave me is not what it seems."

"Really? What is it? Can we see it?" Cora asked.

I shrugged. "Sure." I saw the question in Torin's eyes and added, "It's upstairs."

I got up and headed upstairs. Onyx was on the window seat staring outside when I arrived. Cora was supposed to be behind me, but I heard her voice mingle with the guys' downstairs. "Did you find Eirik?"

No, but I'll keep looking. He could be using dark magic to hide his whereabouts.

"Dark magic? He wouldn't use that. He could just not be in this realm. Have you thought of that, Miss Glass Half Empty?" I pulled out the bed, but the dagger wasn't there. "Where is it?"

Why?

"I want to show it to my friend."

The blonde? I don't like her.

"So? You don't have to like all my friends. Where did you hide the dagger?"

Onyx sat up, her ears twitching. *How can you be friends with her? She has dark runes. Dark runes are associated with dark energy. Then to make it worse, she is dating a Grimnir. Grimnir will fight against the gods, our enemies.*

I counted down from ten to one and prayed Cora didn't catch me strangling my cat. "For starters, Fur-ball, I haven't decided yet whose side I'm on, so I don't care who fights who or where. Second, dark runes or not, she's a good person. She didn't ask for the stupid runes, but she's doing what she can with them, so back off. Third, I choose my friends, not you."

Then I don't want to meet her. I don't want her to know anything about me. If she touches me, I will scratch her eyes out. She hopped onto the floor, but I picked her up and put her back on the window bench.

"Where are you going? I need my dagger."

Top shelf in your closet. Can I leave now?

"No. How did you get it up there?" I found the dagger and turned around when she didn't respond. She was still on the window seat. "Are you sulking?"

I don't sulk. Can I go now?

I sighed. "It's up to you if you want to go or stay," I said. "And if you're nice, I'll take you downstairs a—" I heard Cora coming. "*And introduce you to Cora and Echo, and you'll see that they're really nice people.*"

No. Keep her away from me and don't tell her anything about me or why I'm here.

She sounded scared.

Cora entered the room. "Who are you talking to?"

I glanced over my shoulder and made a face. Standing, I tried to block her from seeing Onyx. The poor cat was petrified. "A cat."

"You have a cat? Since when?" Cora moved closer and peered at Onyx.

Please, don't let her touch me.

"Since last night," I fibbed. "She refused to leave my room, and now I'm stuck with her."

"Oh, she's cute." She reached out to pet Onyx and the cat hissed. Cora snatched her hand back. "Is she feral?"

"No, just weird. She hates everyone, except me." I hoped that would stop the questions. I even lifted my dagger, hoping her attention would shift away from my petrified cat, but Cora was fixated.

"Even Torin?" Cora asked.

"Yep. He calls her Evil Claws while Femi insists I name her Bastet or Isis." I rolled my eyes and waved the dagger again. "Anyway, I got the dagger."

For a moment, I thought I had her attention, but Cora continued to study Onyx. "Is she your familiar?" she asked.

"She's an *unwanted* guest. I'd tell you how I got her, but that's a story for another time. Let me show you how the dagger transforms."

Cora grinned as she watched the dagger shift and grow longer. "It's just like Echo's staff. You have to show him."

I found myself looking at Onyx. She didn't look so scared now. Still… "Can we do it another time? Torin is leaving for California for a game and I promised I'd go with him." I left the dagger on my bed and ushered her out of the room. "Oh, do me a favor and be careful. These dark souls are not kidding."

"I'm sure they're not all bad," she said.

"Oh, yes, they are. If one approaches you, find me."

Cora rolled her eyes and said, "Fine."

~*~

We headed downstairs to rejoin the boys. Soon after, Cora and Echo headed out the front door.

As soon as they drove away, Torin created a portal to his place. "I need to be at the stadium before the students start arriving. Where was the dagger?"

"Onyx hid it."

He chuckled. "Why?"

"Long story. I'll tell you later. Now you need to go." I pushed him through the portal and waved.

"I'll save two seats for you and Ingrid," he said, already changing his shirt. "Remember, two o'clock."

It was cute to see him so excited. Before heading upstairs, I grabbed a can of catnip. Onyx deserved a treat after that mess with Cora. Once she knew Cora and Echo, she'd change her mind.

When I got to my bedroom, she wasn't there and the dagger was gone again. Damn cat.

I sprinkled some catnip near her favorite sleeping spot and changed my shirt, replaced my jeans with Capri pants, and applied makeup. I checked my watch. Cora should be arriving at the nursing home.

I opened a portal and kept an eye on her. She was talking to the two Grimnirs. I couldn't hear their conversation, but if they tried something, I was ready to help her. In fact, the male Grimnir could see me. I sighed with relief when Cora left them and disappeared inside Mrs. J's room. I waved to the Grimnirs. The man bowed his head. The woman finally saw me. She wasn't amused.

I closed the portal and left for the mansion to find Ingrid.

~*~

She was with Blaine in the kitchen, and was still in her bathrobe although she'd put on makeup. Blaine was dressed like a mechanic again. "You're not dressed?"

"Why?" She took a bite of her sandwich, gave me a look that said she had no intention of moving, and sank back into her seat. "I'm not going anywhere today."

My jaw dropped. "What? We talked yesterday about watching the soccer game at the StubHub today. And I texted you two hours ago."

She shook her head. "California? I just woke up, Raine. Haven't checked my phone, still fighting a hangover. All I plan to do is crawl back in bed and watch a chick flick."

I plopped onto the nearest chair. "I'll watch anything with you if you come with me. It's been a crappy day, and I don't want to sit alone with a bunch of parents screaming their kids' names and waving stupid posters." When she just shrugged, I glanced at Blaine. "Want to come? I'll wait for you to wash up."

He shook his head, his expression unreadable. "Sorry. I have to work."

I groaned. "Doing what?"

"Helping out a bunch of bikers."

"You'll watch a movie with me?" Ingrid asked, standing up.

"Yes! Any time. You name it, and I'll be there."

"Okay." She removed her robe to reveal shorts and a tank top. Then she picked up a sign she'd put upside down, lifted it. I saw what she'd written.

'GO JACE!'

"You stinker!" I punched her arm. I shot Blaine a look. "You knew?"

"Nope." But his smile said he was in on it.

"Let's go then." I jumped up, but Ingrid caught my arm.

"Wait. I made this one,"—she extended her hand and Blaine gave her a second sign—"for you." She lifted it.

'GO GALAXY!'

She'd used bright yellow on a blue background. Both were the club's colors. White, sparkly stars added pizzazz to the poster. "When did you have time to do this?"

"Torin stopped by on his way, uh, ten minutes ago. I sent Blaine to get the supplies, so it took about two minutes to do both." Hyperspeed had its perks.

I'd never attended a soccer game. Driven past a few, yes, but never cheered for anyone. I guess I was going to carry a stupid poster after all. Ingrid insisted on redoing my makeup, and then we left.

~*~

We got to the stadium before the game started. In fact, the players weren't even warming up yet. There were a lot more people in the audience this time. Parents and siblings of the players were wearing team colors—navy-blue T-shirts and jerseys with gold/yellow writing and the Galaxy logo—and carried posters with the name of the team and their kids.

Andris waved us over from the front seat. "Nice turnout," I said.

"Serious rivalry between Galaxy and the team from San Diego," he explained and winked at Ingrid when he saw the posters. "Like old times, huh?"

She just grinned, but I was intrigued. "So this is not the first time she's made posters?"

"No," she said. "I've been cheering for whatever team they're coaching or Torin's playing with for as long as I can remember. It's either pom-poms or posters. I can make them in my sleep."

And she wasn't kidding about cheering. Ingrid morphed right before my eyes. Granted she'd been doing that the last week, but this Ingrid... She cat-whistled when the teams entered the field. It was a little embarrassing. Okay, it was really embarrassing. The way she was going on, one would think she had a kid on the team. I slouched low in my seat and tried to make myself invisible. Andris noticed and laughed.

"You'll get used to her," he whispered. Then he nodded at someone behind us. I figured it was his latest conquest, until I turned and my eyes met Taylor's, Jace's father.

Taylor senior didn't carry a poster like the other parents. But then again the mothers were the ones who did the carrying. Most fathers acted like the game wasn't that important, but they were probably living vicariously through their children. If they knew their kids would be dead in two weeks, I'd bet they'd cheer their hearts out.

No morbid thoughts, please. I couldn't afford to start thinking about the plane crash now. There was nothing I could do about it.

Andris left to join the coaches. Torin looked toward us once before the referees blew the whistle and the game began. I didn't know anything about soccer, except the basics—players kicked the ball to the opposite goal and the goalie blocked it or they scored. According to my father's brief tutorial during the week, players could use any part of their bodies except their hands. I assumed they had offense and defense like in football. Prepared to be bored, I sipped my bottled water.

The other team's uniforms were red, making them stand out. Galaxy wore white shorts and shirts with slanted navy-blue stripes crossing from their left shoulders to their right hips. The word

Herbalife dominated the shirt on the chest. I wondered what *Herbalife* meant. Maybe they were into herbs and this was their way of saying Have-a-life. I almost giggled at my thoughts. This was going to be a long game.

Fifteen minutes into the game, I joined Ingrid. We cheered and screamed. We high-fived each other when the team scored and voiced our frustrations when the opposing team came too close to scoring or did score. Ingrid had no problem yelling at the referees when they gave a penalty to one of the Galaxy kids. If the parents thought we were crazy supporting kids we didn't know, they didn't show it. They were right behind us and we high-fived them too.

Jace was amazing. He was possibly the smallest player, yet he was unstoppable. Agile. Torin knew when to play him and when to pull him out. At half time, his father joined us.

"I'm Zachary Taylor, Jace's father," he said, offering his hand.

I shook it. "I'm Raine and she's Ingrid." I indicated Ingrid who waved.

"Do you teach at my son's school?" he asked, his eyes flickering between Ingrid and me.

The makeup Ingrid had put on me must make me look older. "No, Mr. Taylor. We are friends with Coach St. James. We thought we'd come and cheer the team and, uh, Jace. Ingrid made the signs."

The look he threw Ingrid was full of gratitude. "Thank you. Both of you."

The second half went faster, and when the referees blew the whistle, Galaxy had decimated San Diego nine to two.

"Semifinals!" was whispered and shouted as parents left the stands and ran into the field to congratulate and hug their sons. The fathers puffed out their chests, but none as much as Taylor senior.

A woman brushed past me, gripped my arms, and said, "Thanks for the support..." The rest of her words faded away with the field and empty seats.

The stadium was packed, the screaming deafening as the large airplane nosedived into the crowd. I wasn't on the grassy bench anymore, but on the stands on the east side. Around me were the Academy students and their parents, shoving and jumping over each other to get out of the way. They weren't seated in the path of the plane, but that didn't stop the mass exodus or their hysterical screams. People pushed and scrambled away from the stands, most heading toward the upper seats and exits.

"Dad!" a voice rang out and I followed the sound to Jace.

"Jace! I'm coming." His father must have gone to get something for them to eat, because he was the only one pushing through the crowd in the opposite direction.

"No, Dad. Go back! I'm com—"

His words were cut off by a woman who knocked him down as she dragged her younger daughter. Her foot slipped off the seat and the heel of her shoes connected with Jace's ribs. My stomach lurched as he screamed, the sound mingling with others. His father didn't see the incident because the wing of the plane detached and flew across the stadium like a Frisbee, catching him and several people with it, including the woman who'd stepped on Jace. It flung them across the field and stopped right smack in the middle of the seats behind where Ingrid and I were seated minutes ago.

I didn't think Jace's dad and the woman in heels were going to make it. Jace wasn't moving. People kept stepping on him, kicking him. Not intentionally. He just happened to be on the ground as everyone was looking up and not watching where they were stepping. Because of my position, I could finally see the name of the airline written in English.

The vision cleared and I found myself seated a fair distance from the players and their parents, who were still at the edge of the field. Ingrid's arm was around me, and her hand gripped mine. From the way she was seated on the arm of the chair, she was also shielding me from prying eyes.

"You okay?" she whispered.

I stared at her in bemusement. Funny how she'd been the other girl for months. Maliina's sister. Andris' Immortal. Now she was becoming not just a friend, but someone I could depend on. I nodded.

"The woman bumped you and you froze, then your eyes started to glow. That was my cue. I caught you before you fell."

"Fell?"

"Your legs kind of gave out." She smiled at someone, and I followed her eyes to Torin, who might be talking to the parents, but was keeping us in his line of vision. Usually, Torin didn't trust anyone to watch over me. Ingrid had gained his trust.

As though she'd heard my thoughts, Ingrid added, "He was ready to take you home, but I told him the team needed him, and he actually listened." She chuckled. "Men just need a firm voice."

Or maybe he wanted me to see the entire vision. Our eyes met and I saw the concern dancing in the depths of his. I sat up as though to reassure him I was okay. The problem was I wasn't. How could I be, when so many were going to die? Jace was going to lose his father, right after losing his mother.

The parents started across the field for the American Express Stadium Club. Andris was missing, so he must have been in charge of food again. Some parents looked at us and warmth crawled up my cheeks. They must think I was a wimp. Today was the second time Torin had deserted their children and ran to my side.

"I want to go home," I whispered to Torin when he joined us.

He looked at Ingrid and without speaking, she moved away to give us privacy. Torin squatted and studied my face. "You sure?"

I nodded. "I can't eat with them and act normal when I know what's going to happen to them. And no, you're not coming home with me or I will not leave."

He grinned, stood, and offered me his hand. "Whatever you say."

Somehow I didn't think he'd give in that easily. "I mean it, Torin. I'll be okay."

"I know." He glanced at Ingrid who was a few seats away. She smiled at us, shrugged, and went back to studying her fingernails. "She'll tell me if you're not. You want to come to the club and create a portal in the restroom, or do you want to do it form here? I can shield you."

I glanced over his shoulder. The team and their parents were already across the field. The other team had already tucked their tails and left the stadium. Losing sucks.

"Shield us." I pulled my artavus from inside my boot and created a portal. It opened into my bedroom. But it wasn't empty.

Eirik was stretched out on my bed fast asleep, one leg dangling to the floor. Torin and I looked at each other.

"Were you expecting him?" Torin asked.

"Yes. I sent Onyx to find him. I'll explain later." His eyes didn't leave Eirik and he opened his mouth to argue. "Please, just feed your team. Oh, the woman that bumped into me before I got my vision?"

"Yes."

"Find out who she is."

16. Eirik

Ingrid and I stood at the foot of the bed and studied Eirik. I still couldn't get over how much he'd changed. His Chex Mix hair was longer and more wavy than curly. The guy I had known was gone. In his place was a mysterious man full of secrets and a body... Wow. He was either on steroids or some magical juice because he seemed taller and more buff. I wasn't sure how to treat this Eirik. He, on the other hand, still treated my room like his own.

"Damn, he's hot," Ingrid said.

I grinned. Eirik used to be lean with a swimmer's body and was a little on the pale side. Now, he was tanned and buff. His T-shirt had ridden up in his sleep, giving us a view of some serious six-pack.

"Yeah. He's even prettier." He'd worn black the last time I saw him. Today, he wore Levis and a T-shirt with a black trench coat.

The first time he'd appeared after visiting Asgard, he'd carried a mace or flail with a spiked round head. When he wasn't using it, it had coiled around his arm, from his hand to somewhere under his sleeve. I couldn't recall whether it was his right or left arm. He now had a mace tattooed on his right arm. The handle disappeared between his thumb and forefinger as though he was holding it.

"Aren't you going to wake him up?" Ingrid asked, walking to the other side of the bed and studying Eirik from a different angle.

"Why? Want an introduction?" I teased her.

"Why not? The first time we met I didn't know he was a god. I've never really met a god before." She tilted her head to the side and studied him from yet another angle. "He's changed. A lot."

"Yes." Yet in some aspects he hadn't. He still slept with one arm across his eyes and hogged the bed. Part of me wanted to wake him up, but another part was uneasy.

"You're just going to stand there?" Ingrid asked.

Before I could respond, Onyx entered the room. Well, not exactly entered. She stopped in the threshold and hissed.

"What, Onyx?"

Get that thing out of our room.

Thing? I was so not in the mood for her drama. I nudged Eirik's knee. He mumbled something and turned his head sideways toward Ingrid, his hand fell away from his face. He was all skin and muscles, his jawline more defined. He might be eighteen now, but he looked more like he was in his late twenties. I pushed his knee again. Harder.

His eyelids lifted to reveal unfocused amber eyes. Then they sharpened and locked on Ingrid. But instead of saying something, he turned his head and found me.

I swallowed, waiting for, I don't know, the old Eirik. Or the new, mean Eirik. Or maybe even the evil Eirik. A smile tugged at the corner of his lips as he swung his feet onto the floor and stood.

"Where's my hug, funny face?"

I leapt into his arms, tears rushing to my eyes. The old Eirik was back. I hugged him tighter. He chuckled and turned towards Ingrid, his arms not letting me go either.

"Hey, I'm Eirik," he said.

"Ingrid."

"Sorry, she's having a meltdown or I'd shake your hand," he said, talking about me as though I wasn't there, still refusing to let him go. "We've met before, right?"

"And fought on the same side. I better leave you guys. Raine..." She paused and chuckled. "Tell her I'll be at the mansion... Oh, your former house. I don't mean it's no longer—"

"It's okay," Eirik reassured her. There was a draft accompanying the portal opening and closing as she left. Only then did I lean back from Eirik. I still held on to his shirt. Fists of it in case he decided to pull a fast one and disappear again. I was being a girl again and didn't care. Eirik was back.

"You're such a drama queen," he said, wiping the wetness from my face.

"Shut up." I pushed him until he sat on my bed and sniffled as more tears threatened to fall. "You're not moving until you tell me everything. And I mean it, starting with your trip to Asgard."

"Can I get something to eat first? I'm starving."

I laughed. The old Eirik was definitely back. But I didn't want to share him with Femi and Mom or even Dad. Not yet.

"Stay here. I'll get you something. Do not move." I created a portal and was about to go through when I looked back at him. He was leaning forward, his elbows on his knees, his expression serious. He could disappear again.

I walked back and grabbed his hand. "Changed my mind. You're coming with me." He chuckled. "Cut that out. I'm not taking chances with you. You have a nasty habit of appearing to play the hero, then disappearing." Luckily, no one was in the kitchen, but there was a note on the fridge door.

'Food for you and Eirik in the stove.'

I turned and glanced at Eirik, who was already eating an apple. "How long have you been here?"

"An hour,"—he checked his watch—"and a half."

"You should have come to find me." I removed the roast and potatoes from the oven and placed it on the counter.

"You were busy cheering for Torin's team. Didn't want to get in the way." He got up to throw away the apple core and took the plates from my hand. "Besides, I got to catch up with your mother and Femi. And I decided not to eat until you got here."

"I could have gone to eat with Torin's team." I would have if I hadn't gotten that traumatic vision again.

"I knew you'd be home." He served himself enough food to feed ten people. "Remember, I'm a Seer just like you."

I got some food, but it was too early for me to eat, so I ended up watching him shove food in his mouth. He reminded me of Beau.

"So you saw me come home early in a vision?" He grinned and nodded. "Do you also project images to people's heads?" Not that I thought he was behind the visions I'd been seeing of Torin, but it didn't hurt to ask. "Do you?"

"I can, but choose not to."

"Can you tell if there're Witches in town?"

He swallowed, lifted a finger, and got up for a drink. He removed a bottle of orange juice, twisted the top off, and chugged.

"You're still as disgusting as ever," I scolded him, getting him a glass. "Mom will kill you if she finds out you're drinking her favorite juice from the bottle," I said.

"She won't know if you don't tell her," he shot back and we both laughed. It was like old times. It didn't matter how often I warned him and threatened to tell on him, he always chugged from the bottle, unless I served him the drink.

"There're Witches in town, but they came with me. Why?"

"Someone has been putting visions in my head."

"What kind?"

Warmth crept onto my face. The visions were too personal to share with him. "Can you see premonitions about yourself?"

"Nope, and my friends know better than to mess with you."

"They know about me? You mean the Norns didn't delete their memories?"

Eirik smiled mysteriously and went back to his food. I nibbled mine and watched him instead. He demolished the contents of the plate, then he started on the pie—one of the two Cora had dropped off.

"You know this withholding of information never works with me. I need answers, Eirik, so start talking."

"I'm still eating," he complained.

"So talk while you eat. Never stopped you before."

He shot me an amused look. "You do know I'm a god, right?"

"And you do know I don't give a shit, right? You're my best friend. No, my brother and I have…" My voice trembled to a stop. I took a deep breath then finished. "I've missed you."

"Here comes the waterworks," he mumbled.

I kicked him. "Shut up! I want to know what happened, so I can find a reason to forgive you for putting me through so much grief and crap for the past seven months."

He leaned back and inhaled deeply. "I've been waiting for that."

"What?" I asked.

"You getting pissed."

I took a deep breath and slowly counted backwards. Yes, I was angry with him and hurt, but this was not the time to bring that up. My eyes went to the tattoo peeking out from under his sleeve. I took his arm and pushed the sleeve back, my eyes following the mace. When I looked up, he was staring at me with sad eyes.

"I'm not mad," I said.

He snickered.

"Okay, I am pissed and hurt, you jerk. You can't disappear on me and not even bother to let me know you're okay. You are a freaking portal away. And I swear, if you ever pull a last minute appearance again and then disappear without talking to me, I will hunt your sorry ass down and make you regret it." I blew out air. "There. I'm done. Not going to rant and rave again." His lips twitched as though he was trying not to smile and I pretended not to see it. Instead, I traced his tattoo. In the next second, I dropped his arm like it was a snake and jumped. "It's alive."

"Sorry about that. I should have secured it properly."

"What do you mean?"

"I store it in me." He pushed the pie aside. "See? Unbond." He flexed his arm and runes appeared on his skin. The spiked ball of his mace peeled off his skin like a Band Aid. By the time it reached his wrist, it had leapt into his hand. He placed the weapon on the counter.

"How do you do that?"

"Magic. I project it to the mace and will it to meld with me."

"Nice. Who taught you?"

"The Witches. Everywhere I've visited, they've come out to meet me and teach me stuff. I've made friends across the globe."

I frowned. "Do they know what you are?"

He nodded, grinning. "That's why they came when I called."

He didn't seem too worried about the laws or hiding the existence of the Norse Pantheon from Mortals. Or maybe that didn't apply to the gods. "How was Asgard?"

"Beautiful." He picked up his fork and went back to eating the pie. "All they do is party and train. There's an occasional threat from the evil giants and monsters, but it's nothing like Hollywood movies depict."

"And Hel?"

A weird look crossed his face. "Complicated. Demanding. Mean and unforgiving as the realm itself. Can we talk about something else?"

So he and his mother still had issues. Onyx had said that he'd chosen her. "Why haven't you gone back to Asgard?"

"Who says I haven't?"

"My cat. Onyx."

He chuckled. "She's a crazy one. I swear I was sure she'd scratch out my eyes when I appeared in your room. She doesn't like me. Do you remember how cats and dogs would go crazy whenever we went to the animal shelter? Now I know why."

I didn't care about Onyx's hatred for my friends or the past. Eirik had neatly avoided answering my question about returning to Asgard. "Did they kick you out of Asgard? Force you to choose a side?"

He licked the fork. "This is really good." He checked the box and saw the logo. "Of course, it's from Cora's mother. She makes the best pies. Can I have whipped cream or ice cream with it?"

"Get it yourself."

He stood and pointed his fork at me. "You're forgetting again that I'm a god."

"Who happens to know his way around this house and doesn't need me waiting on him. Get over yourself."

He laughed and planted a kiss on my forehead. "I've missed you."

Before I could respond, my phone buzzed. It was Cora. She was going to be surprised to hear Eirik was back. "Hey!"

"If you don't hear from me in five minutes, find me," Cora said.

"Cora, what's going on?"

"I'm dealing with an unusual soul. Make it two minutes." Then the line went dead.

"Cora! I cannot believe that girl."

Eirik came back to the table with a can of whipped cream. "What's wrong?"

"She said she's dealing with an unusual soul, and if I don't hear from her in two minutes, I should call her. I hope she's not doing something she'll regret."

"Are she and Echo still together?"

There was no anger or animosity in his voice, just mild curiosity, but I wasn't an idiot. His refusal to answer my questions only made me more determined to find out what was going on. Why would a god spend so much time in this realm unless he couldn't go home?

"They're still together, but I'm sure you already know that. I swear if Asgardians made you choose between your mother and them…"

He chuckled. "You sound like you're ready to kick some serious ass. Whose side are you on?" He sobered up. "Have you thought about it? Where you want to live? Both sides have different things to offer. In Asgard, you'll probably have a hall with servants and your every need met. In Nornsgard, you'll be treated like their exulted leader despite being the youngest. In Hel… well, it's the same."

Material things. Who needs them? "I have, if you must know. Not that it's any of your business." He continued to watch me. "If they were to ask me now, I'd choose us."

His eyebrows shot up. "Us?"

"Earth, or Midgard. Humans. Mortals and Immortals. I'd rather warn them before I announce the beginning of the battle. Fight with them to make sure some survived, not just a select few."

Eirik smothered the pie with whipped cream. "Okay. Sounds like you know what you want."

"You're not going to lecture me about how humans are not important in the final battle? Or what the prophecy says?"

"Nope." He stuffed his face with pie while I played with my food. I dumped it in the garbage and put the leftovers away. Cora called just as promised, which was a relief. I hadn't felt like leaving to help her out while Eirik was around, which made me feel kind of bad. "Which side are you on?"

He shrugged. "I don't know yet. I'm just enjoying watching them squirm."

I shook my head. "You'd better be on my side when the battle begins."

He laughed. "The Norns want their dagger back," he said.

"Yeah, about that. Why did they come to you?"

"Because the last time they saw it, I had it pressed to your throat. They didn't see me give it to you, so they came to me and demanded I hand it over. I told them I'd lost it."

He'd slipped the dagger in my pocket the night we battled the Earl. "So you came to my room in the dead of the night to warn me? What happened to stopping by during the day? Texting? Calling? Returning the next day?"

He grinned. "Cell phone reception in Hel sucks, so I dumped mine, and your cat went feral on me that night and became a giant cat. Don't give the dagger back, Raine."

"Why do they want it so badly?"

"I don't know, but the fact they do means it's important to them, so screw them."

His sudden show of hatred surprised me. "Have they been messing with you too?"

Pink crept onto his cheeks and his eyes grew fierce. "They've been messing with me all my life. They tried to probe my mind to find it, but I surround myself with Witches, some nearly as powerful as you. Anyway, expect them to probe your head."

I remembered the incident at the stadium when they'd visited me. I'd felt a thick impenetrable shield messing with my ability to link with them. "They might already have."

"But you still have it?"

"Yes. Onyx is very good at hiding it."

He chuckled and rubbed his stomach. "Thanks for the food. Let me check something with your father, then I need to hear all about you and Torin." He picked up his mace, propped his elbow on the table, and said, "Bond."

The weapon wrapped around his arm. Runes blazing. When they dimmed, his tattoo was back. It looked awesome. He stood and started toward Dad's room. I was right behind him.

"So how long are you staying?" I asked, dodging his steps.

"A few minutes."

"A few minutes?" I screeched.

"With your dad. Dial it down a notch there, owl. I'm going to be around." He knocked on Dad's door and turned the handle, but I was right behind him. "I need to talk to him *alone*."

"And I need your cell phone number and how to contact you *before* I let you leave my sight. I'm not buying that cell phone reception crap."

"I'd forgotten how stubborn you are. I wasn't lying about my cell phone. Got rid of it a long time ago." A thoughtful expression settled on his face. "Or was it taken from me? The memories keep merging." He chuckled, his mood changing so fast I was struggling to keep up. "If you need me, send Onyx. She might not like me, but she knows how to find me. Now can I go?" He didn't wait for my response, just pushed the door open. Mom, Dad, and Femi were all in the room watching something on TV. But as soon as we appeared, Mom and Femi got up and came to join me.

"You guys were here all this time?" I asked, closing the door slowly, watching Eirik to make sure he was actually sitting down and not disappearing again.

"Let them talk," Mom said, prying the handle from my hand. She closed the door, took my arm, and pulled me away. "We figured you two would want to catch up without us hanging around."

~*~

"So did you two cover everything?" Mom asked.

"Some," I mumbled absentmindedly. I still had questions and so much to discuss with Eirik. That part about his cell phone being taken from him bugged me. Taken by whom? Asgardians or Goddess Hel?

"Like what?" Mom asked. "Did he tell you where he's living now?"

I stared at her and wanted to smack myself. That should have been my first question. "He mentioned traveling all over the globe, which any of us can do in an hour."

"Did he say what he's been doing?"

Another question I should have asked him. The last thing I wanted was Mom grilling me and making me feel worse. "I thought you guys talked. Didn't you ask him?"

She exchanged a glance with Femi, and then she nodded. "Oh yes, we did, but he was more interested in what we were doing." Mom glanced at Femi. "Isn't that right?"

Femi nodded. "He wanted to know about the Valkyrie Council, who was in it, and how long it took them to reach a decision on Svana's case. Then he asked about my life and Hawk's and how often I got together with other Immortals. Whether there was an organization of Immortals to keep in touch with the others. He said Witches were very organized."

"Then he wanted to know if the Norns are bothering you again," Mom added.

Sounded like he was gathering information, but why? I stared at the den. Tap. Tap. Tap. Tap-tap-tap-tap... Mom covered my hand. I'd been tapping on the table. I got up and paced.

"That's it," Mom said. "Go to Torin's."

I shook my head. "I want to be here when Eirik comes out."

"We'll call you when he does. I can't stand listening to you tap and watch you pace anymore. Go."

"Mom," I whined.

"I'll keep him here, even if I have to sit on him," she reassured me. "Now, go."

"Fine. But if he leaves..." I opened a portal to Torin's. The lights were on and there was something cooking on the stove, but he wasn't in the kitchen. "Torin?"

An air portal opened from his bedroom and he appeared. "You two done catching up?"

"Getting information out of him is like trying to rob Fort Knox. Frustrating."

He went back to his cooking. "Talk to me."

I filled him in on what I'd learned from Eirik. "I have no idea where he lives or what he does, whether he's going to school or not. How often he visits his mother or Asgard. Or even whose side he is on. He's so vague." I looked out the window at my house. Mom and Femi were still in the kitchen. Torin turned off the stove and served the food on two plates. "How come you don't just eat with the others at the mansion? The housekeeper's cooking is great."

"Yeah, the same dishes every week gets boring fast." He handed me a plate. "I like variety in my diet."

"Let's eat at my place," I suggested.

"Why?"

"I want to be there when Eirik finishes with Dad."

Torin leaned against the counter, obviously reluctant to go with me. "You think he'll take off again?"

"Oh yes. He dances circles around Mom and despite changing physically, he's the same Eirik. Stuffing his face and drinking juice from the bottle."

Torin chuckled. "Go. I need to see Blaine about something. I'll join you as soon as I'm done."

I gripped his hand and pulled him toward the hallway mirror. Unlike him, I didn't walk around with an artavus, creating air portals wherever and whenever. We stopped by the mirror and I studied his expression. Then something else registered. His chuckle had seemed forced.

"You're not jealous of him, are you?"

He made a face. "Of Eirik? That show off who appears when we don't need him, plays the hero, then disappears, making all of us indebted to him when we don't need to be?"

It was hard to tell whether he was serious or not. "You know, a wise guy once told me only puny minded people are insecure and jealous," I said.

He ran his knuckles down my cheek. "He's an idiot."

Now I knew he was goofing around. "Later, idiot. We'll talk about the plane crash and Jace later." I shuddered. "Hopefully that's the last time I see that particular vision. I got everything I need to... I mean, I have all the info you need." I went on my toes and pressed a kiss on his lips.

Femi was in the kitchen alone when I entered. "Where's Mom?"

"She joined Eirik and your father."

I sat and ate the food I'd picked up from Torin's, my eyes on the door.

"So our food is no longer good enough for you?" Femi teased.

"It was too early to eat, and Eirik eats enough for five people. I hope there's some left for everyone else."

She laughed. "We'll make do."

"How long has she been in there?" I asked.

"About five minutes."

A bad feeling washed over me. I engaged my speed runes and was at the door to the den in seconds. I knocked and opened the door without waiting for an answer. Just as I'd suspected, Eirik was gone.

17. The Ultimatum

I was so sure Eirik would be back, but no such luck. I sent Onyx to find him, but the cat came back pissed because she couldn't.

"He'll appear when he thinks you need him," Torin said, and received a glare for his efforts.

He took me shopping on Sunday to get my mind off Eirik. He knew exactly where to go, which shops and restaurants were open.

I got several leather jackets, gloves, and a nice Gothic spiked choker and wristband. I found a present for Torin too and paid for it without him seeing it.

Sunday night after we came back, I knocked on the door to the den and Mom opened it. Instead of letting me go inside and say goodnight to Dad, she stepped outside. I pulled out a scarf I'd bought her and draped it around her neck. She rubbed it against her cheek and smiled. It was pure silk.

"Thank you, honey. Come on. I'm making tea."

"Is Dad okay?" I asked, peering into the room before she closed the door.

"He's resting now." She took my arm, but I refused to move.

"I want to see him, Mom. I bought him something."

She sighed, nodded, and opened the door. Dad was propped against a pillow. He looked tired. "Hey," I said.

He patted the edge of the bed and took my hand after I sat. His hands felt warm and dry, his skin paper-thin. "I'm okay," he said answering my unspoken question.

I studied his face. "You sure?"

He nodded. "Where did you go?"

"New York. We did a little shopping." I reached inside the bag, pulled out a robe, and shook it. It was fluffy and monogrammed just for him. It was also his favorite color, green like Mom's eyes. "I thought you'd like this. Oh, and we watched Les Miz. You would have loved that too."

He chuckled. "I'm happy you get a chance to do things like that. Your mother and I travelled a lot in our days, but we flew."

I rolled my eyes. His mistrust of the supernatural world started way before I was born. "I wish…" My voice trailed off. "Nah, never mind."

"No, say it."

I was going to sound stupid and childish.

Dad leaned forward and tilted my chin toward him. "Out with it."

"I wish we could visit places together. The four of us."

"Maybe we will. You never know," he said mysteriously.

"What about you, Dad? If you were to get one wish,"—I couldn't bring myself to add *before you die*—"what would it be?"

"That's easy. To walk you down the aisle and officially hand you over to someone who will love, cherish you, and fill your life with laughter and joy. Someone who will willingly spend sleepless nights worrying about you and get a few gray hairs." He chuckled. "That would be my greatest wish."

My throat closed. I'd assumed Torin would propose when I turned eighteen, but that was four months away. Was Dad going to be around then?

"Maybe it will come true. On the other hand, I'm insulted by the 'hand me over' part. You raised me to be independent."

"I know and it's going to take a special man to appreciate that in you." He patted my hand and added, "Get your mother for me. I need to rest now."

I kissed his forehead and left the room. Mom was making tea in the kitchen. "Do you want a cup?"

I shook my head. "He wants you. He looks tired."

"He's been pushing himself too hard this past week. He'll bounce back."

Somehow, I doubted it. I kissed Mom goodnight and headed back upstairs to run a bath. I had barely sunk into the frothy bubbles when Torin appeared. His hair was wet and he'd changed into his sweatpants and T-shirt. Dad had mentioned graying, but we both knew Torin would never gray, unless he ditched his runes.

I started to sit up, remembered the bubbles wouldn't cover all of me, and sank back under. He'd seen me naked, yet I couldn't bring myself to be indifferent to my nudity.

He settled on the edge of the tub. "What's wrong?"

"I don't think Dad is going to make it to my birthday. He sounded sad and nostalgic."

Torin took the bath sponge from the edge of the tub, dunked it, and gently washed my shoulder. "What did he say?"

He was distracting me. I struggled to focus on my thoughts and words. "He wants to walk me down the aisle and hand me over to someone else so they can lose sleep worrying about me. Can you believe that? Oh, and whoever I marry will go gray with worry. I guess that means you're not a candidate."

He chuckled, not bothered by my words. I didn't know how to feel about that.

~*~

Torin and I arrived at the school parking lot Monday morning to see Cora talking to the two Grimnirs from the nursing home. Andris stood a few cars away with some girl, but he kept glancing at Cora.

"What's going on?" Torin asked when he realized I was distracted.

"Those are the two Grimnirs I met at Beau's. I wonder what they want with Cora. I saw her with them at the nursing home."

Torin hoisted my backpack to his shoulder. "She's dating a Grimnir, so technically they're her people now."

"Does that make Valkyries my people?"

"No, you are mine. Two different rules. One day, you will be Mrs. St. James or Lady Worthington." Despite his blasé attitude, he didn't move away from the bike and was busy sizing up the two Grimnirs. "I don't like that girl's body language."

Cora turned as though to walk away, when all of the sudden the female Grimnir grabbed her by the neck. The male Grimnir clasped her hands together.

"They're kidnapping her!" I exclaimed.

One second Torin was beside me, the next he was gone. My reflexes weren't as fast. I looked around to see if anyone was watching, ducked behind the Harley, and engaged my speed runes before following him. Torin yanked the male Grimnir away from Cora while Andris went after the female. Sometimes Torin and Andris forgot that we were still getting used to their world. The force with which they attacked the two Grimnirs had knocked Cora sideways. I caught her before she landed on her ass.

Andris pinned the girl on the ground while Torin had the man against the tree, his feet dangling.

"You okay?" I asked Cora, aware of students walking by and glancing at us. Andris and Torin were cloaked and so were the

Grimnirs. Cora and I weren't. The girl Andris had been talking to remained standing in the middle of the parking lot with a bewildered expression. He really needed to stop taking chances like this around Mortals.

"Get off me, Valkyrie," the female Grimnir screamed and tried to dislodge Andris who was straddling her and pinning her hands to her sides.

"Come on, sweetheart," he crooned. "You know having me on top is the closest you'll ever get to Asgard, so enjoy the moment. Cora, sorry I was late to the party."

The Grimnir hurled insults at Andris, twisting and bucking.

"Nara!" her partner snapped, and she stopped. She glared at Cora as though blaming her for her humiliating position. Her partner looked down at Torin, violet eyes narrowing. In daylight, those eyes looked even more gorgeous, and I hadn't noticed the studs on his ears before. "I don't want to fight you, Valkyrie, so let me—"

"Shut up," Torin cut him off. Ooh, he was pissed. "Cora. Come here."

I let Cora go and watched my man do his thing. Torin was a natural born leader and from his expression, he was ready to kick some serious boo-tay.

"Did they hurt you?" he asked Cora.

"No." She glanced at the woman, Nara. I still didn't like her attitude. I had warned them to leave Cora alone, I wanted to add, but that would only make matters worse.

"When I let you go, Grimnir," Torin said calmly, which meant he was pissed, "disappear. If I catch you anywhere near her, you will not like it. Cora is under our protection. You mess with her, you mess with us."

"But she has a soul that belongs to us," Nara protested.

We all turned to stare at Cora. She bristled.

"He is under my protection. I promised to help him," Cora said.

"Dev betrayed our people," Nara interjected.

"We don't care," Torin said. His voice was calm and deadly. "If Cora gave him a promise, she'll keep it." He let go of Nara's partner, adjusted his collar and brushed invisible lint from his duster. Then he added, "Now be a good Grimnir and get out of town."

The Grimnir didn't like that. "Others will come for him."

"We'll deal with them, too," Torin vowed, then glanced at Andris and nodded. Andris let Nara go and even offered her his hand, which she ignored.

"We'll meet again, Valkyrie," she said through clenched teeth.

"I'm free Wednesday nights," Andris said, opening his arms. "Don't bring anything but your lovely self."

I fought a smile. That was Andris for you. Once the Grimnirs disappeared through a portal, Andris and Torin used the trees to hide as they decloaked. Luckily, the parking lot was empty except for a few late students. No one made a move to leave. I wanted to hear about this soul Cora was protecting. She tried to get out of explaining with the lamest excuse.

"Guys, the bell already rang," she said.

Andris rolled his eyes while Torin crossed his arms, legs slightly apart. That stance said he wasn't moving until he got answers.

"School can wait," he said. "You're protecting a soul? Why?"

Cora bristled. "He came to me for help, and I promised to give it to him."

Was this the soul she'd called me about on Saturday while Eirik and I were talking? I opened my mouth to ask, but Torin spoke.

"Is he one of the old people at the nursing home?" he asked. "Why do the Grimnirs want him?"

"Is he someone Goddess Hel wants?" Andris shot at her.

"Does Echo know about him?" I jumped in.

"Okay, stop with the Qs." She lifted her backpack from the ground and gripped it tight. "We shouldn't be discussing this now. One of you will have to rune my English teacher, or it's Saturday makeup class for me."

We still didn't move, but I wondered whether I should have sided with Echo and Torin on Saturday. They'd suggested a freeze on helping souls until we took care of the rogue Immortal souls.

"Fine," Cora said. "His name is Dev. He was once one of them. A Druid. Echo turned him into an Immortal during his rescue mission. Then Dev betrayed them, or they think he betrayed them, and they're still pissed. Even Echo won't talk to him."

"Was he one of the Immortals we fought last week?" Torin asked.

"No. Echo killed him thousands of years ago. He's, uh, a dark soul."

Holy crap! Our eyes met and hers begged me to understand.

"I know what you're going to say," Cora said.

"No, you don't," Torin said.

"Yes, I do," she shot back. "I can see the disapproval on your faces. I know what I'm doing and why, so just respect that."

Andris grinned, obviously amused by her bravado. I wasn't. "Is he the one you were with on Saturday when you called me?"

Cora nodded. "I was careful. I only agreed to help him once I realized he wasn't after me. And please, don't tell Echo. He cannot know about this morning with those two. I mean it, Andris. He's already alienated enough Grimnirs without making things worse."

I could just imagine Echo's reaction. He'd go on a rampage.

"What were you doing when she got attacked?" Torin asked. His blue eyes flashed as he focused on Andris. "You were supposed to keep an eye on her the second she left her car."

"I did," Andris shot back. "Besides, I was to protect her against *dark souls*, not idiotic Grimnirs. She was done with them and was walking toward me, and that's when it happened." He glanced at Cora. "Sorry about that, blondie."

"No need to be sorry." She shot Torin a glance. "It's not his fault. I told him they were Echo's friends, and I wanted to talk to them alone. I didn't know Nara would lose it when I refused to tell her where Dev was hiding."

Silence followed.

"Since he's not tethered to you, where are you hiding him?" Andris asked.

"What does he look like?" I asked.

Cora just shook her head and clammed up as we entered the building.

~*~

Officer Randolph saw us, and I groaned. How many times had we runed him to make him forget what he'd seen us do? Too many times to count. It started the day he caught me talking to an invisible Torin.

"The bell already rang, and the five of you were just standing there in the parking lot, St. James," he said, singling out Torin because being the QB who won us state, he could do no wrong.

"There's a perfectly good explanation for that, Officer Randolph," Torin said, pulling out his artavus. Poor guy.

While Torin dealt with the security guard, I went upstairs with Cora, cloaked using invisibility runes, and took care of Cora's teacher before heading to my class.

Amber's hair was back to normal, and she seemed nicer. Or maybe I wanted to believe that to feel less guilty. Halfway through class, I felt a familiar tug.

Norns.

I looked around the class to see if they'd replaced regular students. Nope. Same old faces. For the rest of the morning, I felt them hovering in the periphery of my subconscious. It messed with my concentration and sucked all my energy.

You want something from me, show yourselves! I screamed at them.

By lunchtime, I had a headache. Beau and his friend were on their way out of school, but he stopped when he saw me.

"Hey, you okay?" he asked.

"Yeah." I even flashed him a big smile.

He frowned. "Okay, see you tonight." He thumped his forehead. "No, tomorrow."

Lavania was coming back tomorrow. I had more free time today. "Can we change it to tonight?" I asked.

"Really? Great. Tonight. Smile. You're wearing a long face."

I rolled my eyes. There was really a nice guy behind all that macho crap. I caught up with Cora at the lockers. She was fiddling with her phone, but quickly put it away.

"Please, tell me you're eating lunch here," I said.

"Why?"

"I don't feel like going home." I put my books away, and we headed to the cafeteria arm-in-arm. She asked about Torin, Andris, and Mom's present assignment. I was sure I'd explained Torin's new job at Carson before. I answered her, but I couldn't remember what I said. I just wanted the day to be over.

We turned a corner and Cora's feet faltered. I knew why. Drew. He and a few football players stood by the cafeteria entrance. I slowed down too. Drew had slept with Maliina during the weeks she'd mimicked Cora, but he didn't know about it. He believed Cora had slept with him, and then ditched him for Echo, a college guy.

"Ignore him," I said, my arm tightening around hers.

"I can't," Cora wailed. "Part of me feels sorry for him. He must have really been into her, and seeing me just reminds him of what they had. Can't you erase his memories or something? Make him forget their affair?"

I had Beau's memories to worry about without adding another person's. "I'm not ready to do something that grand."

"I just hate the way he stares at me like I'm lower than a worm."

"Actually, when you're not looking, he wears a different kind of look."

Cora grimaced. "Yeah, like he knows intimate stuff about me. Maybe I should just talk to him and apologize."

"No. You don't want to do that. Just stay away from him. Come on. Paste on a smile and no eye contact." As we walked past I threw out a casual, "Hey, guys."

"Where's St. James?" Slade Peterson asked.

"Working. Are you guys going to Ellie and Justin's party on Saturday?"

There was a collective, "Yeah."

"Will you guys be there?" Drew asked, but I was sure he meant Cora.

"Torin might be working. I'll ask him. Promise." Cora and I continued to the cafeteria, but her relief was obvious. A shiver crawled up my spine.

Norns were nearby.

I searched the cafeteria as we waited in line for lunch—chicken nuggets, mashed potatoes, and gravy. Cora was talking about the three girls she'd pissed off earlier. I only half-listened to her as I catalogued faces.

Kicker and Sonya caught my eye and waved from the swim table. Lunch was terrible, or maybe Torin had spoiled me with his cooking. The chicken nuggets were hard, the mashed potatoes lumpy, and the gravy watery.

A telltale prickly feeling in the back of my head told me I was being watched. Once again, I looked around the cafeteria without seeing anyone staring at me.

Where were they? I wanted to connect with my magic, but I couldn't. My eyes would glow, and I didn't have an explanation to give my swim friends.

"I'm so ready for the prom," Kicker said and twirled a lock of her hair, her eyes on Cora. That hair-twirling habit of hers was becoming annoying. "You're still planning on doing our hair and makeup, right?" she asked, looking at Cora.

"Depends. Will you drive out to the farm?" Cora asked.

Kicker and Sonya glanced at me, but I ignored them. Ingrid had already volunteered to do my hair and makeup for the prom. I tuned out of the conversation at the table, until someone mentioned prom king and queen.

"When are they posting Junior Prom Court?" I asked.

"You shouldn't even worry about it, Raine," Kicker said. I wasn't. "You and Torin are the most popular couple, so you'll be nominated to the court and maybe even win. The only problem is you," she pointed at Cora, "will be nominated, too. Everyone reads your blog, so you're a shoo-in. The question is who will we," she pointed at Sonya and herself, "vote for?"

"Cora," I said and buried my nugget under a pile of mashed lumps. "I don't want to be nominated."

"Too bad," Cora said. "You might even be a princess in the senior court because of Torin."

The conversation shifted to books and their movies, and I went back to trying to communicate with the Norns. They were beginning to piss me off. First, they'd refused to take care of the forest, letting me deal with it. Now they were taunting me with their presence.

When we left the cafeteria, I expected them to appear like they had a few days ago. They didn't. But then again, they never did when I was with other people. I felt their presence as though they were inside my head probing for information. To thwart them, I gave them naked jocks, full frontal, all the way to class and in-between.

Yeah, get a load of that, you celibate hags.

I was on my way to the band room for my last class when I saw Matt Langer, the boy genius I'd spoken with at the library last week. He was talking to Mr. Finch. But that wasn't what shot anger through me. It was the presence of the Norns hovering above them.

What were they doing? Surely, they weren't messing with my charges.

I jabbed a finger at them and at the nearest room, but it was occupied. The students stared at me when I opened the door since it wasn't my class. Frustrated, I backtracked and hurried to the band room, entered the little office the band teachers used, and closed the door. The few students in the band room glanced my way and went back to assembling their bassoons and oboes. I had my oboe with me, which I placed on the table.

Seconds later, they floated in, but stayed invisible and in their true wrinkly forms. They must have decided to stop mimicking regular people because I could always see past their disguises. The fact was I preferred their average teenage girl forms because I could be rude and annoying without feeling puny and insignificant. They were intimidating in their true forms.

I engaged my invisibility runes. "What do you want? I've already taken care of the forest."

"That was something any witch with elemental magic could have done," Marj said. "We have your first training assignment. It is a test of your other powers, so don't disappoint us."

"Training assignment? I'm not one of you."

"Oh but you are, my dear," Catie said in her annoyingly sweet voice. "How many destinies have you altered since we made contact? Let's start with your swim team members."

"Samantha Mathews," Jeannette said and continued to list every swimmer who didn't die the evening lightning hit the pool at the swim meet months ago. "Autumn Byron, Abby Rose Penworth, Trevors Knox, Josiah Evans, Shon Baker, Gabriela Molina, Ryan Jacobsen, Piper Stone, Cord Kincaid, Liv Thomas, and Daniella Greene."

I stared at her in shock. "What are you saying?"

"We're saying you've been doing the work you were born to do for months now," Jeanette continued. "Your friend Cora would not be Immortal if it weren't for you. That boy in the hallway, Langer, would have committed suicide before he hit his thirties but now has a bright future ahead of him. Then there's Beau." She looked at the others and they smiled, wrinkles creasing their gray faces. "The gifted young man you're fighting so hard to help. You won't just alter his destiny, you'll alter his stepfather's and mother's."

A hollow feeling settled in my stomach. "Are you saying I haven't altered his yet?"

"He's a work in progress, Lorraine," Marj said. "Anything could still go wrong."

I swallowed, feeling a little sick at the veiled threat. "Leave him alone."

"Of course, we will," Catie chimed in, her sweetness so fake I hoped she choked on it. "We don't interfere in the lives of Mortals under a different Norn's care, even if she is a Norn-in-training. However, if he were in a witch's care, we would be free to do as we wish."

They had to be kidding. "Are you saying I can only help others as a Norn or not at all? Students here tutor each other. People around the world go out of their way to help others."

"Yes they do, dear," Catie said. "But they don't change destinies. They all follow a path we've set for them, the heroes and the victims. You, on the other hand, alter paths already woven. You have done that over and over again."

"So if I decide I'm not one of you…"

"You can't deny what you are," Catie said, smiling. "We saw it the night of the battle when your powers emerged. Not because you were one with nature, but because the Immortals who were supposed to die that night, including the Earl of Worthington, survived. By immobilizing them with vines, you changed their destinies. And because they couldn't fight, the Witches they were meant to kill that night survived too, their destinies changed. That night we knew you were one of us, and that when you were ready, you would come to us."

How the heck was I supposed to know different rules applied to me? Had I played straight into their hands by helping people? "So I'm supposed to do nothing when I see people suffer?"

They looked at each other. "You want to explain?" Marj asked Catie.

Catie shook her head. "No, go ahead."

"There's a reason we keep away from Mortals," Marj explained. "A reason we don't live or interact with them. Everything we do, think, or say alters destinies. A smile, a handshake, a pat on the back, a spell to change hair color, or an instruction to a boy to chase his dreams. It doesn't last an hour or a day; the effect is sweeping and life-changing. Your abilities came too early, not after your eighteenth birthday like other future Norns. We tried to steer you, but you're a stubborn young woman. Like Catie said, when you're ready you'll come to us."

"I'm never—"

"Let's finish here before they break down the door," Jeannette interrupted me, and I realized that someone was trying to open the door. The jiggling said they were trying different keys. One of them must have stopped the door from opening.

"We want you to erase everyone's memories here at school," Marj said. "No one should remember the Valkyries or Grimnirs, except the Immortals. Memories that include your association with them should also be erased. Memories of you and Eirik should also be altered. You didn't attend any schools here. You were both homeschooled. Your neighbors will remember you as the girl raised by eccentric parents. You'll create new memories for everyone, including your neighbors."

I shook my head. "No, I'm not doing it."

"Yes, you will, Lorraine," Catie said, her voice once again sweet and cajoling. "Tap into your powers now and project your wishes. Recreate new memories and replace those that need to be replaced. The Valkyries are done here."

Helping people and healing the forest were things a witch would do. Erasing memories was Norn territory. I refused to get into bed with them.

"I won't," I shot back.

"Yes, you will," Catie said. "You are one of us. If you don't then all your work and all the good you've done will have been for nothing."

"You said you don't interfere with works by other Norns," I shot back.

"But a Norn who rejects her calling is not a Norn, is she?" Marj asked. "Think about what's going to happen to all the people you've helped."

"Or those you could save if you stopped that airplane next weekend from crashing."

One by one, they disappeared. The person on the other side of the door finally succeeded in opening it and it swung open.

I engaged my invisibility runes and went into hyper-speed, grabbed my oboe and slid past Mr. Zakowsky, who was looking around the room and scowling. Still invisible, I went to the back of the class, opened my oboe case and attached the pieces. By the time he stepped out of his office, I was on my way to my seat.

"Sorry, I'm late," I called out.

"Were you in my office?" Mr. Zakowsky asked.

I shook my head. "I just arrived. My reed broke so I went to get a spare one from my locker."

Mr. Zakowsky glared at Grayce Shephard, and I knew she'd seen me go into the office and told him. A confused expression settled on her face. I guess I should care that I'd gotten her in trouble, but I couldn't. I had Norn problems. I refused to believe the things they'd said. I'm not supposed to interact with people now?

What were they going to do if I didn't do as they asked? Go after everyone whose destiny I had changed?

The bleak reality of my existence hit me. I played without hearing a sound. I had two choices. Either I embraced my calling as a Norn and did as they'd instructed, or ignored them and people died.

I must have put on quite a performance because Mr. Zakowsky didn't single me out once. He had an ear and could always tell when someone was out of tune. I left the band room just as Beau left his class.

Should I cancel tonight? Tell him there will be no more tutoring?

Even as the questions flashed in my head, I knew I could not abandon him. What had the hags said? Whatever I did, however insignificant, changed destinies. I didn't buy it.

"Hey, Raine," Beau said when I reached him. "So you play the oboe?"

Yeah, Einstein. I gave him a side glance. "No, just carrying it for show."

He chuckled. "I play guitar."

"I don't recall seeing..."—one in your room—"or hearing that you play. Are you any good? And please don't say your dream is to be a rock star, because a professional baseball player is perfect."

He laughed. "You're weird."

You have no idea. "See you."

He frowned. "You okay?"

I pretended to think about it. "Yeah. Later." I wondered when I was supposed to erase memories. I hoped it was after I finished helping Beau. He would forget I had ever tutored him. What fillers would I use?

Sonya and Kicker were at the front of the school when I left the building. "Look who's waiting for you," Kicker said and pointed. Torin was at the curb.

He was cutting across the street before the door closed behind me. Someone called my name, but my focus was on Torin. I ran the last few steps and jumped into his arms. The tears threatened to fall.

He scooped me up, and I buried my face in his neck. Last week when he'd carried me away from Beau, I'd felt a little embarrassed. This time, I didn't care. By the time I was done with this school, they wouldn't remember any of this anyway.

Andris approached us and asked, "What happened?"

"Something," Torin said. He sat me on the bike, pushed my hair out of the way, and looked into my eyes. "Whatever it is, I'll fix it."

The vow was meaningless because I knew he couldn't fix this, but I loved him for saying it. He said something to Andris, and then he snapped my helmet on.

"Engage your speed runes," he whispered over his shoulder. I wrapped my arms around him, rested my head on his back, and closed my eyes.

18. Empty Threats

When he slowed down, we were exiting I-84 and pulling up into the parking lot of our favorite spot: Multnomah Falls, the tallest waterfalls in Oregon. This was the place Torin first confessed to me what he was.

"Do you want to go inside for a bite first?" Torin asked. We visited the falls and ate at the lodge so often that the staff knew us by name.

I shook my head. He didn't ask what had happened at school, and I didn't ask how he'd known. I didn't bother asking him anymore, just accepted that he knew when I needed him.

His hand was firm and warm, infusing me with confidence. We took the underpass and walked past the lodge. The forestry workers were still at their tables explaining Colombia Gorge National Park and its animals. We'd heard all this before and didn't stop to play tourist. We went up the walkway and didn't stop at the first viewing area, either. It was crowded, the view of the falls spectacular. As usual, the water flow seemed heavier in the spring than summer or fall.

We continued up the steps and hiked the steep climb to the bridge. At the top, we stood by the rail and stared at the waterfalls. Torin wrapped his arms around me, his cheek pressed against my temple. He still didn't speak. His patience never failed to amaze me.

For a moment, I just rested in the cocoon of his warmth. His love. The crashing sound of the waterfalls was soothing. I savored the moment.

"Let's run away," I said.

He smiled. I knew he did because his lips moved against my temple. "To where?"

"England. You have land there, right? Or we could hide at any one of the homes owned by the present Earl of Worthington. Maybe the Norns might not look for us there."

He chuckled this time. "Noblemen don't own a lot of places anymore. The upkeep and taxes are a killer, but uh, I own a place."

We'd never discussed what he owned. I turned to look at his face. "Where?"

"England."

"Is it nice?"

He nodded. "It's adequate."

"Isolated?"

"Very."

If I stopped living around people, I wouldn't influence them. "Can we go there?"

He chuckled. "Now?"

"Yes. We could create a portal in the elevator of the lodge or the bathroom. Or head up there." I pointed at the top of the first waterfall. Not so many people made the trek this late in the day. My watch said it was almost four. "And create one once we're at the top and away from people."

He looked at my watch and shook his head. "I think the house can wait for another day. It's around midnight, and the people house sitting it are in bed."

I pouted. "When can I see it?"

He stroked my cheek, his eyes serious. "Soon. Are you ready to go back or maybe go in the lodge?"

I looked around. There were not as many people down at the first viewing area anymore. The lodge was probably packed. "Let's get something to drink, then go home and talk."

We took our time going back down, stopped by the lodge for lattés, and headed back to the parking lot. We threw away our cups, hopped on the bike, and headed home.

Five minutes later, he closed the garage door behind us and led me straight to the family room couch. He gripped my hands, pressed them to his lips, then stared straight into my eyes. "Are you ready?"

I nodded. I blew out a breath and started to talk, not leaving anything out. My eyes stayed locked with his, drawing strength from the love in his eyes. A few times, my voice trembled to a stop, but he steadied me with a nod, a squeeze of my hands. When I finished, I waited for his verdict. He always knew what to say to make my pain and problems go away.

"They are manipulating you, luv. They don't know what my father told us. That you can choose. And yes, I know we have no reason to trust him, but he's right this time. Don't cry," he added, wiping my cheeks. "How do I know? Because I got it from reliable sources that you have a choice."

The tears kept flowing. "Who?"

"Eirik. In a few days, you'll get a chance to do that."

I blinked. "I will?"

"Yes. And I'll be there with you every step of the way, because there's no way I'm letting those hags take you away from me. Never." He pressed his finger to my lips. "Don't ask me to explain. Just trust me. Okay?"

I nodded. "Okay."

He pulled me into his arms and stretched out on the couch. He wiped the wetness from under my eyes. "One day I'll make them pay for every tear you've shed."

He said the nicest things, and I was a sucker because I loved hearing them even though I knew they were impossible. No one could make the Norns pay. They were the weavers of destiny. On the other hand, maybe he could wreak havoc on their senile butts during the end of the world, mother of all battles: Ragnarok.

"I'll cheer for you when you do," I said and Torin chuckled. Then I saw the time and sat up. "Shouldn't you be at practice right now?"

"Nope. No practice today. They deserved a break. The teacher I was subbing for is also back, so I'm done teaching." He removed my jacket. It was one of the few things we'd bought over the weekend and had the smell of new leather. He threw it aside as though he hadn't spent a fortune on it, then ran a hand along my shoulders. "You're tense."

"I know. I couldn't relax today at school. I swore to have a long bath when I got home, your surprise was better." I rotated my neck and lowered my chin to my chest as he worked the knotted muscles. He changed positions and worked on my feet. I hated my toes being touched, but his touch was more sensual. He moved to my calves and kept going...

After thirty minutes, I jumped up. If I wanted to accomplish anything before dinner and Beau, I had to leave. "Homework."

"Chicken," he said.

"I have no idea what you're talking about." But I was running. His laughter followed me all the way through the portal.

Onyx was waiting when I arrived. *Where have you been?*

"Nice to see you too, Onyx." I put my backpack on the desk, dropped my shoes in the closet, and changed the shirt I'd worn to school.

Goddess Freya wants to see you, Onyx said, watching my every movement.

"What? Why?"

I don't know. Don't meet with her.

She sounded worried. I studied her. "Why not?"

She wants something, and she won't care if you get hurt.

"Oh. Is that concern for me I hear?"

This is not funny.

"I know. Don't worry." I rubbed her head. "I'm not going anywhere, except downstairs to get water, then I'm coming right back here to work on my magic."

Despite my words she followed me downstairs, watched as I got bottled water, and was right behind me when I checked on Dad. He was still not doing great. Mom wasn't back yet, and Femi was around somewhere.

"Why are you following me around?" I finally asked when Onyx followed me back upstairs.

Making sure you don't go anywhere without me.

"Believe me, the last thing I need is another conversation with a deity. The one I had with the Norns was enough."

Her ears twitched. *Norns? Where?*

"At school today. Nothing I couldn't handle." I sat cross-legged in front of the mirror and Onyx, nosey and refusing to be ignored, climbed into my lap. "But I'm not letting anyone force me to do things I don't want to do."

Like what?

I closed my eyes and worked on controlling my magic. "Like talking to you right now when I'm channeling my powers. Shhh."

For an hour, I worked on creating various illusions while Onyx watched without saying a word. I was impressed. I started with those closest to me: Torin, my parents, and Andris, then Femi, Cora, Ingrid. I moved to those I knew at school and in town. Finally I pulled images of various people from my favorite TV series.

Who's that? Onyx asked.

"I said no talking. You're messing with my concentration."

Well, excuse me! You'll have to learn to change while you're talking, running or fighting. Scared or panicking. Multitasking is how a witch survives. He's hot. Who is he?

I grinned at my reflection and flashed a cocky smile. "That's Dean Winchester, demon hunter, owner of a family business. I sound just like him too."

Oh, fictitious character.

I let my jaw drop and faked outrage. "Shut up! I thought he was real. He even likes Taylor Swift's song."

Onyx smirked. Or maybe it was a snarl but the sound that accompanied it was definitely a snicker. *And that one?* she asked when I changed.

"His brother, Sammy."

He's hotter.

I glared at the cat. "Take that back or I'm kicking you off my lap. In this house, Dean is the hottest guy and if you don't like it I'm—"

Torin is the hottest, daufi, she shot back, stressing the word is.

"Nice comeback."

Thank you.

"And you're right. Torin is hotter than all of them put together. And FYI, I don't like being called *daufi* because I'm not stupid." I lifted her off my lap. "Go and see if Mom's back."

She took her time, and it was another thirty minutes until Mom knocked on my door. She watched me for a few minutes, smiling. We exchanged a grin when I shifted seamlessly into her.

"One week and you can do that so easily," she said, offering me her hand. She didn't let go once I stood. "I got word that Freya wants to see you."

I wiggled my hand out of hers. "I know, but I can't. Not now. I have so much going on." I could feel her eyes on me. "Maybe next week."

"Okay. I'll let her know. What's going on?"

I put some distance between us, then turned and faced her. "If I tell you something, will you promise not to tell her?"

Mom's green eyes clouded. "Honey, of course. She might be my protector, but you are my daughter. You come first."

"Promise?"

She pulled out the chair from under my computer desk and sat, then indicated the bed. Her expression was serious. "If it makes you feel better. I promise that whatever you tell me stays between us."

I sat, feeling a little guilty for doubting her loyalty. "I know you once trained under Norns and chose to leave them. What I don't know is how you did it."

"Oh, honey. Your situation is completely different from mine. I was first a Valkyrie, then was handpicked with a bunch of others girls to join the Norns. You, on the other hand, are special. You're going to foresee the exact moment Ragnarok starts and announce it to—"

"Mom, I know all that," I said, raising my hands. "I need to know what you did to make them back off. You see, the Norns visited me at school today and they said…"

By the time I finished talking she was pacing and calling them all sorts of names. I got up and gripped her arms. "It's okay, Mom. They don't scare me anymore. Even when they appear in their true forms, I'm not scared of them. Intimidated, yes. But not scared. I have you and Torin, and all the Immortals around here who—"

"Would die to protect you," Mom finished and pulled me into her arms. She stroked my hair. I knew she was fighting tears and I was a sympathetic crier. "You sound so brave sometimes I forget you're only a child." She leaned back, and I was surprised when there were no tears in her eyes. She wiped the wetness from my cheeks. "I petitioned the Valkyrie Council, and Freya fought for me to marry your father. That might not work for you because you're not a Valkyrie, but we will fight for you to follow your own destiny and not be the Norns' puppet." Her eyes gleamed with determination.

I nodded. "But what if they hurt those I'm helping?"

"Empty threats made to scare you," she retorted. "This is just another attempt to manipulate you."

"Is it true that whatever they do changes people's destinies? A smile, a nod, a pat on the back?"

"Hogwash. They must think you and I don't talk. I don't recall that being taught in Nornsgard. Remember, you're not one of them. Therefore, their laws don't apply to you. You're also not a Valkyrie, so our laws don't apply to you either. You're an Immortal bound by earthly laws."

I had a feeling Mom was trying to tell me something, but I wasn't getting it.

"Have you talked to Torin?" she asked.

"Yes. He told me to ignore them. That they were trying to manipulate me."

"Exactly." Her eyes went to the window as though searching for someone.

I followed her glance. In spring, the sun didn't set until after eight, so there was still daylight. The leaves on the trees in our cul-de-sac waved gently in the evening breeze, reminding me of the forest.

"Are you tutoring Beau this evening?"

"Yes, which means I have to do my homework now. Thanks for listening, Mom." I gave her another hug, and then took the chair she'd vacated and rolled it to my desk. "I feel better now that you know everything." I threw a smile over my shoulder. "Oh, you should have seen the forest when I was done with it last weekend. The trees danced."

She chuckled and patted my shoulder. "I'm sure they did. Your grandmother was an elemental witch just like you."

I turned and stared at her. She rarely talked about her past. I'd just assumed she'd either forgotten or it was too painful. Then there was the gag order the Valkyrie Council had slapped her with when she quit being one of them. "She was?"

"Oh yes. I left to train under a high priestess when I was young, but I remember she used to make these amazing vases and pots using magic, and people would come to our house to get special herbs and ointments. Witchcraft was openly practiced during my time."

"Which was…?"

She dropped a kiss on my forehead. "A long time ago. She would have been proud her powers remained in our bloodline. I'll let you finish your work. Your dad and I want you to join us downstairs for dinner. Torin too."

"Okay. Wait, Mom? What happened to my prom dress? It's missing."

Mom paused by the door. "I took it to a local seamstress to make a few adjustments. It'll be here before Friday."

"Adjustments? It looked completely fine when I tried it on."

"I want it to be perfect."

I groaned. "As long as you don't turn me into mini-you."

"I heard that," she called out from the hallway and I grinned. I pulled out books from my backpack and got to work.

~*~

We had dinner without Dad.

"He's a bit under the weather," Mom explained, but she didn't seem worried. We ended up eating just the four of us—Torin, Femi, Mom, and me.

Torin helped me with the dishes, while I put leftovers in a bowl. Femi raised a questioning brow when I put a helping of leftovers on top of my copy of *The Scarlet Letter*.

"For Beau. His mother broke her arm, and last time he came without eating."

"Oh, isn't she a doll," Femi said.

"No, she's not," I retorted, cradling the bowl of meatloaf and mashed potatoes.

"Maybe she should tell you how she knows Beau's mother broke her arm," Torin added.

If looks could kill, he would be charbroiled. I waited until we were at his place before saying, "She doesn't know I snuck into his house."

"I figured as much. Your mom?"

"She knows. We talked this evening. I had to tell her about the Norns. Her attitude is exactly like yours." I put the bowl on a tray and got juice from the fridge. "I trust your opinion, so I'm not going to worry."

"You know, if I didn't know that you are crazy about me, I'd be jealous of the way you're fussing over this boy."

I chuckled. "You are jealous of him." I put the fork and the glass by the bowl, stepped back and shook my head. It seemed too pre-planned. I removed the bowl and stashed the tray.

"Why can't he get a girlfriend to feed him and fuss over him?" Torin asked.

"There's Ellie, but she doesn't look like the fussing type." I walked to Torin and invaded his space. "If you taught me how to cook, I'd feed you."

He chuckled. "Nah. It's my job to feed you. Yours is to love me. Everything else is window-dressing. He's here."

I looked toward the living room. "I didn't hear the doorbell."

"He doesn't need one. That truck of his has a distinct annoying sound." He planted a kiss on my forehead and lifted me out of the way. "When will people ever understand that an engine is like a relationship? You have to take care of it or it falls apart."

I giggled. His love affair with engines was comical. Sure enough, when I peered out of the window, Beau had pulled up into Torin's driveway. He was early. I moved away from the window before he could see me.

"That's his stepfather's truck. Yes!" I pumped my fist.

Torin eyed me with a dubious expression. "What's so great about that?"

"The old goat is changing. It doesn't matter what the Norns said." I moved toward Torin, smiling triumphantly and doing a little dance. "I have changed their relationship."

Torin rubbed his chin. "I don't know. Once a drunk and a wife beater, always a drunk and—"

"Shut up." I covered his mouth. "You're not allowed to steal my moment. Besides, I'd like to see you do better."

He pulled my hand down. "I can't, but I know one thing that could spook his old man and keep him on that path."

"What?"

"Pay him a visit."

I frowned. "Like in the middle of the night in my pjs?"

He groaned. "Never. I meant stop by Beau's house. Imagine his reaction."

He opened the door and was gone before I could react. By the time I reached the front porch, he was talking to Beau. Mrs. Rutledge peered out of the window. I wondered how long before she complained about Beau's truck and music, which he had blasted as he pulled up.

Torin and Beau were having a bro moment, so I went back inside the house. Was Torin right? What if the poor guy had a heart attack?

There was a brief knock at the door, and then Beau entered.

"Kitchen," I called out.

He looked a little sheepish. "Sorry I came early."

I shrugged. "It's okay, although my neighbor will call the police if you continue playing your music that loud."

He smirked. "You don't have a noise ordinance around here, do you?"

"No, but don't be surprised to see one. Mrs. Rutledge owns this cul-de-sac. Is Torin outside?"

"Yeah. He said he's good with engines and was going to take a look at my stepdad's truck. It makes this weird sound whenever I step on the brakes." He sat and his eyes went to the bowl of food. He actually swallowed. An engine started, and I knew it was his truck from the way he angled his head. He jabbed his thumb toward the garage. "Is he good with cars or is he going to screw my stepdad's up and get me in trouble?"

"Oh, he's good. He's better than good." Except he could spend hours tinkering with the engine and we only had an hour. I opened a drawer, pulled out a fork, and handed it to Beau. "I know it's my fault you came here before you had dinner, so I put something aside for you." I pushed the bowl closer to him.

He looked at the food, then me. "How is it your fault?"

"I chose the time, which works in my favor." I waited until he pulled the bowl closer, then added, "I'm going to check on Torin."

I left Beau munching. Torin was dismantling the engine at super-speed, which explained why he'd brought the truck into the garage and closed the door.

He slowed down long enough to say, "Keep him away from here. I'll come inside when I'm done."

Like I needed to be reminded. I went back to join Beau. He was halfway through the food. I grabbed him a can of soda. He asked about my father, and I asked him about his love life. It took guts, but dating a Valkyrie and having tangoed with Norns had given me extra confidence I had never had before.

"Anyone I know?" I asked.

He just smirked and shoved more food in his mouth.

We went to work as soon as he finished eating. An hour later, we were still at it and Torin hadn't come inside. An hour and a half, and I excused myself and went to check on him.

My jaw dropped.

The entire engine was on the floor. Some of the parts looked new, which meant he'd used a portal and gone shopping for parts. He had grease on his clothes, his face...

"Now, I put it back together," he said, flashing a kid-in-a-candy-store smile that sucked the anger right out of me.

"How long?" I asked.

"Ten minutes."

"Do it in five," I said and left. Beau looked up when I rejoined him.

"I should be going." He started collecting his things, and I began to panic and curse my boyfriend and his obsession with engines.

"So what do you think of Ellie Chandler?"

That got Beau's attention. He shrugged. "She's cute."

"Cute? She's beautiful."

"Your friend, Ingrid, is beautiful."

"Ingrid is taken," I fibbed. "Would you date Ellie if she weren't with Justin?"

He frowned, but at least he stopped putting his books away. "No."

"No?"

"I like the chase. Once I've had the girl, they lose their appeal."

My jaw dropped. "OMG, you're so rotten. So who *haven't* you slept with?"

He made a face. "I'm not having this conversation with you."

"Who am I going to tell? Come on? Don't pretend you're a gentleman now."

He laughed. "I'm not that bad. What exactly do people say about me?" The sound of the engine starting reached us and I sighed with relief. I wasn't sure how long I would have kept that going. I had zero interest in his conquests. Still, I pointed at Beau. "Saved by the truck. I think he's done."

We were still laughing when we joined Torin outside. I left them talking engines, grabbed my jacket, and headed home. Voices came from downstairs, but I didn't join them. Onyx wasn't in my room.

Where are you? I asked.

Busy eavesdropping downstairs.

I sure loved that cantankerous cat. I showered and was changing into my pajamas, when Femi knocked on my door. I held the pjs in front of me and opened the door.

"Hey, doll. Your mom and dad want to see you downstairs."

"Is he okay?" I asked, my stomach dropping.

"Your father? Oh yeah, he's fine."

"Then why do they want to see me?" I asked, pulling on my pajama bottoms, which wasn't easy while trying to cover my chest.

"You'll find out when you get downstairs. Come on. Hurry." She left.

My heart pounding with dread, I dressed quickly and used the portal, something I rarely did. The first person I saw was Hawk.

Something was definitely wrong. This was the first time I'd seen him in my house, although I knew he visited to discuss the store. I didn't think tonight's visit was about business though. He and Femi sat side-by-side, talking to Ingrid and Blaine in low tones. They stopped talking when I appeared and stood.

"What's going on?"

"Go on in," Femi said, detaching herself from Hawk's side.

I knocked on the den's door and pushed it open. My eyes widened and my stomach hollowed out when I saw who else was in the room with my parents. Torin and Andris. The Earl of Worthington, Eirik and Goddess Freya. Onyx sat on her lap.

This was not good.

19. Black Bears

"What's going on?" I asked, closing the door, my eyes moving from face to face.

No one spoke.

Torin stood and came around the couch to take my hand, his eyes intense. "Remember I'd said I had a surprise for you on my birthday?"

I nodded, glanced at the others, but he moved and blocked my line of vision, forcing me to concentrate on him.

His birthday was on Friday, prom night, and I had already decided on his present. We were going all the way. "Yes."

"I was planning to ask you to marry me."

My eyes clung to his, the panic receding. "Really?" Then I processed everything he'd just said and my chest started to hurt. He looked nervous, which was bad. Very, very bad. "Was?"

He smiled reassuringly. "That was the plan. Things have changed, so I'm asking you today. Now. Because—"

"Yes." I tried to look at the others, but Torin blocked me again. "The answer is yes, I'll marry you."

His expression grew serious. "I haven't finished explaining."

"You don't have to. I will marry you." I smiled and lowered my voice, "Are they against it? I hope not because I'm not going to choose the Norns or the gods,"—this time I managed to make eye contact with Goddess Freya—"I don't belong in their realm. I belong here on earth with those I help. With you and Mom, and—"

Torin covered my mouth. "Slow down. They are on our side. My father found out that the Norns have the means to do something terrible and he contacted Eirik. Raine, they are going to try and separate us."

He had my full attention. My stomach started to churn.

"Eirik talked to your father the last time he was here about it, then me," Torin continued. "We discussed what to do about it, and I came up with a solution. Eirik contacted Goddess Freya, who confirmed what my father had said. Remember I told you you'd make a choice and I'd be with you every step of the way?"

I nodded, trying to follow his convoluted conversation. Plus I'd gone to selective listening at, "Separate us?"

"The Norns found a loophole in their binding law and plan to use it to bind you to them," Torin explained. "Once bound to them, you'll always be loyal to them. No one knows what this loophole is, but they're all here to stop that from happening."

"How?" I asked, my eyes finding Freya's. I didn't trust her, and I sure as hell didn't trust the Warlock.

Mom got up and walked to where I stood. "Sweetheart, let Torin finish."

Torin was on his knee. I'd missed watching him go down on his knee. This was not how I'd pictured him proposing. Not with my father watching us with concern, my mother hovering and trying to act like everything was perfect, and Eirik looking like he wanted to seriously hurt someone, while Freya and Worthington smiled smugly. This was too much like a shotgun wedding. I wanted flowers, candles, and a romantic setting. How did we know whether we should trust the Goddess and the evil Warlock?

"Freckles, focus on me," Torin said.

I did and the love in his eyes pulled me into that place where nothing else mattered but us. I heard music. Saw candles floating in the air. Inhaled the scent of flowers swirling around us. Then Torin spoke, and every word was an affirmation of our love. Of us.

"Lorraine Cooper, you are the love of my life, the keeper of my soul, and the realization of my dreams. My life would be empty if you weren't in it. You drive me crazy, yet you keep me sane. You are the reason I wake up in the morning and spend sleepless nights, yet you complete me. I dreamed of you before I ever met you. Loved the idea of you before I knew you. Wished for you without hope of ever finding you. Then we met and I couldn't see beyond making you love me, want me, and need me. Sometimes I wonder if I'm worthy of your love, and think up ways to prove that I deserve you. But you keep showing me that worth and proof have no place when it comes to love. Love is selfless. Love is kindness. Love is you, Freckles."

His face grew hazy, and I realized I was crying. He had an amazing way with words. I blinked and his face came into focus.

"Will you marry me?" he finally asked in a voice gone husky.

I could swear I heard sighs from around the room. Wasn't sure whether it was a that-was-beautiful sigh or thank-goodness-it's-over sigh. I didn't care. He made the moment perfect.

"Yes, Torin St. James. I will marry you."

Then he was sliding a ring on my finger. It looked old, yet the hazel and green stone looked new and the diamonds surrounding it shone like a pool of a billion stars.

"Now get rid of these and let's talk," the goddess said impatiently. I looked up. Candles hovered around the room, flowers were on every surface, and I could hear music. I hadn't imagined them.

"I did this?" I asked.

Torin nodded, grinning. I closed my eyes and let the image of the study as it usually was fill my head, then I willed it. When I opened my eyes, the room was back to normal. Mom hassled us to join the others. I sat at the foot of my father's bed while Torin stood beside me.

"Your marriage must take place before they know you're onto them," Goddess Freya said.

"Tristan and I will fill out the paperwork first thing tomorrow morning," Mom said. "The state allows seventeen-year-olds to marry with parental consent."

"Lorraine, for the next several days, until you two get married on Saturday, act normal at school," the goddess continued. "Your friends cannot know about this, including your Immortal friend, uh, what's her name?"

"Cora," Mom said.

"Yes, Cora. Do not do anything differently. The ring is beautiful, but you cannot wear it."

I looked up from admiring my ring. "What?"

Torin squeezed my shoulder. "It's okay. You'll have it with you at all times. I have the perfect necklace."

"If the Norns approach you, act the way you've always acted," Goddess Freya added. "We do not know what this loophole is, but we know that the first step is separating you from your family. In past eras, most young Witches were sent from their homes to study under a more experienced witch or a high priest, priestess, shaman or medicine man. This was done to remove parental influence over them or their decision to become an Immortal, a Valkyrie or a Norn. They believe that Torin has had a major influence on your choices and they want the two of you separated until you're old enough to decide. While under their care, they'll bind you to them."

"They can't do that." I looked up at Torin. "Can they?"

"Not if we are legally bound to each other first," Torin said.

What should have been the best moment of my life was turning into a nightmare. I heard them discuss places and people, but my mind was locked in one place—a place without Torin. I slept in his arms every night, ate breakfast with him, discussed everything that happened to me with him. He was so much a part of my life I couldn't imagine going a day without seeing him.

I studied the people gathered in the room. They were being given parts to play, and I sat there like a zombie, listening without really understanding. The Earl wasn't talking much, but he listened and watched.

Onyx hopped up on my lap and I sank my hand in her fur.

It's okay. This will work out, the cat said.

How do you know?

Because I now know what this is about. She wants revenge for what happened to her husband and winning means beating the Norns. The same with Frigga. She also blames the Norns for what happened to her son, Eirik's father. The Norns punished them for refusing to join them. The two of them, powerful Witches in their days, chose love and became goddesses. They want you to win.

Now I was a pawn. Great. But what would the Norns do to punish me for refusing to join them? Would they take Torin like they'd done to Goddess Freya's husband, or my child like they'd done to Frigga?

~*~

The meeting ended, and I went upstairs to bed. Onyx curled up beside me and for once, I didn't shoo her away. When Torin arrived a few minutes later with a platinum chain, I was staring into the darkness, my mind a jumble of scenarios that solved nothing. Either I married Torin and had a few centuries of happiness before they take him from me or joined the Norns and never know life as Torin's wife. Either way, I could lose Torin.

"No, I'm not removing my ring," I said.

"Yes, you are. Come on. You know that they'll know the truth if they see it."

"I don't care. I'm sleeping with it." I turned over. Yet I couldn't fall asleep. And when I did, I was trying to stop the plane from crashing while the Norns chased me with my dagger. Worse, Torin wasn't there to help. I woke up screaming for him.

"I'm here," he whispered. "I'm not going anywhere."

Yet I had the same dream again and again. When I woke up in the morning, I was in a crabby mood.

~*~

I finally agreed to wear my ring around my neck. I kept touching it to make sure it was there, or maybe to remind myself there was still a chance for us. I should be happy, darn it. I was going to be Mrs. Torin St. James. But I could be leading him to his death.

I didn't see Cora until lunch when she dragged me to Echo's place to discuss her boy problems and the dark soul she was helping, Dev. Was it just last week I'd worried about souls and fought *Draugar?* It seemed like ages ago.

"Echo and I fought," Cora said, looking ready to cry. "I know. Shocking. I don't know if I should really call it a fight. He refused to help me with Dev and I, uh, got pissed."

I listened and tried to be supportive. Part of me wished I could share my problems with her too. I stroked my ring through my shirt, finding comfort from it, and made appropriate responses as she talked. We got lunch ready, soups from a nearby restaurant.

"I told him I didn't want to see him for forty-eight hours," she continued.

"And he listened?"

"Not really." She went on and on about their fight and his attempts to reconcile. "I miss him."

Forty-eight hours was nothing compared with what the Norns were planning for Torin and me. Would we have a year if we married? Ten? A century? Or a day?

She frowned and studied me as though she knew something wasn't right. "Once he finds out about what happened yesterday with the Grimnirs," I told Cora, trying to act normal, "he'll be here breathing fire and threatening to decapitate someone."

"He's not going to find out because Rhys, the walking ad for tats, used to be the third member of their trio and they don't talk. And you guys are..." she zipped her lips.

"You're forgetting the girl," I reminded her.

"Nara is a pain. Everything about her bugs me." She yanked her cell phone from her pocket. "Dev said she and Echo dated."

"Oh. I don't know what I'd do if Torin's ex appeared," I said. At this point, I wouldn't be surprised if the Norns unearthed one to mess up my relationship with Torin. "Probably put a hex on her."

Cora laughed. "You wouldn't. You know he loves only you, and you'd ignore her the same way I've been ignoring Nara. The problem with her is she keeps saying things that make me want to punch her in the nose."

"She's jealous, that's all. You have the power."

Then Cora did something weird. She lifted the phone to her lips and said, "Hey, Dev. You there?"

"You talk to him on the phone?" I asked.

"He likes to commandeer my electronics to communicate. He's not back. Come on, let's eat."

My stomach still churned and food was the last thing I wanted. I studied Cora's phone. I didn't care that Dev was a dark soul. Any soul who used electronics rather than dead bodies or dogs had to be worth knowing.

Cora noticed that I wasn't eating and pinned me down with a speculative glance. "How are things with you?"

The soup smelled amazing, but it tasted like salted water. Fighting my gag reflex, I shrugged.

"Not you, too," Cora griped. "I have had enough of reading body language, so talk." She moved closer. "Watching you do magic is amazing. Does it affect you?"

I couldn't come up with an answer to such a simple question and stared blankly at her. Concern flickered in her eyes.

"Oh yeah," I said lamely, wracking my brain for a decent response. "The rush is off the charts. Scary."

"And?"

"That's it."

"There's a lot more going on with you, Raine. Spill it."

She wasn't going to stop digging until I gave her something. Since I couldn't tell her the truth I tried to give her clues. "I need to marry Torin."

She choked on her soup. I thumped her back, trying hard not to laugh at her expression.

"Really?"

"Really. I need him in so many ways it scares me, but marrying him is at the top of my list. It's the only way we can survive all this mayhem. We need each other."

"Does he know how you feel?"

I nodded, but she didn't see it because a gush of frigid air swept through the kitchen and Echo entered the room. I was forgotten as she jumped into his arms and they got lost in each other. When she lifted her head, our eyes met and I indicated the pool deck. I disappeared outside, giving them privacy.

It was three o'clock in the afternoon and the Miami sun hit the deck at just the right angle. I kicked off my shoes and settled onto one of the deck chairs. I wasn't hungry, so I ignored my soup.

A sudden chill rushed over my skin and shadows blocked the sun. I didn't have to open my eyes to know who my visitors were. I wanted to ignore them, but I was told to act normal. How could I act normal when these hags could rob me of everything?

"Do you mind? You're blocking the sun," I asked in the nastiest voice I could muster, squinting at them. They didn't move.

Their wrinkly faces creased even more.

"We asked you to delete the memories of the students at your school," Marj said.

I sat up, my hand creeping up to cover my necklace, but I stopped just in time. "I'm not one of you, so I won't." I looked at my watch. "Come back in three months and twenty-three days. I'll be eighteen."

"Do you know what will happen to those you've helped?" Catie asked.

"Go ahead. Reverse what I did and see what happens." Were they the Norns responsible for making sure Eirik's father died young to punish his mother? And did they take Goddess Freya's husband to punish her for refusing to join them? Or were different Norns involved? According to Lavania there were many. Some good and some bad. An idea popped into my head and I ran with it. "I have lots of opportunities. Sides I could join and still do what you do."

Silence followed.

"Sides?" Catie asked.

I squinted at them. "Maliina did it when she joined your evil sisters. Push me hard enough and that's where I'll end up too, with them. Neither you nor the gods are going to know what happened when the shit hits the fan. The giants are going to slaughter all of you while you sleep and Hel will sit on Odin's chair."

Their eyes glowed with rage and fear slammed into me. But I refused to back down. I was fighting for the right to be left alone, to decide my future. My heart hammering and my stomach heaving, I faked indifference, leaned back on my lounge chair and closed my eyes. The silence was ominous. Any second, I expected them to strike.

When they didn't speak, I wondered if I had I pushed them too far. I didn't need to add the part about Hel, but dang it, I was between a no life with Torin and a short life with him. I was desperate.

The moment they left, relief rushed over me so fast I felt faint. Not wanting to wait around in case they decided to return, I picked up the bowl of soup and went back inside. Luckily for me, Echo and Cora were eating instead of making out.

~*~

Once we went back to school, the rest of the afternoon passed quickly. I was about to get in my car when Beau caught up with me.

"Is St. James going to be home this evening?"

"Yeah, I think so. Why?"

"My stepfather wants to thank him for what he did to our Dodge. Do you have his digits? I need to pick his brain about my truck."

"Just drive it to the house. I'm sure he won't mind taking a look at it."

"The engine conked out on me this morning. I had to hitch a ride with a friend."

"Oh. Yeah. I'll let him know."

"Cool. See you tonight."

I got in my car and headed home. I did not feel like tutoring him this evening, but I couldn't cancel. Tonight was the last night.

Femi was in the living room watching something when I got home.

She switched off the TV and jumped up. "Hey, doll. How was school?"

I gave her a tiny smile. "Same ol' same ol'. Is Dad up?"

"He's not home yet."

Something shifted in my stomach. "He and Mom..."

"Left with Torin about an hour ago to get your marriage license. They'll get it, don't worry."

From what I'd read online, I had to be there in person with an ID and my parents to sign consent forms. Or they could rune some clerk and have her issue them one. I knew in my gut that something was going to go wrong.

"I'll be upstairs. I've got lots of homework," I fibbed.

Onyx got up from her window seat and stretched when she saw me. I didn't even know when the seat became hers. It was mine, then Eirik's, and now my cat's.

How was school? she asked.

"Good." I put my books away then removed my engagement ring from the chain and slipped it on my finger. I studied it, smiling. It really was a beautiful ring. I didn't know how long I'd get to wear it, but I was going to enjoy every minute of it.

It's beautiful. It matches your eyes.

I studied the diamond. "My eyes are not that amazing."

Okay, smarty pants. Whatever you say.

I studied her. "You're sure we should trust the goddess?"

Onyx sighed. *As far as you can trust someone using you to get revenge.*

"Blunt as usual. I like that about you. I gotta go." I admired my ring one last time and engaged my runes. The mirror responded. In seconds, I was in the foyer of the mansion.

"Oh, Ms. Raine. You scared me. I didn't hear you come in."

Crap! I'd been so preoccupied I didn't stop to think about the housekeeper. "Hi, Mrs. Willow. I, uh, I'm looking for Lavania."

"I haven't seen her today, but Ms. Ingrid is home. She's in her room."

"Thanks." Lavania was supposed to be back today. I didn't really want to talk to Ingrid, but I couldn't leave either, not with the housekeeper around. It was either a portal or a long walk home.

I knocked on Ingrid's door and she called out, "Come in."

I pushed open the door and our eyes met in the mirror. She was changing and was down to her panties. She didn't even cover her breasts when she saw me. "Hey, you. I thought it was Mrs. Willow. Come in."

I closed the door behind me, but I didn't move from it. Her room was done in purples and lavender. It suited her. "Can I use your mirror? Mrs. Willow almost caught me using the one downstairs."

She just sat there watching me, completely comfortable being half-naked. "I tried to find you during lunch, but you were gone."

"I was with Cora at their place in Miami." I stared at my ring to avoid looking at her. "Portal, please."

She got up and closed the gap between us. "Come here." Then she proceeded to hug me.

I stiffened.

If she noticed, it didn't stop her from rubbing my back or saying, "This should be the happiest moment of your life, and you're dealing with all this mess."

At first, I wanted to push her away. Then I found the situation so ridiculous I chuckled. She leaned back and scowled at me. "What's so funny?"

"For starters, you're going to getting wrinkles scowling like that." She rolled her eyes. "Second, cut out the mothering. I already have a mother."

"I'm hundreds of years older than you."

"Doesn't mean jack. You look my age. Third, put something on." I wiggled out of her arm and gave mock shudders. "You can't go around hugging people when you're naked."

"Yeah, well, I like being naked." She picked up my hand and studied my ring. "That is truly one-of-a-kind. You should have heard him talking to the jewelers." She lifted my hand and placed it next to my face. "But he got what he wanted."

I frowned. "What?"

"A diamond that looks exactly like your eyes. The amount of green had to be right. I think he had several jewelers and diamond dealers around the world looking for it. Andris set up the meetings, so of course Torin complained to him about how incompetent the dealers were for not finding what he wanted."

I teared up. Onyx had gotten it right.

Ingrid pulled on leggings and reached for a sports bra. "You should have seen him when a dealer finally did," Ingrid continued. "He didn't even blink at the outrageous price. Mind you, he had already offered a finder's fee for whoever got it. Then they had to cut it for both the engagement ring and your wedding band and mount them on these old family rings Echo found for him. Hey… I didn't mean to make you cry."

"Sorry. It's… This is supposed to be my moment, damn it!"

"I know." She returned to my side and rubbed my arms. "But you know what they say… If you don't fight hard to love someone, you don't appreciate what you have."

I wiped my cheeks and shot her a dubious glance. "Never heard of it."

"I just made it up. What are you doing now?"

"Since Lavania is not back, heading home to work on my powers and have a pity-party. Want to join me?"

"Hel's Mist no! But you can join me. Go change into your workout gear. We're going to burn some energy."

"You hate sweating." I remembered her complaining at StubHub.

"I hate sweating in high heels while dolled up. As you can see, I'm not dolled up right now."

Except her workout outfit was just as trendy as her regular clothes. But like me, she chose ones with hidden pockets for hiding artavo. In fact, I watched as she slipped the tiniest artavus, a portal stillo, in the interior pocket and zipped it up.

"Okay, I'm in. Where are we going?"

She grinned. "To your forest. We Immortals need camouflage when we work out and the woods around here love you."

I used her private portal, changed at hyper-speed, and told both Onyx and Femi that I was going for a run. Torin and my parents were still not home. Ingrid joined me and we headed to the forest. I looked around at the green foliage and smiled. I felt better already.

"Thanks for asking me to come. I needed this," I told Ingrid.

"Catch me if you can," she said and took off.

I kept up with her easily. Then passed her.

"Cheater," she yelled.

"Not my fault," I called back. The trees and the bushes created paths for me, making the run even easier. After an hour, we stopped.

I leaned against a tree trunk and tried to catch my breath. The forest floor was thick and lush with spring sprouts.

"Look at these babies," Ingrid said, and I followed her gaze. She was staring up. The trees were endless, but sunrays shot through to feed the undergrowth. Ingrid disappeared and came back with ice-cold bottled water. Perks of air portals. She threw one to me and twisted the cap off of hers.

"Do you know where we are?" she asked.

We'd headed north and the trees along the coast were the same. "Mount Hood National Forest or somewhere in Washington."

"Or Canada," she added and chuckled.

"Or Alaska," I said. I closed my eyes and enjoyed the crisp air and the warm glow of the sun. Then I heard the whispers and my eyes flew open. "Something is coming."

Ingrid stopped guzzling her water. "I can't hear anything."

Twigs broke and the ground shook. "More than one. We gotta go, Ingrid."

We jumped to our feet, but it was too late. We were surrounded by black bears. About a dozen of them. Most of them full-grown. From Animal Planet, I knew black bears didn't hunt in packs or live with extended family.

We moved closer to each other and away from them, and reached for our hidden artavo. They closed in. I tried to connect to the source of my magic, but I was too rattled. I needed to calm down.

"They are behaving weird," Ingrid whispered. I couldn't tell whether she was scared or not.

"I know. They're not pack animals and rarely attack people." Come on, magic. Work with me.

"So do we open a portal and disappear or run?" Ingrid asked. This time, I heard the excitement in her voice. "We can outrun them easily."

"No, we subdue them."

"Why?" Once again, I didn't hear fear. Maybe she was an adrenaline junkie. Might explain the cheerleading.

"They're possessed. See how they're behaving more like humans than animals? Torin and Andris fought possessed dogs last week. We need to knock them out, not hurt them." I tried again to connect to my magic, but it was as though something was blocking me, or it.

"Okay," Ingrid said slowly. "Strength and speed runes," I heard her add.

"Right. Ready?" I asked.

She grinned. "Yep."

"Now." We charged. Ingrid headed in the opposite direction.

I barreled into the nearest bear and hoped the trees helped without me asking. The force of my attack propelled it backwards, but this was a huge animal. It stood on its hind legs and swatted me like a fly.

The impact sent me across the forest, but the pain radiating from my thigh said the claws had left their marks. I landed on another. It reached for me. I watched the claw come closer and closer as though time had slowed to a crawl. My magic had deserted me. Why?

Help us, I begged the forest.

Vines and roots from nearby trees shot out and coiled around the bear's arms. Relief coursed through me, but it was short-lived when I saw the terror in the bear's eyes. Damn it. These souls had no business possessing helpless animals. Maybe I could connect with my magic in a different way.

ONYX! I NEED YOU! BRING THE DAGGER!

Ingrid yelled. She was on the ground, her hair a mess and grass stains on her pants. She was pissed. Two were gunning for her, the one she'd attacked and a bigger one that had broken free from the vines and roots. Worse, the one that I had attacked was lumbering towards me. Roots shot up from the ground and started wrapping around its legs.

No, the big guy. I hoped they knew which one I meant.

The roots changed direction and went after Ingrid's bear. I went after mine, running circles around it at hyper-speed, hoping to confuse it. But their reflexes were not like those of regular black bears. They were fast like *Draugar.*

I pulled the move I'd seen Torin pull—I hopped on its back and wrapped my arms around its neck. I dug deeper and a spark flickered.

"Got one!" Ingrid yelled just as her bear came down. She was hanging on to its neck. "Squeeze their necks but not too hard to snap it."

The bear growled and tried to shake me off its back. Black bears didn't have the upper body strength like grizzlies. I squeezed my knees around its midsection and hung onto its neck while fighting to hold on to the spark. It was there, but very weak. Hoping for the best, I projected my thoughts into the bear's head.

The bear's body relaxed, the legs giving away. I jumped off its back as it crashed to the ground. Thank goodness. Now for the rest of them. A scream from Ingrid distracted me and I saw why.

Onyx had arrived in her glorious, shifted form. She looked like a panther. Walking around, she bared her teeth and growled at the struggling bears, some close to breaking free from the vines and roots holding them down.

I took my dagger from between Onyx's teeth. The spark became a surging wave so powerful my connection with the dagger was immediate. It shifted and elongated into a staff, the runes at the tip glowing. Now that my magic flowed clean and pure, I could help these poor bears. They were thrashing and trying to break free, probably going insane.

Turning slowly, I made eye contact with each, got inside their heads, and calmed them down. One by one, they fell asleep.

Ingrid wore a perplexed expression. "Did you...?"

"Yes." I walked toward Onyx.

"Take care of the cat too," she screeched.

Oh, so much drama. Didn't you tell her? Onyx asked.

"No. You look badass like this." I extended my hand and stroked her head. Her fur was sleeker. The night we fought the *Draugar*, her fur had seemed glossy too, as though washed or brushed.

"Raine?"

"It's okay, Ingrid. Come here. Don't change," I added softly to Onyx.

I'm not a pet you show off, meylar.

"That's new. What does it mean?"

Little girl. You're lucky I like looking like this.

"Ingrid, meet Onyx, my familiar."

Muse.

"I thought she was a *cat*," Ingrid said.

"She's still a cat, just bigger. Lick her hand or something and reassure her, Onyx," I said, walking toward the first bear while Onyx called me all sorts of nasty names. I stopped in front of the first bear, pointed my staff at it, and muttered, "Come out you vile and evil fiend."

The soul slithered out of the bear. It was completely black with no features or form. Before I could react, the soul slithered into the glowing tip of my staff.

Okay, not sure whether it was sucked in or it dove in, but that couldn't be good.

No time to worry about it now. I moved on to the next bear, then the next. When I was done, I stared at the staff. Now what? I dimmed my runes and pushed down the energy associated with it. The staff transformed back into a dagger, but coldness radiated from it. I even felt it in the handle. I shivered.

No, that cold wasn't coming from the dagger.

I turned and growled. Ingrid was staring at me with rounded eyes, but she wasn't the reason I was getting pissed. Standing near the trees were the three Norns.

Twice in one day? They must be getting desperate. Onyx growled and crouched low, ready to pounce.

20. Crypt

"Onyx! Down!"

I walked to the cat and patted her head. The Norns moved closer. Ingrid turned, saw them, and gasped. She moved closer to us.

One of them pointed a staff at the unconscious bears. I'd never seen them carry staffs before. The vines and roots uncoiled from around the bears. They lumbered to their feet and trudged off.

I moved forward, so that Ingrid and Onyx were behind me. "So to what do I owe the pleasure of this little surprise?"

"We want the dagger," one of them said.

Funny I couldn't tell which one was doing the talking. I usually could distinguish between their voices. Maybe it was because she was pissed. No, she sounded constipated.

"Sorry, you can't have it. We've bonded. See?" I raised the dagger and something weird happened. Runes appeared over my arm and the handle slowly bent as though the runes on the blade were responding to the ones on my skin. The blade touched me and goose bumps raced across the surface of my skin. It was that cold. The runes continued to blaze until I couldn't see the blade anymore. Then they dimmed and my jaw dropped. The outline glowed, then darkened. Just like Eirik's mace, I was now the proud owner of a tattoo of my weapon.

Okay, not sure how that happened, but I liked it.

I looked at the Norns and showed them my new tattoo. "Sorry. Anything else?"

They looked at each other and grinned, which was something Norns shouldn't do because it made them look quite grotesque and it meant I'd done something I shouldn't have done. They disappeared and silence followed. Even the birds and the trees were quiet.

"Raine," Ingrid whispered.

I glanced at her. She was shivering. "It's okay. I can remove it."

"Were those *Norns*?" she whispered.

I nodded.

"How can you talk to them like that? They were creepy with glowing eyes and gray, translucent skin and... and... I'm still shaking. They were so cold."

I heard her, but I was busy staring at my tattoo. My arm felt different. Cold. Heavy. I covered the handle with my other hand and said, "Unbond."

The dagger lifted from my skin, starting with the blade. The coldness and heaviness disappeared. That was going on the Never to be Repeated list.

"We need to take this to Echo," I said.

"I know a club where Grimnirs hang out," Ingrid said.

I didn't mask my surprise, "Really? Let me guess, you've dated a Grimnir."

She laughed. "Can you imagine how Andris would react to that? No, but we, Andris, Maliina, and I have been to a few clubs frequented by Grimnirs. Crypt in Los Angeles is very popular and most of the clubs are run by Immortals, so I know their owners."

"The problem is that Echo doesn't hang out with other Grimnirs." Then an idea popped in my head and I went with it. "Actually, I owe a pair of Grimnirs some souls."

"Who?"

"Rhys and Nara. I stole a soul that belonged to them and they weren't too happy. Oh, no, Onyx. You're not going home. You're coming with us."

Why? I hate Grimnirs. Just because you choose to associate with them doesn't mean I have to.

"Oh, quit your whining. We need you to protect us. If you haven't noticed, Torin didn't run to our rescue today. We're on our own." Just like in my dreams. Was this how things were going to be when he was gone? I pushed the ugly thought aside. I needed to stop thinking our marriage wouldn't last. "Lead the way, Ingrid."

"Shouldn't we go home and clean up first?"

"No way. I'm not taking a dagger with twelve evil souls to my house. We need to look badass, not dolled up. I have an idea." I let the image from one of Mom's favorite TV series fill my head. My tank top changed color and texture until I was wearing a laced up brown leather tank top and my Capris became a leather skirt with an uneven hem. My sneakers and socks shifted into knee-length leather boots, and a dagger sheath dangled on my waist.

I shoved my dagger into the holder and spread my arms. "What do you think?"

Ingrid laughed. "I love it. Do mine." She was practically hopping. "Just make my top smaller and the skirt a little shorter. More skin the better. Oh, and give me arm braces with pockets to hide my artavo."

Shaking my head, I took care of Ingrid's outfit, making her top the same size as her sports bra and her skirt a little shorter than mine. She and I were about the same height. Her boots and arm brace matched her outfit. With her bob cut and pale skin against the dark leather, she looked striking.

"You look amazing. Well, Onyx?"

Make me wear something leather, meylar, and I'll smother you with a pillow in your sleep, she vowed.

"No, grumpy. I meant, how do we look?"

I'm not sure whether you're supposed to be Phoebe or Piper, but Valkyries don't dress like that.

I grinned. "Nice to have a cat that appreciates a good witch TV series." I glanced at Ingrid, who was making sure her artavus fit inside the pouch on her arm brace. "Ready?"

She looked up and studied me. "You should bond with the dagger again."

"I don't know. I don't like the way it feels."

"That's because you're not used to it. We'll be in and out of there in five minutes. A tattoo of the dagger makes you look badass. You'll fit right in. No Grimnir will dare question our presence."

I frowned. Grimnirs and Valkyries didn't exactly get along. "So there will be no Valkyries?"

"There will be some. Oh, and you might want to send Onyx home."

I love this girl, the cat said.

"You're sure we'll be done in five minutes, because I really, really don't like the way the dagger feels when I bond with it."

It's probably the dark souls trapped in the blade, Onyx said.

Why hadn't I thought of that? "You're probably right, Nyxie."

Not another nickname. Can I go now?

I stroked her head. "Okay, you big baby."

Onyx's runes glowed, and then she opened a portal large enough to accommodate her new size. She disappeared through it. I squatted and our eyes met.

"Get off my bed and change back to your normal size, Fur-ball."

I hope you catch something while cavorting with Grimnirs, she retorted.

I rolled my eyes, stood, and gripped the dagger. "Bond."

~*~

The portal Ingrid opened led to the women's restroom. It was huge with full-length mirrors covering the walls. There were runic writings on the frames. Portals. At the corner of the mirrors, I recognized the initials TC for Tristan Cooper, my father. Before he became ill, Dad had made the frames for our store.

Some of the reapers were leaving, while others were arriving using the portals. Most wore long coats with scarves, gloves, and heavy boots. Others dressed in leather pants with midriff tops under their leather jackets or coats. We were way underdressed in comparison. Somehow, I didn't care. We almost bumped into two guys as we entered the room.

"Is there a *Charmed* convention in town?" we heard one ask.

Ingrid turned and said, "No, a Charmed-themed party, and you guys are welcome to join us." She paused before adding, "If you can handle it."

My jaw dropped. She was terrible. "What if they decide to join us?"

"I'd throw a party."

Ingrid was officially the craziest woman I'd ever met. We entered a long room packed with men and women. More leather trench coats and fingerless gloves. A long bar ran from wall-to-wall, with pool tables on one end of the room, and booths with chairs on the other end. Waitresses in tiny tops and shorts moved between the bar and the tables. The noise level made it impossible to hear a thing. And there was no way we were going to find Rhys and Nara in this mess.

Or maybe not. Those closest to us stopped and stared, then whispers followed. More turned to stare at us, but Ingrid seemed oblivious. She tapped the back of a black guy with dreadlocks and said, "May I borrow your stool?"

The Grimnir looked at her and then me, and gave us a slow smile. "Sure, sweetheart."

"Don't call me sweetheart, reaper," Ingrid said. "But thanks for the stool."

She climbed onto it and stepped up on the bar. The ceiling was high, so she stood, bold as you please. I expected her to start dancing or doing something else equally scandalous, but she just stood there, hands on her hips, until the room became quiet and all the attention was on her.

"My name is Ingrid. No last name necessary. I'm an Immortal. My sister would like to have a word, so please focus on her," she said, then indicated me.

Eyes turned toward me and necks craned for a better look.

I sure hoped she didn't expect me to climb on the counter. She extended her hand toward me. I shook my head. She and I were going to have a serious talk after this. But a new whisper started and I heard Norns mentioned. Someone recognized me. Just great!

"I'm looking for Rhys and Nara," I said, my voice not projecting far.

The guy whose stool Ingrid had taken turned and yelled, "Rhys! Nara! Get your asses over here."

I gave him a tiny smile. "Thank you."

"You're welcome, Raine Cooper. Would you like a seat? Maybe a drink?"

I started to shake my head, but Ingrid said, "Yes. Absolutely." She sat and stayed there on the counter, legs crossed. Like moths to a flame, the guys moved closer.

"Is it true you have the powers of a Norn?" a guy to my right asked.

"Did you really talk to real Norns?"

"We heard you fought Warlocks and won."

The crowd grew. Ingrid answered the questions and offers of drinks followed.

"Give us room," a familiar female voice said and the guys parted ways for Nara and Rhys. "What do you want, young Norn?" she asked rudely.

"It's always nice to talk to you too, Nara," I said. My eyes volleyed between her and Rhys. "I owe you guys a soul, but I'm bringing you a few more because I know our paths will cross again, and I will stop you from reaping souls I plan to save." A few snickers followed. My eyes locked with Nara's. She smirked. When I unbonded with the dagger and removed it from my arm, her eyes widened. She took a step back when the dagger shifted into a staff. The others followed.

"Do you want the souls or should I offer them to someone else?" I asked.

"We don't need—"

"Yes, we'll take them," Rhys said, interrupting Nara, but I noticed his eyes kept going to Ingrid, who was flirting with several Grimnirs.

I pointed the staff. *Come out.*

Nothing happened.

Crap. This could get embarrassing fast. Then I remembered how Andris had talked to them.

I took a deep breath then said, "Get out of my weapon you scums of the earth before I disperse you for eternity."

The first soul shot out of the staff. By the time the last one left, I had the attention of the entire room. Most of the souls were dark with no features. A few were gray and I could see their fingers. I wondered what Dev, the soul Cora was protecting, looked like. Excitement swept the room, but my eyes returned to Rhys.

"Thank you," he mouthed.

"Where did you get them?" someone asked and my focus shifted. While I explained our fight with the bears, without bringing up the Norns, someone put a drink in my hand. Ingrid. She was behind the bar, helping the bartenders. She must have been one sometime in the last several centuries. She looked too comfortable.

I took a few sips of my drink and realized it wasn't my usual nonalcoholic drink. When I grimaced, Ingrid grinned and raised her glass. I saw the challenge in her eyes and rose to it. I raised my glass and the crowd cheered.

Time lost meaning as she served drinks and flirted with the men and bumped fists with others. Rhys and Nara returned from dropping off their bounties. I knew because Rhys joined the group of Grimnirs trying to catch Ingrid's attention. Some of the women hugged Ingrid and she introduced them to me. I guess you couldn't live for several centuries without knowing other Immortals.

Faces and names blended, but I could only tell the warmly dressed Grimnirs from the casual Immortals and the Valkyries among them. Some seemed hard-core with tattoos and piercings, and crazy hairstyles. Others were like Nara, very model-like. All were athletic and beautiful. One asked when I was getting married. She had silver and electric blue hair, and looked like a China doll.

Ingrid and I looked at each other, and I cringed. I'd forgotten to remove my ring. I hid my hand under the counter.

"That's just for show so guys wouldn't hit on her," Ingrid improvised, then she changed the conversation by adding, "Raine, tell them how you fought *Draugar* last week."

Even the men joined in the discussion, until they learned how we defeated them. I think I just gained a few more admirers and an open invitation to hunt with them. Then they wanted to know about how we fought the Warlocks.

"Oh-uh, look who has decided to grace us with his presence," a guy called out to my left.

"Shut up, Orias," Rhys snapped.

From the resentment in the guy's voice, I assumed it was Torin, but I didn't feel the telltale sensation I always felt whenever he entered the room. I turned my stool and realized why. It was Echo, which explained the resentment and envy on their faces. After all, he was Hel's number one reaper. Some of the men looked ready to throw him out.

"Echo! Over here." I stood and the room spun.

Echo caught me before I hit the floor. He chuckled. "What are you doing in a den of reapers, young Norn?"

I grinned and studied his blurry face. My first time drinking and I had gotten wasted. On two glasses. I decided that I got a better buzz from using magic. Things were more beautiful, not blurry. And the room didn't spin. I was sure the only thing stopping me from kissing the floor was the death grip I had on Echo's leather coat.

"Celebrating," I said. "We captured a dozen scumbag dark souls. They should have been yours, but I said, naaah! Echo had enough."

Echo glanced around the room, then back at me. "And where did you put them?"

"My dagger." I lifted my arm, and showed off my tattoo. Okay, maybe the only thing stopping me from falling over was his arm. "I gave them to Rhys and his sour-puss partner." That generated a few snickers. "I owed them a soul and I'm investing in the future."

"I think it's time you went home, Raine," he said.

"No, she's fine here," Orias said and reached out to grab my arm.

Echo caught his hand and snarled, "You touch her and you'll—"

"We know," Orias shot back, his voice filled with hatred. "Her Anglo-Saxon Valkyrie boyfriend will hunt us down. Ingrid already warned us. I meant she's safe here with us. We have no problem with *her*." They had a problem with Echo.

"I know what *safe with you* means, Orias," Echo said, speaking slowly as though the other Grimnir was an idiot. "I meant, touch her and I'd make your life so miserable you'll beg me to kill you."

"Screw you, Echo," Orias snarled.

"Enough," Rhys said, speaking with an authority that surprised me. After the encounter in the parking lot at school, I'd assumed he hated confrontations. Even more surprising was the fact that both Echo and Orias backed down. Rhys looked at Echo. "What do you want?"

Echo hesitated as though he meant to say something, then shrugged and smirked. "Nothing. I'm taking Raine home." Echo glanced at Ingrid, and a silent communication passed between them.

Too much past history was mucking up things in this club. I might be drunk, but I wasn't blind. I remembered everything Cora had told me about Echo and his Druid brothers. Chances were Orias was a Druid.

"Before we leave, just one more thing. Next time we face Warlocks or *Draugar,* can I count on you guys?" I lifted up my glass.

Cheers and raised glasses were my answer.

"Thank you. Drinks are on m..." I had no money. I glanced at Echo and grinned. "Drinks are on Echo." Another round of cheers.

"I'm not spending a dime of my money on them," Echo growled.

"Oh yes, you are, Grimnir. Time to start playing nice," I said.

"No."

I smacked his chest. "For Cora's sake, or she'll be very unhappy. I've seen it."

He glowered. "You're not supposed to read her."

"I didn't. This is all from you. Going once... going twice..." I raised my hand and yelled, "Two drinks for everyone."

"I don't have a credit card with me," he barely snarled.

"Start a tab. I'm sure you're good for it."

He sighed. "You're worse than Cora," he grumbled, then nodded at the bartender. "I'll be back to settle it." Then he scooped me up.

Only one guy ever cradled me in his arms and made me feel safe. Torin. I missed him. Tears rushed to my eyes. I closed them and tried to hide my face in Echo's shirt since I was hanging on to him like he was my lifeline and praying the room would stop spinning.

"What is it?" Echo asked.

"Nothing."

He lowered me down, and I realized we were no longer inside Crypt. We were in my bedroom. He placed me on the bed and glanced at Ingrid, who had turned down the covers. I ignored them both, but their whispered voices sounded so loud.

"You let her drink?" he asked. "She and Cora don't drink or even know how to vibrate and stay sober."

"I have my reasons. Thanks for carrying her, but I'll take it from here."

"Where in Hel's Mist is Torin?" He didn't sound like he was leaving.

"Busy."

"Doing what? She's his first priority."

"Echo, just go. I have this."

"I'm getting Cora to help."

"No!" Ingrid sounded angry now. "You don't want her involved in this."

"STOP IT!" I yelled. "Both of you out!" I could still feel them. I waved my arm and yelled, "OUT!"

Silence followed. Then they left. Onyx crawled from wherever she'd been hiding and climbed onto the bed.

I knew you'd catch something from Grimnirs. Love for Mortal brew. Disgusting.

Shut up, Onyx! I was sure the bed was floating away. My stomach rolled.

~*~

I woke up with a headache, a ringing in my ears, a weird taste in my mouth, and my stomach growled. A chuckle resounded in my head.

"Go away, Onyx."

"You'll have to wake up eventually," Torin teased. He didn't sound angry.

I opened one eye, waited until the brilliance of the lamp wasn't hurting anymore and then opened the other. Torin lay on his stomach on my bed, a big grin on his handsome face.

"I was in danger, and you didn't come," I whispered. I was going for accusatory, but the words came out whiny.

He pushed hair away from my face. "The Norns blocked me, and I don't think this helped either." He touched the tattoo of my dagger. "Come on, engage your pain runes."

I did and the headache quickly ebbed.

"If you're going to do this sort of activity, I'm going to teach you how to vibrate while engaging your speed runes and burning off the alcohol without leaving the bar."

Why wasn't he mad I'd disappeared? And what did he mean about my dagger? "That was my first and last drink. If I want a high, I'll use magic." I sat up and my stomach made so much noise I cringed.

"When was the last time you ate?"

I shrugged. "Lunch." No, I hadn't eaten the soup at Echo's place in Miami. "No, breakfast this morning."

"You mean yesterday morning?"

My eyes flew to my clock. It was six in the morning. No wonder I was starving. "Oh crap! I missed my session with Beau."

"He understood and forgave you because I worked on his truck. Took hours. I don't know how humans do things at a normal pace. Come on, I'll make you breakfast while you shower. Lucky for you, your parents didn't know you and Ingrid decided to have a bridal shower in a bar full of Grimnirs while wearing nothing but animal skin."

Bridal shower? Yeah, crazy Ingrid would definitely call it that. As for Torin... "Why are you so pleased with yourself? The Norns have a way to separate us," I said grumpily. "If I marry you, they'll kill you the way they killed Goddess Freya's husband or our child like they did to Eirik's father."

"No wonder Beau said you looked unhappy at school. He thought someone had hurt you. Namely me." Torin jumped off the bed, picked me up, and started for the bathroom. "Have a little faith, Freckles. Soul mates always find each other. Look at us. I found you despite being separated by eight centuries. If the Norns succeed, and that's a big if, I'll find you again."

Tears rushed to my eyes.

"No, no, luv." He lowered me on the counter beside the sink and cupped my face. "Don't cry. I want you pissed, because you're good at sticking it to them when you're pissed. Crying is bad. Crying is weak. Worthingtons don't marry weak women, and you, Freckles, are not weak. You are about to become my wife."

I punched him, starting to see hope in the middle of despair. If he could be optimistic after all the crap he'd dealt with, I should be too. And he was right. I was about to marry him. It couldn't get any better than that.

He tugged at one of the laced up strings. "I like the outfit. In fact, I think you should keep it. On one condition." I caught his hand when he was halfway done. "You can't wear this when I'm not around or I'll have to punch the men who look at you."

On a different day, his show of possessiveness would have thrilled or amused me. Not today. "You're not my keeper."

His eyebrow shot up. "Wanna bet? Reaping was my first priority for eight centuries. Now I have a new priority. You, Raine Cooper. Loving you. Watching over you. Laughing with you. Crying with you. Making babies with you." He grinned. "Oh yeah. I'm going to be the best father in the world. You can run around and save the world while I take care of our family. And when you need me, I'll come and rescue you."

I rolled my eyes at his silliness. "I did great without you yesterday."

"You did *okay* without me. You ordered Mother Earth to help with the bears and you got drunk, big whoop. I don't need help from Mother Earth and if I'd been at Crypt, we would have made out at the bar and been the envy of every Grimnir in the room."

I gave up. When he was in a teasing mood, it didn't matter what I said. Besides, I was too tired and hungry to come up with a response. My stomach growled. Someone ought to come up with runes for hunger pangs.

He went back to unlacing my top. "Let's remove this and get you in the shower. You smell like Grimnirs and Hel."

I pushed his hand away. "No. Go away."

"I'm scared you might keel over if I—"

"Leave."

He chuckled again as he left the room. The shower didn't make me feel better, but at least I was clean. My crazy leather outfit was gone. Torin. He wasn't really serious about keeping it. It was made by magic, which meant it would eventually go back to its original state.

It was about six-thirty and my house was quiet. I put on lotion and paused to study the tattoo of the dagger. It was so convenient to carry it this way. I bet I could do the same with the rest of my artavo. I removed it and handed it to Onyx for safekeeping.

Afterwards, I headed to Torin's. He was making steak and eggs for breakfast. I walked to where he stood and wrapped my arms around his waist. "I'm sorry for being such a grouch."

"You'll make it up to me this weekend." He turned to face me and ran his fingers down my cheek as though memorizing its texture. "Do you know why?"

I shook my head.

"Because we're getting married on Saturday."

21. We Know the Truth

How could I focus on anything else after that? It was one thing to discuss the possibility of something happening and quite another to know it was going to happen.

I can't recall what happened after that. I was in the house then at school. My ring was on a chain around my neck, the diamond digging into my skin, but I didn't care.

"I'm getting married on Saturday!" I wanted to yell. According to Torin, they were working on setting things into motion, but keeping it quiet. "Does your father know?" I asked him when we walked toward the school building.

"Yes."

I still didn't trust that man.

"Remember, you can't tell anyone about it, including Cora."

"That's going to be hard." I saw Cora enter the school with Ingrid, but she was gone by the time we reached the lockers. Torin walked me to my English class, which was in the opposite direction from his one class.

As soon as he left, I felt them. I looked up and down the hallway, but didn't see them. Refusing to let them take away my moment, I shrugged and entered the classroom. Mr. Q was already in class.

But I couldn't focus, my thoughts wavering between the plans for Saturday and the Norns. When class ended, they were waiting in the hallway. Part of me wanted to ignore them. Today was supposed to be my day. Refusing to get pissed, I entered the bathroom, locked it, and waited.

They floated in, looking smug. Yeah, I was becoming quite the expert at reading their wrinkly faces. I didn't speak.

"We know what you're up to," Marj said, the annoying voice scraping on my nerves. "It's not going to work."

My stomach dropped. How did they know? Before I could respond, someone started banging on the door. I ignored her.

"What is not going to work?" I asked, faking ignorance.

"Your defiance will have serious repercussions," Marj continued as though I hadn't spoken. "Your mother and the Valkyrie, they'll all suffer because of you."

I swallowed, my stomach starting to hurt. Who'd told them? The Warlock? I'd bet he was spying for them. The banging on the door continued.

"Think about all the people you've helped. Do you want to destroy their lives?" Jeannette asked.

"Don't do it, Lorraine," Catie said. "You want us to back off, we'll back off. Just don't destroy your gift this way. You'll be forced to do disgusting things." She reached out as though to touch me and I cringed.

"Despicable things," Jeanette mumbled.

"Destroy your life," Marj said, moving closer too.

"Damn your soul," Jeanette mumbled. They were crowding me in.

"And the souls of those who help you," Catie added.

"For eternity," Marj added.

"GO AWAY!" I screamed.

They stopped and backed away.

"Don't do it, Lorraine," they said it together. "Don't do it."

I blocked my ears, but the words echoed inside my head.

Don't do it, Lorraine... Don't do it, Lorraine...

A loud crack filled the room and the entire bathroom door came crashing down. Officer Rudolf, Mr. Q, and students peered into the room.

"Are you okay, Miss Cooper?" Mr. Q asked.

"We heard a scream," Officer Rudolf added and entered the bathroom, eyes darting around as though searching for an intruder.

This didn't look good. Some of the students were taking pictures, others videotaping me. Yes, I might be pissed at the Norns, but I wasn't going to live this down if I didn't think fast.

"Miss Cooper?" Office Rudolf asked.

"There was a spider," I said, standing up. "A giant, hairy spider with big eyes and it kept coming for me." Students snickered in the hallway. "I'm allergic to spiders, so I have this pathological fear of them."

"She does," Ingrid's voice added from behind the crowd. "I've seen her swell up like a balloon when bitten. Last time we had to take her to the ER," she added. "Move aside, please." The students stepped out of her way. She grabbed my hand. "Are you okay? Were you bitten?"

If I read her expression correctly, she wanted me to say, "Yes. I think so." I grabbed my arm, faking a swelling.

"She needs to see the nurse. Move aside, please. I need to take her to the ER." She added over her shoulder, "The school needs to do something about these pesky bugs or someone might sue them." When we were a fair distance away, she asked, "A spider?"

"I couldn't tell them the Norns were there and at their meanest."

She pulled me into a room and closed the door. "What did they want?"

Their words returned to haunt me and with them came anger. How dare they take something beautiful and make it seem dirty and evil. Just because they chose not to marry didn't mean marriage was horrible.

"To stop me from marrying Torin. They think I'm going to destroy my gift, damn my soul for choosing him. In which universe does that make sense? I don't care what they say. I'm going to marry Torin."

Ingrid grinned. "Engage your invisibility runes." She pulled out an artavus just as students poured into the room. She created a portal and pulled me through it.

My feet sank into plush carpet and I looked around with interest. We were in a gorgeous bedroom decorated in gold, teal, and burgundy. The bed was huge and looked like an antique. Same with the chairs and chest of drawers, and there was the most beautiful tri-fold vanity mirror and stool.

"Where are we?" I asked, looking past an arched doorway with pinned back, heavy draperies to a patio. I started forward, drawn to the incredible greenery visible out the window and a swarm of voices that came from outside. So many voices.

Ingrid caught my arm. "Not yet. You can explore some other time. Right now, sit down."

She pushed me onto the bed. I bounced on it once, and touched the duvet. Silk. Soft. "Seriously where are… What are you doing?"

"Removing your boots." When I tried to stand, she went into hyper-speed, removing both my boots and my jeans. "And before you ask for the third time, we are in England. At Torin's… since you're getting married in"—she looked at her watch—"the next thirty minutes, I should call this castle your place. Remove the shirt. I'll get your mom and Femi."

My mouth opened like a fish out of water as she hurried to the inner door and said to someone, "Tell them we're here, Mrs. Donovan. I'm getting her ready."

Ready? I wasn't ready. Not mentally. "But... but... Torin said Saturday."

"That was in case the Norns got inside your head. As soon as they got the license yesterday, he wanted the deed done today." She lifted a bag I hadn't seen from the floor and placed it on the vanity. "Hawk has officiated many Immortal weddings, so he's marrying you two. You have me as your bridesmaid and Torin has Andris. Oh, and your father gets to give you away. He's in the den downstairs. Come on. I need to finish your hair and makeup before your mom and Femi get here."

I couldn't move. My eyes went to the window. Torin owns a castle? He'd said he owned a place in England, not a freaking castle. Was it old? New? I wanted to explore. "A castle?"

"Yep. Built in the 1600s but he's modernized it as technology has changed. I love the stairs, but the place needs elevators. Make sure you put in some when you're the mistress." She patted the vanity seat. "Sit."

I didn't think I could stand or walk. I wanted to see Torin.

"Listen, we need to have this wedding before your next class, so move your ass." She went into hyper-speed and by the time she was done, she'd arranged makeup on the vanity counter.

I stared at her. "Are you kidding?"

"Not today. No one is going to suspect anything. Your spider stunt worked to our advantage. Two classes are the maximum we can miss."

"Where's Torin?"

"Getting ready in the east wing. Seriously, Raine, get over here." She plugged in a curling iron and pulled out facial cleansing towels from a bottle.

I sat facing the mirror, but she turned me around. It took her under five minutes to do my face and my hair. My jaw dropped when I faced the mirror.

I grinned. I had a lot of hair that could look overwhelming when curled, but she'd created soft waves, until halfway down and then had made the curls tighter and kind of layered. The front was pinned away from my face except for two strands near my temples. I reached up and touched the hairclip.

"Something borrowed. What do you think?"

"It's amazing."

"I know. I'm good," Ingrid bragged.

The door opened and Mom and Femi walked in carrying a white organza wedding dress. Femi described it as a princess Chantilly lace gown with sequins and a full skirt. A designer friend of hers had gotten a team of seamstresses to work on it using the measurements from my prom dress. They'd worked for thirty-six hours straight and had barely finished the gown.

Mom and Femi refused to let me see my reflection as they fussed and adjusted lace and the bodice. It was a perfect fit. The veil had the same sequins used on the dress, but the earrings and the tiara had the same diamonds as on my engagement ring.

Minutes crept by. I stopped looking at the clock. Femi talked about her weddings and how mothers would not talk about certain things. Mom never had that chance because she'd been told right after her powers showed that she should dedicate her life to becoming a high priestess. That led to her being made Immortal, selected to join the Valkyries and of course, tapped to be a Norn.

"Women in my time were prudes and didn't discuss sex," Mom said. "Not me."

"Mom," I whispered.

"The first time can be scary, Raine, but it only gets better," Mom said.

"Don't," I moaned, my face warming up.

"I made sure you stayed pure until your wedding night, so I'm allowed to be proud and do the traditional thing," she said.

"Don't forget, she chose well," Femi cut it. "Most men would not have waited."

"Most *girls* would not have waited for a man like Torin," Ingrid added and they all laughed.

I covered my face, wanting to die. After another five minutes of torture, they slipped crystal-encrusted sandals on my feet and stepped back. Mom's eyes welled up, her hand pressed to her chest.

"My baby," she whispered. "You look like a princess."

"We did good," Femi piped in. "And in such short notice."

"Can I look now?" I asked impatiently. The three of them nodded and I turned. The girl in the reflection could not be me, was my first reaction. I did look like a princess.

"I'm going to check on your father," Mom said, but I heard the tears in her voice.

"Mom, wait!" I called to her before she left the room and gave her a hug. "Thank you for making this perfect. You're the best Mom a girl could ever have."

"Oh honey, I brought this on you. If it weren't for me, all this mess with the—"

I pressed a finger on her lips. "We're not discussing *them*. Not today. Don't forget that if it weren't for you, I would never have met Torin." We hugged again. Then she left. Next was Femi. Ingrid was changing into a light-blue dress.

Cora was never going to talk to me after this. We'd never discussed marriage or weddings, but she would have loved to be by my side.

Mom returned with a dried bouquet of flowers, a blend of white and soft shades of blue. "Something old and something blue," she whispered. "I carried this when I married your father, and I kept it for today."

I couldn't talk. I was sure if I did, I'd start crying.

We headed downstairs. I was nervous, scared, and excited at the same time. We went down a curving ivory staircase with a polished ebony banister. Soaring ebony columns with ivory and gold accents at the base stood in the main entrance. I forgot about the room when I saw Dad.

Tears rushed to my eyes.

He stood at the bottom of the stairs, his eyes alert and filled with pride. Because he didn't do chemotherapy like most cancer patients, he had a full head of hair, which was combed and styled. His hair was so long it almost brushed the collar of his shirt. He never kept it that long. I wasn't sure why I was thinking about that now. Despite looking frail and gaunt, he had color in his cheeks and he looked dashing in a tux. As I got closer, his eyes grew shiny with tears.

"Pumpkin," he whispered.

"I told you your wish would come true," I whispered back, fighting tears.

"What wish was that?" Eirik asked from the doorway to our right, a camera in his hand. He was here. He raised the Nikon to his face. "Smile."

He took pictures and gave me a hug, then took Dad's arm.

"No, son," Dad said. "I got this. I'm walking her down the aisle and handing her over to Torin," he chuckled, but it sounded hollow as though he was barely hanging on. He cleared his throat and added, "He'd better take good care of you."

I took his arm, a tear escaping. "He will, Daddy. I know he will."

"I'll make sure he does," Eirik added. "More pictures."

"Just a second, Eirik. No crying," Mom scolded even though her eyes said she'd shed a few. "You don't want to ruin your makeup." After a few more pictures, she adjusted my veil, kissed Dad, and whispered, "If you need me, Tristan…"

"No, my love. I'm fulfilling a promise I made to myself the day she was born. Go. We'll be okay." He patted my hand for emphasis. "Won't we, pumpkin?"

I nodded.

He walked slowly and I adjusted my steps to accommodate him. Every few steps, I could feel tremors shoot through him. I wanted to ask if he wanted the wheelchair, but the words he'd spoken and the determination in his eyes told me this was one walk he planned to complete.

It seemed like forever before we left the foyer and entered a small chapel brimming with people. Who were these people?

Even as the question flitted in my head, I recognized them. Witches who'd fought beside us against the Immortal Warlocks and survived. Rita and Gina sat by their mother and waved when our eyes met. Bash and the twins. Their father was missing and I couldn't remember whether he had died the night of the battle. But it seemed like everyone who'd survived that night was here. Had someone issued a Call?

"Dad, these people…" Of course, he wouldn't know.

"Friends of Eirik's," he said. "He said they were here for your protection."

They had lost friends and family, yet they'd come from all corners of the globe to stand by me again, ready to defend me if there was an attack. I saw it in their eyes. I was one of them.

Fighting tears, my eyes followed the rose petals to the arch decorated with lace and flowers and found Torin. He looked handsome in a tux, the brilliance of his sapphire blue eyes taking my breath away. I was going to love this man with every breath in me. It didn't matter whether we had a year or centuries.

Andris stood beside him and to the left of Hawk and Femi while Ingrid was to the right. I supported Dad's weight up the steps, and past the flowers and petals forming a circle around the arch. Someone had created an opening for us to walk through. When Mom whisked him to their seats, Ingrid pushed the flowers and the petals back to complete the circle. My eyes stayed on Dad for a few minutes until he smiled. That walk had been too much for him.

Hawk cleared his throat.

"Friends, family, Witches, Immortals, and Valkyries. The day when two souls finally unite to become one is a day of celebration. It is a day of laughter and joy. A day to thank the ancestors, the gods, and Mother Earth for clearing the path that led to this moment. It takes some of us a lifetime to find the one, our soul mate." He glanced at Femi and I could swear he faltered before taking the silk rope from the tray she was carrying. "But once we do, we must learn to love and cherish them. Clasp your hands," he said. "Torin and Raine, are you ready with your vows?"

I hadn't come prepared, but I knew what I had to say. I grinned and nodded. Torin smiled as though he knew I wanted to go first.

"Torin, I didn't know it was possible to find someone like you. You love me for who I am, not what I am. You've taught me that it's okay to walk on my own, yet you're always there to carry me when I can't. You've taught me it's okay to run, stumble, and fall, and pick myself up because a fall is nothing to be ashamed of. You've taught me it's okay to fly because the sky is the limit and you'll catch me if I fall. You inspire me, challenge me, and celebrate me. You are the first man I've ever loved and you will be the last man I'll ever love. You are my one and only true love, and I promise I will love you for eternity."

Hawk draped the silk rope around our wrists and picked up the second one.

Torin looked into my eyes as he started to speak, his voice sure, his words sincere. "Raine Cooper, from the moment you opened your door and our eyes met for the first time, I knew I had reached the end of my quest, yet I didn't even know what I was searching for. I just knew you were the one, my omega. Where there was cold, you've brought warmth. Where there was sadness, you've brought happiness. Where there was pain, you've brought relief. Where there was darkness, you've brought light. You know me better than anyone, my fears, my shortcomings, my habits, yet you still love me. My vows to you are a privilege because I get to laugh with you, cry with you, walk with you, run with you, and fight with you for the rest of our lives. I promise to be patient. Most of the time," he added, smiling. "I promise to be faithful, respectful, attentive, and to become even a better man for you. I promise to celebrate your triumphs and step back so you can shine like the star you are, but I'll always be there when you need me. My shoulders are yours to cry on and to carry your burdens. My body is the shield that blocks the blows that might harm you and yours to do with as you wish. My hopes and dreams will always start and end with you. Yours will be the name I cry when I'm in need. Your eyes are the balm I seek when I'm in pain. And your soul is the beacon that my soul searches for when I'm lost. I will love you fiercely, tenderly, and passionately. And when we have children, I promise to be the best father a child could ever want. For you, Raine Cooper, deserve the best and I plan to give it you. You are my one and only true love, and I promise I will love you for eternity."

I was crying by the time he finished. I didn't hear the rest of the words Hawk and Femi said as they wrapped the ropes around our wrists and tied the knot that made us one. I had no idea what tradition we were following. Mom's Celtic handfasting ceremony, or a Native American ceremony, or an Ancient Egyptian marriage. They tied the knots several times.

Then Andris and Ingrid brought the rings, and both Hawk and Femi blessed the rings, invoking the elements, the four directions and the blessing that came with them. They talked about the ribbons and the knots and what they symbolized.

At last, Andris pulled out an artavus and started etching a rune on Torin's cheek. "To seal the bond, I give you the binding rune of love intertwined with Raine's rune."

I had a rune? Torin's eyes didn't leave mine. He didn't even flinch. The rune glowed. Then it was my turn as Ingrid took my chin and whispered, "Engage your pain runes." She added louder, "To seal the bond, I give you the binding rune of love intertwined with Torin's rune." My cheeks tingled.

They stepped back, then Hawk ended the ceremony with, "You may now kiss the bride."

The kiss went on forever, and the applause that followed had me hiding my face in Torin's chest. "You're mine now, Freckles," Torin whispered.

Some of the Witches started to sing. Others played instruments. A few shouted something about sending positive energy our way as we left the room. Mom and Dad, I noticed, had disappeared. Eirik took more pictures until I insisted he should be in them.

"You have to go now," Torin said.

"Yes, we do," Ingrid said, glancing at her watch. She grabbed my hand. "The period will be ending soon."

I didn't want to go yet. I yanked my hand from hers and ran back to Torin for another kiss. We clung to each other.

"Remember, no one can know about this," he whispered.

"I know." I left his arms reluctantly, turned, and hugged Eirik. "Thank you for coming and bringing all of these people."

He winked. "That's what brothers are for. And if you ever need them for anything, just send Onyx to find me."

I nodded, gathered my dress, and ran up the stairs. At the top, I paused and waved to the people below before following Ingrid. I changed while peering out the window at a beautiful landscape with lawn fountains and gorgeous gardens.

"We gotta go!" Ingrid yelled. I was ready.

We opened a portal into the upstairs bathroom at school. My rings were once again hanging around my neck. Just as well. The moment we stepped into the bathroom, I felt traces of the Norns. They must know how often we used this bathroom. Whether they knew it or not, I had made my choice. All that remained was appearing before the Valkyrie Council when I turned eighteen and challenging whatever ace they had up their sleeves.

We left the bathroom and bumped into Cora. Dang!

22. Death Comes Knocking

"Hey. Where are you guys coming from?" Cora asked, studying our faces suspiciously. "Don't tell me you ditched class and went somewhere fun without me." She peered at me. "Are you wearing makeup?"

My face warmed. "We went makeup shopping at the mall. The lady tried some on me," I fibbed and sighed. More lies.

"She's good. You look amazing. What's the brand? What shop?"

"I've been meaning to ask you something," Ingrid interrupted, slipping an arm around Cora's. "Excuse us, Raine. See you at the mansion at lunch." She winked and I knew she was deliberately detaining Cora while I escaped. Cora would have noticed my hair.

I didn't look back.

The Norns' presence lingered. Any second, I expected them to float through the walls like ghosts and grab me. I made it to class without seeing them, but I was tense throughout the whole hour.

I called home as soon as the class ended. Femi picked up the phone after one ring.

"How's Dad doing?"

"Not good. I know this is not the day for sad news, but he has slipped into a coma."

My heart squeezed even though I'd known the wedding had put a strain on his frail body. At least, he'd been there for my greatest moment. "Do you want me to come home?"

"What can you do, doll? I'm keeping him comfortable. Lavania is expecting you."

I started upstairs when Beau called my name. "Sorry about yesterday," I said as he and his friends drew closer.

"It's okay. Torin fixed my ride. The dude needs to start his own shop. He and I also went over the last two questions, so I'm good. I owe you one."

"Extra-large caramel Frappuccino?" I asked.

He chuckled. "Got it."

Cora, Ingrid, and Blaine were waiting for me by the bathroom when I got upstairs. Lavania was in the foyer of the mansion in one of her trademark long gowns when we arrived.

"Oh, I missed you, girls," Lavania said, giving us hugs. "I have so much to tell you. Come here, Blaine," she added when Blaine kept his distance.

"Nice to have you back, Lavania," he said without moving.

Lavania chuckled, walked to where he stood, and gave him a hug anyway. "As long as you live in this house, you put up with my idiosyncrasies. Where are my boys?"

"StubHub Center," Blaine said, extricating himself from her arms.

"Oh no, not one of the teams," Lavania said. "They're so young. Come along. I brought pastries for lunch." She led the way to the kitchen. Mrs. Willow wasn't around, which meant she was either out grocery shopping or running other errands for Lavania.

Once we sat, Lavania took a stool next to mine and asked, "How are you holding up, dear?"

"Fine," I said and wondered if Femi had told her about the wedding. I tried to redirect the conversation to the meat-filled pastries before she blurted out something. "These are really good."

"Thank you. I stopped by to see your father. I didn't know he'd slipped into a coma."

"He's not been lucid since yesterday," I fibbed. I didn't know whether she knew about the wedding or not. "I don't think he's going to come out of this one." The conversation stayed on Dad, until Lavania changed the subject to Asgard.

As we headed back to school, Lavania gave me a longer hug and whispered, "Congratulations. You two are perfect for each other."

I grinned. "Thanks."

The rest of the day was perfect. Blaine stayed with me when we went back to school, while Ingrid and Cora went ahead. It was obvious he wanted to talk.

"S'up?" I asked.

"You and Cora are going dress shopping this afternoon?"

"Yeah, for her prom dress. Why?"

"Can we tag along?"

I shook my head in confusion. "Why?"

"Echo stopped by the mansion this morning. Cora was attacked last night by a dark soul. We're to keep an eye on her just in case."

I shrugged. But I was worried. "I don't mind, but she might."

"I can deal with her," he said. "Just wanted to give you a heads up." Funny how I used to think he was the hottest guy in school. He and Beau, one preppy and wealthy, the other dirt poor and dressed like he slept in his clothes, yet girls had drooled over both of them. The difference between them was Blaine always stayed faithful to his girlfriend while Beau did his bee dance—circle, sting, and fly away.

Speak of the devil. He was waiting outside my class with a caramel Frappuccino. He'd probably spent all the money he had. "You know that I was only kidding."

"I don't play, except when it comes to…" his voice trailed off as he stared after three girls who'd just walked by.

"Later Beau, and good luck with the test."

"Thanks."

~*~

I was finishing band when the Norns entered the room. Seriously?

I took my time putting away my oboe, and then locked the door after the room became empty. I didn't speak, just waited to see what they were going to say. It wasn't often I saw them twice in one day.

"Did you do it?" Marj asked.

"Do what?" I asked warily, gripping the handle of my oboe case even tighter.

"Don't waste our time, Lorraine," she snarled. "You know what you threatened to do yesterday."

Wait. This wasn't about my wedding? Could it be possible they didn't know? "I threaten a lot of things when I talk to you guys. It's the only language you understand."

"You've become so insolent," Jeannette said.

I'd better watch it or they'd become suspicious. "Honestly, I don't remember."

"You threatened to choose a different side, like Maliina did. We can't let you do that."

Relief was sweet. No wonder they were here. I'd scared them. "I was just letting you know that I have options." I stood. "Leave me alone, and I'll stay away from them. All I want is to help people. Not control destinies."

"But you are changing their destinies," Catie cut in. "We explained everything to you already."

"There's nothing I can do about that. I can't live in a bubble." But I could live in a castle in a small village surrounded by trees. I smiled and skirted around them. They turned to watch me with their ancient, wise eyes. They didn't detain me or speak, and I wasn't sure if that was good or bad.

I hurried out of the building and found Blaine and Ingrid by Blaine's car. "Cora's not out yet?"

"She's probably talking to the soul she's helping."

When she joined us, Cora wasn't amused that Echo had stopped by the mansion and now Blaine and Ingrid were babysitting her, but she couldn't stop the Immortals. They followed us downtown while Cora talked about quitting the business of helping souls.

"A dark soul attacked me," she said.

"I know, but Echo said it will never happen again."

"And how will my all-powerful and all-knowing boyfriend guarantee that? He can't be with me all the time."

"You have us too, Cora," I said, rubbing her arm. "You love helping souls find closure. Don't let the dark souls stop you from doing that. Just like I won't let the Norns stop me from doing what's right."

She started the car and we eased out of the parking lot. Blaine and Ingrid followed closely behind. Cora talked about her soul problems, but my mind was in England reliving my wedding, Torin's vows, imagining my life in the castle. We found a spot to park near Angie's Boutique and waited for Blaine and Ingrid to catch up with us before we went into the shop.

Conversations swirled around me, but I was back at my wedding. I kept playing with my rings underneath my top, until Ingrid shot me a warning glance and shook her head. Even Blaine chuckled when he caught me staring into space. But I must have made appropriate responses to Cora's questions because she didn't suspect a thing.

I helped her choose a prom dress and accessories. I usually shopped here too, but Mom had bought my outfit online this time. While I helped Cora out of her dress in the changing room, scuffles and shouts came from the other side of the door and I reached for my artavus. I created a portal and could see inside the store and the sales girl sitting at the counter. Ingrid and Blaine were missing.

"Outside," Cora said, and I followed the direction of her eyes. Rhys.

We joined them.

I noticed the way Ingrid stared at Rhys as though seeing him for the first time. Those violet eyes and dimples were totally irresistible. He was looking for Echo.

"He's not here," Cora said.

"I can see that. Could you tell him he and I need to talk?"

"Why?" Cora asked, not ready to trust him yet. He didn't indicate that he'd met me or Ingrid, but he couldn't take his eyes off Ingrid and neither could she from him.

"The dark souls are restless, and quite a number of them are headed this way," he explained.

Cora swallowed. "How do you know?"

"We reaped a few not far from here. Dark souls are loners by nature and territorial. We saw a group of them. If they're coming here because of you, Echo is going to need help dealing with them."

"Are you offering to help us?" Cora asked, taking the question from my mouth.

"Yes. It's time to bury the past." This time, Rhys glanced at me.

"So this has nothing to do with Dev and the fact that you guys want him?" Cora asked.

"No, but chances are the dark souls followed him here. Dev tended to act without thinking, and I'm sure that hasn't changed."

Cora sighed. "Okay, I'll talk to Echo. How will he contact you?"

"He knows where we hang out." Again he glanced at Ingrid before walking away.

Ingrid's eyes followed him. I was going to tease her about him. For now, I focused on Cora. She was spooked by the news about dark souls. After fighting *Draugar* and possessed black bears, dark souls didn't bother me. As long as I had my dagger, I could just suck them up and dump them at Crypt.

Ingrid and Blaine were almost at his car when I realized something. As soon as they got home, she would tell Lavania what Rhys had just told us. "Don't drop me off at my place," I told Cora. "Let's stop at the mansion and talk to Lavania. I'd rather she hear what's going on from you rather than me, or someone else."

I texted Ingrid and explained my plans, then added, "That Rhys is sure hot."

She sent an emoji of a sweating cartoon.

I laughed. "Did you see how the Grimnir, uh, Rhys couldn't take his eyes off Ingrid?" I asked, looked up, and caught Cora's expression. She glared at me. "Yeah, I know, we have enough to worry about without thinking about romance. But peaceful moments are meant to be enjoyed. Worrying about what might happen will only paralyze us. Torin often says we shouldn't let our enemies dictate how we behave. Let them come and think we're not prepared, until they attack and realize we are way ahead of the game."

She sighed and gripped my hand. "Thank you. I needed to hear that. Oh crap. I can't believe I forgot to ask Rhys about Maliina."

"I'm sure Echo would know if she's on Torture Island or not," I said.

Cora frowned. "I don't know. Remember, he never left my side after the battle, and when I recovered, he left with Eirik. The other Grimnirs were envious of his reaping record and hated him. Maliina could have escaped them, and they wouldn't have bothered to tell him."

Now Cora was beginning to have me worried. "Did you feel anything that could connect the dark soul that attacked you to her?"

"You mean other than the pure evil spewing from her core? No."

I felt a little sick. I'd just threatened to follow in Maliina's footsteps if the Norns didn't leave me alone. She was a vindictive bitch and was once in league with evil Norns. If she was back, chances were she was working with them again. Could she be after me or were the evil Norns the ones I should be worried about now?

~*~

Cora explained everything to Lavania. Then Andris and my husband arrived, and I lost track of who was saying what. My husband. I loved the sound of that. I couldn't take my eyes off him.

He inched his way to my side, sat on a stool and pulled me onto his lap. While the others discussed dark souls and the possibility that Maliina was back, he stroked my arm and whispered naughty things in my ear. It was a wonder I wasn't a puddle on the floor.

"You're not coaching this evening?" I asked.

"Nope. The assistants are in charge today." He ran the tip of his fingers up and down the palm of my hand. I always loved that. His other hand rested around my waist, his thumb slowly working its way under my shirt. Luckily, the counter blocked us from the others' prying eyes, except Andris'. He threw us mocking glances and smirked.

"Want to get out of here, Mrs. St. James?" Torin whispered in my ear.

My entire body flushed. I turned my head to glare at him and caught the naughty gleam in his eyes. Our lips were only a few inches apart. All I had to do was lean forward. Yes, I wanted to leave, but we couldn't. Cora would think we didn't care about her. Rhys shouldn't have told her about the dark souls.

Still, I said, "Yes."

"Then, listen," he whispered and turned my head, so I could look at Lavania. I wasn't sure what I was supposed to be listening to and only caught the tail end of her sentence.

"...start a new school," Lavania said. "A special school to train Immortals and future Valkyries. We should be up and running by fall."

I'd mentioned it jokingly when she and I had discussed this. "I didn't think they'd go for it."

"Why shouldn't they? As soon as they learned that the idea came from you, they were happy to oblige."

"Perfect place to send my Immortals too," Torin whispered, his warm breath fanning my ear. I shivered and he chuckled. He was deliberately messing with me.

Lavania continued, "I'm still searching for the perfect location, but once I find it, I expect you three to be in my senior class."

Ingrid liked the idea. Cora not so much. Me? I just wanted the meeting to end, so I could spend the evening with my husband.

"I think she needs our help," Torin whispered.

"Sure, she does." He was driving me crazy.

"She really does," he added.

"Who? Lavania?"

"No. Cora."

I studied Cora. She kept checking her phone, probably worried sick about Echo. She looked up and her eyes confirmed it. She was losing it. This business of dark souls and Maliina had her spooked. I sighed. My wedding night was going to have to wait.

I leaned against Torin and whispered, "For someone who's so intuitive, you don't know how to read your wife."

"I don't think a reading is what you have in mind tonight, Freckles," he whispered.

True. I got up and followed Cora outside the kitchen. As soon as she mentioned going to look for Echo, I knew Torin was right. We couldn't send her home alone. I gathered up the troops. Cora protested, but no one listened to her.

We used a portal to go to Echo's place in Miami, but it was empty. Since her parents didn't know what we were, we couldn't just create a portal and appear at their home. We had to go there like Mortals.

We headed back to the mansion, piled into cars, and headed to her place. Cora's family lived on a farm. Her parents were former school teachers, but her father wrote science fiction now, while her mother did organic farming. When we pulled up outside the farmhouse, her parents were at home. They didn't appear surprised.

We stayed on the deck while her mother prepared dinner. Torin took the swing and pulled me down onto his lap. It was five, the sun still high in the sky. I tried not to think about what I could be doing instead of talking and listening to Ingrid's dating stories. Cora was surprised by her stories. I wasn't. The Ingrid I'd gotten to know these past weeks was not as sweet and innocent as she looked. She was fun and unpredictable.

When Echo finally arrived, I was ready to go home. Mrs. Jemison was an amazing cook, but I don't remember what I ate. I couldn't focus while the guy I was crazy about watched me as though every movement I made mesmerized him.

When we left the farm, we took the back seat of the SUV, and I slipped into his arms, our lips meeting like we were starved for each other. I know I was.

"Keep it PG-13 back there," Andris called from the front seat. Blaine was driving for some reason.

"Leave them alone, Andris," Ingrid said from the middle seat.

The two traded barbs. After a few seconds, I was lost in Torin and stopped hearing anything. His hands were everywhere, his mouth relentless. He lifted me so I straddled his hips. With both our runes glowing, he watched me as his hand left a heated trail up my back to unclasp my bra. Somehow, we managed to pull the straps through my sleeves.

On a normal day, I'd be self-conscious that we were making out with the others seated a few feet away. Not this time. I'd waited for this kiss since he'd pledged he would love me forever in front of my family and friends.

I shuddered as his touch became intimate. I expected him to smirk. He enjoyed the way I responded to his touch, but tonight, he was intense, blue flames leaping in the depths of his eyes. I wrapped my arms around his neck and pressed my face to his, nuzzled actually, loving the feel of his heated skin against mine. Our lips inches apart, we exchanged a breath as we stared into each other's eyes. They say eyes are windows to the soul. They were right. I saw his and it was beautiful.

"I love you," he whispered.

"Forever," I finished it, and then kissed him, pouring my hopes and dreams into that single kiss. I wanted to touch him, feel his skin with my hands and lips. No, with my entire body. I wanted to drape myself all over him and let my skin soak him in. I had the right to now.

I yanked his shirt up and sighed blissfully when his stomach muscles contracted underneath my palm. He drew in a sharp breath and groaned. I crept up, loving the way his muscles trembled as though wanting to leap through his skin and blend with me.

A sudden cold draft filled the car and my first thought was Norns, but then I remembered they weren't exactly cold. It was their essence that was cold and induced revulsion and shudders.

"Goddamn it! There's no time for that now, you two."

I recognized Echo's voice and yanked my lips from Torin's.

"Get lost, Grimnir," Torin snarled.

"You want to hear this. I got a text from Cora. It's about your father, Raine."

My senses dulled by passion, I was slow in processing the information. When it finally hit me, I got off Torin's lap and looked at Echo. "What?"

"Your father's gone," he added, voice softer.

Tears welled in my eyes. I knew he'd been dying slowly for days. This morning, or this afternoon in England, I'd seen it in his eyes after he'd given me away. Felt it in his body as he'd placed my hand in Torin's. Still...

Torin opened a portal, the first time I'd seen him do that from a moving car. He picked me up and hopped into our living room, not missing a step. Echo followed before the portal closed. We raced to the den. Dad's body was still on his bed, but I couldn't see his soul.

Had Mom reaped him already?

Cora stood in the middle of the room covered with dark runes. On someone else, they'd look ugly. On her, the contrast between her skin and the inking was striking. I didn't even know why my mind went there. My father's soul was missing. If the Norns had taken him...

Snippets of the conversation between Echo and Cora reached me. They were discussing the medium runes etched on her by Ingrid's evil sister. The same dark runes inking her body now.

"Where's my father?" I asked in a voice I didn't recognize. Torin's arms tightened around me.

"He's inside her," a voice said from Cora's phone as she moved closer to us.

"Who is that?" Ingrid asked from behind me, but I already knew. Dev, the soul Cora was trying to help.

"Dev, the dark soul, who will be in trouble if he doesn't shut up," Cora warned. Her voice softened as she added, "Your father bonded with me, Raine. He wants to talk to you, Torin, and your mother."

Hel's Mist! "Mom, I have to tell her," I whispered.

"Lavania went to get her," Femi said. The entire group was inside the room, but one by one they left. Dev explained to Cora what to do. As a soul who'd possessed others, he had firsthand knowledge what the effect was. Now he possessed electronics.

Echo left with the phone, leaving us alone with Cora. She didn't hesitate before she started to speak, but her voice was no longer hers. It was Dad's. He sounded weak.

"I love you, pumpkin, and I'm so proud of the woman you've become. You are loving, fiercely loyal, and a fighter. But then again, from the moment I held your frail body in my arms and the doctors said you needed me to survive, I knew you would be. You were determined to live and you did."

Dad's voice grew stronger as he reminisced about my childhood, the little things I'd forgotten, yet he remembered with such clarity. "I remember when you were five and insisted on climbing the tree near your bedroom window, fell, and scraped you knees. You looked me straight in the eyes and said, "No, Daddy, it doesn't hurt. I'm okay. I'm going to do it today." Tears raced down your face, but you'd made up your mind. I stood under that tree and my heart swelled with pride with every step you took. You were a fighter then and you are a fighter now."

I cried harder and somewhere along the way, Cora started to cry too. I left the protection of Torin's arms and hugged her.

"Today, you made my dreams come true and I will cherish those memories forever," he finished, sounding more like the man I'd known growing up. "Torin, I expect a lot from you. I know you love my daughter, so live up to all your vows. Eirik reassured me that he'd keep me informed on what's happening, so I'll know if my princess is not happy." There was a pause and I thought he was done. Cora was sweating, and she looked drowsy. "I expect you to be a good father to my grandchildren. If possible, I hope you'll bring them to see…"

Mom must have come in while Dad was still talking to Torin. His voice stayed strong as he talked to her, but Cora looked terrible. Her eyes were glazed and sweat dotted her forehead. I didn't know what happened next. One minute Dad was still talking and then next he had left Cora. Her legs gave away.

Torin reached for her, but the door flew open and Echo was by her side. He caught her and lifted her in his arms. Echo threw us an unreadable glance. "She'll be okay. Dev said she shouldn't have done it for so long."

"You can take her upstairs to my bedroom. I'll find her some Twizzlers." After a possession, Cora usually needed sweets to rejuvenate. Twizzlers was her candy of choice.

Echo left the room with Cora in his arms.

"Do you want to join the others or stay here and talk to your father?" Torin asked.

"Let's stay here." New souls were like newborn kids, able to hear, but not talk. The difference was they understood what was said to them. They were also confused about what was happening to them. Not Dad though.

It took nearly two hours for Cora to recover and Echo refused to leave her side. I took her some Twizzlers then went downstairs to wait when I overheard Mom say, "Echo will find him the best resting place in the hall."

I entered the room, my eyes locked on her. "What did you say?"

Mom got up and walked around the bed to where I stood. "Sweetheart…"

I pushed her arm away. "What do you mean? Echo is reaping Dad? You went back to being a Valkyrie so you could reap him. You said so yourself, Mom." Torin was by my side in seconds. "Tell her. She promised. I... She was away at that stupid Council hearing so she could be reinstated as a Valkyrie just for him."

"I tried, honey," Mom whispered.

"No. Dad is not going to Hel," I whispered. He gave me a pained look and my heart broke. He didn't understand. Hel's Hall was cold and miserable, and the Goddess Hel was just like the place.

"Freckles," Torin said.

"No. They did this, Torin. The Norns are behind this." I was going to make them pay. Tears flowed again. I had thought I didn't have any left.

"No, they're not." Torin wiped my tears and added gently, "They didn't do this, luv."

"You don't know them like I do. I'm going to make them wish they'd never crossed me. They're not doing this to my father. Not *my* father. I won't let them. I won't..." My voice ended in a wail.

Torin hauled me into his arms and held me tight as sobs rose and shook my body. He murmured words, but I didn't hear them. Those conniving hags had crossed the line this time.

I wasn't sure how long I cried, but Torin's shirt was drenched when I pulled back, and my eyes landed on Mom crying a few feet away. Dad was trying to console her although his hand didn't exactly make contact with her. When our eyes met, he smiled reassuringly and realization hit me.

"You knew?" I asked Dad.

He nodded.

I looked at Torin. "You too?"

"Yes. Do you remember where and when I found your father after the plane crash? Echo was going to reap him, and I talked him out of it. He is meant to reap your father. It didn't matter how much time passed. But he and I talked, and he promised to find him the best resting place by the gods. He'll be surrounded by memories of his life. He could recreate this morning and relive it over and over again, or the day you were born, or when he met your mother. The gods' wing has private rooms so his world will not be corrupted by another soul."

I wanted to believe him, but I couldn't think beyond Hel. In Asgard, he could see my mother often, eat, sleep, run, and talk to others. In Hel, he'd be alone with nothing but his memories to keep him company. What was the point of having powers and knowledge when I couldn't secure my father a place in Valhalla? I didn't care what Torin said. The Norns engineered this.

Torin lifted my chin and wiped the tears from my cheeks. He was hurting for me. I saw it in his eyes and the way a muscle ticked on his jaw. Tonight was supposed to be our night. Our wedding night. Instead we had death and Hel.

Someone was going to pay for this.

23. Our Moment

The rest of the evening was a blur. I said goodbye to my father's soul, and watched as Echo and Andris escorted him away. Echo might be part of our group now, but my father was too important to trust him to do the right thing. Andris volunteered to go with them. Each step they took was like a dagger through my heart. I kept imagining Dad, not his soul, in Hel. Alone. Miserable.

My tears ran unchecked.

Once he was gone, I just wanted to crawl into Torin's arms and make him take my pain away. The moment Cora left he whisked me away to my room, lowered me on a chair, and said, "Don't move."

I watched him shove a few of my belongings in a bag—panties, tops, and pants—and didn't bother asking him what he was doing. He disappeared in the bathroom to get more stuff. Then there was silence. He must have opened a portal to his place. I closed my eyes, wishing I were in bed. I wanted to shut out the world for a long time.

My father was in Hel. Tears threatened to fall again. Onyx hopped onto my lap and purred. I couldn't remember hearing her purr. I stroked her fur.

So sorry for what happened tonight.

"They'll get what's coming to them."

I was sure she'd repeat the same thing everyone kept telling me, that the Norns weren't responsible. She didn't. Instead she said, *your friend Cora is not so bad after all.*

I didn't respond.

I had no idea she could do what she did. And her Grimnir... We'll see.

I really didn't care what Onyx thought of my friends. My father was in Hel. Torin reappeared without the bag, runes blazing. Onyx hopped down to the floor.

"Come on, luv. We're going home." He scooped me up and engaged his runes. My bedroom portal responded, but I couldn't see where we were going. One second we were in my room, the next at a front door. The sun was up. I realized where we were—the castle where we'd gotten married this morning, or yesterday afternoon UK time.

We could have teleported straight into the bedroom, but my wonderful husband was doing the traditional thing and carrying me across the threshold. Tears rushed to my eyes again.

A man opened the door. "Welcome home, Sire. Madam."

"Thanks, Donovan. Don't mind the cat. Her name is Onyx, and she belongs to my wife. We're not to be disturbed for the next twenty-four hours."

The grandfather clock in the foyer chimed. It was a quarter after eight.

There was no indication there had been a wedding feast. The flower petals were gone. Sounds from our left let me know that there was more than just Donovan living in the house.

Torin didn't slow down until he reached the bedroom I'd used to get ready for our wedding. My bag was on the bed, pajamas already laid out. The curtains were drawn, so little light came inside. Lamps covered with golden shades cast a warm glow over the room.

Torin lowered me to the floor and smiled. "Welcome home, Raine St. James. This wasn't how I'd planned the day to end, but I promise you that once we lay your father to rest, I'll give you a honeymoon to last centuries. Right now, I just want to hold you and make—"

I attacked him. It was the only way to describe it. I threw my arms around his neck and shut him up the only way I knew how. With a kiss. I broke the contact and whispered, "I don't want to sleep. I don't want you to hold me. I don't want to wait. I want you to love me. Make the pain go away."

He forgot I was new to all this because his primal instinct to claim, own, and brand took over. His mouth covered mine as he scooped me up. The bag and my pjs flew off the bed, but I think I might have used magic to do that. Or the burbling energy unfurling in my core had flowed into him and given him some of my magic.

He lowered me on the bed, reached over his shoulder with one hand, and pulled off his T-shirt, his eyes not leaving mine.

Shirtless, he tugged mine over my head, and then removed the chain necklace with my rings on it. One by one, he slipped them onto my finger. He raised my hand to his lips and pressed a kiss on the rings, then my palm. He grinned, joined our hands, and lowered his body until our chests touched.

The feeling of his skin against mine was heavenly. Maybe it was the runes or my magic, but every touch was heightened, every kiss toe-curling, and every nip erotic.

"Thank you for saying that," he whispered, his warm breath fanning my skin and teasing my senses. "I was trying to be noble, but..." He paused and kissed me, the moment endless. He lifted his head, his breathing as harsh as mine. "I want you. I need you." He ran the tips of his fingers along my collarbone. "I will take your pain away. *Our* pain away, because when you hurt, I hurt." His hands moved lower and stroked my chest, focusing on sensitive areas. His mouth followed.

He trailed kisses all over my bare skin. From my lips to my belly button, he lingered in some places, nipped with his teeth and soothed with his tongue in others.

I arched into him, the sensation so overwhelming I cried out. He went into hyper-speed, removing everything so our skins could breathe each other in, feel, and memorize the textures of each other. He paused for a moment and studied me, from my face to my feet.

"Perfect," he whispered.

Something flashed in my head. A memory, but it disappeared so fast I thought I imagined it. Stroking my calf, he started the slow torture of awakening my senses. New ones and old ones.

I had no idea what he could do with his hands and tongue and mouth until tonight. His touch was so intimate, I begged him to stop, when I never actually wanted him to. I bucked as though to push him off, yet held him tighter. Fought hard to breathe in oxygen, when all I needed to breathe was him, his scent and his essence. And yet my mind continued to tease me with images of moments like this when this was our first.

When he looked me in the eye with love and anguish, and then whispered, "I never want to hurt you. Not ever, yet I must," similar words echoed in my head.

"It's okay," I reassured him. "I'm ready."

He hesitated, fighting demons that I understood, yet didn't. I urged him with kisses and gentle caresses, reassured him in every way, yet he still agonized.

"Please," I whispered, hating that everything seemed like a replay when I wanted to cherish this first moment.

He kissed me and whispered, "I belong to you, Raine St. James. My heart. My soul. My body." Then we were one.

There was no pain, just memories crushing, overwhelming my senses. We'd done this before and the old hags must have wiped our memories. Why? Tears rushed to my eyes, until I met Torin's.

There was confusion in his sapphire blue depths and I read the questions. Had I been with another before him? When?

Then he jerked as though prodded and his eyes widened, and I realized I'd sent him the images. A growl escaped him when he realized what had happened. Rage washed across his face and he roared with it, but I refused to let them spoil our moment. They will not win. Not with us.

I pulled him down and kissed him, until passion and love once again ruled his head. With every movement, the memories receded. With every sigh and whispered love, we created new ones.

They could steal them as often as they wanted, but we'd always create new ones. Better ones. With our runes blending, my magic flowing into Torin, my senses exploded and I cried out his name.

Curled in his arms, I listened to his heart pound and slowly return to normal. His kisses became languid. He wasn't done. His, "I'm just starting," came out near my chest as he caressed me again.

"Don't you want to talk—?"

"No. *They* don't belong in our bedroom." He turned me around and continued to kiss his way down my back to my waist. I squealed when he nipped my butt. He chuckled and laved the spot with his tongue.

"Scoot back, luv," he whispered seductively.

He was relentless. Unstoppable. It was as though he planned to replace all the memories the Norns had stolen in one night. When I couldn't take it anymore, he amped up things until I thought I would die from sensations. This time, I think I blanked out.

When I came to, he was watching me, head resting on the heel of his hand.

"How long have you been watching me?"

He smirked. "Not long enough."

"That's creepy," I said.

He twirled a lock of my hair, spread the strands on the pillow, then leaned back and grinned. "I often wondered what you'd look like with it spread out like this."

I stroked his arm. "And?"

"You're breathtaking." He kissed my knuckles. "You want to try something different?"

Like I said, he was determined to create new memories and I was his willing accomplice. "Yes."

"You are going to engage speed runes when you're ready." He settled on the pillows with his arms behind his head and said, "You're in charge. You set the pace. You're allowed to make me beg. Just once, or I'm taking over."

To actually make him beg? I loved the idea.

By the time we finished, I learned something new about myself. I was bossy and a tease, and I loved watching him beg. But more than that, I loved giving him whatever he wanted.

~*~

We didn't venture out of the room until six in the evening, which was ten in the morning in Kayville, Oregon. We showered, changed, and headed downstairs.

Onyx was being spoiled by Mr. and Mrs. Donovan, the elderly Immortal couple who'd lived in the castle since Torin had bought it in the sixteen hundreds. I didn't remember meeting either of them during my wedding, but Torin insisted they'd been around. Mrs. Donovan was preparing our lunch, but she'd already baked fresh scones.

"I'll show Raine around before lunch," Torin explained and we left the kitchen, Onyx on our heels. "I've made renovations over the centuries," he explained as he showed me around. Us, I should say since Onyx came along and had something to say.

This is my new home. Plenty of places to hide your dagger.

I chuckled and explained to Torin.

"Why do they want—" He shook his head. "No, we're not talking about those hags. Not today. Let me show you something amazing."

He grabbed my hand and we headed upstairs to a hallway with a ceiling shaped like an upside down boat. It was beautiful. We moved from room to room. The paneling showed how beautifully he'd blended wood and rocks when fixing the place. Gilded mirrors and picture frames complemented the furniture and each room represented an era down to the area rug. We were in the drawing room, whatever that meant. I'd already seen the living room and it was cozy with fluffy chairs.

I pretended to faint on a lounge, which Torin insisted was called a fainting lounge. It had only one arm. Like most of the furniture in the room, it was Victorian with ivory legs and gold accents. I noticed he favored that era when decorating bedrooms.

"I always thought these were uncomfortable," I said, resting my head on the arm of the lounge and resting my feet. They weren't.

"Try this one," Torin said, dropping on a chaise lounge. I joined him and he pulled me onto his lap. For the next thirty minutes, we forgot about the tour. Onyx made herself scarce.

Sounds came from outside and I jumped up and raced to the window. Mrs. Donovan was cutting flowers from the flower beds. I could see a pond and a garden. "I want to go outside."

"Not until I finish showing you around Castle Windhaven," he said and grabbed my hand.

"Are you going to be one of those bossy husbands?" I shot back.

"Oh yes. Putting you in charge is detrimental to my health, as I found out last night."

I laughed. He'd loved it. "What is a drawing room?"

"It's where you receive guests. That's why it's close to the main entrance. We also withdraw there after dinner. Or the ladies did while the men smoked their cigars."

So happy I wasn't living during those times. My feet were beginning to hurt when we finished. The castle had twelve bedrooms, eight bathrooms, a large ballroom and a smaller one in the main tower, which he called a banquet room, a dining room, a modernized kitchen with an old fireplace, and a library. The wine cellar was huge and fully stocked.

When we finally made it outside, I was happy to explore. I'd seen a town from the tower, but it wasn't visible from the grounds. The castle sat on two hundred acres of land, Torin had explained. It had landscaped gardens, an orchard, a green house, and an ornamental lake, stone fountains and even stables. I could spend the rest of my life here and never care. There were three staff houses, the biggest one occupied by the Donovans. The other two were empty, but fully furnished.

After lunch, which was dinner for the Donovans, I disappeared into the bedroom while Torin talked to the two Immortals. When he joined me, we found ways to pass the next several hours. Once again, he helped me forget my worries about Dad and Hel.

We were resting when a portal opened and Ingrid yelled, "Is it safe to come in?"

"No," Torin yelled back.

I yanked the sheets to my chin then called back. "Yes."

Ingrid stepped into the room, her cheeks pink. Funny how one moment she could be so confident and cocky and the next shy. Then I noticed why. Torin's only cover was a pillow.

"Sorry to intrude. In my defense, you left your phones in Oregon."

"Because we didn't want to be bothered," Torin said.

I elbowed him and mouthed, "Be nice. What is it?" I asked louder.

"Cora and some of the swimmers are coming over to see you after school. That is in," Ingrid glanced at her watch, "less than an hour."

"Thanks, Ingrid. We'll be there."

She nodded. "Okay. Have fun."

"We were," Torin said. "Now where were we?" he asked before the portal was fully closed.

We barely made it before Cora arrived with Kicker, Sonya, and Nara, the three co-captains, and several other members of the swim team. Torin and Ingrid played host and hostess, while I sat there and wished I were back at my castle. The house reminded me of Dad. Everything reminded me of Dad, and the fact that he was in Hel's Hall. Worse, Andris and Echo hadn't returned.

Mom, Cora's mother, Lavania, and Femi were in the den. They'd cleared it of Dad's things and they must have called the morgue to take his body. Tears rushed to my eyes. I knew that Echo and Andris would do their best to make sure his soul was okay. That belief was the only thing that kept me sane. Still, I missed him.

Mom and I spoke briefly. I wasn't angry with her anymore. I was slowly adjusting my thinking about her situation. It wasn't her fault she couldn't reap Dad. The blame was on the Norns' laps. Just like how they did this to Goddess Freya when she'd refused to join them, the Norns were now punishing me.

As soon as Cora and the swim team left, Torin left for Carson to talk to his soccer team. I headed upstairs to rest. Onyx was still at Castle Windhaven.

Someone had left my prom dress on the chair. Seeing the dress reminded me that tomorrow was junior prom night. I had no interest whatsoever in going. I went next door and crawled into Torin's bed. I guess it was our bed now. His scent enveloped me and a sense of comfort coursed through my tired bones. It was early, but I was exhausted after staying up last night. My thoughts naturally shifted to Dad. What if they couldn't find his soul a place? Tears welled in my eyes. I hated feeling helpless and useless.

Exhausted, I drifted. I was half asleep when my phone rang. I didn't recognize the number, but I answered it anyway.

"Before you hang up on me, this is Ryder Copeland. I'm just calling all numbers on Beau's phone to tell you he was in an accident. They don't think he's going make it."

My stomach dropped to my feet. "When?"

"This morning. It would be nice to see some of his friends at the hospital. His parents are out here alone."

"I'll be there." They did it, the manipulative hags. First Dad and now Beau, someone I had come to care about. I grabbed my jacket and started to leave the room, but an idea popped into my head. They wanted the dagger, didn't they? Let them have it.

I went home and opened the drawer where I usually kept it, but it wasn't there. Then I remembered. *ONYX. I NEED YOU.*

Could she hear me from across the ocean? I started for the mirror just as it turned into a portal and she walked into the room.

What's with the ruckus? I was sleeping on an amazing bed Mrs. Donovan made for me. You've been crying again?

"Where's my dagger?"

Gee, hold your horses. What happened?

"They went after Beau," I practically snarled.

Our first case? Onyx asked.

"Beau stopped being a case and now he's dying."

Onyx disappeared into my bathroom and came back with the dagger. I grabbed it and said, "Bond."

Can I come? Onyx asked.

"No. Stay here." I left for downstairs. My rage must have been obvious because Mom took one look at me and jumped up.

"Sweetheart, what is it?" she asked. She, Femi, and Lavania were now in the living room. Cora's mother must have left.

"They did it again. They weren't just happy manipulating things so Dad could end up in Hel, they took our memories—"

"What memories?" Mom asked, her voice rising.

"Mine and Torin's. Now they've gone after Beau."

"The boy you've been tutoring?" Mom asked.

I nodded, so mad I wanted to scream. "He was in a car crash this morning. They don't think he'll make it." I started for the front door.

"Oh, no. Not so fast." Mom caught me by my elbow. "I'm coming with you. You're in no state to drive." She pried the keys from my hand. "And don't forget these." She removed the rings from my fingers.

In my rage, I'd completely forgotten about them. I shoved them in my left jacket pocket and zipped it up, wishing I had the chain. I liked having them touch my skin.

I didn't realize Femi and Lavania were coming with us until we reached my car. They squeezed in the back. The registration for Mom's car had expired weeks ago and we never renewed it, so taking it was out of the question.

~*~

No one spoke during the drive, but the closer we got to the hospital the angrier I got.

"Where's Torin?" Mom asked.

"Carson," Lavania answered. I was too pissed to talk.

"Rune anyone who tries to stop us," I heard Mom say and I saw why. Lavania and Femi had their invisibility runes.

Inside, Ryder, Seth, and several baseball players were in the waiting room. I blinked when I saw Ellie and Amber. Justin wasn't around and she'd come? And she looked like she'd been crying. I went straight to the information desk.

"Yes?" the nurse behind the desk asked without looking up.

"What room is Beau Hardshaw?"

The nurse continued to fidget with something behind the desk. "Are you family?"

"No, but his father will let me see him," I said.

"Sorry." She looked up and smiled. "Only family members are allowed to visit."

I glanced at Mom. Her eyes were locked on the nurse's face. "Rune her," she ordered.

The nurse smirked and two others joined her. Everything clicked as I stared at them. In my anger, I must have turned off my Norn radar.

"No, Mom. I'll take care of this." I leaned toward the nurses. "Screw you, you bitter old hags," I said through clenched teeth. "I'm seeing him and if you don't like it, do your worst."

Varying expressions crossed Mom, Femi, and Lavania's faces when they realized who the nurses were. The people from my school and the others waiting for their relatives stared at me in shock. My voice had carried.

I turned and cursed. I had no idea where his room was. Just before I turned and demanded they tell me, Hardshaw senior stepped out of the room and saw me.

"Mom, stay here." I hurried toward him. He stared at me with a look I couldn't describe—hope and fear. "Mr. Hardshaw—"

"It's you," he whispered hoarsely.

"Yes."

"Help him. You promised you'd watch over him." He pushed opened the door for me to enter, but pressed against it to put as much distance between us as possible. "You said he has a great future, and now he's dying."

My heart broke. Beau was hooked up to every machine imaginable, his face swollen and purple with bruises and stitched up lacerations. It was like the windshield had exploded on his face. His mother's eyes flickered between her husband and me.

"Janice, this is the guardian angel I told you about. She will help Beau."

Beau's mother scrambled to her feet and came around the bed. She gripped my hand. "Please. Help my boy."

"Leave the room," I said. They looked confused. "Please. Just go."

They left, and I moved to the bed. Beau looked really bad. Since hospital security wasn't breaking the door down, I knew I was right about the three nurses. I didn't wait long before they joined me.

"Fix this. Now."

They looked at each other, then Marj asked, "Why would we do that?" No matter what form she took, she was always the taller one.

This time, she was a redhead. She wore her arrogance and condescension like a cloak. "You don't listen to us, so why should we listen to you?"

"I have the dagger you want." I lifted my right hand and showed them the tattoo. "Heal him, and I'll give it to you."

"What's wrong with you? Get that dagger off you!" Catie snapped. Like Marj she had a distinct size she favored, short and a bit on the chubby side. Today she was a brunette.

"Why would I do that?" I shot back.

"Because you're not supposed to bond with it that way!" she yelled, face turning red. "That staff is the most powerful weapon of our people. You think you are the first one to wield it? It's been wielded by more powerful Norns before you and they all fell victim to its seductive power. You are to connect with its magic and channel yours, not absorb it into you. That's the kind of thing that turns Immortals into Warlocks. This one turned our sisters evil."

My first instinct was to remove the dagger, but I hesitated, remembering Eirik's warning and the incident in the forest. Eirik bonded with his weapon and he seemed okay. Unless he was slowly becoming evil or power hungry like Torin's father.

"How do I know you're not just saying that to trick me? I know you want it."

"Why would we want a weapon that doesn't respond to us?" Catie asked, annoyance lacing her words. "It's yours now. Every few centuries, a child is born who can bond with it. When she does, we know that she is our future leader and the first announcer of Ragnarok. We've already lost three Norns to that weapon and each time, we had to fight them to pry it from their evil hands."

If these hags weren't responsible for the attack in the forest, then that meant I was dealing with a different set of Norns. They even sounded differently. They were probably former wielders of the dagger wanting their dagger back. No wonder they'd grinned smugly when I'd bonded with it.

And if they controlled dark souls, they must have sent the *Draugar* too, just like Torin's father had said. As for these three, my threat to join the dark Norns must have hit them hard. They'd thought they were losing me to their evil sisters.

I touched the tattoo of the dagger. *Unbond.* The blade lifted and peeled off my skin. I grabbed the handle, hating that I had to touch it, that it was the cause of all my problems. If I hadn't bonded with it, I would be just another witch. I must warn Eirik about the dangers of bonding with his weapon.

"Now do you see why we are the only ones qualified to instruct you?" Catie asked.

She was right even though her condescending tone grated on my nerves.

"So give me private lessons, and try not to take me away from those I love." They looked at each other and laughed. "What's so funny about that? I've spent the last week helping Beau with his lessons and we did just fine." Beau. I couldn't believe they had sidetracked me. "What do I have to do for you to fix him?"

They watched my hand, a strange expression on their faces, and I realized they were watching the dagger. It must have a powerful pull on them. I shoved it in my pocket and zipped it up.

"So what do you want? And just so you know, I've decided on the side I'm supporting and it's not you or your evil sisters."

Silence followed.

"And it's not the Asgardians or Hel and her army."

More silence. Eyes watchful.

"I'm staying right here, supporting Immortals," I continued. "The rebellion by the Warlocks a few weeks ago happened because you and the gods neglected them. I may have your gifts, but I can never be one of you."

"We told you before, Lorraine," Catie said. "You cannot escape your destiny."

"I'm not escaping it. I'm embracing it, but I'm doing things my way. I'm going to have a life and I'm going to help those that need it the most—magical Mortals and Immortals. I am one of them. I am a witch and an Immortal. If they need help, I'll give it to them. If they need to talk to you or the gods, I'll be the intermediary. I've no interest in living in Asgard or your hall. I'm staying right here. And when Ragnarok draws closer, I will inform them first. Not you or the gods."

"You don't understand, you silly child. The gods will fight for humanity," Marj cut in. Catie touched her arm and they had another one of their silent communications.

"No, the gods will fight for themselves. They only care about the survival of one man and one woman to repopulate this realm. If you haven't noticed, Mortals come in all colors, shapes, and sizes. More will survive with my help and the help of the Immortals. Since I get to decide who goes inside the Yggdrassil, I'll make sure the mix represents them. When I appear before the Council on my eighteenth birthday, this will be my position. I'm telling you now so you're prepared."

This time the silence was longer, but I felt the vibes that said they were communicating. I was tempted to link with them and eavesdrop on their conversation, but that would mean they'd hear my thoughts. The last place I wanted them was inside my head. They'd know I'd regained the memories they stole and about my marriage.

"Does your decision have anything to do with your Valkyrie boyfriend?" Marj asked.

For one second, all thoughts flew from my head and my stomach dropped. Did they get inside my head? I wouldn't put it past them. Then I remembered the last discussion with Goddess Freya. They'd blamed Torin for everything and wanted us separated.

"Of course not. This is the path I've chosen for me. You've told me over and over again that he's just a passing phase. I see that now. I'm destined for something greater than my youthful obsession with him."

Another stretch of silence and conferencing among them.

"Fair enough," Catie said. "Support your Immortals. But if you want this boy back on his feet, you must do a task we each give you. It's the least you can do for all you've put us through with your shenanigans."

My jaw dropped. "Me? What about what you've stolen from us?"

"Stolen from you and...?" Catie asked, latching on to my blunder.

"Me and my family," I corrected myself, talking so fast my tongue tripped. "My father is in Hel because of you. I'll never see him again. You know what? Forget it. What do you want me to do?"

They studied me as though trying to see beyond my words, and then Catie looked at Jeannette and nodded.

"Erase every memory of the hospital staff who treated the boy," Jeannette said.

"Then the students at your school so they don't remember the Valkyries or you," Marj said.

"And finally the Witches who answered the Call," Catie added. "That impossible boy refused to do as he was told."

I studied their faces, hoping they weren't tricking me. I hated the very idea of erasing someone's memories. It was diabolical, like being mentally violated. Yet I saw no way out. Not if I wanted to help Beau.

"How do I do it?" I asked, feeling a little sick to my stomach.

"Link with me and I'll walk you through it," Jeannette said.

Yeah, like I was going to fall for that one. "No. Just explain it."

"Fine. Will it," she explained. "Mentally go over what they know and will it away, then go over what you want them to remember and plant it as new memories."

She talked and I listened, and then I followed her instructions.

"These are the new memories. Beau fell asleep at the wheel and rolled his truck. He was thrown clear at impact and became unconscious. The doctors are baffled because he has no external or internal injuries. In a nutshell, he's a medical anomaly. He's just a boy in a coma, who will slip right out of it after this and surprise everyone. And all the original records should also be erased and replaced with the ones matching his new medical status."

I studied Beau, his banged up face, and the machines, and I knew I was doing the right thing. With my eyes on him, I connected with the source of my magic and repeated everything Jeannette had said, until I could see the sequence of events.

A chill crawled up my spine as the bruises on Beau's face disappeared and the sterile tapes covering the stitches melted away.

Jeannette smiled, and nodded at the other two.

"Good job," Catie said and glanced at Marj. "Your turn."

"Remove the memories of the Valkyries and Grimnirs from the people here in your town," Jeannette said, "so they don't recognize them. Instead of the Valkyrie playing football for your school, replace him with the Immortal." She glanced at the others. "What's his name?"

"Blaine Chapman," Catie said.

"That's right. Blaine Chapman. The memories of you will also be erased from everyone you've known most of your life. You and Eirik never attended this school. Your neighbors across the street will only know you as the girl who was homeschooled by an eccentric mother and father. This way, when you leave, no one will wonder what happened to you."

I shook my head. "Leave? I'm not going anywhere."

"You must continue your studies, and since the Valkyries and your instructor are leaving, we assumed you and your mother will want to leave with them," Catie said, smiling benignly.

I nodded. "I do."

"Good. We plan to help with your education whenever we can now that you've decided on your future." She looked at the others and added, "But right now, your focus should be on Beau Hardshaw. You've chosen to help Immortals and Mortals. Save him."

I swallowed and wavered. They were too calm and smug, which meant they were up to something. I just couldn't see it yet. The one thing they still didn't know was that Torin and I were married. That should screw up whatever plans they might be concocting.

"Do you need more time to decide?" Catie asked.

"No." Beau looked so peaceful. If it weren't for the machines monitoring his vitals, I'd think he was dead. "I'll do it."

I closed my eyes this time and wove the memories in my mind: Blaine winning state with the football team, Torin, Andris, Ingrid, and Maliina never setting a foot in our school. Instead of completely erasing memories of Eirik and me, I changed it to Eirik and I leaving after the swim meet incident. If I hadn't attended middle school I would never have met Cora. Erasing those memories meant erasing hers too. I refused to erase her memories or her parents'.

The cold I'd felt earlier was creeping toward my chest. If I didn't know better, I'd say that with every memory-manipulation the coldness spread.

The door flew open, and so did my eyes as I whipped around to see Torin standing in the doorway, looking like my champion. The problem was he couldn't afford to fight these women. He wouldn't win. He took the scene in with a sweeping glance and reached a conclusion.

"You," he snarled. "No wonder everyone out there is on a time loop doing the same thing over and over. Stay away from her."

"This is none of your business, Valkyrie," Catie snarled. "Lorraine, you're almost done."

"Whatever they're asking you do, Freckles, don't do it," Torin begged.

"I'm trying to save Beau, Torin," I explained, torn between listening to him and helping Beau.

Torin pulled out an artavus and moved to my side. "I'll save him for you."

"You wouldn't dare," Marj said, moving closer to the bed. "Your status will be revoked and it will be another millennium before you'll ever be considered for the position of an Idun-Valkyrie."

"I don't care about being an Idun-Valkyrie. You will not manipulate her when I'm around." He gripped my hand.

"What about when you're not around, Valkyrie?" Catie cut in. "You won't just lose your new position, you will be assigned to Goddess Hel and posted in her realm, not here on earth."

My stomach sunk at the threats. Torin and I belonged together. I tugged his hand. "I told them I was on the side of the Immortals and Mortals, and I was staying here."

Fear flashed in his eyes. Torin was fearless, so this couldn't be good.

"What did they ask you to do?" he asked me, but his eyes were on the Norns.

My eyes flashed between him and the Norns as I explained erasing the memories of the hospital staff, the students at school, and the Witches.

"I don't like it, but this would prove—"

"Nothing," Torin cut in. "They're liars, Raine, and they're still trying to trick you. Each Norn gives a task to a novice. If she accomplishes the tasks, she's bound to them for as long as they deem fit. That's how they recruit Valkyries and Immortals who resist them. Remember the loophole in their binding laws we talked about last week?" He glanced at me. "I wasn't subbing at CC High. I went to find answers." He went back to glaring at the Norns. "This has nothing to do with saving Beau. They're trying to bind you to them."

"It is done, Valkyrie," Jeannette said triumphantly. "You've lost. She's bound to us already."

"I didn't complete the last task," I protested.

"Oh, but you did," Catie said. "I asked you to heal the forest and you did. That was your *first* task."

"And you just erased the memories of the hospital staff," Jeannette chimed in. "Task two."

"And I believe you completed fixing the memories of people in this town," Marj finished. Her eyes went to Beau. "Too bad about the boy. We didn't cause his accident. We don't do that sort of thing.

Whatever did you do to anger our evil sisters, Lorraine? Let me guess. They know you have the dagger."

I stared at them in shock. "You knew all this time?"

"About the attack by the dark souls in Carson and in the forest?" Catie asked. "Yes, we did. We hoped you'd realize there's no one who can help you but us."

"She doesn't need your help," Torin said. "She has me."

"No, she doesn't. She's now bound to us, Valkyrie. Check her arm. She has our rune now." They laughed gleefully.

One by one, they disappeared.

Torin took my hand and pushed up the sleeve of my jacket. A glowing *valknut*, the three intertwined triangle rune of the Norns, appeared on my skin. And with a last evil smile the Norns vanished.

24. Turning Tables

I stared at Torin and moaned, "No."

A grin touched the corner of his lips. "Look again," he said.

I stared at my arm. Two runes appeared, both attached to the rune of love.

"Those are our bonding runes. The runes Andris and Ingrid etched on us yesterday when got married. One etched on you and another on me, yet we carry them both. We are connected now. Bonded. Mated."

The two runes were bigger and brighter than the Norns' *valknut*. They reminded me of Beau's tattoos, the bigger butterfly dominating the menacing dog. Love always wins.

"They're wrong, Freckles," he said. "You and I bonded first and our bond is stronger, and that's why our runes are bigger and brighter than theirs. What they don't know is that we're going to kick their asses when we face the Valkyrie Council. We are going to win this battle."

I exhaled and hugged him tight. I hope so. I really, really hope so.

"Now what are we going to do about him? Should I heal him?" he asked.

"No." I shook my head. I refused to let him throw away his future. "I need to think. I plan to stick it to the Norns. What do they fear the most?"

"Exposure," he said.

The door opened behind us, and Mom peeked in. She saw us and rushed forward to give me a hug. "Thank goodness you are okay. Those hags put us on a time loop we couldn't escape. The worst part was we were aware we were doing the same thing over and over again." She studied my face. "Are you okay?"

I nodded. "They tried to trap me. No, they tricked me and bound me to them, but we won."

"What?"

I looked at Torin and he explained to her what had happened. She looked worried, but tried to downplay it. "And the boy?"

"We'll figure something out."

The door opened and Femi stuck her head inside, "Lavania says his parents are coming back. She can't rune them again."

We filed out of Beau's room. The father saw us and frowned. "Who are you?" he asked, not recognizing me.

"Friends from school," I said.

"Have they figured out what's wrong with him?" he asked, looking at Torin.

He shook his head. "No, Mr. Hardshaw."

"What good are these doctors when they can't heal a simple boy?" I overheard him object as we walked away, but I was still reeling from the fact that he hadn't recognized me.

In the waiting area, Seth and the others were still there. Amber and Ellie saw me and smiled, then their eyes slid to Torin. There was no recognition, just curiosity. Had I really scrambled their memories?

Mom, Femi, and Lavania disappeared into the nearest bathroom to create a portal home. Torin and I took my car. "How did you know where I was?"

"You mean other than the fact that we're even more bound to each other than before and I know when you need me?"

I rolled my eyes. "Yes."

"Onyx found me. I love that cat." He revved the engine and eased out of the parking lot. "I had tracked down my father to some gentlemen's club in London and was asking him how he'd known about the loophole in the Norn's binding law when Onyx arrived. She likes to make an entrance."

"Let me guess, she was this high,"—I indicated the area near my nose—"with a shiny coat and piercing green eyes?" I asked.

Torin chuckled. "Yep."

"She did that when I called her to the forest the other day."

"Is that the day you were attacked, and you somehow forgot to give me the details?"

"No, it's the day I got drunk and swore never to touch alcohol again. As for the loophole, I think it's more like the green light to trap unsuspecting, naive Immortals into Norn servitude."

Torin reached for my hand and brought it to his lips. "It works both ways, luv. If you don't follow their instructions, the bond loses its impact. If you have a more powerful bond with someone else first, like we do, that bond dominates."

"Does that mean if you piss me off, my Norn bond will dominate?"

He shot me a quick glance. "I refuse to believe my bride would think of something that horrible."

I grinned and rested my head on his shoulder. "About your father, do you trust him now?"

He laughed. "Not in this lifetime. He's a self-serving opportunist who will hitch his wagon to any winning horse." He brought the car to a stop outside my house. "Not that you are a horse, but I think he realized you're more important than going to Asgard. He won't tell me where he gets his information though."

"Probably from the evil Norns." I explained about the dagger, the attack in the forest, and the *Draugar*. "He knew about the attack by the *Draugar*, and that I was the target."

"Nothing he does surprises me anymore. Are you sure you don't want me to heal Beau?"

I shook my head. "I can't risk losing you. Once the Norns find out we're married, they'll be pissed and I'm afraid they'll take it out on you to punish me."

He sighed. "I can take anything those hags dish out."

"Including being banished to Hel?"

He gave me a lost puppy look. "Would you come with me?"

I kissed him. "Of course I would. Someone will have to keep the goddess away from you, but I'd rather live here than in Hel's Hall, so no healing Beau. I'll come up with something."

"Come on, I need to talk to your mother and the others about something my father said."

That was the second time he'd referred to him as his father, not the Earl. "What?"

"Inside." He walked around the car and grabbed my hand then frowned. "Where are your rings?"

I touched my pocket. "I had to remove them before going to the hospital."

Mom, Lavania, and Femi were in the kitchen peering at something on Femi's laptop when we entered the house.

"I like that better," Femi murmured. "It has more room for the students and the staff."

"This one is more secluded and has a drawbridge," Lavania said.

"What is secluded?" I asked and they looked up.

"We're trying to narrow down properties for the school," Mom said when she looked up and saw us. "What do you guys think?" One window showed a Gothic castle in North Wales, England, worth five million pounds. The second one was in Great Barrington, Massachusetts. The last one was a secluded château in France.

"The Gothic," Torin and I said in unison.

Mom grinned at the other women. "They're starting to think alike." Her face became serious. "Okay, sit down. We want to hear everything."

There was only one chair, so Torin sat and pulled me down onto his lap. I told them everything, and then Torin added the information from his father. "He thinks there will be more attacks by dark souls. He's not sure when, but he insists someone is organizing them. I was sure he was the one doing it, but after what Raine learned, it might be someone working with the evil Norns."

Mom sighed. "Who else would be stupid enough to work with evil Norns after what happened to Maliina? Now they're after my baby." She rubbed my arm.

"Sorry, Mrs. Cooper, but she's mine now," Torin teased, removing the rings from the pocket of my jacket and sliding them back on my finger. He got a smack on his hand for his pains.

"She'll always be my child, Torin. We're ordering dinner, then sitting down in earnest to figure out this school business once Hawk gets here."

"I think I might offer Dev, Cora's soul, a teaching position," Lavania said. "It might quicken his recovery. Do you guys have anyone else in mind?"

"Blaine and Ingrid might like the positions," I said.

"They're already shortlisted," Lavania said. "I decided Ingrid is too old to be a student."

"My father," Torin said, and the shock in the room was palpable. No one spoke. I turned to look at him. Not to put his idea down, but come on. His father was a total douche and even he didn't trust the guy.

"Why?" I asked.

"To keep an eye on him. What better way than in a school full of Witches and other Immortals? Besides, he has enough experience warring. He could be in charge of martial arts and battle strategy."

"Well, we'll have to think about that, Torin," Lavania said. "As the founders of the school, we'll also have put it to a vote."

"Founders?" I asked.

"Oh yes. There's your mother, Femi, Hawk, and me. We have three months to get the school going and send out admission letters to all eligible Witches around the world."

I stood, wanting to be alone with Torin. "Well, good luck. We'll see you tomorrow."

They stared at us with knowing expressions and heat rushed to my face. I could swear one of them muttered, "Young love," as we walked away.

"We'll be next door if you need us," Torin said.

"Let us know when Andris comes back," Lavania added. "Oops, we need Ingrid here. She had some wonderful suggestions earlier about classes."

Just before we entered the portal, I glanced back and caught Mom watching us. She wore a haunted look, and I wondered if she was thinking of Dad or worrying about me.

~*~

We went back to the castle and spent another night fulfilling some of Torin's fantasies. He had so many of them. I would never look at a mirror again without seeing our reflections. He made me forget about the Norns, but not Beau.

I woke up before Torin did and watched him sleep. The clock on the wall said it was one in the afternoon, which meant it was five in the morning in Kayville. I wondered if my memory deletion thing worked. Every time I thought about it, I felt guilty. Since Beau was in a coma when it happened, did it affect him?

"Still worrying?" Torin asked, and my eyes flew to his face.

"I was actually watching you sleep."

He stroked my cheek and grinned. "You should have woken me up."

"You looked so peaceful."

He leaned in and kissed me. The kiss grew intense fast. It was another hour before he left for the bathroom. Then I heard the water running. He came into the bedroom and whispered in my ear, "Want to have a bath with me?"

For an answer, I turned and looped my arms around his neck. He scooped me up.

"Do you know today's your prom night?" he asked.

"So?"

"So do you want to go?"

"No. Oh crap! I meant to call Cora last night and warn her."

"About?"

"The memory erasing thing. If it worked, she shouldn't talk to people about you guys or me. They'll think she's lost it. Is there a way you can find out if it worked?"

"Sure. I'll call one of the football players and see if he remembers me."

I pushed the matter aside and enjoyed the moment. Torin had invested a lot in modernizing the castle. The tub was big enough for the two of us. The bath lasted longer than we'd planned, and then Torin disappeared through a portal.

I stared at my arms and thought of him, and our runes appeared. The more I thought of him, the brighter they appeared. The feeling of love and wellbeing washed over me. I dozed off with the runes still on my skin. I probably had a dopey expression on my face.

When Torin woke me up, he had breakfast and flowers on a tray. He was wearing my favorite sweatpants. As usual, they were indecently low. My stomach growled and my attention shifted to the tray. The setting was for one.

"Aren't you eating?" I asked, sitting up.

"Later. I need to take care of something first." He pressed a kiss on my temple, but I felt the tension pouring from him.

"What is it?"

"I'll explain when I come back, luv. Rest." He pulled on a T-shirt and left.

I was tempted to follow him and find out what was going on, but I refused to be that woman. You know the kind who was so insecure she spied on her husband.

Oh, who was I kidding? We had so much crap going on, this could be a matter of life and death. Or Andris and Echo could be back from Hel. I wanted be sure that Dad's soul was safe.

I changed and opened a portal to his place in Kayville. *Our* place. I stopped at the top of the stairs and angled my head to eavesdrop. I heard Blaine. It was the morning ritual at his place. He made coffee and all the non-tea drinkers at the mansion moseyed over to get some. I didn't hear Andris, which meant he wasn't back.

This was stupid. I should either go downstairs and join them or find something else to do. Like check on Beau at the hospital.

Instead of turning into a stalker, I opened a portal to the hospital. I'd been to Kayville Medical Center so often over the last eight months I knew the place inside out. There was the night we kept vigil after several swim team mates got injured at a club. It was my seventeenth birthday. Seemed like a long time ago now. Then there was the time I was first admitted after Maliina hurt me. I hated thinking about the bitch because my thoughts automatically switched to evil Norns. She'd been an evil Norn-in-training. Amazing how different she was from Ingrid.

I engaged my invisibility runes before going through the portal, and then headed to Beau's room. His mother was asleep in the chair by the bed, and a female with a smooth dark-chocolate complexion and curly black hair with red streaks sat in the corner playing a game on a tablet while munching on Lays potato chips. Invisibility runes glowed and dimmed on her skin. Her trendy hip-hop clothes left too much skin for her to be a Grimnir.

She looked up and blinked when she saw me. "Sorry, hun, but he's mine."

I couldn't think up anything to say, but various thoughts went through my head. There had to be a mistake. A Valkyrie could not be here for Beau. He wasn't supposed to die.

She glanced at me again and frowned. "You look familiar. Have we met?"

"No. I'm here for him. I mean, I'm his friend."

She swiped the screen of her tablet, her lips scrunched as she studied the contents. Then she looked at me, her eyes widening. She got up, wiped her hands on her pants and came to shake my hand.

"I'm Attie, short for Atieno. You are Raine. Torin's Norn. I recognized you from pictures my cousin sent."

"Pictures?"

She showed me her tablet and I found myself staring at my wedding photos. "How did she get those?"

"She's a witch and was lucky enough to attend your wedding. I call her cousin but she's really my... Let's just say we are centuries apart and somehow related. She took them with her cell phone. She even taped a few segments. I can't believe I'm meeting you. The first

Norn to break the celibate tradition. You go, girl. We're rooting for you."

Crap! The Norns were so going to hear about this. "Thanks. Uh-mm, is he supposed to die?"

She glanced at Beau. "Honestly, I don't know. We're supposed to collect four of them from here this week, so we do our rounds twice a day. I check on all the coma patients while my partner checks the ER, then we switch. So I can't say for sure. What's wrong with him?"

"He had an… The Norns put a whammy on him to punish me."

Her eyes widened. "No way. What can I do to help?"

"If he gets worse, find me or Torin."

"Sure, hun." Then she gave me a sheepish smile. "Uh, can I take a selfie with you?"

I touched my hair. I was sure it was a mess, and I had no makeup. So much for the girl the Valkyries were rooting for. "Sure."

~*~

I got out of the hospital fast and went in search of my husband. He was in the kitchen taking care of all the coffee cups. I slipped my arms around his waist and rested my head on his back. He turned around and studied my face.

"What is it?" he asked.

"I went to the hospital and there was a Valkyrie in Beau's room."

He cursed softly. "I'm sorry."

"It's not your fault. I just want him to get better."

"I know." He rubbed my arms. "We need to talk. Cora stopped here on her way to school. Maliina is definitely back."

I groaned. "You're kidding."

"And she's not alone. She's leading an army of dark souls into town to take over the students tonight at the prom. The evil Norns are behind this, and they probably expect you to be there. They don't know you're no longer a student. I called one of my former football buddies and he thought I was pranking him."

I listened to him, but I was still trying to wrap my head around Maliina being back. The woman was the ultimate villain. Even death didn't stop her. "What? Did you just say you're going to use me as bait?"

Torin chuckled. "That was to confirm that you were listening. Of course, I'd never use you as bait. Dev, Cora's dark soul, will lead them straight to the gym, where we'll be waiting."

"Isn't that where the prom is? You can't have all those Mortals around dark souls."

He groaned. "I knew you weren't listening."

"I'm trying. Start from the beginning. Please?"

He sighed. "If I wasn't crazy about you, I'd wring your neck."

"And I'd survive it and wring yours. Start talking."

He grinned, his eyelids lowering in a sexy look I found totally irresistible. "I love it when you're bossy."

"And you have a one-track mind."

"We're supposed to be on our honeymoon. I'm allowed to have a one-track mind." He lifted me onto the counter and settled between my legs, then wrapped his arms around my waist and pulled me closer. I sucked in a breath. "The others are taking care of things. Why don't we continue this conversation upstairs and talk later?" he asked in a husky voice.

What were we discussing? Oh yeah, prom and dark souls. An idea popped into my head. It was bold, but it could work. I had to get rid of my husband first.

"No upstairs and no distracting me until you answer my question. What's the plan for tonight?"

"You're a spoilsport."

"Hmm. Yeah. You and I know that's not true. I give in to you whenever and wherever." I kissed him then leaned back and said, "Tell me everything."

He shook his head. "You can't do that and then ask me to... Okay. We are having two proms, one in the cafeteria attended by the juniors and the other in the gym attended by us, Grimnirs and Immortals. Any dark soul crazy enough to follow Maliina is going straight to Hel. Blaine is talking to the student council to change the venue as we speak. He's promised to bring a live band to perform and acoustics are better in the cafeteria. Your mom and the others have gone shopping since they'll be chaperoning the second prom, or helping capture the souls. I'm going shopping for the theme paraphernalia. School is half-day today, so we have time to add runes on the buildings to protect the students and some to let the souls in, but not out. It will be like a roach motel. What do you think?"

Like he needed me to validate him. "It's brilliant. Since the gym is in a separate building, the students won't know what's happening."

"We'll also add bind runes with a dampening effect so anyone driving by the gym won't hear a thing. So what's your idea?"

"I'm going to trick the Norns into helping Beau."

He frowned. "Now?"

"No, tonight. After we're done with the souls."

"From the gleam in your eyes, I don't know if I'm going to like this."

"Oh you will." I did something I'd been meaning to do every time I saw him wear his sweatpants so low. I slid my hands under the elastic band. He took it from there, the dishes forgotten.

~*~

Assuming I was resting, Torin got dressed and left. As soon as the portal closed, I jumped up and headed to my home. My parent's place. My throat closed thinking of Dad. It was now just Mom's place.

The place was quiet. Mom and Femi must still be shopping. I wondered if Ingrid went with them. Maybe I should invite her along. No, I wouldn't want her caught in the crossfire. Besides, she might foil my plans and contact Torin. He was the last person I wanted there.

I shrugged on my jacket. The dagger was still in the pocket. I pulled it out and bonded with it.

That weird sensation crept up my arm and I shivered. I still didn't like the feeling, but I needed the Norns to know I meant business. Besides, now that I knew what was going on, I could control it. The source of my magic stirred as though trying to connect with it, and I let it.

I removed my rings, slipped them onto the chain, and snapped it around my neck. To hide it, I added a Gothic spiked choker. The platinum chain looked like it was part of the choker.

I let the image of Torin fill my head and then willed the transformation. In seconds my reflection showed Torin in his trademark leather jacket and fingerless gloves. I adjusted the hair length and added a shadow of a beard. Perfect.

ONYX!

The mirror shifted and flowed and a portal appeared.

What's going...? The cat started to ask, entering my room. *Oh no. This can't be good.*

I grinned, channeling my husband's cocky smile. I loved saying that even if it was only in my head. My husband. So surreal.

"Where have you been?" I asked, adjusting the collar of the jacket.

Do you need to ask?

At the castle, of course. "I want you with me. In your fiercest form."

She groaned, but runes appeared under her skin as she shifted and grew bigger, her hair becoming sleeker, until a beautiful jaguar stood beside me. I stroked her head. "You are beautiful."

You too.

"He is beautiful, isn't he?"

She rolled her eyes. *I can see past the illusion, Raine, to the real you. And yes, he is. Where are we going?*

"To find the evil Norns and there's only one person who can do that."

Not him. He scares me.

"Nothing scares you, you faker. Lead the way."

She turned and faced the mirror, and in seconds I could see the inside of a heavily paneled hallway. On the walls were paintings of men who looked like they were ready to conquer the world. Warlocks. They probably owned the world. A gentlemen's club. They should just call it a Warlock's club.

I stepped into the hallway, and a man walking with a cane headed toward me in a spiffy suit and a trench coat. He had white hair and carried himself like he expected everything and everyone to bow to him.

The silence was spooky. As I followed Onyx, I studied the faces on the walls. I expected to see Hitler, Mussolini, and Stalin. No, members of this club, I was sure, were shrouded in shadows. Yanking Mortal leaders' chains like puppet masters.

We entered the main floor. It was huge and heavily paneled with statues of the gods on the walls. Interestingly, they represented gods and goddesses from known civilizations. I spied Thoth holding a book. Venus in her flowing robes. Freya riding a chariot pulled by her cats.

My mother would get a kick out of that one, Onyx said.

I chuckled. *Freya too.*

The Earl of Worthington was talking to two men as we approached his table in the center of the room. He saw us and said something to the men. They got up before I reached them.

"My son, Torin," he said, then waved to indicate the two men, "Lord Westmoreland and Lord Paddington."

Bet they lost those titles centuries ago. I gave a curt nod and received nods before they walked away.

The Earl indicated one of the chairs the Warlock lords had just vacated. "You didn't need to bring her familiar with you, son. I told you, you're safe here."

I'd fooled him. Now for the real charade to begin.

25. The Norns

"Onyx knows how to find you, and Raine insisted," I said, stroking Onyx's silky coat. *Sit.*

Don't believe anything he says, Onyx warned.

A cynical smirk touched the Earl's lips. "Raine has nothing to worry about from me. I made my position very clear. I'm here to help both of you in any capacity."

No wonder Torin had called him self-serving. I glanced around, studying the members interacting with each other. Very few were walking around. They sat in twos and threes, talking and laughing, yet not a single sound escaped their tables. I wondered if this is what inspired most gentlemen's clubs, where silence was the golden rule. Of course in here, the runes on the chairs and tables had a dampening effect on the sounds so you only heard those sharing your table.

I focused on the Earl. His hair looked grayer, the white concentrated along his temples. "I need to meet the Norns."

He blinked. "Excuse me?"

"You heard me, so let's not play games, *father.* You knew about the loophole in their binding laws. Not even Norns-in-training like Svana knew about it. How could you, an Immortal? You have to be at the top of the Norn hierarchy to know something that damning. Or know someone that powerful. You also knew about the *Draugar* targeting Raine, and that dark souls were getting organized. Again, information that can only come from the top. I want to meet them."

"Son—"

"Don't call me that," I retorted reacting as me and not Torin.

A cynical smile touched his lips. I still hated that he looked so much like Torin down to his sapphire blue eyes. Except his were cold. And his hair had gray.

"I'll always be your father, Torin. I vowed to help you and your fiancée as much as I can, but dealing with Norns directly is foolhardy."

"I can handle them. Just take me to them."

He leaned forward, something flashing in his eyes so fast I might have missed it if I wasn't trying hard to read him. He was afraid.

"What do you want with them? These deities are unpredictable. And once they have their claws in you, they don't let go."

I saw through his cold voice to the fear he tried hard to hide. He might be a bastard, but he cared for Torin on some subliminal level. "They're the ones who made you challenge the status quo and demand entrance into Asgard, aren't they?" I asked, watching his expression for signs of any emotion. Guilt. Remorse. Fear.

"No one makes me do anything." He sat back, his face unreadable. "I made a mistake of seeking their counsel. You don't want to negotiate with them. Let Raine deal with them. She seems to have the ability to make them heel."

"No. She's been through enough and needs a break from dealing with them. They'll negotiate with me once they realize what I have."

His eyes sharpened. "You have the weapon?"

I ignored his question, but his reaction confirmed what I'd suspected all along. I also remembered what Nikos had said the day the Warlock and I met in his café. The Earl had met with Bash and the twins, who were really my Norns.

"I know you've used both of them to your advantage. I want to meet them all, starting with the malevolent ones."

He sat back. "You're starting on a perilous path, son. A path that will bring you nothing but problems. Go home and marry your young love and stop them from interfering with your life. I already told you, bind her to you as soon as you can before she's bound to them."

Okay, the Warlock was trying to make up for what he'd done to my fellow Seeresses. That was good. I might actually forgive him. "If you do this for me, I will tell Raine what you've done for us. She has a kind heart and will see past what you did before."

He studied me so intently I was sure I'd given myself away. "You think she'd forgive me? Maybe let me be a part of your life?" he asked, speaking slowly.

"If it's what I want, she'll try."

He looked around the room and sighed. "If anything goes wrong, I'll do my best to protect you, but don't say I didn't warn you. Come on. We're going for a drive." He stood and buttoned his jacket, picked up a trench coat, a hat, and a walking stick. I noticed that each chair had a hook for walking sticks, and almost all of the Warlocks had one. They were probably weapons of some kind.

Onyx stood and walked by my side as we left the room. I also noticed something I'd missed earlier. There were women in this club. I wondered what you called a female Warlock.

Eyes followed us, and I fought the urge to turn around and stick out my tongue at them. I bet they'd fought on the Earl's side, the smug, power-hungry fiends. Or I could be wrong and they were just Immortals with more money than any Mortal needed and nothing to do with their time.

The sun had set and darkness was spreading over the land. It wasn't even noon when I had left home, which meant this club was somewhere in Europe. The parking lot had high-end cars and golf carts were parked by the building.

"We'll take a cart," the Earl said.

Onyx sat in the back seat, while I took the front seat next to the Earl. The drive seemed to take forever, or he was deliberately taking a longer route.

"So when is the young Norn's family burying her father?"

"Tomorrow morning," I said.

"Isn't your wedding tomorrow?"

I almost smirked. "Maybe."

"Don't postpone it. The sooner you bind her to you the better off she'll be, or her loyalties will always be with the Norns."

I don't know why I said what I said next. Maybe it was to test him. "I'm not sure I'm ready to marry her. She's so young."

He brought the cart to a stop. We were so far from the club building I could only see a section of the roof. Instead of getting out, he turned and faced me.

"I've seen you together, Torin. I may not have the right to advise you, but I know what I saw. The girl adores you, and you her. Don't throw what you have away. Marry her. The sooner the better."

"So if I wanted to join you..."

"There's nothing to join," he warned. "I'm done. I thought..." His voice trailed off. "Marry the girl, Torin. I will offer her an apology for the things I said to her in the café when the time is right, when my actions are not all she sees. Maybe she'll forgive me. Maybe not. Just know that this life is long and lonely, and if you can share it with someone, do it." He stepped down and started across the hilly slope. I followed.

I didn't speak. Onyx had plenty to say.

As I live and breathe. I think he's actually sincere. Maybe he's worth forgiving, huh, Raine? You're not saying anything. Please, don't tell me you're getting teary over him? He'll see through your disguise.

Stop talking, Onyx. The Earl had stopped ahead on a sandpit. There were trees behind us, another patch of sand to our right, and a pond to our left. I wasn't sure what the Earl was doing, but he hung his head low as though he was praying.

Lightning speared the sky. Dark clouds appeared, but I wasn't sure whether the lightning was real or the malevolent Norns were behind it.

"What is the meaning of this meeting?" a voice crackled and I whipped around.

Damn, they really looked like corpses—long white hair flowing down their backs, eyes of indeterminate color glowing, white gowns cinched in at the waist by a sash of the same color. And that voice was the same one in the forest the evening of the bear attack. I'd thought Marj was just constipated.

"Who gives you the right to summon us?" she added. She did sound constipated. The thought took my uneasiness away. Or maybe knowing I had something they wanted gave me the courage. That and the magic surging inside me from bonding with the weapon.

I transformed back to myself. The shock on the Earl's face was comical.

"*I* called the meeting," I said. "You can go now," I told the Earl. He looked unsure. "Really, you should." I didn't check to see whether he left or not. My attention had shifted to my cat. Onyx's large body pressed against my legs, but she was trembling. *Go with him.*

No. My place is by your side. I think I peed on myself, so this had better be worth it.

I almost smiled. I focused on the three Norns. These were the ones who'd tried to get inside my head at the stadium and later sent the dark souls after Ingrid and me in the forest. They'd even seen me wear my ring, but they hadn't cared because they were only interested in one thing, the dagger.

"Dark souls will be attempting to possess students at my school this evening. Call them off."

"That is none of our business," Constipated Norn sneered.

"Actually it is. Before my usual Norns arrive, I thought I'd give you a chance to call off the attack."

"We are not responsible for tonight's attack. That's Maliina showing her rage," Constipated Norn continued. They looked at each other and cackled. "Your friends should have killed her."

"I'm happy you find it amusing and yeah, we should have a long time ago," I said, getting pissed when I'd sworn I'd be in control. "Tell her to back off, or I'm going to have a problem with you three."

"Are you still mad because of the forest incident? We were just having a little fun," another malevolent Norn said and chuckled darkly. "You were in no danger whatsoever."

"I'm so happy you enjoyed yourselves, but if anyone gets hurt tonight, I will be forced to retaliate."

"Lorraine, what do you think you're doing?" Catie asked.

My usual tormentors had arrived. I didn't even have to call them. They were also in their true forms.

"Giving both of you a fair warning." I rolled up my sleeves and showed both groups my dagger. Since they were on the opposite side of the sandpit, I had to move my arm and turn my head. I saw the Earl watching from the top of the first hill we'd passed. Idiot. They could easily hurt him.

"What warning?" one of the malevolent Norns asked.

"That I will not sit back and be treated like a chess piece. I have the dagger. It's mine. No one. And I mean, no one, can take it from me." *Unbond.* The dagger peeled back and slid into my hand. I let the magic flow between me to it, and the runes on it lit up. It shifted and elongated into a staff. The Norns watched and even took a step back. Something about the staff fascinated and repulsed them. I saw it in their eyes.

I pointed the staff at the malevolent Norns and they cringed. Hmm, that wasn't disgust or fascination on their faces. It was fear. Interesting.

"Just because I bond with it doesn't mean I'm like you. I will bond with it whenever it suits me. I'm neither on your side or theirs,"—I inclined my head to indicate my usual Norns—"and I'm not on the side of the gods or Hel and the giants. When it comes to you people, I'm neutral. I'm not your tool or servant or someone you can manipulate. If you push me, I'll push back. If you hurt someone in my care, I will retaliate in kind." I glanced at my usual trio and caught their grins. They were so sure they had me.

"You cannot stay neutral," another malevolent Norn snarled, her voice brittle.

"I'm not." I pointed the staff at Marj, Catie, and Jeannette, and they actually stepped back. Something about this staff really scared them. I wondered what it was. "I'm siding with Mortals and Immortals here on earth. I'll try not to interfere with your work because I understand that you're both necessary for the world to function. You," I pointed at the malevolent Norns, "and your firm control over tragedies and mayhem and them," I pointed at my usual trio, "and their kindness toward mankind." Not that I had seen it. "I understand about good and evil, yin and yang balancing each other. But I don't believe in a destiny being set in stone. If anyone needs my help in changing their lives, I will help them, and you will not stand in my way. If you do, I will do everything I can to expose you to this world. You will not be able to hide from Mortals and Immortals anymore. I'll make sure they know who is responsible for their misfortunes, who destroys their lives, and they'll find ways to fight back. Humans are ingenious that way."

"You cannot control us," Constipated Norn said.

"Or dismantle a system that has been in place since the beginning of time," her malevolent partner piped in.

"I don't want to, but I will if you don't stop messing with me and those I love and care about."

Catie and the other two were still grinning as though they thought I was just blowing steam. They thought they had me in their back pocket.

"For starters, there's a young man lying in the hospital in a coma," I continued. "His name is Beau Hardshaw. I hold all of you responsible." Catie and the gang stopped smirking. "I want him back with his family. He has a prom to attend tonight, so if I don't see him there, be ready for my response."

The look on their faces was comical.

"Come on, Onyx." I turned to leave and they all started talking at once.

I whipped around. "No! This was not a meeting to discuss my behavior or rudeness. I'm just a girl who wants to be left alone, except you won't let me be. So I'm making sure that you at least try."

I turned and walked away, but I could hear them yelling. I wasn't sure whether they were yelling at me or at each other. Lightning cracked. I didn't look back, but the Norn's *valknut* runes appeared on my arms. They were dim and kept disappearing. I laughed. I couldn't believe those old hags were trying to reel me in. I engaged our runes by thinking of Torin. Our runes appeared and dominated theirs.

The Earl wasn't alone when I reached the hill.

Torin, Mom, Ingrid, Femi, Lavania, Hawk, Blaine, and Andris stood with him. Torin was brushing off his pants and shirt as though removing dirt and looking furious. The anger left him when he saw me. He reached me in a fraction of a second and yanked me into his arms.

"I'm okay."

"Mimicking me?" he whispered. "Facing the Norns on your own. *Evil Norns*, Raine. If they hadn't stopped me..."

I squeezed him. "Sorry I worried you. I didn't mean to."

"Next time tell me. The hags blocked me again."

The dagger probably contributed to that too. I left his arms and went to Mom. She looked like she'd aged. "I'm okay," I reassured her when we hugged.

"Don't do that again. I've already lost your father. Don't make me bury you too." My eyes welled.

"I won't." I moved from person to person, until I reached Andris. I searched his face. "Is Dad okay?"

He nodded. "We found him the best room, right next to Eirik's father's," he whispered when we hugged.

I squeezed him hard. "Thank you."

~*~

"You are the craziest woman I've ever known," Ingrid said as she applied my makeup.

"I knew they wouldn't touch me." At least I'd hoped. I glanced at my phone, tempted to call Beau and confirm he was okay. The last several hours had been a nightmare worrying about him.

"You should have come for me," Ingrid said, pouting. "I need adventure in my life too."

"I'd trade places with you in a heartbeat if it meant keeping Torin. I'd give up everything except him."

"You should have seen him when he couldn't find you. They'd blocked you from him again. Like that day in the forest. Instead, he locked on Onyx. We had to hold him down when we got to the golf course." She stepped back and studied the result. "You're now officially a flapper girl."

Tonight's theme was All That Jazz and the outfits were supposed to represent that era. My dress was moss-green. Mom had gone all out on accessories—the heels, the gloves, beads, and frilled headpiece with real jewels. Ingrid managed to hold up most of my hair with it, which showed just how creative she was.

Her outfit was white, but the black gloves matched her feathered headpiece and mid-thigh tights. Her short, blond hair was perfect for that period too.

"I wonder what the boys are wearing," Ingrid said.

I didn't care. This evening was about stopping souls and sending them to Hel. I was still pissed the Norns hadn't taken me seriously. "I'm just happy Andris is back."

"Poor guy. He was frozen when they came back. Echo went straight to Cora's. He's pissed."

Cora was resting after Maliina tried to possess her. Happened right after my meeting with the Norns. Her dark soul buddy, Dev, had to help Cora fight back in the only way he knew how—by possessing her. She was still recovering. Apparently, possession by a dark soul was worse than by a regular soul.

"She was supposed to do some girls' hair this afternoon," Ingrid added.

"Yeah, the swimmers, Kicker and Sonya."

"I sent the ladies who do my hair to take care of them. They're good with makeup too. Come on, let's join the others."

Lavania, Femi, and Mom were reminiscing about the twenties. They looked amazing in their outfits complete with long cigarette holders. I debated again whether to call Beau or not.

Then Torin arrived and distracted me.

He was dressed in all white except for the green vest, the bow tie, and a fedora. He looked amazing. Hawk and Andris looked dashing in three-piece suits, vests and bow-ties, though Andris opted for a sweater. Blaine was missing.

"You look amazing," I told Torin.

He tilted his hat. "And you look miserable."

I shot him a mean look.

"You take my breath away, Freckles, but that's not what you want to hear right now, is it?"

"Of course. I worked hard to get this look…" I sighed. "No, it's not. I'm a mess."

"Do you want me to check on him?" Torin asked.

I nodded. "I didn't want to in case I jinxed it."

He chuckled. "The most powerful woman I know is worried about bad luck. Oops, I forgot. You're also a witch." As soon as we were away from the others, he created a portal into Beau's room. He was still in a coma, and his parents sat by his bed.

"There's still time," Torin said, trying to reassure me.

I shook my head. "No. Let's go."

While others created a portal to the Sports Complex, which was separate from the school's main building, Torin and I headed to the cafeteria. It was decorated with All That Jazz paraphernalia—black and silver tulle with gold, red, and silver stars, and a city skyline draped the walls, lamp posts covered with black gossamer and silver cutouts of a jazz guy, flapper girls, and twenties cars. Jazz music played in the background.

We stayed invisible and watched couples saunter by in twenties fashion. Even the teachers stayed true to the theme. I spotted Sonya and Kicker. Sonya's outfit was made by her mother, but I couldn't tell by looking at her.

Reapers—an underground band made up of Grimnirs—had already set up their instruments in the cafeteria. According to Cora, Echo used to be a member until they kicked him out. Echo rubbed most people the wrong way.

Blaine was the opposite. He was charming. And thanks to the new memories, he was the QB who'd taken the Trojans to state and brought us home champions. Convincing the student council and teachers to change the venue of the prom must have been a piece of cake. Getting the band here was another story. I had no idea how he knew Reapers, but the guy kept surprising me. They weren't just here for entertainment. They were to keep the students within the walls of the building tonight. Apparently, their music had that effect on people.

More students arrived. Still no Beau. Torin tried to keep me entertained by explaining what was wrong with the outfits. He had lived and breathed the twenties.

Then the band started to play. They weren't bad. Couples moved to the floor. I'd never been to a prom, so I didn't know whether it was normal to have so many seniors and sophomores attend it.

"Did you hear about Beau?" a girl to our right said, and I whipped around. They'd just arrived and were shouting to be heard above the band.

"Yes. I got a text from Amber."

My stomach dropped. Amber had been at the hospital with Ellie. I exchanged a glance with Torin, and then strained to hear the rest of their conversation, but the music was too loud. All I got was, "Tonight." And "Weird, right?" Then their dates joined them and they went to the dance floor.

I pulled out my artavus and created a portal straight to Beau's room. It was empty and the nurses were stripping down the bed. They only did that when someone died.

"Don't jump to conclusions," Torin warned.

"I have a bad feeling..." my voice trailed off when I saw the three girls who'd just entered the cafeteria. I saw through their disguises. Norns mimicking teen girls—a blonde, a brunette, and an African-American. How dare they come here.

"What is it?" Torin asked, sensing my anger. His eyes followed mine to the three girls. "Are those—?"

"Yes. It doesn't matter what race they choose. I always know them."

"Okay, what do you want me to do?"

One hundred percent support. No wonder I was crazy about him. "Tell them I'm about to be their poster child."

He frowned, concern flickering in his eyes. "How?"

"I'm going to broadcast what I am to these students and through technology to the world."

Torin's eyes narrowed. "You're sure about this?"

"No, but they leave me no choice."

He nodded. "Okay, luv. I got your back."

He walked toward the Norns while I went in the opposite direction toward the band. The Grimnir behind the mic saw me coming and cocked an eyebrow.

"Can I have the mic, please?" I asked.

He covered it and said, "You are invisible, Raine."

I blinked. "How do you know my name?"

"From Crypt."

"Oh. The mic, please," I said firmly. He shrugged and complied. I signaled the band to stop playing. "Can I have your attention, please?"

Students looked around curiously, some not too happy that the music had stopped, until they realized the mic was floating.

"Get your cell phones out because part of tonight's entertainment is magic. I'm going to reveal to you the world's best kept secret."

Some looked at each other. Others reached for their cell phones.

"Come on, people. I need this trending tonight," I said, my eyes going to Torin. He appeared to be arguing with the three Norns.

"How many of you know about Norse mythology?" The students looked at each other, shrugged, or made faces. A few hands rose. "Other than Thor and Loki, that is." Sputters of laughter filled the room, but their bewilderment was genuine.

"How are they doing this?" Allyson Pine, a girl from my history class asked her date.

"I will tell you how Allyson, as soon as you take out your phone."

Her eyes widened, then she looked at her friend, Jessica Lauders.

"Come on, Jessica, tell her to get out her phone. You all know the password for the school's Wi-Fi. Log in." Some did. Others followed the floating mic, already taking pictures. Across the hall, Torin was no longer talking to the Norns. He wore a smile that said he was utterly proud of my crazy performance. And it was just that, a performance. I could never expose who and what I was. One of the Norns was missing and the other two were talking to each other. "Videotape this moment, guys. Take pictures and post them on Twitter, Instagram, Snapchat... Tag your friends and share your pictures. Tell them to come here now because there will be more revelations tonight."

Students moved closer, their cell phones raised high. Those closest to me swept their hands under the microphone to see if something was holding it up. I backed away.

"You don't want to do that, Kaitlyn," I told one of the girls. Torin had his arms crossed. He indicated with his finger that I should wind it up. The two Norns glowered. "I'm here to tell you that I am a deity. I can appear and disappear right before your eyes. Like Thor, I wield a magical weapon. Anyone want to see me appear and disappear?"

There was a sputtering yes.

"I didn't hear that. Was that a yes?"

"YES!"

Beau entered the hall with Ellie. I sighed with relief. That was way too close.

"Maybe next time," I said. "Thank you for giving me this chance to entertain you." I pushed the mic into the guy's hand. "Make up something about the mic," I whispered to him.

"Are you kidding? You've just given me an idea for a new act," he said.

"Really? Great." I ran to where Torin stood. He opened his arms and I flew into them. "We did it!"

He laughed. "No, you did it. I don't know how to deal with them. They were threatening to do all sorts of crazy stuff if I didn't stop you. I actually believed them. They threatened to put me on Hel duty for eternity. I told them you'd only come with me."

Yes, I would follow him to the darkest, coldest parts of any realm. I hugged him. The band was back to playing, and most of the students went back to dancing as though nothing had happened. A few were still staring at their phones, probably trying to figure out the microphone trick. As for Beau. He had Ellie in his arms and they looked so happy.

"I knew he was into her," I said.

Torin pressed a kiss on my temple. "I hope he doesn't disappoint you. You went through a lot for him."

"I know."

"If he screws up, can I straighten him out? I have an amazing method of dealing with Mortals that try my patience."

"I know. You turn them into Immortals."

Torin chuckled, twirled me around, caught me and dipped me over his arm. "How about a dance? We didn't dance at our wedding."

"I don't think we have time for one now either. The dark souls will be here any minute. It's time to do some reaping."

"I'm not a Valkyrie anymore," he protested. "I want to dance with my bride."

I wanted to dance with him too. "We'll have our dance, but right now, you have someone who expects you to be by his side."

He faked ignorance. "You're here."

I pulled out an artavus and created a portal. We could see inside the gym. Not only were our people there, Grimnirs and souls in flapper outfits also stood around in groups. Regular souls ready to fight dark souls. It was surreal.

I had my support system—Immortals, Valkyries, and Witches, but I didn't need the Witches tonight. Cora had hers—Grimnirs and the souls she helped. Word about how she helped souls find closure had spread fast and they often waited for days, even weeks, to see her. But tonight, they came to support her. They must have heard about the attack on her by a dark soul.

"Go help your brother reap some souls," I said.

"You do know Andris is not really my brother," he grumbled teasingly. As soon as we appeared, Andris left the people he'd been talking to and came to meet us. He demanded to know what had happened and Torin obliged him, both chuckling over my craziness. No matter what positions they held, they'd always be brothers.

Cora and Echo were the last to arrive. They looked amazing together. No matter where I went and what I became, Cora would always be my best friend. I had to find the best time and place to tell her about my marriage. I hoped she wouldn't disown me.

When the dark souls arrived, we were all ready.

Epilogue

Ingrid and I sat on the grass and watched Team USA play Uruguay. A week and one day had passed since my showdown with the Norns. Onyx and I had gathered the Witches since their leader Eirik had disappeared again. I didn't get a chance to tell him to stop bonding with his weapon, so I hoped he was okay. The Witches were now scattered around the stadium, ready to act at my signal.

It was a beautiful sunny afternoon, the perfect day to foil some evil Norns' dastardly plot. The fans were out with Team USA paraphernalia—the foam fingers, the flags, and the pom-poms. The little girl in braids played with her sister on a blanket a few feet away from us. The boys with their trading cards were to our right. My eyes went to where Jace and the other Galaxy Academy players sat.

I found Torin seated at the end of their row. He continued to coach the Galaxy Academy U-16 team, and I hadn't missed a single practice or game.

As though he knew I was looking at him, he waved. I waved back and the light caught the diamonds on my rings. I now wore them openly. I wasn't worried about the Norns. They'd left us alone since prom night. I knew it was temporary, but I wasn't complaining.

Then there was Cora. Where to begin? She'd refused to talk to me for a whole day. Then she'd yelled and scolded, and vowed not to invite me to her wedding. Finally, she'd cried over the wedding pictures that had mysteriously appeared in my room, thanks to Eirik. When the tears stopped, we'd gone to England to inspect my new home. She now wanted a castle of her own.

The sound of an airplane flying too low reached me, and I turned. It moved closer and closer. Instead of watching my vision replay itself, I raised my staff and pointed it at the plane.

Luminate.

The light from my staff shot up to the plane. The Witches, using their staffs, and magic joined me and we slowly lowered the plane above the scrambling and screaming fans onto the middle of the field. We even made sure it slid on its belly and stopped at the end of the field.

I glanced back at the sky. I couldn't see the evil Norns, but I hoped they were cursing and finally realizing they shouldn't mess with me. Okay, so I was flexing my muscles a little bit, but they started it with sending *Draugar* and those bears after me. I was sending them a message—I wasn't sitting back and cowering while they laughed.

People stopped running when they realized the plane had landed safely. The wings didn't fall off and the tail was still intact. Emergency doors opened and passengers slid down the chutes to the field. Fans poured into the field. Some taking pictures others videotaping. I wondered if Torin reached Jace in time.

"Let's go," I said, opening a portal.

Ingrid was busy searching the stands for Rhys, I was sure.

"I think I'll stick around for a little longer," she said. She must have found him.

I grinned. She was so transparent. "Good luck. Onyx, come on."

The cat, or jaguar really, got up from the fence where she'd been enjoying the sun and went through the portal.

"What do you mean good luck?" Ingrid asked before the portal closed. "I just want to make sure no one is hurt. I do have a nursing degree."

I laughed. "Sure you do."

She stuck out her tongue at me.

Mom, Lavania, Femi, and Hawk were busy at the new school, preparing it for the fall. I wasn't sure when Ingrid and Blaine would join them. Ingrid was going to teach. Male Witches were going to crush on her like crazy. Blaine was somewhere in the stadium supporting the witches. The females were already drooling all over him. Andris still hated witches. I hoped to find out why some day. He didn't have a partner yet, but we were all staying together as a group. For now.

Onyx and I headed home. I stared out the window at my old house. It was up for sale. Mom now lived at the mansion, but Torin kept the house at our old cul-de-sac.

He didn't arrive for another hour and found us watching TV. He picked me up and took my seat, wrapping his arms around me.

"How did it go?" I asked.

"Good. I went with him to the hospital and waited while they tried to revive him. I gave the doctors a chance. They did everything they could. The dad was going to stay with him until the end. I runed his father and talked to Jace."

"Did he accept your offer?"

"Yes. I am systematically giving him more runes until he recovers. His asthma will be gone by the time we are done. He wants the final change to happen when he's eighteen. I told him about Lavania's Academy and he wants to go there. After all, he's a witch."

That explained how he'd sensed our presence in his room. He'd felt the magic. "So who's your next case?"

He stroked my nose. "This really hot girl in Seattle," he said, and I hoped he was teasing. "Tell me about yours. I noticed the boxing gloves in the closet."

"Well. There's this hot boxer…"

He didn't let me finish. He captured my lips in a soul-melding kiss. Just as well. I didn't really want to talk.

THE END

A SPECIAL MESSAGE FROM EDNAH WALTERS

I hope you enjoyed this next installment in the Runes series. If you want to read more about the memories the Norns stole from Raine and Torin, download your copy of Losing It: A Collection of VCards.

To get notified about new releases (I have a few planned this year, including Eirik's book 1), sign up for my mailing list and newsletter: https://mobile-text-alerts.com/TeamEdnah

BIOGRAPHY

Author Ednah Walters writes about flawed heroes and the women who love them. From her international bestselling Runes series (which focuses on Norse mythology and legends) to her Guardian Legacy series (which focuses on the Nephilim, children of the fallen angels). Whether she's writing about Valkyries, Norns, and Grimnirs, or Guardians, demons, and Archangels, love, family, and friendship play crucial roles in all her books. When not writing YA and NA books, she writes contemporary romance under the pseudonym E. B. Walters.

You can visit her online on:
Her websites: www.ednahwalters.com
Facebook: https://www.facebook.com/AuthorEdnahwalters
Twitter: https://twitter.com/ednahwalters
Blog: http://ednahwalters.blogspot.com